THE SYNDICATE TEAM

To David
Best wishes
Paul

PAUL LAMOND

Paul Lamond asserts his moral right to be identified as the author of this book.

Published by Paul Lamond 2021

ISBN: 978-1-5272-9134-8 (Paperback)

Printed by
Dolman Scott Ltd
www.dolmanscott.com

ACKNOWLEDGEMENTS

I would like to give a huge thankyou to:

Jacky McHugh, who spent many hours of her own time diligently reading through my work and correcting, and querying innumerable subjects, without her encouragement and continual perseverance this book might never have got to print.

Also to **Susan Isbister** whose help in ensuring I didn't lose work, and if I did how to get it back. Taught me how to use 'word' correctly and whose vast experience in so many fields was of enormous help.

A big thanks also to **Sue Saville** who was kind enough to guide me through the minefield related to the undertaking profession, ensuring I had followed the correct procedures.

My niece **Emmy Gray - Winter** , who at the launch of her first book encouraged me to finish this book.

Wikipedia provided me with many facts required to give the book some authenticity.

And finally to my wife **Lynn**, who, when she was we well, put up with my preoccupation of finishing a life-long ambition.

FOREWORD

This book took me in the region of twenty years to actually produce, since the thought of the inception of producing a piece of fiction with football being its main theme. They always say that the first book contains an awful lot of yourself in it and this certainly does.

To Brentford, Fulham and Queens Park Rangers Football Clubs, Their directors, management, staff and supporters...

I wish you every success in the future and may you all remain as independent clubs going forward... but to link you together gave me the opportunity to invent a new club; West London Football Club. It was also important to include another fictitous club; Kirklees County.

The period chosen is 1999, just prior to the continual use of mobile phones; the advent of computers; the influx of foreign players; the massive wages and ridiculous transfer fees.

Sky Sports was in its infancy.

THE SYNDICATES TEAM

New Years Eve 1999

It was a typical cold, damp winter evening and the happy revellers at Trafalgar Square's annual "New Year Party" seemed much noisier than most years. The square had been fortified to protect the historic site and the public themselves. Nelson's Column was defended from exuberant climbers with twelve foot high wire fencing, held into position with concrete blocks, and the fountains had been switched off. Scaffolding was prevalent throughout the area, with enormous signs indicating entrance directions to the Square and stipulating that all forms of drinks, and the vessels that carried them, were strictly forbidden. But, typical of the youth of today, they had been totally ignored. Drinks carried in glasses, bottles, flasks and cans were in abundance. The masses had journeyed in from the suburbs to celebrate in the many pubs, clubs and restaurants which adorned the streets of the City. The theatres and cinemas did not escape either, each reporting full houses as the London streets became crammed full of bodies.

The party had enveloped nearby Leicester Square and Piccadilly Circus, as the overspill attempted to get closer to Trafalgar Square. The streets of Haymarket, Piccadilly, The Mall and Pall Mall had all been shut for some hours as the merrymakers approached in disarray; drunk on the tubes, singing their way to the hallowed zone. Those that were wishing to leave were caught up with the influx of revellers. At every subway, train and platform throughout the City they were confronted by youth, booze in hand and a song in their hearts. Wishing all and sundry "Happy New Year."

"Would you like a swig?" or "Cheer up it might never happen."

Families kept their children close to them as the boisterous, but normally good-natured, groups ventured towards the epicentre of activity. The excitement in the square grew as they awaited the chimes of "Big Ben" to announce the beginning of a new era. Those chimes were accompanied by hundreds of the City's churches, each ringing out their own particular tribute to the dawning of a new year: 2000. The crescendo descended on the masses through the cold night air, to be greeted with the customary "Happy New Year." The hugs, the handshakes and the kisses, more often than not with total strangers, all bound together with a singular mind: to celebrate the future, and to remember only the good moments from the past.

One hundred and twenty thousand revellers tried to form themselves into human chains and all around could be heard the slow melodic (and in some cases the not so melodic) renditions of *Auld Lang Syne*. *"Should auld acquaintance be forgot, And never brought to mind? Should auld acquaintance be forgot, For the sake of Auld Lang Syne?"* They swayed, danced, drank, vomited and, in some cases, urinated in the well of the dormant fountains. The massive police presence tried, in vain, to keep the requisite peace and order and some became over- zealous in their attempts to do so. Arrests were inevitable; hundreds were made; but it did not deter those remaining.

Whilst everyone seemed to be more than happy, one drunk was becoming aggressively unhappy. Dave McLeod, West London's Scottish International Goalkeeper's evening had started badly and had not improved. He had already lost, quite involuntarily, £5,000 in a casino somewhere in Soho. He was too drunk to remember which one and, after the unsuccessful evening at the roulette table, he had split with girlfriend Penny. Penny had begged him to stop when he had quickly speculated, and lost, the £1,500 cash he had taken with him. The casino's owners, however, were more than happy to allow a celebrity like Dave McLeod credit. As his losses increased and the effects of the free booze prevented him from rational thought, Penny's appeals for sanity became tiresome to him. After a few angry words, she finally realised that she was wasting her time, walking out and leaving him to it. Unrecognised, Dave McLeod stood stationary, whilst all around him danced and sang. An occasional well-wisher shook his hand and an occasional woman volunteered a kiss, but he was in no mood to join in the celebrations, his mind continually dwelling on the past. He felt sorry for himself, feeling more inclined to hit somebody than wish them a happy anything. He felt totally isolated and lonely, and his eyes began to fill with tears. As the time ticked on, Dave McLeod's anger at being jostled and manhandled became too much and he punched a nearby fellow drunk. McLeod very soon became another statistic in the police records, joining an already full black mariah; with the help of two burly police constables; for a short trip to Bow Street Police Station and a night in the cells.

The Justice Taylor report, following the Hillsborough disaster in 1988, had seen major football stadia throughout Britain replaced with or transformed into all-seater grounds. The financial encumbrance carried by the country's professional football clubs caused many of them to refinance themselves. This forced several of the sides playing in the lower leagues to become semi-professional and others into insolvency and out of existence all together. Some old established names had disappeared completely, now to be only found in the record books.

New clubs emerged, mainly a combination of several former clubs. West London Football Club had been formed from the demise of Brentford, Fulham and Queen's Park Rangers, who had formed themselves as an alliance. Their combined shared assets, along with the financial interest of three major banks, had seen the construction of a 45,000 all-seater stadium on a 50 hectare brown field site within easy access of the M4, M40 and M25 motorways. The £300 million stadium; Heathrow Park; had a sliding roof; its own multi-screen cinema; squash courts; indoor tennis courts; golf range; gymnasium; solarium; an international- sized swimming pool; an indoor shopping complex and a multi-storey car park for over 25,000 vehicles. The shopping area, named The Heathrow Mall, had attracted major retail stores Marks and Spencer; Bentalls; British Home Stores and Tesco's, along with another two hundred smaller retail concerns, and had become West London's major commercial centre. The facilities were further enhanced with the construction of overland railway and tube transportation which connected the site to Heathrow Airport and Waterloo and Paddington Stations. The Heathrow Mall competed strongly with established shopping centres at Kingston, Ealing, Hounslow, Richmond and Staines. The ground and the facilities afforded to it were the envy of most.

West London Football Club's formation in 1992 coincided with the first season of the FA Premier League, which had broken away from the Football League after 104 years. The Football League had been formed many years back, in 1888. Twelve clubs competed in a single division: Accrington; Aston Villa;

Blackburn Rovers; Bolton Wanderers; Burnley; Derby County; Everton; Notts County; Preston North End; Stoke; West Bromich Albion and Wolverhampton Wanderers.

The new Premier League was to be contested by 20 clubs and West London's inclusion had been a bone of contention as they had taken up the 20th place. In the 7 years since its formation, the club had never come close to the expectations first envisaged. Now red-faced, the FA Premier League no longer found it easy to justify the merits of including them in their membership, after they had waived the formalities of having them compete in a process of promotion from the lower divisions of the Football League. The decision had caused considerable resentment from The Football League, driving an even bigger wedge between the two main footballing bodies

In April 2000, West London Football Club were entrenched in a relegation battle. It was vital to remain in the Premiership and reap the financial benefits (estimated at some £45 million to the Club) whilst the remaining clubs in the lower leagues would struggle to survive. The initial interest at the beginning of the season had seen large crowds, enabling the Club to achieve its cash flow forecasts and attain an average attendance of 30,100. The newly-found fans, however, had not taken long to become disillusioned and, in-line with the abysmal performances, attendances had more than halved. The once imaginative brain-child of three ambitious chairmen now looked a forlorn joke. Relegation to Division One of the Football League could well see its final nail in the coffin.

1

It was back in the 50's when floodlights were first introduced into professional football. The quality would never meet the standards required today, but they attracted thousands of spectators. Friendly matches were arranged and kit was specifically designed, very often of a silk-like appearance. The lights allowed later kick-offs and made for brilliant spectacles. At times, the floodlights failed and everything was plunged into darkness.

Right now, the twenty thousand fans at Zion Park would most likely be wishing this would happen. They looked on motionless; the stadium radiated a deathly silence as they waited for the referee's whistle, knowing it would sound but hoping and praying that it wouldn't. Life appeared, momentarily, in slow-motion as Mike Stephenson's late last ditch tackle in the penalty area on Darius Vassell had sent him sprawling head-long through the wet, muddy top surface of the pitch. The home crowd held their breath. The referee raced into the penalty area, whistle tightly grasped in his left hand, slowly raising it to his lips. The brightness of the powerful halogen floodlights exacerbated the eeriness of the evening, as the expelled carbon dioxide from the breath of the crowd hit the unusually cold April night air and transformed itself into masses of vapour. That vapour being gently lifted up by the slight breeze and allowed to disperse into the atmosphere.

The whistle reached the referee's lips, Vassell looked up and stared at Stephenson in total disbelief and turned to the referee for ratification. The sharp shrill of the whistle pierced through the momentary silence and echoed around the half empty stadium, halting play. The Villa players looked surprised but elated. Conversely, the West London players looked dejected and miserable. The electronic scoreboard told the tale; **87 minutes 28 seconds** and, brilliantly displayed underneath; **West London...0 Aston Villa...0.** The referee pointed to the spot.

The scoreboard operator, seated in his small console overlooking the proceedings, high on the top tier of the main stand, leaned forward and reluctantly pressed the appropriate button on the console which represented 'penalty'. The board sprang into life as it lit up again, figures dancing intermittently on and off the display in regular monotony.... **Penalty.... Penalty.... Penalty** flashed up. The clock ticked on. **87:29, 87:30, 87:31, 87:32, 87:33, 87:34, 87:35, 87:36, 87:37, 87:38, 87:39, 87:40.....**

Dion Dublin, the Aston Villa striker, retrieved the ball, stepped forward and placed it carefully onto the penalty spot, manoeuvring it subtly until it was positioned to his liking. He took a few steps backwards but wasn't happy; its position wasn't quite right. He slowly walked back to the ball, bent down and readjusted it slightly. The referee halted the kick and told the West London defence, in no uncertain manner, to remove themselves from the penalty area, warning them about the consequence of any encroachment.

The home crowd were becoming anxious as they awaited the outcome, they began jeering, heckling and making disparaging comments as to Dublin's parentage. The goal to them seemed to be getting bigger, and the goalkeeper smaller, with every passing second. Dublin stepped backwards again, this time in a gentle arc. As he commenced his run-up, the crowd whistled and booed in the hope of putting him off. Dave McLeod, the West London goalkeeper had watched many of the Villa striker's previous penalties on TV and was confident where he would place it. He guessed correctly, but Dublin's right boot connected with the ball with such ferocity it was on its way before he was really ready. It wasn't the best placed penalty ever taken by Dublin; the ball being a good three feet off the ground. McLeod flung himself despairingly to his right and was fortunate to get the tips of his fingers to the spherical white blur, deflecting it onto the inside of the right-hand post. The ball rebounded, hit the now prone goalkeeper on the shoulder and bounced into the the goal, entwining itself into the netting. A handful of visiting supporters and the whole of the Villa team leapt for joy.

Dave McLeod looked up, viewed his disconsolate team mates and pulled himself dejectedly up from the ground to retrieve the ball from the back of the goal. Thousands of West London's fans did not witness that insignificant event, for they were already making their way to the exits, disgusted with their team's performance, the sound of the seats emptying simultaneously making more noise than the excited Villa fans.

The electronic scoreboard danced once again in to life;

Goal..…...Goal..…....Goal..…......Goal..…......Goal..….… West London...0 Aston Villa...1 ...Dublin (penalty) 88 min.. Attendance: 20,105.

Nor did they witness the sickly, sly grin that covered the face of a little sturdy bald headed gentleman who seemed more than pleased with the outcome, though he was certainly no supporter of either side, so his reactions seemed somewhat dubious. Positioned near the corner flag, the man turned and joined the mass exodus, listening intently to the comments of the frustrated exiting throng of home supporters and relishing in their dissatisfaction. With the exception of Watford, who were already relegated, only two points separated West London, Sheffield Wednesday and Kirklees County.

Fortunately for West London, none of the others had gained an advantage.

Everton 2 Kirklees County 1
Manchester United 0 Watford 0
Sheffield Wednesday 0 Manchester City 3
West London 0 Aston Villa 1

	P	W	D	L	F	A	GD	PTS
WEST LONDON	35	8	8	19	36	65	-29	32
SHEFFIELD WED	35	8	7	20	34	58	-24	31
KIRKLEES CTY	35	6	12	17	40	68	-28	30
WATFORD	35	5	6	24	32	72	-38	21

As he reached the top of the stairs, the referee's whistle sounded the end of the game. West London Football Club had lost crucial points in their fight to stave off relegation from the F.A. Carling Premiership. The funereal-like walk came virtually to a standstill as the crowd in front tried to squeeze their way through the wrought iron main gate. Directly in front of him, a young boy adorned in West London's yellow and blue; scarf, ski-hat and an assortment of badges, stumbled alongside his father, whose attention was totally absorbed in a typical post-match dialogue with a friend. The boy gave the appearance of abject misery. Not only had his much loved team taken a step nearer relegation but his father was intent on ridiculing Mike Stephenson, the boy's hero.

"They should get rid of Stephenson. He's not worth the money. £15,000 or whatever a week the Club pay him."

"That's the third time in as many weeks he's given the bloody game to the opposition!"

"There was no need to even tackle Vassell, was there?" He was never going to score from that position!" he said.

"Yeah you're right." said his friend "But the whole team's performance was pathetic."

"They seem to have stopped trying."

The father continued his onslaught. "Stephenson's just not good enough anymore. He's rubbish!"

The boy sobbed but his father didn't notice as he unmercifully carried on with his attack.

"How does he continually get picked for England? Christ! No wonder we can't win the World Cup. I still haven't forgiven him for that bloody awful penalty miss against Germany!"

The crowd were becoming packed closer together, everyone pushing hard to get through the limited space at the main gate. The boy tripped and fell to the ground amidst a deluge of legs. The man, close behind, reacted before anyone had time to think, picking the boy up in one swift movement and standing him back on his feet. The boy felt the strong hands and fingers of the man biting into his arms and the soreness in his knees from scraping them on the ground. Their eyes met. The boy froze. Fear reached up inside him, he suddenly felt cold, stepped backwards into his father's arms and began to cry. The father thanked the man without giving him a second glance, more intent on quieting his off-spring and herding him towards home than paying attention to the man. It was not the fall that made the boy cry. The little man had frightened him.

When Mike Stephenson tripped Vassell in the penalty box, West London's manager John Crowther was sitting in the draughty dugout alongside coach Rob Dyson, physiotherapist Tony Pullen and one of the unused substitutes, Eddie Dillon. The blanket that had been wrapped around their legs had fallen to the ground as both Crowther and Pullen had leaped to their feet in annoyance. Eddie banged his head hard on the top of the dugout but still managed to gesticulate with one hand whilst rubbing the bump vigorously with the other.

"You pratt!" he shouted.

"Mike what are you playing at!" groaned Crowther, almost to himself. Substitute Eddie Dillon just sat with his sore head in his hands, in resignation. Crowther reseated himself next to Dillon, whilst Pullen remained standing to witness executioner Dublin nearly miss the opportunity, as the ball ended up on the wrong side of Dave McLeod, smacking against the post and then being deflected in off of his shoulder. The electronic scoreboard continued to clock up the time **87:49, 87:50, 87:51**. By the time the ball had found its way back to the centre spot for West London to kick off, barely a minute of normal time was remaining, plus three minutes of additional play. Striker Jim Fellows touched the ball to Dennis Harper who showed his inexperience by trying to take on the Villa defence single-handedly and inevitably lost possession. Jim voiced his annoyance when he called him "a wanking little tosser!"

Villa found it easy to play out time, continually playing keep-ball by the corner flags, frustrating and committing the West London players into what could only be described as wrestling, as they manhandled their opponents in an attempt to get possession of the ball. The referee was lenient in not collecting names for his book and let the players get on with it. Many others would have booked at least two of the West London players for their overvigorous efforts, but maybe this particular ref thought that defeat was a large enough price to pay. The sound of the final whistle saw John Crowther leap from the dug-out, quickly shake Villa manager John Gregory's hand along with a few of his associates, and disappear down the tunnel, leaving behind the inane comments being hurled at him by some of the home supporters. The tunnel echoed with the sound of his footsteps as he walked briskly down the slight gradient towards the dressing rooms.

On reaching the door he could hear the clattering of boots on the concrete floor behind him and the mutterings of the players who had now reached the end of the corridor. Crowther entered the home dressing room and opened a window to let out some of the steam already seeping in from the adjoining plunge bath, which Stan Dark the caretaker was busily getting ready. The players began to emerge through the open door. The first, big Jim Fellows, was still moaning about young Dennis Harper to anyone who would care to listen. He was followed closely by full-back Paul Sulley and his close friend, right mid-fielder Eddie Hirst. The remainder of the team sombrely strolled in, with the last two players, Mike Stephenson and then Dave McLeod, looking very down in the mouth, as they plonked themselves down on the benches. Crowther scrutinised them and decided that this was not the time to have a post match inquest. He clapped his hands and a deadly hush fell around the dressing room, everyone waiting for the bollocking, but in a calm voice he said;

"Okay lads. Let's just try and forget tonight's performance, we'll dissect the game tomorrow after training. I'll see you in the bar in about half-an-hour."

Mike Stephenson looked up as if to say something but thought better of it.

John, now in his fourth season as Manager, hadn't experienced anything similar in all his time in football. The club had finished the previous seasons in sixth, eighth and tenth place respectively and had started this current season well. The first eight games had seen them accumulate 18 points with home wins against Newcastle United and Spurs and away wins at Wolves and Sunderland. The front two partnership of Jim Fellows and Adrien Belmonte, which had been nicknamed 'FAB', was providing the goals on a regular basis, until tragedy struck in a match at Everton.

The Frenchman, bought in the close season from Paris Saint Germain for £850,000, tragically broke his right leg earlier in the season when he collided with two Everton defenders and a post as he slid in attempting to score. The players close by knew immediately that it was bad and the scream from Adrien, plus the sight of his tibia protruding through his sock, confirmed the seriousness of the injury. A number of the players turned away in horror and one had thrown up.

The Red Cross made him comfortable on the stretcher and fed him oxygen continously. He was taken to the Royal Liverpool University Hospital, where his leg was operated on and placed into a splint. In a few days he had been flown back to his family in Paris for recuperation. From then on, Jim Fellows had struggled. John tried to sign a replacement but good strikers were not available, unless you had more money than sense. He did, however, manage to sign 31 year old Bob Gaze from Huddersfield very cheaply.

Bob, who had once been capped by England, had plied his trade with nine other clubs and came with loads of experience, and he initially looked as though he would fit the bill nicely.

His skills were good but he was unable to achieve a fitness level sufficient for Premiership football. He never lasted the whole 90 minutes and struggled with a recurring hamstring problem. It was no surprise when both parties decided that it was time that he should retire. The loss in form saw West London Football Club drop into one of the three relegation spots.

In the dressing room, whilst the players removed their kit and threw it unceremoniously into the centre of the floor, Tony Pullen wandered round tending to the minor injuries. Meanwhile Don White, the Club skipper, got up and wandered over to Mike Stephenson in his stocking feet. Resting his hand gently on Mike's shoulder, he said in a reassuring voice;

"Don't worry about it Mike, it could've happened to any one of us." Mike retorted without even looking up."But it didn't did it. Piss off Don and go and patronize someone else."

White looked deeply hurt and said;

"All right. All right. Sit there and feel fucking sorry for yourself."

Jim Fellows, never the diplomat in the side, blurted out;

"You're becoming a clown Mike. I just hope you can make us all laugh when we're playing in the poxy Football League."

"Fuck off!" replied Stephenson.

Whilst this was going on, the rest of the team, with the exception of little Barry Thomas, had discretely vacated the dressing room in preference for the plunge bath and showers. Barry had been sitting daydreaming, picking the mud from the sole of his boots, half listening to the row whilst thinking of several chances that had come his way and that he had squandered. In a sudden fit of temper he leapt to his feet and hurled the boot towards them. The boot narrowly missed Mike Stephenson, thudding against the wall above their heads, the loose mud showering both as it finally came to rest on the floor by their feet. The two of them looked up startled as the little Welshman yelled.

"For Christ's sake shut-up!"

He grabbed his towel and rushed towards the plunge bath, banging the door shut behind him.

2

Ray Prince considered whether James Lowdnes was involved in the impending intimidation of Mike Stephenson. Normally, activities of this nature were influenced by money. In the past, he had never allowed the underworld to be connected with his beloved Kirklees County Football Club, and, if current events were solely being directed by James' younger brother Douglas, then the potential consequences worried him. He pondered over ringing James Lowdnes in the States to discuss it but decided against it. Douglas Lowdnes had given him specific instructions. The initial plan was to set the 'holier-than-thou' international footballer up with an offer of big, easy money; a beautiful woman and an opportunity for sex. Providing he took the bait; bingo….. one extremely worried man. With so many businesses in London already contributing to the funds of the syndicate's protection racket, it would not be long before an opportunity presented itself.

Prince enjoyed working for the Lowdnes brothers, he found the work varied and the pay good. He enjoyed his trips abroad and travelled under various guises. He was in possession of five European passports and two American; the names Ray Prince and Phil West were not amongst them.

His lack of a good education had left him unprepared for any position that would have been advertised in the press. The jobs he went for more often than not required *'street skills.'* Streetwise he was, and had been since his school days. At a very early age he learnt the art of persuasion. Not from having in-depth discussions and debates, nor an interchange of ideas, but from terrorisation. His sadistic behaviour came naturally to him.

People feared him. The boy grew into a man totally devoid of a conscience. His adrenaline flowed when he inflicted his power over other human beings. Obviously some humans had been stronger than others, both mentally and physically, but the few that were did not possess the same kind of sadistic tendencies Prince thrived on.

Personal possessions were often damaged beyond repair, whilst beloved pets were not excluded from his torturous acts. Dogs, cats, horses and the like had fallen foul to his wickedness. Eyes had been gouged from their sockets, legs and heads severed with an axe and some creatures even boiled alive. It turned most people's stomachs. Most of all though, he revelled in the suffering of man. It amused him to make them plead for their looks, or their lives.

Both James and Douglas Lowdnes became respectable pillars of society. As their wealth increased dramatically they bought various major franchise operations and began making associatons with likeminded business people: the wealthy and the people that mattered. They donated to, and supported, many charities and became well known. James, Douglas, Eddie Bezer, Micky Pearse and Prince had attended the same secondary modern school in Finsbury Park and became good friends in the 60's, starting a gang they called the *Finsbury Boys Syndicate.* From the very start Prince, Bezer and Pearse bullied the other pupils and controlled everything possible, those that objected were singled out and beaten up. They refused to tell the teaching staff who the assailants were, knowing full well that to do so would render themselves as cripples. The Lowdnes brothers set up the protection racket and were taking 10p weekly from many of the pupils, which they would split between themselves each weekend.

One of the teachers, Mr Sawyer, who took the boys for football every Wednesday, insisted that the boys should not wear any pants under their shorts, as it was unhygienic. To prove they were not, they had to line up whilst he sat huddled up in his chair at his desk. Each pupil would pull their shorts open so that Sawyer could peer down at their genitals, obviously getting himself aroused as he did so.

The Finbury Boys decided to act and confront Mr Sawyer. The Lowdnes brothers found him in a classroom one break time, just as he was about to go up to the staff room.

"Could we have a word with you Sir?" asked James.

"Yes certainly boys, what can I do for you? Please make it quick, I have a tea and bun waiting for me in the staff room." He chuckled.

"Are you some kind of queer Sir?"

Sawyer's face physically flushed and he exploded. **"No I'm certainly not!"**

"We think you are Sir. Looking at all the boys' willies excites you, doesn't it? And you with a wife and two little girls."

"I'm going to thrash you two now."

"Maybe you will Sir, but it won't stop us telling your wife, or the headmaster. Mud sticks Sir."

"What do you want?" he said aggressively.

"£2.00 per week to keep our mouths shut Sir, a small price to pay. Better than losing your job, or your wife. Place the money in my desk every Friday and nothing more will be said. Thankyou for your time Sir."

They turned and left through the door, leaving Sawyer totally dumbfounded.

There were many things they were allowed to do and get away with over the next two years, before they left. The sense of power gained was immeasurable. Sawyer paid for three weeks and then stopped. Nothing happened, everything seemed normal on Monday and the Tuesday, but during the pre-football ritual on Wednesday, James spoke softly to him as he opened his shorts. "I saw your wife and daughters yesterday, did she say that she had met me? Let's make it £4 a week." Sawyer paid up every Friday afterwards.

It didn't take long to begin the protection racket when they left school, there was no outlay of capital required. It was easy to continually frighten shopkeepers and alike to pay up; from having their windows regularly smashed to being physically assaulted.

The syndicate progressed rapidly under Bezer and Pearce, covering most of England and Scotland, the States and Europe. Money laundering, prostituition, armed robbery, killing, smuggling, human and drug trafficking were amongst their crimes. They were thought to be responsible for over twenty murders and earned themselves a criminal fortune of £200,000,000.

3

On closing the dressing room door, John Crowther heard the outburst and was deeply concerned that the moral of the side had dropped to this level. He was caught in a dilemma whether or not to go back in and calm it down, but thought better of it. He briskly walked down the corridor and up the stairs to the VIP Suite.

On entering, he found the room exceptionally warm and full of the regular complimentary ticket hangers-on, local dignitaries, directors friends, sponsors and such like all proceeding to drink the lavish cocktail bar dry. It always irked him how much people could drink when it was a free bar, as well as the amount Bert Little had told him, was left at the end of the evening, pints of beer still half-full that wastefully had to be poured away. Crowther threaded his way through the highly vocal mass of bodies, acknowledging the familiar faces, giving the occasional nod, "hello." and a few hand shakes.

Bert Little the Club's Steward spotted John Crowther as soon as he came into the room, and immediately commenced pouring his customary post-match double Balvenie single malt whisky. By the time he had reached the bar, Little was grappling in the ice bucket with a pair of tongs. He finally prized a few suitably sized pieces of ice free and placed them carefully in the scotch and placed the glass on a paper doily.

"Good Evening Mr. Crowther. A bit of bad luck tonight Sir." said Little diplomatically. "Evening Bert. Thank you." said Crowther smiling, but totally ignoring the opportunity given to make comment. He turned and was surprised to see the Chairman Alfred Wade. The Chairman very rarely left the boardroom on match days. He was usually inclined to remain with his fellow directors and that of the oppositions. Wade beckoned him over, with a wave of the hand that resembled more of a command than a friendly gesture. Crowther had begun to wish he had gone directly to the Players Bar.

Alfred Wade was a large, rotund, balding Yorkshireman in his late fifties. A typical, self-important, self-made man. If the opportunity presented itself, he would embark on his own life story, pompously boring the unfortunate listener with his own inflated version of how he made his fortune and the circumstances, which led him to become chairman of West London Football Club. His dress sense was from a bygone era; dressed in a crumpled blue three piece suit, with a solid gold chain trailing from his waist coat pocket, affixed at one end to a button-hole and the other to the Hunter watch which had been given to him by his long departed father. On the little finger of his right hand sat a large, gold monogrammed ring with the letters *A.W* finely engraved in an oval shape, with a small diamond embedded in it depicting the dot between the letters.

At regular intervals, the hand made its way to his mouth, taking huge gulps from the vintage red wine he consumed at every opportunity as he talked down to Gregory Shaw the managing director of Zion Electronics. Shaw looked uncomfortable in his conversation with him but Wade was in full flight. Shaw occasionally flapped his arms in a waving motion, undoubtedly to clear the air of the foul breath being emanated from Wade after several cigars, wine and the considerable amount of garlic from the meal he had ingested a few hours earlier. Wade remained totally oblivious to his obvious discomfort, and continued.

"I'm amazed that this is the first time you've been down here." Stated Wade.

"Well normally I leave it to one of my staff to make an appearance. Not being that interested in football myself." Shaw replied curtly.

"But I felt that I should come along and see how secure our investment is at this time. I can't say that I am not worried. Ten million pound investment is a huge outlay for a company such as ours and it looks as though the Club could end up playing in the Football League next season, a situation I don't relish."

"Nor do I!" barked Wade in reply.

"But it won't happen."

Alfred Wade was becoming more and more agitated with this overpayed university educated comedian signifying very strongly that he had the audacity of even considering withdrawing their sponsorship from the Club. Wade did not like Shaw and the feelings were mutual.

Undoubtedly Zion Electronics had supported them well in the past and even the name of the ground name had been changed from the Heathrow Park Stadium to the Zion Stadium and all four roofs had the slogan *'In future watch Zion Sports Channel'* along with a huge logo projected skywards to the mass audience of passengers watching from the enormous jet-aircrafts landing every three or four minutes as they dropped gradually making their way to the awaiting runways at Heathrow Airport. It was an ideal adverting spot missed originally by British Airways.

4

Alfred Wade had, on paper, literally billions. As a boy he picked up waste paper in a small trolley and sold it off for recycling and, by the time he had reached 17, had made his first million. The small beginning expanded rapidly into a vast empire. He reached multi-millionaire status after he bought a papermill in Dartford, Kent, which he drained of any assets and managed to dispose of at a considerable profit. To coincide with its sale, he acquired a major mill in Austria which employed 1,500; it produced high quality multi-coated paper which was produced for premium quality publications all over the world. It manufactured 950,000 tonnes each year.

Originally, along with the chairmen of Brentford, Fulham and Queens Park Rangers football clubs, he agreed to invest in a totally new football club, which would be called West London Football Club. All three original clubs would be liquidated. He never thought for one moment that, one by one, the other interested parties involved in the original negotiations would cut and run. All of them had great difficulty in associating themselves with the new club and didn't have the capital to continue. Wade had never been associated with football before and, whilst his inclusion was part monetary, mostly it was egotistical. Nostalgia was increasingly becoming part of the many discussions. It had taken many hours to establish the name, through which Wade had been more than patient, but he became tired of the other three somehow trying to keep this or that about the demised clubs. *'Should we play in blue, red, white?' 'With stripes, hoops?' 'The name of the ground, the badge?'* It went on and on and on.

They argued relentlessly. They also realised before long that Wade wasn't interested in the nitty-gritty. He made his feelings clear that he would rather employ someone else to deal with the infinitesimal details. They then realised that Alfred Wade was in a position to repay them their interest free loans and pay an exceedingly over inflated share price to gain control of the club. Alfred Wade had already secured the requisite land close to Southall and architects had formulated many drawings for consideration. With a major share holding of 81%, Wade now totally dictated the club's every move. It took nearly two years to obtain approval; the go-ahead was granted by the local council at a public meeting and construction work commenced.

Whilst he didn't mind Zion Elecronics's ten million pound sponsorship deal, Wade couldn't lower himself to grovel. He let Chief Executive, Roy Peters, undertake that as he seemed pretty good at it. It was surprising that this had been the first time Gregory M. Shaw had availed himself of the hospitality of West London. The last year had seen him decline invitations to every home game, two sportsman's dinners and an inauguration dinner, all held at The Hilton Hotel in Park Lane. But, unknown to Wade, the Zion Electronics Board of Directors had pressurised Shaw and insisted on the visit. The board had begun to ask pertinent questions in light of the current economic climate and the club's poor league position. It was important that the company's high profile should be maintained and board members now realised that the proposed new eight and a half million pound, three year, sponsorship agreement (which was less than the previous one) was due to be confirmed in the next couple of weeks and would not achieve its objectives if the club fell from the top echelon of football. The money would not then be wisely spent.

Shaw had been reluctant in requesting his secretary to ring the club and obtain two tickets. He was not surprised when he received the two tickets with additional entry to the Club's VIP Suite. The hospitality, as expected, was second to none. Chief Executive Roy Peters, who had originally negotiated the sponsorship deal, had fussed about him all afternoon like an old mother hen looking after her brood. He was relieved when the much more likeable Commercial Manager, Paul McCormick, had ushered him away to sort out a problem with the police.

But, the time spent in the Club Chairman's company, he found unpalatable. Shaw had always been a good listener but the man's conceit, bigotry and sheer arrogance had made him long for the attention of his secretary, who he had brought with him and could see was being well looked after by a hoard of young men in the far corner of the suite. Periodically, their eyes would meet and a knowing smile pass between them. Opportunities to gaze at her were infrequent due to the vast amount of people that were amassed between them. He felt envious of the young men who were surrounding her and wished he were one of them. His time with her was limited as he would have to despatch her to her home within the next hour or so.

Andrea Carpenter was, at twenty six, some twenty years younger than Shaw and the affair had been taking place for the past sixteen months. The Saturday afternoons making love at her apartment, whilst on the pretext of watching West London and the official dinners, which had given him the ideal opportunity to stay out overnight with her looked as though they might now come to an end. Then what excuse could he make to his wife? He glanced over and gave her a slight tilt of the head. She got the message, bid farewell to her admirers and started to make her way towards Shaw and Wade.

Shaw watched her as she walked over. The long blonde hair, lovely face with angular cheek bones and hazel coloured eyes caught most of the men's attention, which evoked a slight smile from her; enough to melt most men. As she passed, their eyes could not help continue to gaze at her perfect little waist, long legs and snug little bottom. Just watching made Shaw feel randy. He felt proud that he had seen everything that they were imagining, and it wasn't disappointing. If he could get her back to her home reasonably quickly he still might have enough time to make love to her.

John Crowther and Andrea Carpenter arrived at the same spot simultaneously. John could not stop himself from staring at her. She was stunning.

"I would like to introduce you to the manager, John Crowther." said Wade, gesticulating towards John with one hand.

'Ignorant bastard' thought Greg Shaw, 'he hasn't even got the courtesy to introduce me.'

Greg Shaw stuck out his hand and shook John Crowther's firmly.

"Greg Shaw, managing director, Zion Electronics. And this is my secretary Andrea Carpenter."

John Crowther took her hand in his and shook it gently, momentarily not wanting to let go. He finally did as she proffered her hand to Alfred Wade. Wade did not let go, putting his other hand to hers and holding onto her. Looking her straight in the eyes he said;

"What a beauty. How lucky you are Greg." She blushed, feeling quite uncomfortable and as though she was being mentally undressed there and then. The conversation between them lasted a few minutes before Shaw had had enough, made a weak excuse and left with her.

"I bet he's screwing her." said Wade as they walked away. John Crowther didn't know what to say.

Zion Electronics' original investment of ten million pounds, and the impending eight and a half million three-year deal, was money West London would find it difficult to survive without. Sponsorship had taken many forms, shirt advertising being the most effective. This deal was providing the Club were successful in attracting the TV cameras to the games which, whilst being guaranteed large income, didn't match Manchester Utd, Chelsea and Liverpool who were continually being shown. which provided even greater income to the chosen few. Massive full-colour advertising in the Club programme was available as was sponsorship of every home game; the supply of all the playing and training kit of the whole team; all the match footballs and the occupation of an executive match-day box throughout the season.

The forty air-conditioned executive boxes, each with a capacity to accommodate twenty people, were totally self-contained with a well stocked bar, refrigerator and television. They were dutifully serviced by a local catering company, who provided a group of attractive young ladies, suitably attired in the Club's bespoke uniforms, to ensure the clientele were spoilt. The boxes were well designed with glass surround for unobstructive viewing and, in addition, there were a further twenty seats to the front and outside the cubicle. These seats allowed those who wished to sit in the open air and capture the atmosphere, whilst still having the luxury of downing their tipple.

The injection of capital was important to the Club; the overdraft facility was already in excess of seven million pounds and the Club were in no position to raise further funds. Alfred Wade had made it abundantly clear to the board of directors that his ten million pound interest free investment in the club was as far as he would continue with his financial support.

The lower echelon of the football market was a diminishing one and had been for a number of years and, for a club like West London, be being relegated would be financial suicide. Zion Electronics were one of the largest satellite television companies in the United Kingdom. Their tremendous success in both the home and European markets had seen them take up the challenge of satellite television giant Sky and begin to infiltrate into their market share, spending billions of pounds on its development. Whilst others struggled against cable TV and the capture of large audiences, ZETV as it was called had more than its fair share of the viewing public and caught their imagination with unique 'sports only' channels. Live Saturday afternoon sport relayed direct to the home. The audience, without moving from their favourite chair, could sit entrenched in front of the television set, selecting at the flick of a button; more often with the help of an infra-red remote control unit; a full coverage which included horse racing, golf, cricket, wrestling, snooker, ice-hockey, American football, baseball, motor racing, rugby, darts, motorcross and almost any other sport you could think of.

It was too much for football to compete with. Even the television football coverage tended to discourage likely paying customers from attending matches. The critics all too often highlighted the seedier and less comforting aspects of the game, inventing clichés such as the 'professional foul' and continually showing the players bending the laws and attempting to con the referee. The continuous play backs in slow motion, placing the referee on the rack whenever they erred, made matters worse. Thankfully they had curtailed the close-ups of mindless morons fighting each other in the crowd, but it all had its negative ramifications. The beautiful game had become attractive to the wealthy and the average, Tom, Dick and Harry were being priced out. Many sons and daughters were restricted to watching on ZETV and the like.

John Crowther chatted for another twenty-minutes with Alfred Wade before circulating with some of the other guests. Half-an-hour, and three scotches, later discreetly provided by the Club Steward, he left the VIP Suite and made his way down the stairs to the Players Bar. The bar was still full with many of the players, their wives, girlfriends, friends and members of the select '100 Club'

This congregation seemed a lot more despondent than those he had just left. Striker Jim Fellows, as always, was surrounded by his fan club. The same four or five members of the '100 Club' regularly cornered him, pestering him for internal tit-bits. The recent dressing room argument had already reached their ears and set their tongues wagging.

"What's this we're hearing about a punch-up in the dressing room?" was the first question asked.

"Who threw the boot at who?" asked another.

"What's wrong with Mike Stephenson?" prompted another.

"Do you think John Crowther will resign?" asked a fourth.

They stared at him intently, awaiting his replies.

Big Jim used his vast experience to evade giving direct answers to any of these questions, without offending the enquirers.

He wished tonight though he that he didn't have to be subjected to this barrage, The '100 Club' members did, however, feel that the £1,500 per season paid to the Club, did somehow allow them more than just a season ticket and a chance to rub shoulders with the players, although most of the players were rich in comparison and earned far beyond most of the members.

5

John Crowther had been born in Bristol and was the youngest son to parents Jack and Elizabeth. His brother Martin was two years older. The two bedroomed terraced house in Fishponds had been big enough until the arrival of younger sister Caroline several years later. Jack, a compositor in the printing trade, decided to look around for another job, feeling that London held the key. After several months of interviews and laboriously travelling to and from the city, the family finally moved to a three-bedroomed semi-detached house in Greenford, Middlesex. Jack had accepted the position of Composing Room Overseer with The Daily Telegraph in London's Fleet Street.

Although commuting daily by underground to and from Chancery Lane was at times tedious, the additional income allowed Jack and his family the luxuries they had never before been in a position to enjoy. Their very first acquisition, albeit on a rental basis, was a television from the Puratone TV Rental Company, which received transmission for two channels; BBC and ATV. This was to everyone's liking and the evenings were spent glued to the little black and white screen, watching programmes like 'Fabian of Scotland Yard', 'Lassie' and 'Dragnet'. The family had become one of the better off. Not many households had one, or could even afford one. The next addition, a washing machine, was soon followed by a refrigerator and record player. Jack's spending spree continued when he outlayed further on a greenhouse and then a car. The greenhouse afforded him many hours to potter around in total isolation and the car; a brand new cream Austin A30 two-door, bought for £507, gave him a freedom he had never thought possible. Although driving became one of his great joys, he never relished driving in the congested streets of London and, whenever possible, shirked the problem in favour of public transport.

One day, thinking that Jack would pick him up in the little Austin, a car-less work colleague asked him whether he would like to go to see a football match with him one Saturday afternoon. It had been a long time since Jack had followed Bristol City and witnessed the talents of the great John Atyeo, it didn't take him long to decide that he would like to. The match was at Queens Park Rangers. Jack arranged to meet his work-mate at South Ealing tube station. His work-mate, disappointed that Jack wasn't there to pick him up, was not impressed when they had to catch the train. Jack wasn't invited again. Jack, however, didn't need another invitation; he went the next time on his own and became an avid fan of the little West London club, attending every home game over a period of three years. On the Saturdays the R's were completing their away fixtures in the Third Division South, Jack began to think about other London clubs playing at a higher level and with more quality. There were both Fulham and Chelsea not too far away and he decided to alternate between QPR and Chelsea.

His wife Elizabeth didn't mind his obsession but was taken aback when, after arriving home immediately after Chelsea's 1-0 victory over Wolves at Stamford Bridge, he announced his intention to travel to Portsmouth the following Saturday and support them! Elizabeth argued with him, not understanding his sudden allegiance to a club he had been only watching for a few weeks, and wondered how he could have become so involved. She was not interested to learn of Chelsea's quest to win the league championship for the first time in their history. Her argument to prevent him going was fruitless and, regardless of what she said, he was selfishly still determined to go. Typically, as she had done throughout their marriage, she gave in. But being fed up with forever being left with the family when he made his football sojourns, she suggested that the boys be taken to the next home match he attended. Jack readily agreed.

Elder son Martin, disappointingly to Jack, had never shown any interest in the game, being a studious and academically-minded type of boy. Although, on the occasions he had to play, he showed a great deal more ability than most. Young John, on the other hand, had always been very keen, forever kicking a ball, or anything else he imagined to be one, whether it be in the garden or the street. He also possessed the requisite aptitude and ability for the game.

Jack set off on the journey to Portsmouth on his own; it took over two hours in the little A30 but it was an enjoyable experience for him.

The game at Fratton Park was played in front of 40,230 people and it looked to have been won when Les Stubbs crashed the ball into the Pompey net. Joy, however, very soon turned to disappointment when Mr R.E. Smith from Newport, Monmouthshire, ruled the effort offside. The full-time whistle finally sounded without either side registering a goal and the point gained by Chelsea was to set up an historical encounter a week later; a home game against bottom of the table Sheffield Wednesday.

John Crowther's baptism into professional football on Saturday 23rd April 1955 would go down in the annals of the club's greatest achievement. A crowd of 51,421 assembled in expectancy to witness a buoyant Chelsea team - Charlie Thomson in goal; right back Peter Sillett; left back Stan Willemse; right half

Ken Armstrong; centre half Stan Wicks; left half Derek Saunders; outside right Eric Parsons; inside right John McNichol; centre forward Roy Bentley; inside left Seamus O'Connell and outside left Frank Blunstone - totally outplay and slaughter Sheffield Wednesday convincingly 3-0 to win their first Football League Championship. The Wednesday side, which included the young mercurial Albert Quixall; *The Golden Boy of English football*; were already doomed to the Second Division and were no match for the rampant Chelsea side. John Crowther's recollection of that occasion is still vivid to this day:

The tube journey from Greenford to Fulham Broadway via Notting Hill Gate; on the Central and then District Line; watching the miles of piping on wiring on the dark tunnel walls and excitedly waiting for the train to emerge into the daylight or the well lit stations. Walking up and down the rattling wooden escalators, along with hundreds of other commuters fighting their way on and off the trains; looking wide-eyed at the many adverts covering the walls..... He remembered being quite embarrassed when his eyes had focused on a young lady, stripped down to her bra and pants, advertising underwear. It was the first time he had seen anything like it.

He remembered the short walk along the congested Fulham Road. The jostle with his father to buy the sixpenny programme from the overworked, besieged programme seller. The long, bustling queue of fans fighting their way to get through the turnstile, and his elder brother crying because he wanted to go home. When they finally reached the top of the stairway, the view of the huge mass of heads before him, already assembled and positioned waiting expectantly for the teams to take the field. He remembered the pushing, and the fight to get down to the front by the railings, where all the young boys were allowed to stand. The loud speaker announcements, and the quite unforgettable tones of the then 'hit' number *Stranger in Paradise,* sung by Tony Bennett.

He remembered the excited, almost deafening, roar as the eleven men in their royal blue shirts, silky white shorts and black socks with blue and white hooped tops, ran onto the pitch, in what became to him the most wonderful colours he had ever seen. The two goals by Eric 'Rabbit' Parsons, and a penalty slotted home by Peter Sillett, turned the game into a one horse race, with the day culminating in the awarding of the Football League Championship Trophy, at the end of the game, to the Chelsea captain, Roy Bentley.

Roy became young John's favourite player. Whether it was because he was born in his own home town of Bristol, or maybe because his father Jack continually sketched footballers (always fictitiously autographing Bentley's name beneath them) could never be established. Photographs of the English International adorned John's bedroom, along with a number of others in the Chelsea team. As time went by, John's own ability on the pitch improved dramatically. When his father had first seen him play in a games lesson at school, John had run around the pitch along with the others, hovering around the ball like bees around a honey-pot, with no semblance of positioning and very little know-how. The years ahead saw young John Crowther become a gifted right-half, captaining first Parkfield Junior School and then, after passing his eleven-plus, Pendry Grammar School. Whilst at Pendry, he also impressed his games master, Mr. Miller, so much that he recommended John to the county selector. After seeing John just the once, his selection was a formality;

he was head and shoulders in advance of his age group and, by the time he reached the tender age of fourteen, was a regular in the South West Middlesex team. Off the field however, John was causing his father and mother some consternation. Unlike his academically adept brother and sister, he showed very little interest in his school work and no application to his studies. His obsession with football had caused considerable conflict between his parents, the two having spent numerous late nights arguing about John's future. John's ambition was to become a professional footballer but in the early sixties the wages, facilities and opportunities the youth of today are afforded like the Y.T.S. schemes, then were non-existent.

With elder son Martin now working for Coutts Bank in the Strand, Jack and Elizabeth Crowther decided, when John reached fifteen, that it was time sit him down and discuss the future with him, to ascertain what he wanted to do when he left school. John was confused, the future profession he wanted more than anything else was to become a professional footballer. Thoughts of being anything other had not even been considered. His father said that, as good as he was, the chance of becoming a footballer and to get paid for it was very unlikely, and he must be sensible and think of other ways to earn his keep. It was days before he could even formulate a list of occupations he might consider doing, but none of those chosen seemed to have anything in common. A chef, a tailor, or, like his dad, a printer. Lengthy consultations with the local Youth Development Officer however proved more rewarding, as after one such meeting John arrived home to announce that he wanted to follow his father into the printing trade.

The request, though, was not that easy to fulfil. Apprenticeships were normally gained on a father-to-son, or a who-you-know basis, but apprenticeships in the printing industry were difficult to obtain, due to so few being available. The vacancies that did come up, were very much sought after. Jack tried without success to persuade the management at The Daily Telegraph to offer an apprenticeship to John, as other fathers with sons also at school leaving age, and who had put in longer service than his own, had already reserved positions for their off-spring. Unperturbed, Elizabeth Crowther sat down and, with the help of the London telephone directories, wrote to every printing company in and around the City, requesting an interview for her son. Out of the thirty or so enquiries, only one had the courtesy to reply. The Lawyers Stationers offered John the opportunity of an interview. The interview, which took place in the company's head offices in New Fetter Lane, included a series of I.Q. tests in the form of shapes; picking the odd one out within a predetermined time. Unknown to John, he passed with very little difficulty, but it seemed an eternity until the letter relating to the interview finally fell on the doormat of 21 Barber Drive, Greenford.

The family excitedly waited for John to open the envelope. He nervously slit it open with the help of a kitchen knife and carefully withdrew the contents, unfolding the single sheet of paper. The letterheading was printed in sepia with raised ink on a thick, expensive looking white laid paper, he was later to find this process called die-stamping. The typing was set out immaculately. It read:

The Lawyers Stationers Limited

Holroyd Buildings,55-66 New Fetter Lane,London E.C.4.
Telephone: CHAncery 2233

Master J. Crowther,
21 Barber Drive,
Greenford,
Middlesex.

Tuesday, 19th January 1960.

Dear Master Crowther,

Thank you for attending the recent interview at these offices for the position of apprentice compositor.

We are pleased to offer you the position at a weekly wage of £3.11s.6d per week. You are entitled to two weeks holiday per year plus public holidays. We require you to commence employment on Monday 12th February 1960 on the first day at 9.00 a.m. and thereafter at 8.00 a.m.

You will be responsible to Mr. L. Jacks, the Composing Room Manager, but initially would you please report to the Personnel Department, bringing this letter with you.

We look forward to seeing you on the 12th.

PNC Robinson

Yours faithfully,
P.N.C. Robinson,
Personnel Manager.

John started his apprenticeship on the 12th February and left the house on that morning with his proud father. After being introduced to his new environment, John was sent rapidly to the company doctor for what was for him a most embarrassing medical. Having to show his private parts came as a shock! When he arrived home and told his mum what had happened, she laughed so much she nearly wet herself, and his further predicament of having to provide a specimen the following day without picking up any utensil to contain it, set her off again. She managed to find a used medicine bottle which he filled to the brim, she found and wrapped it in a paper bag, sealed with a rubber band. Having to carry it around discreetly for several hours until his appointment added further to his embarrassment, until finally he felt the relief of leaving it with the doctor.

6

Whilst John was learning his trade through the week, his weekend was totally devoted to football. Saturdays were taken up travelling the country, watching his favourite club Chelsea, and Sunday mornings playing for local West Middlesex Sunday League side Pendry Park. The club won every conceivable honour available to them in the three years John played for them. Rumours regarding Football League club scouts being in attendance at some of the games were rife and believed, as many strangers regularly stood and watched the games on the touchline. The approach inevitably arrived; disappointingly to John; from Arsenal and not his beloved Chelsea. As he was making his way to the dressing room at the end of one the Sunday morning games, he was quickly approached by a tall man dressed in a large camel coloured duffle-coat. The man, in his late forties, virtually stood in John Crowther's way stopping him in his tracks.

"John Crowther isn't it?" he said.

"Yes." replied John, looking hard into the man's face and noticing his deep blue eyes and a faint smile that showed warmth and friendliness.

"My name is Len Morris and I represent Arsenal Football Club." he said, slipping him his business card. John felt excitement reach up and grip him by the throat. He stared at the business card without really absorbing its contents. "I've been watching you, young man, for a number of weeks now and I've been more than impressed with your performances." he continued. John was speechless, and just stood trance-like, looking straight back at him. Len Morris could see the shock in his face and it was not the first time; his many years as a coach had seen him approach countless young boys and the reaction was nearly always the same.

"How would you like to come down to Arsenal for a trial?" he asked.

John had a fleeting desire to look around and see whether there was another scout from Chelsea before accepting the invitation, but the feeling passed as rapidly as it had arrived.

"That would be great." he replied.

Len Morris left John with all the details showing him how to get to the trial venue in North London. John couldn't wait to get home and share the news with his family. He was surprised that they didn't have quite the same enthusiasm...... they were concerned over whether he would still want to continue with his apprenticeship if the trial proved successful. The trial, a few days later, was being held at a small school playing field near Barnet and John was concerned as to how to get there. He studied the underground map intently: Greenford on the Central line to Tottenham Court Road, change to the Northern Line, get off at High Barnet and then about a thirty minute walk. Miles!

'*How long will that take?*' he thought.

It took him the best part of two hours and the trial was attended by over forty other boys and four officials from Arsenal. On arrival, John approached one of the officials holding a clipboard and gave his name. The man scanned though the names with John peering anxiously as he said,

"You did say Crowther? It should be in alphabetical order..... That's strange. It doesn't seem to be listed." The man continued looking through the file, flipping each sheet over. Finally he reached the very bottom of the last page where he found John; his name had been hand-written at the bottom, like an after thought.

"Go over to the changing rooms and get changed. I hope you have something warm to wear, whilst you're waiting around." said the official. '*Someone to make up the numbers. That's what I am.*' John thought to himself. He couldn't see the man Morris, who had originally approached him, anywhere. He was surprised and disheartened that there were so many boys and felt a pang of disappointment, seeing the likelihood of his dream not being realised with so many boys like himself trying to capture the scouts' attention. John was not selected in the first twenty two players, his disillusionment grew deeper as he sat watching the ones chosen exhibit their talents. He was becoming bored with watching the others and fed-up. The whistle blew repeatedly as boys were removed and others sent on in their place, but not John. He sat on the touchline, itching to get on and waiting for the signal from the man in charge. The game went past half time and five minutes into the second half; John felt more and more disconsolate as time ticked by; before he heard a familiar voice.

"Right lad, now it's your chance to show what you can do. You'll be playing right-half." It was Len Morris. Morris stood clutching the hand of a small boy in one hand and signalling the man with the whistle with the other. The game stopped and a young lad was called off, removing the number four shirt he had been wearing as soon as he knew his time was up. John took the shirt; it smelt like the worst case of body odour and was damp from the boy's sweat. John nervously pulled it over his head, tucked it into his shorts and raced to take up his position on the field. It didn't take long for the ball to find its way in John

Crowther's direction. The opposing inside left had already evaded two tackles, leaving two players on their backsides as he came hurtling towards John, skilfully stroking the ball with his left foot. Unlike the two before him, John held off the tackle, allowing his opponent to come closer to him with the ball. His timing would have to be immaculate to dispossess him. The forward feinted to go one way and pushed the ball on the other side with a deft flick of his right foot. John had moved firstly in the wrong direction, nearly being sold by the dummy, but he held his balance, swung his body in the opposite direction and took the ball away from him in one movement. He progressed with the ball into the midfield and put a glorious through ball inside of the left full-back for the right winger to run onto. John moved up to the edge of the box, hoping to receive a reverse pass, but it never materialised. The winger greedily struck hard towards goal from an oblique angle and missed by a considerable margin. John continued to feed the winger, giving him every opportunity for a reverse pass, but the boy, trying hard to impress, continued to waste the chances. The only bright spot came when the winger managed to secure a corner. The ball was swung into the near post and a defender headed it away to the edge of the penalty box, where John was positioned. He watched it drop, his timing was near perfect and he half-volleyed the ball, driving it hard into the top right hand corner of the goal, beating the 'keeper and finding the back of the net. He couldn't have wished for anything better! Although he thought he had played well, John was himself taken off after half an hour; he looked hard for Len Morris, but he was nowhere to be seen. Dejectedly, John headed for home.

Exactly four weeks later to the day and without any communication, John had ruled out any chance of progressing any further with Arsenal and concentrated on continuing his apprenticeship as a compositor with The Lawyers Stationers. As he caught the train home that evening, little did he know what would be waiting for him. On his arrival home, he wondered who the little Ford Anglia parked in on the kerb outside his home belonged to and, after opening the front door, questioned whose was the third voice he could hear talking to his mother and father.

As he walked towards the lounge where the voices were coming from, the door opened and his mother greeted him with a large grin. There, on the far side of the room, sat on the couch clutching a cup of tea, was none other than Len Morris, along with the small boy he had brought to the trial with him. Without a word being spoken, Len carefully placed the cup on the side table before getting up and, for the second time in their brief association, shook his hand and handed him a letter with the other. John, with a smile breaking on his face, took the letter and started tearing at it frantically to open it, spilling the contents, unable to control his emotions. The letter said it all; Arsenal wanted young John to sign on professional terms for the club from North London and John was all for it; he could hardly read the letter for the tears that were beginning to fill his eyes.

Len introduced the young boy as his 4 year old son, Terry, and then got down to more serious matters. One main obstacle was the insistence of both Jack and Elizabeth Crowther that he continue with his apprenticeship. It was obvious that this subject had already been well discussed prior to him arriving. A suggestion was made that maybe becoming a part-time professional would satisfy all parties. Len Morris sat and listened to their argument then explained to them the workings of a football club and what would be expected of him. John sat back reluctantly, seeing the conversation transform into an agreement that he really didn't want to agree to. An hour later, at the conclusion of the meeting, it was agreed that John would continue with his apprenticeship and play as a part-time professional for Arsenal. It was a decision made for him, but one he would never regret.

He undertook his apprenticeship with an enormous amount of enthusiasm, knowing that his time spent as a *Printer's Devil* would culminate in him becoming a full-time professional. The company were more than obliging, letting him off to play in mid-week games during the day. Not that they paid him for the time, but the expenses received from Arsenal more than covered his loss. In fact the company were becoming quite proud of the budding celebrity in their midst. His footballing ability saw him make a couple of games in the first team. No mean feat for a semi-professional. His debut was on Saturday 13th February 1965 v Leeds United at Highbury; he played at right-half in a disappointing 2 – 1 defeat, in front of a crowd of 31,132 supporters.

7

John's lovelife though was a different tale altogether. He longed to have a steady girlfriend but, whether he was too choosy or he just hadn't met the right one, he wasn't too sure. But one morning, whilst visiting the Personnel Dept, he held the door open for a petite, very attractive brunette with a bob hairstyle who worked in one of the company's offices. In his daily life, John didn't associate with many of the gentle sex and working in the Composing Department with 100 other males full of testosterone didn't help him. He was out of his depth as to what do next. Chatting up girls was alien to him, but he couldn't get this girl out of his mind. Then, making his way home on one fine winter's evening, walking briskly down Fetter Lane, there she was; strolling along slowly, almost aimlessly. As he approached her he felt his heart begin to race and his breathing quicken. He wondered what he could say and more importantly what her reaction would be. He plucked up courage and just said "Hello. Where are you going?"

She looked up at him, smiled and shrugged her shoulders indifferently.

"Just following my nose." she replied.

John was taken aback by her reply so he just nodded to her and carried on walking, bitterly disappointed, not knowing what on earth she had meant and actually thinking she had been quite rude.

After arriving home and eating with the family, it was obvious to his mum that he had something on his mind. His conversation was minimal and he wasn't absorbing anything being said. His mother began collecting the dirty dishes and was surprised when John, unusually, helped her and then grabbed the teacloth in readiness to dry up. This came as a bit of shock as, like his father and brother, he never ever considered this to be something 'manly' to be doing. She looked at him quizzically a few times, expecting something but unsure what.

"Mum, if someone said to you that they were 'just following their nose', what would they mean?"

His mother looked at him and grinned. She knew at that moment that her son had a girl on his mind.

"It means 'I'm not really going anywhere. I'm just following my nose.' Get it?"

"I met a girl and …."

His mum quickly finished his sentence "And that's what she replied!"

"I thought she was being rude to me Mum."

"No, no, not at all."

John was now more determined to ask her out but, working in the composing room and never having any access to the offices, he felt frustrated. One idea did however come to mind. He knew that everyone in Head Office had to sign in when they arrived every morning. Eric, the commissionaire on the South Exit, was reponsible for looking after the book and drawing a red line at 9am; everyone after that was deemed as late. On leaving work one evening, John discretely questioned Eric, describing what she looked like. Eric, who must have been well into his seventies, thought about it for a while.

"Well there are two girls Shawna, who works in the Pensions Office; that's Shawna Owen; and the other is the junior secretary to the Company Secretary's secretary, Mrs French, and she is

Sandra Farrer. Shawna is a brunette with long hair, slim, tall and wears glasses." John shook his head. "Well then it is Sandra Farrer."

"Actually Sandra has just left, about five minutes ago. She turned left heading towards Fetter Lane." he said.

John purposefully strode out of the building and within ten minutes he had caught up with her.

"Hello again." he said, as he drew up next to her.

She gave him that same smile he had seen a few days earlier. "Hello."

"My name is John Crowther and I work in the Composing Dept at The Lawyers Stationers. Have you got a boyfriend?"

His approach startled Sandra. Her eyes opened wide, her head tilted backwards and she blurted out:

"Wow, I didn't expect that approach. No actually, I haven't! By the way, my name is Sandra."

"I know." he said.

They walked and talked, telling each other about themselves; where they lived and what their hobbies were; but whilst he told her of his love for football, he never mentioned Arsenal.

When asked for a date, Sandra agreed without hesitation. They planned to meet at 7pm at Charing Cross station the following Saturday and go to the cinema. This fitted in with John's football commitments as the Arsenal Reserve games always took place on Saturday mornings. Their dates continued for over two months. Every Saturday, Sandra would travel up from Kidbrooke and John would meet her at Waterloo; a trip to a cinema in Leicester Square and a meal at The Lancaster Grill in the Strand (usually a mushroom omelette and chips) before seeing her off on the train home. On their first date they watched

It's A Mad Mad Mad Mad World, the following Saturday, *Move Over Darling and then Charade.*

Sandra rang John every Sunday afternoon and they monopolised the line for ages. John became besotted with her; he walked with her to Waterloo Station every evening after work, Waterloo because her ex always caught the train from Charing Cross. His friendly commissionaire every evening told him how many minutes ago she had left and he would soon catch her up, then they would walk hand in hand until saying goodbye at the station. Every Thursday lunch-time he would alter his lunch hour to coincide with hers and they would stroll around happily together. At one time, one of his colleagues had seen them both looking in Bravington's the jewellers window and asked whether they were trying to choose an engagement ring.

As Easter approached, Sandra mentioned coming up to the city and spending a day with her Mum and Dad at the Easter Parade, but before that Mum decided she wanted to meet John. Her mum was Dutch and Sandra had often said that when she lost her temper, she could not understand what she said. They met one Thursday evening to go late night shopping and they wandered around, buying bits and pieces and specifically a winter coat. Her mum invited John to join the family for the Easter weekend and maybe re-visit London to see the Easter Parade, John was elated at the prospect.

Sandra had not long broken up with a long-standing boyfriend, James, when they first started dating. John knew this, but he didn't expect what happened next. On one of the evenings, walking back to Waterloo, Sandra told him that she had seen her ex earlier in the week and she was sorry but they were going to give it another go. She gave John a peck on the cheek, said she was sorry again and departed through the gates to the platform. John felt sick, empty, heartbroken, and for weeks walked around feeling miserable, lonely and unwanted. He felt that the whole world was against him. His life seemed to be meaningless. His football went to pieces and the management at Arsenal couldn't understand why he was playing so poorly. The composing room overseer, Bill Halls, at The Lawyers Stationery Society was constantly admonishing him for his continual lateness for work and the lack of concentration when he was actually at work. He had made numerous mistakes, including two major incidents causing many hours of rework after unintentionally pieing* two chases of type. Bill was contemplating going higher to find out how he should be disciplined.

*The letterpress printing process is based on utilising hot metal type under impression, each character is produced individually using a Monotype system. Copy would be set on a keyboard by a trained journeyman, producing a large perforated paper tape. The tape is then sent to the hot metal caster and connected with a typeface matrix type which produces individual metal characters in a line and places them in a galley (a metal tray). The compositor will firstly take a galley proof from a hand press and provide proof readers with it, to read and mark the proof for corrections. The compositor would then manually make the corrections. The type would then be made up in a chase/form; a large metal frame; which could have the capacity at times to hold as much as eight pages of A4 type on a stone (a large metal topped table). When completed the chase is tightened by the use of fillers/crap and tightened up with wooden or metal quoins. When lifted, all the type must be secure. In the event that it isn't, the type will spill, which is called pied. A pied chase is *a catastrophe, because of the work that it involves in putting it back together again. Most of the time the work would have to be completely restarted.*

He had not seen Sandra at all in the ensuing weeks; not that he had been looking; he had purposely had taken to entering and leaving by the North entrance to avoid doing so. But, on arriving very late for work one morning, to save time he decided to enter by the South entrance. As he approached he discovered Sandra and her boyfriend James on the steps leading to the entrance to the building. John could just about mumble the words "Good Morning." as he walked quickly past them. His heart was thumping and he had a huge lump in his throat. They say that you always remember your first love, whether it be reciprocal or not. John now felt inconsequential, just one minimal sentence in someone's life. Time went by and the hurt gradually faded. Sandra had left the company but even so, he purposely made sure he avoided places they had been to together and, as the days went by without seeing her, his feelings began to diminish and eventually disappeared.

Finally, his big day arrived; Wednesday 19th January 1966. All apprentices look forward to the day they receive their indentures and become journeymen. But, whilst other apprentices would be apprehensive at having to leave and go off to other places of work (a requisite laid down by the British Federation of Master Printers to encourage greater experience), John knew he was to become a full-time professional footballer.

When he left home, John made sure that he had clean clothing to change into after the customary 'gonging out' procedure, leaving for work with a small holdall containing a fresh shirt, tie, trousers, jacket, socks, pants and a pair of shoes. He knew the practice now very well. Through his six-year apprenticeship he had been instrumental in more than thirty 'gonging outs'; a tradition reserved for the apprentices to perform, to bid one of their colleagues a fond farewell and to celebrate him attaining tradesman standing. The morning saw John carrying out his normal duties in the Composing Room; he worked on the stone, making corrections to the Articles of Association for Kimber, Small and Co. solicitors, based in Grays Inn Road. He diligently removed one piece of type and replaced it with another with the the corrected letter. Ticking off the galley proof as he implemented the corrections made by the proof readers. He stopped a number of times to think of what he would be doing tomorrow, and few times of what was going to happen to him in the next few hours. Many of his work colleagues approached him, ribbing him about the planned activities and wishing him good luck for the future.

John had an appointment with the Works Manager at twelve o'clock. At eleven thirty, he left the Composing Room and entered the toilets to change. He quickly washed his face and hands and opened his holdall, changing from his working clothes into the clothes he had brought with him. He looked hard into the cracked mirror to make sure he looked alright, gave his tie a quick alignment and walked smartly from the toilet. The whole of the Composing Room had stopped work, some forty grown men were standing on chairs and tables, banging encouragement as he walked through the swing doors along the corridor towards the Works Manager's office.

He stopped when he reached the door, pulled his jacket down and again made sure his tie was in place. The sign on the door read in large bold capital letters 'R. M. BAILEY WORKS MANAGER'. He knocked and waited for a reply. "Come in." replied a high pitched voice. 'Blobby' Bailey's secretary was in her mid-thirties and had been with the company since leaving school. He had met her a couple of times before and never knew whether to call her Sonia or Miss Fry. He decided to call her neither and nervously said;

"I'm John Crowther. I have an appointment to see Mr. Bailey at twelve o'clock."

"Yes of course. Have a seat a moment and I'll see whether he is ready for you." She knocked once and a gruff voice replied "Come."

"John Crowther to see you Mr. Bailey. He's the young man I gave you the indentures for this morning."

"Yes. Yes. I do remember. Let him in." came the irritable reply, from a man with obviously too much on his mind. Sonia Fry turned, smiled and beckoned John through the open door. John walked through the door slowly, to be welcomed by the enormous figure of Ron Bailey, and the door was quietly closed behind him. Ron Bailey's physique made the large office look miniscule. He sat perched behind an ornate oak desk, his body was stuffed into a swivel chair on casters, his stomach overlapped his trousers and his shirt looked as though it would escape at any moment. He rose with great difficulty, his body performing unstably as he extended his hand to shake John's.

The meeting was short and sweet. It was well known to everyone that Bailey was a drinker and he had his own private stock of whisky securely stored in the bottom drawer of his desk. As he gripped John by the hand the alcohol on his breath nearly made John gag.

"John Crowther, our little footballing star!" he said sarcastically, he seemed to be intoxicated already.

"Well I wouldn't say that." said John politely.

Bailey reached down to the corner of his desk and handed John a certificate with a large red wax seal and several signatures.

"Your indentures. This, lad, is what you have studied and worked to attain for the past six years. Congratulations." He walked around the desk, opened the bottom drawer and withdrew a bottle of Famous Grouse whisky with two glasses, pouring a large tot into each one.

"Thanks." said John as he took an enormous gulp of the neat whisky, which hit the back of his throat and burnt like hell. He coughed and watched Bailey pour the contents of his drink down his throat without flinching. The bottle was put back in the drawer and John knew at that moment his interview was over. He quickly finished the remaining liquid in his glass and realised that he felt light-headed; he recollected why he shouldn't be inebriated today, today was something very special. The meeting in all took no longer than ten minutes and he returned through the swing doors, where all his mates were excitedly waiting for him.

Throughout the week, the apprentices had collected waste food from the canteen, the canteen staff being more than helpful by providing sprouts, cabbage, tomatoes, eggs, custard and leftovers which, after hoarding for a while, had rotted and now emitted a foul smell. Ink, glue and paper waste (from the bindery's punching machine) along with every fire bucket in Holroyd House (filled with freezing cold water) were now ready for the occasion. John was unceremoniously hoisted into the air and taken to the toilet where he was stripped of all his clothes. His testicles were smeared with cobalt blue ink and he was dressed in sacking cloth. As they dragged him from the toilet, raucous laughter and banging again emanated from the Composing Room floor. He was bound to a trolley and taken to the loading bay, where all the delivery vans had been cleared to accommodate the ritual.

The apprentices, egged on by the journeymen and a considerable number of office staff, hurled all of the stash at him. John was covered in a thick colourful mixture which enveloped his ears and his eyes and secreted into his naval passage and mouth. He felt awful and was relieved when they stopped, when there was nothing else they could throw at him. They then wheeled him into the surrounding streets at hurricane pace, accompanied by what could only be described as the noise from a howling tribe of red indians. At nearby Fleet Street, the barrow was secured; with the aid of a chain; to a lamppost, where he was left to his own means of escapology. John was subjected to the humiliation of jibes and comments from the inquisitive office workers on their lunch breaks, not to mention the many others minding their own business and giving him a wide berth, as though he were a local vagrant. After some ten minutes of wrestling with his constraints, finally a sympathetic passer-by came to his rescue and freed him from his shackles. He left the trolley behind, knowing some of the lads would retrieve it at some time or other. It did not take him long to rejoin his tormentors in the local pub in Fetter Lane opposite the Daily Mirror building, aptly named The Printers Devil. A mate had brought his clothes, so a quick wash in the toilet and change back into his clean outfit brought him back to life. The celebrations, goodbyes and promises to keep in touch took several hours. John left his employ at The Lawyers Stationers' very drunk, but very happy.

8

Whilst John's footballing life progressed successfully, his love life was a series of disasters. His relationship with Sandra at The Lawyers Stationery Society; his first love, his first girlfriend; had been limited to holding hands, kisses and an occasional snog and, even if she had not gone back with her boyfriend, the distance between their respective homes was too far, even if he had had a car or could actually drive. He was lacking in experience, unlike a number of his close friends who were never without a girlfriend. He often thought of Sandra and wondered whether she had married and had any children.

A number of years later he was out with a group of good friends at the local bowling alley. Included in the party was Kathy. He was instantly attracted to her. She was tall, blonde, with deep blue eyes and a curvaceous body. She had a great sense of humour, a welcoming smile, and was extremely tactile. He asked if he could take her home and was astonished when she said yes. He found her easy to talk to and she invited him in when they finally reached her home, on the pretence of a coffee. They went through the front door and she held her hand out and led him up the stairs to the bedroom. Directly after they had made love, and whilst he was preparing for an encore, she told him that she was married, separated, and had three children. It was strange because, if any of his mates had said that they were having an affair in a similar situation, he would have said they were mad. She told him of her estranged husband who continually beat her and had dubious methods of earning money. A few weeks into the affair, whilst in bed, Kathy sat bolt upright.

"Christ, I think the bastard is climbing up the drainpipe!"

John was, to say the least, more than a little frightened. She leapt out of the bed, ran down the stairs and made sure the doors were all locked.

"Don't worry everything is alright, he's not here. But he has done these things before." On his very next visit, Kathy informed John that her husband, Ken, knew where he lived, as he had followed him home. Why he didn't just walk away then, he didn't know.

Then, one evening, there was a knock on the door at his home in Greenford. His father answered it. Returning to the lounge he said "There's a bloke at the door wanting to talk to you." He looked hard at John and said "If you have a problem son, shout." John looked back at him mystified

"Who is it?"

"He wouldn't say…. Be careful son!"

When he reached the door, he recognised Ken from a photograph Kathy had shown him, He was not as tall as John but huge in stature; fair hair; cool blue eyes; and looked ready for anything anyone would like to throw at him.

"John, my name is Ken. Kathy is my wife, come and have a chat with me about my Kathy."

He walked towards a large Ford Zephyr, unlocked the door, reached across and opened the passenger door. John nervously sat down. Ken said "I want to know what your intentions are with my Kathy."

John actually shocked himself when he replied "I don't think it's got anything to do with you!"

The punch came as a total surprise; John's head recoiled backwards and was caught again with a follow up punch directly to the nose; blood spurted out all over the car.

"You fucking shit, keep away from my wife and my kids!"

As he prepared himself to strike John again, the driver's door opened and John's Dad hit him with an old cricket bat, which he always kept by the side of the bed in case of unwanted guests. He then pulled him through the door and head butted him, knocking him senseless. John scrambled out of the car whilst his father continually kept slapping Ken's face; Ken was shaken and very groggy. "Don't you ever fucking go anywhere near my boy again, or you will have me to contend with. Do you understand?"

Ken nodded, crashed the door shut and fortunately never came anywhere near John again.

The affair continued for another year, John didn't know why. The association was a nightmare from the very start and gradually started to fall apart after John helped her move some distance away from her home in Surrey. Directly after the move, Kathy obtained her divorce and became single again, she was free of her husband and wanted to put herself about. John watched her flirt with everything in long trousers and began to wonder whether others were also warming her bed at night. He started to get horrible pangs of jealousy and felt that he was continually being used as a taxi service and occasionally as a lover. He loved her, but he also hated her.

One night he dropped her off and never returned. It must have been mutual as he never heard from her again. He did hear something of her a few years later, when he met a good girlfriend of hers; Pauline. Kathy had been living on her own, the children had departed to live with her ex-husband Ken. Ken had turned into, or always was, a small-time crook. Since then Ken had been sent to prison after committing grevious bodily harm and Kathy had taken custody of the children. Whilst serving his time he was also found guilty of armed robbery. John gulped and thought about what might have happened, Good old Dad!

9

The sudden death of his mother Elizabeth several years ago; a week before Christmas; and then his father Jack on Christmas Day only two years later, had a profound effect on the family. Elizabeth loved Christmas. On Christmas Eve she always spent the evening making mince pies whilst she played her favourite Christmas LP's, Nat King Cole, Frank Sinatra and, repeatedly, her favourite single; Bing Crosby singing White Christmas. John recalled the smell on returning home after a few drinks out with his mates. He would unlock the front door and be greeted by the aroma of the mince pies from the kitchen. They were so irresistible, he would devour several before going to bed.

John's brother Martin and sister Caroline had discussed many times the best way to commemorate their parents lives as a family every year. Many ideas were suggested and Christmas was agreed to be the time for it to take place. Exactly what and where was giving them a headache. Caroline, now separated from her husband and having to bring up her two small girls Lynette and Ritchi, invited her two brothers over for Sunday lunch in Perivale. She was a great cook and Sunday lunch, when offered, was never to be missed. The topic of their parents again dominated most of the afternoon, the photograph albums came out and, as the afternoon progressed, Caroline and Martin were becoming more and more tipsy. The children played with their dolls and entertained themselves as the siblings sat in a relaxed atmosphere on the two leather Chesterfields in the lounge. Caroline was becoming more and more frustrated with their lack of progress and said "Oh come on you two, surely we can think of something!"

Martin, well known for his caustic sarcasm, slurred;

"Hey C-A-R-O-L-I-N-E, your ideas have been brilliant so far!"

"Oh shut up." Replied Caroline angrily.

Ritchi's little voice suddenly piped up, "Mummy why did Grandpa and Grandma call you Caroline?"

Caroline laughed "I don't know love."

There was a long pause as she looked questioningly at her mum, before posing another thought;

"Was it anything to do with Jesus?"

"I don't think so."

"Wasn't Caroline at the birth of Jesus?"

"No."

"So why do we sing Carols?"

"I really don't know Ritchi, but I will try to find the answer for you."

John suddenly blurted out loudly. "Ritchi you are a diamond!"

Everyone looked at him.

"That's it. What about a carol service, there is a huge one held at *The Royal Albert Hall* every year." It was that Eureka moment. They all smugly agreed, sitting back with huge smiles on their faces while Caroline poured out some more Champagne. It was just left to obtain the tickets and their parents' lives were remembered and celebrated from that day onwards.

Another year and another evening at *The Royal Albert Hall* had, once again, reached its climax; the audience fully appreciated the opportunity to sing their hearts out. The evening ended with old favourites Once in Royal David's City; Hark! The Herald Angels Sing and O' Come, All Ye Faithful and everyone was disappointed when it finished. They had enjoyed the convivial atmosphere, superb choir and orchestra. The applause at the end of the evening continued for over five minutes, until finally everyone vacated the stage. John said his goodbyes to his family and, along with hundreds of others, was slowly exiting one of the aisles towards the foyer. Finally he reached it and was heading towards the exit doors when a woman shouted excitedly "It's Johnny Crowther!" Before he knew it, he was surrounded by adoring fans with pens in their hands, handing him the evening programmes and anything they could find quickly to obtain his autograph.

Bill Farrer watched the mass hysteria with amusement, whilst he waited for his daughter to return from the ladies. On her return, she grabbed his arm and asked.

"What's going on Dad?"

"Someone spotted Johnny Crowther and they all went crazy."

She stared at them all and began to smile.

"I don't understand people sometimes. Why don't they leave the bloke alone."

Bill said "He might like the adoration."

"You'd never see me doing anything like that."

"Why? Would it be too demeaning for you?"

She paused and thought about it momentarly, "Yes, I think it would be."

"You are funny sometimes."

Just then Johnny came into view.

"Dad…. I know him."

"Of course you know him, it's Johnny Crowther."

"No, I mean, I actually know him, or knew him."

Bill looked at his daughter with a bewildered frown.

"He plays football for Arsenal and England, that's how you must know him."

"No Dad, No! I know him. I went out with him when I was at The Lawyers Stationers Society. Don't you remember, when James and I split up for about a month or so, I went out with him. John Crowther. Dad I really do think it's him."

"Oh come on Sandra he's always on the box. You must know him!"

"Dad when have I ever watched football, or been remotely interested? I would rather watch paint dry!"

"Well why don't you join the queue and say hello?"

"You must be joking. No way!"

Bill was intrigued by his daughter's reaction, and enjoyed watching her squirm with embarrasment.

"He probably wouldn't even remember or recognise me."

"OK, then I'll line up with everyone else." he said

"No, no please don't."

Bill smiled at her and walked towards the throng of eager admirers, he joined the end of the line and every now and then he would look over at her and make a grimace. Then, at last, it was his turn. "Sorry Johnny, I personally don't want your autograph, but my daughter reckons she knows you. Did you once work at The Lawyers Stationers Society?"

There was a long pause and it became obvious to Bill that maybe Sandra was right; he looked quite uncertain.

"Yes, I did.... Let me just finish signing the last few autographs and I'll come over. Where are you?" Bill pointed towards where he had left Sandra, who now couldn't be seen as she had hidden behind a pillar feeling embarrassed.

"Well we are just over there by the pillar." Bill said.

Bill returned to Sandra and told her Johnny would come over when he had signed all of the autographs. Johnny was unable to see the girl in question and actually thought it might be some hoax. He wondered whether it might just be Sandra, and then dismissed it almost immediately. He continued signing autographs and chatting to everyone, then he began to walk towards Bill.

Sandra watched him approach, standing behind, and half hidden by, her father.

Johnny still wondered if this was a hoax. 'Could it be, no it couldn't be Sandra, wake up, get real'. As he finally reached the couple and Sandra came into view, his heart started to race and he found it difficult to say anything more than "Sandra. I don't believe it."

"Neither do I. How are you? Wow you've done well. I never associated you with the young guy from the Composing Room."

"I'm really good. Are you married? Got kids? I have thought of you. Wondered what had become of you."

Sandra was embarrassed as, to be honest, she had seldom thought about John since their time together. The three sat down in the bar area, John bought two gin and tonics and a sparkling water for himself. The first question was "What's with Johnny? You were John when we went out."

"Oh it was when I started to play for Arsenal's first eleven, there were already a couple of guys called John at the club and, being the youngest and the greenest, they said they would call me Johnny in future and it stuck. My Mum and Dad hated it, all my friends and my brother and sister still call me John."

They were constantly disturbed by autograph hunters. John signed each time without hesitation and always exchanged a few words with each of them. He discovered that James had walked away before the wedding, not long after the invitations had been sent out. Bill was still extremely aggravated about it and had to walk away for a while, his disgust at the way his daughter had been treated could never be forgotten. Time passed quickly and, before anyone realised it, Bill looked at his watch and started to panic. They were close to missing their last train home and it looked more than a possibility that they already had. John would have loved to have driven them home, but his car was miles away.

Bill seemed a little upset. "Look the club use a chauffer driven limousine service, I have one picking me up soon, when it arrives you take it. It will get you home. Don't worry, I'll pay."

"Thank you. I do appreciate it, but I cannot accept charity. You let me know how much it costs and I'll reimburse you."

"Sorry, that's fine, I was only concerned that you ended up in a black cab which would cost you a small fortune."

The limo arrived and Bill told the driver the address in Kidbrooke. They shook hands, Bill left his telephone number and Sandra and Bill departed in the limo while John took a black cab home. As the cab made its way to Harpenden in Hertfordshire, John cursed that he hadn't at least attempted to make a date. The journey home cost him £100!

A week later the invoice from the limo company arrived; £130, which was a lot more than he expected. John was caught in a quandary. He had promised Bill that he would phone him but how could he; the price was exorbitant. But if he didn't, he might never have the opportunity of ever seeing Sandra again. It was a further five days before John plucked up the courage to call Bill and, after he told him the price of the limo, he would ask to speak with Sandra. As he dialled the number he felt his heart begin to race, the phone rang and rang and rang until, finally, the answer machine kicked in. John left a short message, including the price and his home telephone number and hung up. He lied when he said it was £65.

Three hours elapsed before the phone ran; it was Bill and the price didn't phase him at all.

"Are you sure? It took him well over an hour?"

"Yes, no problem."

"Nice to speak with you John, hang on a moment, Sandra would like to have a word with you." There was a long pause and there was muffled talk with an occasional recognisable word.

"Hi it's Sandra. My Dad is trying to play cupid."

John said nervously "I would love to meet up."

"John, I'm sorry but I'm not looking for a boyfriend."

"No strings, we could just have a drink, or a meal."

Bill hadn't left Sandra's side and just looked at her in disappointment, knowing that she had very little trust in men since the wedding had been cancelled. He shook his head. She saw his reaction.

"OK. OK." she said reluctantly.

"Why don't we meet up at Waterloo Station and maybe go to the flicks?" She laughed. "It would be like old times!"

"OK, give me a couple of days and I'll sort some dates out."

"OK, I'll wait for your call." she replied.

He replaced the phone and leapt up, punching the air.

Sandra and John finally met up at Waterloo Station after a number of postponements from both parties. John arrived early by limo and waited patiently at the exit. As the train finally arrived, John felt really anxious. The train stopped, the doors began to open and the platform quickly became full of passengers hurriedly attempting to exit as quickly as possible. John watched intently as the sudden exodus came to a halt at the barrier, as each traveller handed their tickets to the overworked railway official.

He couldn't see Sandra. Momentarily he thought she hadn't come, but that wasn't the case. Within moments she was handing her ticket to the ticket collector and making her way in his direction. The official recognised John and gave him a knowing look, intrigued to see who he was waiting for. He watched him as he met up with Sandra. They said their hellos and she gave him a peck on the cheek. They briefly discussed where to go, gave the cinema a miss, and decided to eat. John suggested "How about *The Savoy* for something to eat?" Sandra was quick in replying "No way, I'm not dressed for it!" John, with a huge grin on his face, looked her up and down. "You look absolutely fine to me."

It was so strange to her to be with someone that was so well known. In the Savoy it was obvious that people were whispering to each other and looking furtively in their direction. Both chose French onion soup as a starter, followed by cod and chips washed down with a Chablis. They both declined the dessert for a couple of white coffees. Two hours passed, discussing what had happened since they had last seen each other and loads of memories from the past.

Sandra started to frequently look at her watch. John beckoned the waiter and asked for the bill. It arrived but before he could look at it Sandra had grabbed it. "50/50!" she said. "And before you say anything….. not negotiable." There was no point in arguing about it. John put his hands in the air in a gesture of defeat. "OK. How much is it?" he asked "£146.00 plus tip say £165.00; £82.50 each."

Sandra opened her purse and counted out her half and John matched it, reluctantly. "I have to go, Dad has promised to pick me up at Waterloo in about ten minutes."

"OK, it won't take us long to walk there. I would love to do this again." he said nervously. There was a very long pause, until she said "I have to be honest with you John, I was not very sure about tonight, but I have really enjoyed myself and yes, I would love to see you again." They walked briskly down The Strand and over Waterloo Bridge until they reached the main entrance, where Sandra's Dad was waiting patiently. They said their goodbyes, but this time it was a full kiss on the lips and a promise to ring.

The dates increased over the coming months and they became closer with every meeting. The first weekend Sandra spent with John started quite bizarrely. John continually glanced out of the window anxiously awaiting her arrival. It had been two hours since she had phoned to say she was setting off from her home in Kidbrooke. Finally she arrived in a clapped out faded red coloured Morris Mini, she climbed out puffed out her cheeks, sighed, gave John a quick kiss and opened the boot, she looked exhausted. She complained bitterly about how long it had taken her and the amount of traffic on the road. John lifted the bag out of the boot and looked at the wreck of a car in disdain, he placed his hand on the bonnet and removed it quickly; it was red-hot. "Come on I'll show you where the bedroom is, and then we'll have a drink." He went upstairs closely followed by Sandra. He entered the bedroom. "There you are, it's an ensuite, I've got out loads of clean towels, and shampoo, conditioner, etcetera. She looked around, grinning and slowly shaking her head.

"You are lovely. It's a nice room, but I'm not going to sleep in here on my own. Where are you sleeping?" He smiled and walked to his room. She looked around. "This will do nicely, which side of the bed do you sleep on?"

"On the left." he replied.

"Ok the right is fine for me. Not that we're going to get much sleep." She said enticingly.

They went back down stairs and ordered a Indian take away and opened a bottle of Moet. "How old is the Mini? Ten years…..more?

"I don't know, it was my mum's." she said defensively.

Look I have a brand new Ford Capri 1600 GT in black which I bought six months ago, sitting in the garage and of course already have the Mercedes. Why don't I get shot of the Mini for you and you take the Capri?"

Sandra went berserk. "Hey this relationship has only just begun, don't try and buy your way in to it. It's to early to start this sort of thing."

There was a long pause, silence….. John had thought of giving her the car as a present, but he quickly realised his error and changed tact.

"No, I'm not giving it to you, just borrow it, until you can afford to buy another, or when you do, or if our relationship flounders, you just return it to me. The Mini isn't safe."

Sandra calmed down, gave him a kiss and and cuddle. "OK thanks, let's just see, don't rush me into anything, let's take it day by day and see whether things work out."

Before long, Sandra was spending nights in his home, a five bedroomed detached house on the affluent West Common in Harpenden, where a number of TV, film and sport celebrities resided. Within fifteen months, in 1974. The relationship grew ever stronger and the Capri was never returned. John and Sandra were married. It was a small affair, a registry office in St Albans and then a reception at The Sopwell House Hotel with just twenty people including Sandra's mum and dad, his brother Martin, sister Caroline, her children Ritchie and Lynette and some close friends including Len Morris.

It had been difficult to keep the wedding out of the press; there always seems to be someone in a trusted position that will, for a few bob, tell all. A number of fans turned up and a few managed to slip security and find their way into the hotel. Fortunately, those that did were in great spirits and only wanted to give their Johnny and his bride their very best wishes. The security staff finally arrived apologetically and were in the process of ejecting them, but John was so happy he stopped them and the five lucky fans were offered a glass of champagne.

Sandra never liked football or the fame she 'found' by marriage. She very seldom attended any of the home matches at Arsenal but, nevertheless, she was proud of her husband and was happy being a wife and mother to their son Bradley, who was born in 1975, followed by daughter Michelle two years later.

His service as a full-time professional with Arsenal Football Club lasted thirteen years; he retired in 1979. He was then 34, his knees had begun to cause him problems and he was finding it difficult sometimes to complete some of the training sessions. It was time to pack up. He played 512 games, capturing three league Championship medals, two F.A. Cup winners medals and one European Cup Cup Winners medal and was capped for England 23 times. On retirement from the game, John was honoured with a testimonial match between Arsenal and local rivals Tottenham Hotspur at Highbury. Sandra attended, along with all of the family. Unfortunately inclement weather reduced the attendance figure dramatically, and his payout considerably. John banked a mere £17,000, adding to the savings of £10,200 that he had already placed in the hands of a major building society, in readiness for the future.

Surprisingly, John decided that his future would not involve football and set about the endless studies required to be a London Cabbie. It took him three years to pass The Knowledge and, from his savings, he bought an Austin Taxi and began self-employment, ferrying the fare paying public around the City of London. It was hard work with long unsociable hours. Hours of sheer boredom, waiting to be hired. He tried for months, along with hundreds of others, parked on the perimeter of Heathrow Airport, just sitting in the cab, or chatting with other cabbies. You could wait for hours before it was your turn and then be called into the airport hoping that someone would want to go to Brighton or Bristol or Birmingham, but you could end up too easily somewhere local.

When approached some three years later to manage a local Gola Alliance Premier League side; Barnet; he readily agreed. The money wasn't fantastic, but at least it wasn't boring and it was regular. His now good friend Len Morris was never far from his side, giving help and guidance when solicited.

It came as a big shock when Len Morris was allowed to leave Arsenal for West London Football Club, to take up the position as manager. An even bigger surprise was forthcoming when, in 1995, Len requested John to join him as his assistant. The association between the two friends ended before the season even commenced; Len suffering a fatal heart attack one evening. John stepped up as manager, even though he was still finding life without his friend hard to accept.

10

Jenny Clarkson was one of those who had experienced Princes' barbarous acts first-hand, and had succumbed. Since leaving RADA, her acting ability and beauty had blossomed appreciably. Her determination to succeed and be recognised in the television and film world, without the use of the directors couch, was at long last paying dividends. A couple of commercials early on; for a hair shampoo and a body lotion; had been quickly followed with cameo parts in Eastenders, The Bill and Holby City. She was now on the verge of capturing a major role in a new six-part T.V. thriller. She was nearing the big time: her third audition was merely a formality and confirmation to the backers that the producer had found the right character to play the female leading role.

As happens all too often, the underworld had infiltrated the profession through the backdoor. The protection racketering again proved a worthwhile source of revenue, together with an additional avenue to peddle their drugs. Douglas Lowdnes had specifically detailed Prince on the method he wished to expose Mike Stephenson and the contacts who would make it possible. The first approach was to be at the Bravo Rehearsal Rooms in Acton; Douglas Lowdnes knew they were in the process of opening a new shop named Redmand Art. Prince used his own persuasive manner to influence them in their selection of a celebrity. The owner, Colin Redmand, had originally preferred the sophisticated Melvyn Bragg but he was a meek man who found it difficult to come to terms with the seedier side of life and paid heavily to protect his investments. T.V. producer and heroin addict Felix Simon, the owner of Bravo, provided another part of the jigsaw, and probably the most important. The bait. When asked whether he had any up and coming beauties, he was quick to offer Jenny Clarkson's name.

Ray Prince invited himself along to what was to be her third audition. He stood leaning against the side wall, watching the various rehearsals and auditions before Jenny Clarkson stepped into the fray. She was stunning. He watched her move gracefully around; the swagger of the hips, the flicker of the eyes and the smile. He began imagining her laying submissively beneath him, whilst he attended to his own desires and sexual fantasies. He wanted her badly. He watched and waited for her to finish and instructed Felix Simon that he wanted his help by way of an introduction. Simon agreed and the beginning of a frightening plan to secure her assistance was put into action.

"Jenny, sweety, I would like you to meet a friend of mine." said Simon effeminately.

"This is, sorry……." The heroin which Prince had given him as his reward had already been taken and had affected his memory. He put a couple of fingers to his lips in a please forgive me gesture.

"I've for…."

He had forgotten his name and before he could finish what Prince was dreading he was going to say, he interjected quickly.

"I'm Phil West."

Jenny Clarkson held out her hand and Prince took hold of it, shaking, it firmly. He threw a look at Simon who knew it was time for him to disappear.

"I'll leave you now as I know Mr West has a proposition to put to you."

Felix Simon departed to the toilets for another snort of heroin.

"Miss Clarkson, let me first say that I feel you have great acting talents and considerable beauty and I have been studying your progress for some time now." he lied.

"Thanks very much. What can I do for you?"

I am involved in another side of the business, closely related to what you are presently doing, and I am willing to offer you a substantial amount of money to become part of a small film, which would last probably thirty minutes with an additional amount of preparatory work prior to it."

"Firstly what are you offering and secondly, what does the part entail?"

"I am offering £15,000."

"How much?" she said in astonishment.

"£15,000." he repeated.

"That's unbelievable!" she said, and a faint smile came to her face as she thought to herself that she had made it at last.

"What is it, an advertising film?"

"Come and sit with me in the refreshment area, and let's discuss it over a cup of coffee."

They walked over to the refreshment area and found a vacant table with a couple of seats. There was only one other person sitting there and he was tucked up in the corner, quietly reading through a large manuscript. The square room was tiled in white and black and was crammed full of old wooden school desks and seats. It was cheap and devoid of any decoration except for the cream emulsioned walls above the tiles, which were once white.

Prince brought the coffees over and sat down.

"Are you now finished for the night?"

"Yes. This evening was just a formality. I've just been short-listed for the female lead role in a six-part war drama." she said excitedly.

He gazed at her as she lifted the coffee cup to her lips and sipped the contents.

"Well come on. Tell me what the part is? I can't wait to hear!" she blurted.

"Do you mind something a little risqué?"

"No, not if it is an integral part of the dialogue."

Prince then told her the outline; a story with an international footballer and a beautiful girl. How she will meet the guy and take him back to her apartment and then seduce him.

"That seems fine to me. When we simulate love making, presumably I will be covered by a sheet or something?"

"No, I think you might well be naked."

Alarm bells started to ring, something seemed wrong. Jenny Clarkson started to become very suspicious.

"Will he also be naked?" she asked.

"I suggest that he might also be. If you've done your job right."

"Will the film show glimpses of my body or will it be a bit more detailed?"

"I think the audience would like to see your body in, as you put it, detail."

"And the lovemaking itself, will he be naked?" He looked at her. The kind face had turned hard and cruel, he was exciting himself with the line of conversation.

"I hardly think he could penetrate you with his pants up around his arse. Do you?"

"What are you saying?! Stop this. This is porn. I'm not interested in having sex with anyone, especially not in front of bloody cameras. I'm an actress. You dirty, pathetic little man. What's this, a big thrill for you? You can fuck off. I'm not interested."

She shot up abruptly from the table, knocking it so hard that the coffees overspilled onto it, and then rushed towards the toilet.

11

Ray Prince felt humiliated, he had totally misread Clarkson. £15,000 to be fucked was an unbelievable sum of money, especially when he himself would do it for nothing. He sat for a minute or so, wiping the coffee splashes from his trousers and wondering what his next move should be. He was determined that Jenny Clarkson would do what he wanted and she would pay for her outburst. He left the rehearsal rooms and positioned himself opposite, in the shadows of a small shop doorway. He watched the door for Jenny to come out for what seemed like hours, but in fact it was only thirty minutes.

Intermittently the door would open and the light from within would cascade into the darkness, casting elongated shadows of the people leaving onto the pavement. They left in groups, talking and laughing animatedly, or singly and silent. He hoped that she would be alone. At long last it was her. The door closed behind her and the darkness engulfed her as she strode briskly towards the car park. Prince followed, treading softly. He slithered menacingly in her path, keeping her within easy reach. She was unaware of his existence as she triggered the central locking system of her old Nissan Bluebird. The key turned in the lock and all four doors were ready to be accessed. Prince knew that as careful as most women were, they very seldom locked all the doors from the inside until they had sat and placed their handbag safely in the car. The other mistake was to strap themselves in first.

Jenny Clarkson made that mistake. She slipped into the seat, threw her handbag on the back seat, strapped herself in and put the keys in the ignition. She was seething and very upset.

Prince seized his opportunity; he leapt towards the passenger door, opened it, climbed in and shut it in a succession of rapid movements. If Jenny had any opportunity to escape it was gone within seconds. He stifled her scream with one hand and punched her hard in the solar plexus with the other. The muted scream turned into a wince as the air from her body escaped involuntarily. She slumped forward in a motionless state.

Prince quickly undid the seat belt, dragged her limp body over to the passenger seat and made his way around to the driver's door. The automatic started first time. He engaged reverse gear and pressed hard on the accelerator, the wheels spun as the car leaped backwards. He slipped it into drive and sped off in the direction of Wormwood Scrubs. On arrival, he found a secluded spot in a small copse of trees, well away from any public thoroughfare. He switched off the engine and waited for her to recover. As he waited and watched her, he started becoming aroused. The diffused moonlight had cast her in a silhouette which made her appear even more attractive. He fought hard against the compulsion to have her, but he could feel himself becoming excited as the blood began to respond to the signals from the brain. He started to undo her blouse. He unbuttoned it and pushed his hands inside her bra feeling her breasts; he wanted her badly. He then put his hand up her skirt, pulled her pants down and then off. He undid his trousers and started to take them down, along with his pants. He wanted to have her there and then. He started to move his hands up her thigh, and then stopped. This had to wait. This could be done somewhere else at some other time.

Jenny came round almost immediately from a nightmare, only to be the subject of another. She was on her back with her blouse open, breasts released from her bra and her pants removed, and him with his trousers and pants down. She could smell the pungent smell of male body odour; in itself enough to make her feel sick; and saw the grinning face of the stranger she had met earlier. She was hurting from the blow to the stomach and was petrified. She screamed loudly, wriggled, scratched and fought for her life.

Prince placed his hand across her mouth, his strength was too much for her and her distress made him excited again. He enjoyed the power he held over her and knew she was totally helpless. "Now shut up and fucking well listen."

He picked a flick-knife from the pocket of his dishevelled trousers and held it closely to her cheek.

Jenny drew back, frightened.

"Life, my dear Jenny, is cheap. And yours is worth nothing to me, or the people I work for. I will still pay you £15,000 to do this little job of work, although I reckon I could probably now get it done for nothing. But I won't be greedy."

Jenny began redressing herself, sobbing as she did so.

"I wont do it!" She said. "I wont do it!"

Prince placed the knife against the upholstery of the car and pulled it hard across its surface. The material separated as the blade cut through it like butter. Jenny shivered.

"You will do what I ask, or your short acting career will be finished. Facial scars do not look too attractive. Do they? No-one will want you when I'm finished with your pretty face."

Jenny tried to get out of the car but Prince was too quick for her. He grabbed her and held both her hands within one of his own.

"You, lady, could easily lose your fucking life here and now. So sit there and shut up."

He released her hands and retrieved her handbag from the back seat. He undid the clasp, opened it and rifled through the contents. He found her driving licence and looked at the details.

"Now let's see where you live. 'Jennifer Anne Clarkson', "So you use your own name, not one of these, pretentious *nom de plume* type stage names Jenny. Or should I call you Jennifer? '112 Primrose Hill Road, Primrose Hill'. Nice, very nice."

Prince pulled his pants and trousers up and got out of the car, opened the passenger door and dragged her out, throwing her to the ground.

"I will never be very far away from you until I need to get in touch." he said as he clambered back into her car and drove off at considerable speed.

She sat sobbing, with her head in her hands, on the wet grass for quite some time, until she knew he was not coming back. She lifted herself up; the wetness of the grass had absorbed through her clothes and her backside felt damp and cold. She tried to examine herself in the dark. She felt relieved, despite the fact that fear had made her wet herself involuntarily. She picked up the remnants of her handbag and looked around for her shoes but couldn't find the left one. She limped bare-footed towards the far off lit road. It took her some time to reach it as she stumbled through the grass, her feet continually digging into the damp soil as she made her way to safety. She tripped and fell several times, falling into wet grass and mud.

12

It was now gone midnight and traffic was scarce on the well-lit road. The few cars that did materialise did not attempt to stop; they drove past and around her as she frantically tried to get them to pull over. She walked in the road, in the hope that someone would stop for her. Relief finally arrived in the form of a local police patrol car. The two officers, one male and one female, were finding it difficult to comprehend what she was trying to say. They could see the state of her. She resembled a bag lady. She was covered in grime; all over her legs, arms and face. Her clothes were dishevelled, she gripped hold of her handbag tightly in one hand and a single shoe in the other. Her mascara had smudged all around the eyes. They sat her in the warm of the car as they fired questions at her, with little response.

"Are you all right madam?"

"Are you hurt?"

"Where do you live?"

"What's your name?"

Whilst one officer asked the questions, the other radioed through to the station and informed them that they were taking her to the nearest hospital. The policewoman again attempted to establish the evening's activities and her identity.

"Come on love, we're trying to help you. Tell us your name. Is there anyone we can contact for you?"

The only thing that the officers could make out from the almost incomprehensible prattle coming from Jenny's mouth was the word 'stranger' which was repeated time and time again. The policewoman prized her handbag from her grip and began to search through it. She found her driving licence and contacted the station, giving them exactly the same details Ray Prince had memorised earlier in the evening. The car shot off with the siren blaring and the lights flashing. Jenny had been given a blanket and she sat in the back, cuddled up in it. Hammersmith Hospital was not too far away and the squad car didn't have any difficulty in reaching it in rapid time.

The overworked Accident and Emergency Department was already stretched to the limit: Several 999 calls had dispatched ambulances to two heart attack victims and a further two to major motor accidents. One car accident, involving two cars and three people, had just seen them brought in for treatment; each of them were on the critical list. There were two victims from a house fire, one of which had subsequently died. Two drunks sat in the waiting area, along with two policemen. They had been involved in a pub brawl and were requiring stitches to the mouth and forehead and one sat there holding a severed ear.

As Jenny waited with her two police officers, the hospital staff rushed backwards and forwards. Curtains were forever opened and closed, showing patients in semi-dressed states, laying prostrate and helpless. Whilst one of the officers gave the details he had extracted from Jenny's licence to the clerk, the other went to obtain some coffee. Jenny sat bewildered. The police would now have to wait until the doctors had finished with her before they could question her any further. They spoke to the Superintendent at Hammersmith and and told him what Jenny Clarkson had said. He was worried that the person who had committed the atrocities was out there in the community and had to be caught. He contacted 'SOCO' to provide a forensic medical examiner as soon as possible.

The doctor's examination was thorough and confirmed that she had not been raped, which was a huge relief to Jenny. The hospital found her a dressing gown and a pair of paper pants and informed her that she could go home, giving her a couple of sedatives to take when she did so. As she left the cubicle some two hours later, she noticed the two police officers who had brought her in get up from their seats in the waiting area and come towards her. She had now regained her composure and was able to speak and think coherently.

"Miss Clarkson, unfortunately, you'll have to go home as you are. We will also get some towels and a dressing gown from the hospital. Your clothes have been taken for analysis. We will run you home to Primrose Hill.", said the female police officer "and, if we may, we would like then to come in and for you to answer a few more questions. We do appreciate that you might not be up to it yet, but it is quite important to obtain as many of the facts as we can whilst it is still fresh in your mind. And we can than act to attempt to catch the culprit."

"Thank you. I appreciate your concern. I will try to answer as much as I can." She knew there would be certain facts she'd be leaving out; she didn't feel now in control of her own life and was certainly not going to jeopardise it at twenty four.

She was relieved to walk up the path of her Victorian semi. She turned the key in the door and beckoned the two officers into the lounge.

"Would you mind if I have a quick bath and a change of clothing before we start?" she asked.

The two officers looked at each other, they had been on duty for ten hours and were clocking up the overtime already.

"No, not at all." replied the policewoman .

They removed their caps and sat on the couch.

Clarkson walked into the dining area, opened the cocktail cabinet, poured herself a large brandy and swallowed it in three gulps. The intensity of her actions saw huge particles of liquid missing her mouth and dribbling down her chin onto her the dressing gown. She didn't care. The response to its consumption was almost immediate. Her heart began to race and her head became woozy. She put the bottle along with the glass on the side table and poured another. She could hear the two officers downstairs laughing and joking and felt secure. She took off the National Health dressing gown and the paper pants and dropped them on the floor as if they were contaminated.

Standing naked, she turned the bath taps on, placed a quantity of moisturising bath cream in the water and examined herself closely in the mirror. She could feel pain from the punch to the stomach and looked closely to see whether it would bruise. All in all, she had survived the ordeal without too much damage. Steam began to fill the room from the ever filling bath. She took another sip of the brandy, felt the temperature of the water, turned the taps off and stepped in. The police officers could still be heard chatting away downstairs. She had virtually filled it to the top and she slipped in until it covered her shoulders and only her head protruded. The water enveloped her body as she relaxed into it. She started to apply the soap to her body far more than she needed to, trying to remove the stench and body secretions from the evening before.

In her preoccupation she never heard the breaking of the glass or the hollow thump of two feet hitting the carpeted floor. As she wallowed in the bath Ray Prince was in her bedroom, carefully rummaging through her personal possessions, looking for something of great sentimental value. He carefully examined each drawer in turn with the competency of a customs official searching cases of contraband. His hands manoeuvred around her underwear, occasionally his rough skins caught in the delicate fabric. He shut each drawer carefully after examination. The chest of drawers provided nothing. He looked about the room and spotted what he was looking for; a signed framed photograph of whom he could only presume were mum and dad, which was sitting next the radio alarm by the bed. *The last thing she looks at before she closes her little eyes* he thought.

He quickly undid the frame and slipped the photograph in his pocket, replacing the empty frame on the bedside table. He tip-toed out of the bedroom to the bathroom door, he could hear the movement of the water and the police officers deep in conversation downstairs. '*Bloody fools, all of them*' he thought. The door was ajar and he gazed through the crack. He could clearly see the corner of the bath and the back of her head and he watched enthralled as she stood up in the bath, bent over and removed the plug. The sound of the water escaping down the drain obliterated the chatter of the police downstairs, which disturbed Prince. He had to leave. She turned to grab a towel opposite and revealed even more of her naked body to the voyeur. He could feel himself once again in the early stages of arousal, he took a deep breath and slowly and reluctantly made his way to the second bedroom. He manoeuvred himself through the open window, slithered down the drainpipe and made his way back to her parked Nissan.

Jenny towelled herself down and finished off the last of the brandy. She wrapped a towel around her head and ventured into her bedroom. She opened the top drawer of the chest of drawers, selected a pair clean panties, stepped into them and then put on a clean bra. She sprayed herself with perfume, repositioned the dressing gown and made her way downstairs to the lounge.

"Do you feel any better?" asked the policewoman.

"Yes, a lot better thankyou."

"I'm WPC748 Susan Fairbrother and my colleague is PC349 Alex Merritt." she continued.

"Start at the beginning and tell us what happened."

Jenny sat on the couch opposite, gave a large sigh and started to tell of her ordeal. She had been thinking, whilst towelling down, just what her story would be. She began....

"I was driving down the Chiswick High Road. When I stopped at traffic lights, he jumped in beside me."

The police officers looked at each other in disbelief.

"What time was this?" asked Merrit. Fairbrother had the job of writing everything down and continued scribbling in her notebook.

"Approximately 10.30pm I think. I'm not too certain."

"And then what?"

"He told me where to drive."

"And?"

"I told him to get out."

"And then?" prompted Fairbrother.

"He pulled a knife out, held it close to my throat and gave me directions of where to drive."

"Where had you been earlier in the evening?" asked Fairbrother.

"Oh, nowhere in particular. I often just drive around at night. I find driving relaxing."

"But why in this vicinity? It's miles away from where you live."

"I don't know. I just go where the mood takes me."

The two police officers again exchanged looks of disbelief and Fairbrother continued with a few questions.

"Alright, sorry I'm stopping you. Then what happened?"

"He directed me to what I now know is Wormwood Scrubs, dragged me across into the passenger seat and used the knife to threaten me."

"To rape you?" said WPC Fairbrother.

"No, well, no I don't think so. No well he obviously didn't." Jenny began to sob a little.

"Afterwards he tossed me out of the car and drove off in it."

"He stole it? You haven't mentioned that at all."

"God, if we had known that we might have caught him by now."

"What's the registration number and make of the car and what does this character look like?" Fairbrother was getting impatient.

"JC10." she replied.

"Its a red Nissan Bluebird."

Merritt radioed the information to the station immediately and held the communication open for the description of the assailant.

"He was average height, medium build with fair hair and blue eyes, aged in his mid-thirties." she muttered.

"If you don't mind I would like to get to my bed now."

"Yes. Yes of course. We can finish this at the station tomorrow if that's alright. The station will be in touch with you sometime tomorrow. I hope you manage to get a good night's sleep. I know it's difficult. Goodnight Miss Clarkson."

The two officers left, neither of them believing the story and with one question WPC Fairbrother was dying to ask……

Jenny fell into a deep sleep immediately her head hit the pillow; the brandy and the pills working well.

As the morning light filtered through the curtains, Jenny woke with a start. The phone next to her bedside table was ringing and it had woken her from her safe dream to the world of reality. She carefully picked the phone up and answered.

"Hello."

"Good morning Miss Clarkson. This is Sergeant Cox of Hammersmith Police Station. We have located your car and it is at this moment in the yard. The fingerprint experts are dusting it. Would it be convenient to send a car over to pick you up and bring you down to the station at 11am this morning so that WPC Fairbrother and PC Merritt can conclude their questions and you can retrieve your car?"

Jenny looked at the radio alarm, it was 9.12am and, fortunately, Saturday morning..

"Yes, that'll be fine."

She replaced the handset and her eye caught sight of the empty frame. Her heart missed a beat and her mouth dropped open. She picked it up and looked around for the photograph. She turned the frame over and saw that it was secure, the picture had deliberately been removed. At that moment the phone rang again. She jumped. She lifted the receiver and answered.

"Hello."

"Good morning Jenny."

She recognised the voice immediately as the menacing little man from the night before. Ray Prince didn't wait for a reply.

"Listen to me. You've probably noticed by now that the picture by your bedside is missing. I presume it's one of your mum and dad. I broke in to show you just how vulnerable you are and how the police are totally ineffective. So if you think you require their protection, it will be a waste of time. I'll get to you. You looked nice in the bath Jenny, but you really should cut back on the brandy. You'll end up waking with terrible headaches if you continue like last night's little session. Yes, you're probably intelligent enough to assume by now that, whilst your friends in blue were laughing and talking downstairs, I was not very far from you. Tell them anything and you are as good as dead. Do you understand?"

"Yes." she replied weakly.

"I will be in touch with you soon. To tell you what I want from you." The line went dead and she replaced the receiver.

As promised, the squad car arrived at eleven o'clock. WPC Fairbrother knocked on the door.

"Good morning. How do you feel?"

"Morning. I've felt better."

They walked to the waiting car where PC Merritt sat at the wheel. The drive to Hammersmith Police Station took just half-an-hour and Jenny could not stop thinking about the telephone conversation of earlier. On arrival, Jenny was subjected to a deluge of questions, many repeated from the previous evening. Her answers followed the same storyline. It was an easy one to remember, but WPC Fairbrother had still held back one question she had been wanting to ask, on one particular aspect which Jenny Clarkson had still failed to even mention. As the discussion came to its end, WPC Fairbrother got up from her seat and went over to the coffee pot.

"Anyone fancy one?"

There was a shaking of the head from both Jenny and PC Merritt.

"Your car has been dusted for prints and is in the yard. The keys are with the desk sergeant. Strangely, the keys were actually left in the ignition." she continued.

"Hey I'm not the guilty party here. I was the one attacked remember. I object to being treated like this."

"Yes of course. I'm not implying anything else, I'm just concerned about you. You leave a great chunk, an important chunk, of the incident out. You wander about having a drive. You pick strange men up in the street and you're in a location that is out of your normal area. You must think we're stupid. I think you know this man. Come on tell us who he is, so that we can put him away. You've been lucky but someone else might be less fortunate than you. This man is a danger to all women in the area. Who knows what he is capable of."

Jenny sat with her head down staring at the table top in front of her. She longed to tell the officer the truth, but was too frightened of the consequences.

"I know nothing more. I want to go home."

"Well there's nothing we can do if you don't let us. Come on Jenny, tell us who he is. Why are you protecting him?"

Jenny sat and said nothing.

"You know, if he does have a criminal record we'll pick him up by either his fingerprints or the DNA tests. Do you know whether he ejaculated? If he did, we might be able to pick up DNA traces from his clothes."

The question made Jenny look up with a start. If they did find out, would they be able to arrest him before he got to her?

She had to control the strong desire to scream at them and tell them to mind their own business.

"Come on, I'll show you the way to the front desk."

WPC Fairbrother obtained the car keys, had her sign the relative release papers and took her to her car. As she clambered in, Fairbrother spoke softly to her.

"Jenny just ring me if you have any problems."

"Thanks."

Fairbrother watched her drive through the gates, knowing that she had major problems, but being unable to help.

13

Mike Stephenson sat quietly by himself in one corner of the Players Bar. The coffee he had ordered some fifteen minutes previously sat cold and untouched on the small table in front of him. His mind continually wandered, from the nightmare of the penalty to his wife Julia and Emma their little girl, and then back to three weeks previous.

Mike had been with his agent, Tony Sale, opening the mail and categorising it. There were a number from his admirers and of course plenty from his critics. Every star had his detractors, those odd people who find fault with anything and anyone; it's part of the British way of life to create a star, place him onto a pedestal and then, once he's up there for a little while, try to knock him off of it. A lot of the letters were not only rude and insulting but obscene. Far different to some of the obscenities some of his female fans would like to have him perform on them!

The majority found their way into the litter bin. The remainder were answered. That afternoon had seen the mail deliver three lucrative offers. The first was from advertising agency Walter P. Coote, requesting his services for a television, radio and press campaign for a well-known but undisclosed sportswear company. The second was from a local Referee's Society, asking him to be their after dinner speaker and the third from a new shop in Bruton Street, London, who wanted him to cut the ribbon and officially open the shop named Redmand Art, which seemed on the face of it to be a shop selling original paintings. The third offer was incredible - twenty thousand pounds for about two hours work.

Mike told Tony to write back and accept all three offers. A decision he would very much regret.

Stephenson's reputation as a sportsman, father and husband was impeccable. His work for a variety of charities was endless and it was known that he not only gave his valuable time for nothing, he also made regular generous cash donations. Happily married with one child, a girl, he had always been aware of the effect that any kind of scandal would have on his popularity. The current England captain at twenty eight, was trying to secure his future and so far his character was unblemished.

Mike Stephenson received all the relevant details regarding the shop in Bruton Street including, as agreed, fifty percent of the fee; a bankers draft in the sum of ten thousand pounds. He spent an hour writing a humorous speech based on the details provided about the shop, linked with his own footballing experiences, which suited the occasion. After the morning's training session at the Club's training ground, he promptly made his way to his detached Georgian house in The Avenue, Sunbury. In three quarters of an hour he had showered, shaved and dressed himself smartly in a dark grey single breasted suit, white shirt and blue spotted tie with matching handkerchief in his top pocket and was speeding up the Great Chertsey Road, heading towards the City. The time was now two-thirty and he was expected to meet the owner, a Mr Colin Redmand, at three o'clock. The Red Alfa Romeo held the road well as he negotiated the series of small roundabouts leaving the Twickenham and Richmond area, but the traffic grew considerably heavier as he approached Hogarth Roundabout and was virtually at a standstill when climbing Hammersmith Flyover.

Mike began to worry whether or not he would manage to get there on time. The traffic, astonishingly, thinned passing through the Cromwell Road. Mike passed the Harrods store situated in Knightsbridge, went down the underpass and made Piccadilly Circus in minutes. He swung the Alfa into Regent Street and fought his way into the inside lane to negotiate the left turn into Bruton Street. The time was now five minutes to three and he still had to find a parking meter. As he neared Redmand Art an elderly man in an old, blue, rusting Ford Focus drove away from a meter and he slipped gratefully into the vacated spot.

Feeding the meter quickly, he hurried to the shop. Colin Redmand and his manager, Ron North, were staring anxiously out of the window awaiting his arrival. When they saw him approach, the anxiety left their faces and was replaced by friendly smiles. Mike apologised for his last minute arrival, shook hands with the two men and accepted their invitation to sit down and discuss the opening in detail. The opening was organised for three-thirty which enabled Stephenson, who always suffered from nerves prior to one of these events, to relax and take stock of the situation.

As the time of the opening rapidly approached, the pavement outside was becoming congested with prospective purchasers and onlookers wishing to get a look at the well-known figure. The opening ceremony, including the customary cutting of the ribbon with gold-plated scissors and Stephenson's speech, lasted no more than fifteen minutes. The champagne corks popped and the bubbly was freely enjoyed by all and sundry.

Mike finally broke away from the official party and wandered around on his own, studying the paintings. Sipping his champagne, he ambled from one to another, tilting his head one way and then the other, stepping back from others, grimacing and frowning at the more outrageous. Suddenly, he was aware of someone standing next to him. A strong aroma of her perfume reached his nostrils. As he struggled to think of what brand it was, a soft voice said;

"That's awful isn't it?"

He turned to face one of the most attractive women that he could recall ever seeing. She was examining the same abstract piece of art he had been trying to make out for the past couple of minutes. Her face was soft and angular, her eyes deep blue, she had a small sensual mouth, the hair was blonde; side parted with highlights; and fell gracefully onto her shoulders. She wore a small-print knee length skirt; pink buttoned down blouse with a low neckline, allowing just a minor glimpse of her cleavage; pink high-heeled sling back shoes and a white Burberry Mac draped over her shouders. She wore no rings, a pair of single pearl earrings and a small thin neck-chain adorned her pretty neck. Her eyes stared straight at the painting. There was a pause whilst he surveyed her beauty. "Yes it is." he said staring at her. "Grotesque. How could anyone think of buying it?"

"I'm trying to buy something to go in my apartment. All of these are not only well beyond my purse, they don't really appeal either." she purred. The girl took another couple of steps and looked at another picture opposite. As if under a hypnotic spell, Stephenson felt compelled to follow her. As he reached her side she tilted her face towards him and gave him a smile. That reaction brought a surge of blood to his face and around his ears, which gave him a warm tingling feeling. She turned away and surveyed the picture, turning up her nose. Stephenson again realised he was staring at her and began looking at the picture. She again acknowledged his presence saying;

"Now, I really think I could've painted this one myself!"

"Do you paint then?" said Stephenson childlike.

"No, silly. That's what I mean. He can't!"

They both giggled like two naughty schoolchildren who had found a dirty word in a dictionary. For the next half an hour they continued to amble around the exhibition, making cryptic comments on the prices and aptitude of the painters, before Stephenson finally plucked up courage.

"Look. I don't know about you, but I fancy a coffee. Would you care to join me?"

She paused and, looking in to his eyes, she said "Yes, I would like that very much."

They found their way to the exit, Stephenson finding the owner Mr Redmand and bidding him farewell on the way out. They walked down Bruton Street, along a small stretch of New Bond Street and then into Maddox Street, busily talking and familiarising themselves with one another as they went.

"By the way, my name is Mike Stephenson. What's yours?" he said, almost apologetically.

She turned and gave him another one of those smiles.

"I know, and the way most people are looking at you, so does everyone else. My name is Jenny. Jenny Rastall." she replied teasingly.

None of the small brassieres or cafes caught their eye and it looked as if the afternoon was about to reach an end when Jenny had an idea.

"None of these places appeal to me at all. My place is back in Berkeley Square. You're more than welcome to come back for a cup of coffee, or something stronger if you wish."

Stephenson looked at his watch, it was now just gone five o'clock. If he started to journey home now he would only join the mass exodus of workers fleeing the City. He might as well sit in her flat as sit in a traffic jam. "Well I have parked my car back there so yes, why not." He said. In agreement, they turned and walked back towards Berkeley Square talking away merrily, they went past the Bentley salesrooms Jack Barclay on the corner and into Berkeley Square. The luxury apartments of 'Tennison House' were only a hundred yards from the corner; at the door there was a huge brass panel of buttons with names alongside them. She punched in a coded number and the door locking mechanism was freed. Once inside, the entrance was plush, elegantly furnished and fully carpeted in a thick red Axminster. They took the lift to the fourth floor and walked down the corridor, similarly carpeted to the entrance, to the door numbered 41.

On entering the apartment, Mike was pleasantly surprised by the simplicity of the decor and the lack of children's toys that had prevailed in his own household for the past ten years. The living room was enormous; rectangular in shape with two loose fitting covered large beige three-seater settees facing one another. A small smoked glass coffee table sat in the centre, placed on a thick ornamental red Chinese rug. The floor was covered in a pale cream Berber carpet. There were two doors on the left hand side, and another to the right. In the left-hand corner, underneath the window, a small CD unit and an enormous selection of CD's sat awaiting someone's selection, and in the right an enormous Sony plasma television and video recorder. Jenny shut the door behind them and made her way to what he could only imagine to be the kitchen, saying;

"Make yourself comfortable and I'll get some drinks."

Stephenson could hear her pottering about, cupboard doors opening and closing and what sounded like a cork exploding. A few minutes later she returned, clutching two glasses and holding aloft a cold bottle of Chablis.

"Something I always keep in the fridge, for that unexpected occasion." she said, as she placed the glasses on the table and poured an equal amount of wine into each of them.

"I've got the coffee percolating. But in the meantime would you care for one of these?"

Stephenson didn't seem to have any choice in the matter. He accepted what was offered without any qualms.

"That'll be fine." he replied.

They both lifted their glasses and drank to each other's health before she moved across to the CD player and selected a Barbra Streisland album. As the first track began to play, he recognised one of her greatest hits in the song Somewhere from the album One Voice. They began friendly banter, questioning when and where the album was recorded, in the end having to find the small booklet in the CD casing to find that it was recorded in Streisland's back garden in Malibu, California on 6th September 1986. Neither of them were anywhere near getting it correct. After satisfying their inquisitive minds, and with the sounds of Streisland still reverberating softly in the background, she settled back down on the settee opposite him. Gently kicking off her shoes and tucking her legs underneath her on the settee, Mike Stephenson could hardly take his eyes off her, observing her every mannerism and movement. He could feel himself becoming sexually excited as certain movements gave momentary glances of a thigh or a glimpse of cleavage.

The Chablis was soon consumed and was quickly followed by a second bottle. The two were tipsy. He established that she was an actress, still striving for the big break, and worked for a sales promotion company, acting as hostess at various corporate events. It didn't pay that well. Stephenson wondered how she could afford to be living in this luxury. When the need arose, she stood up and refilled the glasses. He was still watching her every move admiringly, fantasies filling his inner thoughts. Her movements were sexually arousing and her conversation absorbing. Suddenly she rose from the settee and set off towards the kitchen.

"This bottle's a bit warm. I'm going to get some ice. Do you want some in yours?"

"Please." he replied. "What's happened to the coffee?"

"Do you really want some?" she replied.

"I might, before I go." The music had stopped. Stephenson ambled over to the CD player, knelt down and began to browse casually through the CD collection. From the kitchen he could hear the breaking of ice and the clinking of the glass. She shouted "Why don't you put another CD on."

"OK." he answered.

He was holding another oldie in his hands, this time one from Kenny G called Montage with one of his favourite tracks Songbird on it. He slipped it into the deck and pressed the play button. Still on his knees, he realised that she had returned and was standing next to him. She placed one hand seductively on the nape of his neck and gently caressed the back of his head. She manoeuvred her hand to his scalp and began seductively running her hands through his hair, whilst pressing her body provocatively into his back. He placed his hands behind, gripping the back of her knees. She slowly lowered herself to her knees as his hands gently moved from knee to thigh. She began to kiss the nape of his neck and her mouth moved to his ear, her warm tongue piercingly penetrating it.

He couldn't stand it any longer without reciprocating. He turned to face her, gripping her firmly around the waist and placing his lips inside her partly opened mouth. The kiss was long and sensual, their tongues spasmodically reaching out for each other. He could feel the contours and warmth of her body and smell the sweet fragrance emanating from her perfume and her own sweet bodily scent. The inevitable contact coincided with Mike's desire to venture further; a kiss was just not enough. He had not felt so much passion since the early days of his marriage. He nervously removed one hand from her waist and began to undo one of the buttons on her blouse, wondering all the time whether she would stop him and hoping like hell that she wouldn't. She didn't. His hand kept on working until he had undone them all, then it pulled the blouse apart and moved inside to feel her skin. She wore no bra and his hand found her bare breasts. They continued kissing as he fondled her, wondering what his next move should be. He had not been discouraged so far. In fact, he felt as though he had been very much encouraged.

"Where's the bedroom? Or do you want to make love on the floor?" he said boldly. He couldn't recognise himself, this was totally out of character.

"Well Mr England Captain, I don't really mind. But I think the bed; it's much more comfortable." As they both raised themselves from the floor, even in a state of semi-undress she still looked something very special. They walked arm in arm towards the bedroom door, stopping and kissing every few steps, her slowly undoing the zip on his fly, as if in encouragement. She gently kicked the door open in front of them. The appearance of the bedroom was an enormous shock to Stephenson. The facing wall was a large mirror which reflected the two of them standing in the doorway. Jenny coaxed Mike Stephenson to the giant double-bed and removed his jacket. She kissed him several more times before unknotting and removing his tie, discarding it to the floor, smartly followed by his shirt.

Mike was working slowly, as if at any moment she would change her mind. He removed her skirt and panties in one movement, moved his hand downwards and found her femininity wanting, at just the same moment as she found his masculinity. She helped him to remove his trousers and pants, caressing him all the time. They fell on the bed and he took her. The sex was enthusiastic and satisfying, so satisfying that it was not long before they were repeating the exercise, and starting to explore each other deeper. She had an almost insatiable appetite for sex which, fit as he was, sent Stephenson into a relaxed sleep, the respite allowing their exhausted bodies to recover.

Mike awoke startled, not knowing for a moment where he was; his head ached badly and he felt sick. It didn't take him long to leave his fantasy land and enter the real world. The naked body of Jenny was curled up beside him. Mixed feelings of remorse and pleasure swept over him as he thought first of his wife Julia and their little daughter, and then of the pleasures of total satisfaction he had just been subjected to. He looked hard at his watch and, realising how late he was, left the bed in one large leap. It was twenty past eight! He dressed rapidly, looking at her all the time as he did so and, when ready to go, he bent down to kiss her.

"Where's the fire?" she murmured sleepily.

"It's half past eight. I've got to get home." he replied.

"Bloody married men. You're all the same. Have your fun and run." she said bitterly. "You're a nice man Mike and I'm really sorry."

"Oh come on Jenny. You knew I was married when you met me. You even knew who I was." he retorted.

"Can I see you again?" he asked.

"What, are you going to bring the wife and kid? I think not Mike. Let's just say it was a nice interlude. Goodbye." She turned over to go back to sleep.

As he left the apartment, he stopped in the hall and made a mental note of the telephone number, hoping that when he rang her she would change her mind. He was surprised at the sudden change in attitude towards him, and why was she sorry? He quietly opened and closed the front door behind him, totally disregarded the lift and made his way down four flights of stairs and into the street. The streets were still quite busy as he made his way quickly from Berkeley Square into Bruton Street.

The Alfa was still where he had left it earlier in the afternoon, but the parking meter next to it read Penalty and the car had a £50 parking ticket taped firmly to the windscreen.

"Sod it." he muttered loudly, as he ripped it from the windscreen in anger. The drive home was comparatively trouble free and he reached Sunbury in half-an-hour. Even so, the thirty minutes seemed like an eternity, his mind continually racing; scanning through plausible excuses for his lateness and reliving the events of the past few hours. He pictured the different scenarios with Julia, as he imagined her response to each excuse. Arriving home, he parked the car in the double garage alongside his wife's new four-wheel drive BMW and went through the adjoining door into the main body of the house. The response was not far from what he expected; Julia Stephenson was livid. Her evening's culinary delight had been in the oven for so long it had totally dried up to become nearly unrecognisable.

"Where the hell have you been?" she screamed.

"I've been worried sick about you for the past three hours! Don't you know it's nine o'clock?" she continued, hardly taking a breath. "Your mobile's been turned off. The children are in bed without seeing their father, again."

"I'm sorry. I just didn't realise the time." he said weakly.

"What a crap excuse Mike. Why was your mobile switched off?" "Why didn't you ring?" she screamed.

Mike started to think fast on his feet. Whilst he expected this argument, he didn't expect the ferocity.

"Hey. Look, I'm sorry. I earned big money today and these guys didn't just expect me to walk away afterwards. I just had to stay. I could hardly excuse myself whilst I made a call 'cos my wife would be worried" he said accusingly.

Julia Stephenson's temper cooled, she had worried herself sick and was so glad to see him home in one piece. To Mike Stephenson's relief, the incident wasn't taken any further.

Directly after training the following day, Mike made several attempts to ring the telephone number he had memorised. The phone rang and rang. No-one answered. The next morning Mike was determined to ring her again, he couldn't stop thinking about her. He got up as soon as he heard Julia depart with Emma on the daily school run and hurriedly made his way down the stairs.

As he passed the front door, the postman was pressing the door bell. He opened it. "Morning Sir, I have a special delivery for you and I require a signature please." The postman handed him the proof of receipt, which he signed, and then gave him a large hard back manilla envelope, along with three DL sized letters. He stood for a moment, curious at what it could contain; he didn't recognise the sender. He perused the remaining mail before entering into the kitchen; there were three other envelopes. One appeared to be a gas bill, another from Barclaycard, the third was addressed to his wife. The handwriting looked familiar. He studied it carefully. He wasn't fully awake yet. Of course, it was her sister's.

The fourth, the envelope he had just signed for, had the words 'Photographs Do Not Bend' printed in red on it. He chuckled to himself, presumably some wag from the Post Office had written next to it: 'Oh yes they do!'. The envelope intrigued him; he couldn't remember having any photos outstanding. He walked into the kitchen, placed the letters on the breakfast bar and poured himself a black coffee from the cafetiere. He extracted a knife from the drawer and began to open the manilla envelope, carefully running the knife along its edge. He removed the contents and stared at them in disbelief, feeling his body freeze in shock.

His face went ashen as he gazed at the six colour photographs. 'They were pornographic. He felt panic and fear, firstly because he had committed adultery and he wondered about the consequences when, and if, Julia found out and secondly over who had set him up, and why. He felt extremely vulnerable.' He became nauseous.

The pictures were very clear; the photographer had managed to capture every detail. A number of porno magazines would pay dearly to have them in their collection! The face of Jenny Rastall was not clear, the photographer obviously choosing those where she was somehow obscured in every shot. His, however, was in full focus in every single one. Nothing had been left to the imagination; it was a pictorial collection covering all of his activities earlier in the week.

He picked up the envelope again, the postmark was smudged and the label professionally typed. He shook it to find out if there was anything left in it. It was empty. His brain began working overtime, as many thoughts penetrated it.

'This is surely some practical joke. It's a bad dream. I haven't woken up yet.' He had read many books and newspaper articles covering blackmail and could only presume that this was the first stage of the cycle. Another envelope containing more photographs, a letter, a telephone call…… some other contact would be made soon. But when? Where? And from who? Jenny Rastall was obviously involved, but with whom? Or could the photographs have been activated automatically 'More sinisterly, if not, then there was someone sat watching and taking photographs of them through the mirror! Mirror…., mirror…… bloody hell it must have been two-way! There might have been a whole bloody audience, even a video!!'

Mike Stephenson suddenly rushed to the kitchen sink and was violently sick. Immediately, he stuck his head under the cold tap, dried his face with the aid of a wiping-up cloth and began to compose himself.

He plucked the telephone from the wall and quickly dialled the number. This time he heard a continuous tone, normally associated with a disconnected line. He tried it again and again, the same tone monotonously persisted. He rang directory enquiries. "Hello could you please try a number for me, I've tried it several times but keep obtaining an invalid signal."

"Certainly sir. What number are you trying to connect with?"
"020-7340-4180." he replied.

"And your number sir?" she requested politely.

"01932-771133."

He could hear the operator tapping the numbers he had given her. He waited patiently for the reply.

"I'm sorry sir. That line has been disconnected. Is there anything else I can help you with?"

"Yes. Can you tell me who the subscriber was?" he answered, knowing that it was unlikely she would give him the information.

"I'm sorry sir. We are not allowed to disclose information of that nature. Is there anything else I can assist you with?"

"No thanks, thanks very much for your help anyway." he replied and replaced the phone on its cradle.

Stephenson felt desperate, he could imagine everything he had worked for; his marriage, his family, his career; all crumbling around him. His mind again thought of Jenny Rastall. Accepting that, like everything else, she had probably used a false name. Whilst his softer side thought the meeting was a chance one, the realistic side knew that he had been set up. He had to admit that she certainly could act. It hurt, he felt vulnerable. If someone could pre-plan a meeting such as this, and be certain that he would follow a pretty face, it didn't say much for his morals, or for that matter his family image. But, on the other hand, it could just have been a calculated gamble. The whole set-up must have been quite expensive. How much will they/she/he want, he wondered.

"I've just got to somehow keep this quiet." he said out loud. Realising that Julia would be back soon, he stuffed the photographs back into the envelope, hid them behind a loose panel in one of the kitchen cupboards and screwed the panel securely into position. It was a small job Julia had been asking him to do for a couple of months, and he knew it would be the safest place to hide them, until he could destroy them.

In ten minutes Mike, dressed in his track-suit, was on his way back to Tennison House. On his way to the City in the rush-hour traffic, he thought of going to the police but realised that, in doing so, there was a strong probability that a leak would see the national newspapers and television pursuing the story. The rain that morning hindered the traffic flow, the nose to tail journey taking well over an hour and a half to complete.

He drove around Berkeley Square several times in the hope of finding a parking meter, but everyone was firmly entrenched for the day, probably getting their secretaries to feed their meters every couple of hours. He finally left the Alfa on a double yellow line and walked towards Tennison House. As he reached the front door it dawned on him that he had to get in somehow. He had seen it done before on the TV, so he tried it. Mike pressed ten of the buttons on the panel and voices began to come through the communication panel, finally one of the impatient residents pressed the entry button and the locking mechanism released itself. He pushed the door open and once again viewed the plush entrance hall he had seen a few days before. He briskly mounted the four flights of stairs, striding up them two at a time. He had no idea what he was going to do or say when he confronted her. He reached number 41, hammered on the door with his fist several times and waited for a response. There was no reply. He quickly exited, as the noise he was making was going to attract some attention soon.

It was still raining and the Alfa was still there, when he reached it he started to sweat and shake uncontrollably. The Alfa's ignition fired first time, he slammed it into first gear and pressed his foot down hard on the accelerator. The car screeched away from the kerb into the oncoming traffic, violently cutting up a London Transport bus, much to the displeasure of the driver who showed his annoyance by standing on his horn and giving the back of Mike Stephenson's head a two-finger salute.

Mike quickly immersed himself in the busy London traffic. On his journey home to Sunbury he had time to reflect on the likely repercussions of his actions. 'Who are these people? What do they want from me? Christ, what a mess! If any of this hits the news media, I'm finished.' Mike Stephenson slept uneasily that night and would do so for many weeks to come.

14

Manager John Crowther was surprised that Mike Stephenson had missed the previous morning's training session. Not that he had not missed one before but, without exception, either his wife Julia or Mike himself would ring or get word to the club somehow that there was an illness in the family, or whatever. But this particular Friday morning he still had heard nothing and it was nearly time to start. Mike arrived in a hurry and Crowther was even more alarmed that he had turned up uncharacteristically unshaven, looking tired and drawn. To make matters worse, no offer of apology for his absence was forthcoming. In the two hour session Mike seemed totally out of sorts; looking tired and slow, mistiming too many tackles; and his concentration seemed to wane dramatically. John took him aside directly after the morning session, before reaching the changing rooms..

"Everything all right Mike? Julia? The children?" John inquired diplomatically.

"Yes……....Yes. Everything's fine." replied Mike abruptly.

"Isn't there anything you want to say to me?" asked John.

"No."

"Really. Are you sure?" replied John angrily.

"Oh, ah, yes. I'm sorry I missed training yesterday. Julia wasn't too well and I thought it best if I stayed home." he replied unconvincingly.

"Why didn't you ring the club?" continued John.

Mike struggled to find suitable reasons.

"What's this, twenty bloody questions?" barked Mike.

Crowther was now feeling himself growing even more annoyed and withheld his onslaught for a moment before replying.

"Alright Mike, I know something's up. If you don't want to tell me that's your business. But this club pays you good money to play football and that includes training. I'm not going to fine you this time, but next time I will."

Mike slapped the back of his own hand in a mock gesture of chastisement.

On reaching the dressing rooms, John Crowther and Mike Stephenson were confronted with bedlam. All the clothes were scattered over the floor and benches. Pockets were turned inside out and the players were searching frantically throughout their belongings, swearing and cursing as they did so. Eddie Hirst was retrieving his opened empty wallet from the floor shouting.

"Some bastard's nicked forty quid!"

Barry Thomas discovered his Rolex watch as well as all his money was missing. Coach Rob Dyson, skipper Don White and Jim Fellows had lost not only their money but all of their credit cards. The remainder had been sensible enough to leave their valuables locked in their cars or had left them at home. The two players who said very little were Mike Stephenson and goalkeeper Dave McLeod. McLeod's hunt through his belongings had left him startled. Not only was his wallet still tucked inside his jacket pocket but it was crammed full of notes of all denominations, far more than he originally had in it. He briefly stared at it, it was unbelievable. He calmly placed the wallet back into the jacket pocket and said in his deep Scottish accent.

"They've cleaned me out too."

Mike Stephenson had found his wallet in the middle of the floor like Eddie Hirst. His search had established, like some of the others, a near empty wallet, except for one item that was foreign to him. Pushed into the back was a folded photograph. 'He knew exactly what it was.' He again felt the feeling of panic and the perspiration return to his brow and the palms of his hands. He began to shake.

'He realised that the whole operation had been carried out just to plant the photograph and to show how smart and resourceful this outfit were, whoever they were.'

It took nearly two hours by the time the police had arrived and taken all the necessary details. One by one the players left the changing rooms for their cars. Stephenson slid into the driver's seat and opened his wallet. He carefully removed the photograph and unfolded it. The photo was different from the others, this one portrayed him holding Jenny Rasall's head in both hands, whilst she administered oral sex. He turned it over and written on the back were the words '*You naughty boy Mike*!' Mike slumped over the wheel, close to tears.

John Crowther wondered where the security staff were, they were supposed to guard the whole site 24 hours a day, constantly, ensuring the dressing rooms in particular were secure at all times. Questions would have to be asked.

Crowther immediately drove to the ground to speak with Paul McCormick. When he arrived he was not in his office and so he went looking for him. He finally located him in the one of the dining areas, arguing with a carpet contractor.

"I'm sorry to interrupt, but I do need to have a few words urgently."

McCormick was pleased at the opportunity to curtail his disagreement and dismissed the contractor with "We're not fucking paying for it!" The contractor grunted and swiftly made his way out through the exit with his tail between his legs.

Crowther looked around to make sure nobody else was in the room before he said anything.

"No doubt you know by now that the dressing rooms have been robbed, due to a lack of security staff. This continual penny pinching has to stop and more staff must be employed and quickly. We have to ensure the players and coaching staff come to work in an environment where they don't have to keep worrying whether their valuables will safe, that much we owe them."

"We haven't got the money!" replied McCormick indignantly.

"Well we'd better find some from somewhere, the facilities are bad enough without being subject to very little safeguarding for the players' own property."

This time it was McCormick who walked off in a strop.

15

Dave McLeod now hated living in the south, he longed to return to his native Edinburgh and his wife Margaret. The split up with girlfriend Penny on New Year's Eve did not help. The ex-Scottish International's halcyon days with Dunfermline Athletic, Newcastle United and Rangers had long since passed; he now knew at 32 that he was in the twilight of his career.

The Scotsman was once the life and soul of the party. The comic. The outrageous one, always ready with an answer. The quick wit and repartee though had now hit rock bottom. He had first met Margaret not long after signing for the Pars as a school boy at 16. They married when they were both 18 and set up home together in Dunfermline. His £180,000 transfer from Rangers to West London Football Club at the start of the season seemed, at the time, to be the correct move. For a while, he and Margaret were happy in their new environment, but the distance between their new home - a three bedroomed detached house in Ealing – and her parents in Dunfermline, whom she idolised, was simply too far. She had missed them always being there. She had also found it difficult to make friends. The other players' wives had not found her easy to talk to, she was forever telling them how beautiful Scotland was and all about Mummy and Daddy's lemonade empire.

She became more and more despondent every time her period materialised monotonously each month. She longed for children and blamed Dave for being incapable of making her pregnant. Each month she went into a decline. As time passed,

Margaret became so preoccupied with becoming a mother that she began to treat Dave similarly to a stallion on a stud farm. It didn't matter about his feelings, more about his sperm count and mating at the correct time; lovemaking and fun as such had long diminished. When her yearning was not satisfied, Margaret became bitter. In her eyes Dave could do no right. Before long they were sleeping in separate beds. When he arrived home from training one afternoon in late November, Dave McLeod was devastated to find that she had cleared the whole house of all of her personal possessions and left everything else, along with a short note saying she was going to drive back home to her parents in Scotland. Dave decided then and there to travel up to Dunfermline and confront her.

He made a quick phone call to manager John Crowther and explained the situation; John reacted sympathetically by giving him compassionate leave. Dave rang for a cab and threw a few items in a holdall, the journey from Ealing to Heathrow Airport took him a lengthy forty-five minutes, meaning he could catch the 4pm British Airways shuttle to Turnhouse Airport on the outskirts of Edinburgh. At a quarter to six a taxi hired from Turnhouse, with David McLeod in it, was half-way across the Forth Road Bridge. Gazing at the enormous red oxide coloured bridge directly opposite Dave felt a buzz as he watched the train crossing the nearby Forth Rail Bridge. The bridge was magnificent, standing majestically proud in the water with its three steel columns protruding from the Firth of Forth, as it had done for over one hundred years. As a boy he had taken photographs of it from every conceivable angle. He remembered with much affection the ferries which used to run between North and South Queensferry, before the suspension bridge was built. In those days it was the only way to cross the Firth of Forth, unless you journeyed the long way round out to Stirling and crossed it on the Kincardine Bridge.

He felt like a nerd as his memories brought back many useless pieces of boyhood information connected with the bridge. Designed by Sir John Fowler and Sir Benjamin Baker, the construction started in January 1883 and was completed in March 1890. The cantilever design was hailed as a wonder of the world. It cost more than £3.5 million to build, with a total length of 8,296 feet (over one and a half miles) and a span of 1,710 feet. The highest part of the bridge at high water was 361 feet. 55,000 tons of steel and over 8 million rivets were used. In the past the 45 acres of steel were continually painted, generations of families worked full-time and many lives were lost in both building and painting the iconic construction. He remembered how his father had told him that the Germans had tried to bomb it quite unsuccessfully in the Second World War. It had looked like a pencil to the Luftwaffa from the air and, along with the combined protection afforded to it because of its close proximity to the naval dockyard at Rosyth, it had thankfully remained untouched. Along with the thistle it represented Scotland; it was an emblem. He smiled to himself at the irrelevant rubbish he could still remember.

The taxi's approach to Dunfermline took it underneath the viaduct bridge and past the hospital before it turned into Roland Street. The large four-storied granite house Margaret's mother and father lived in had been beautifully restored, the dirty grey buildings surrounding it looking tired in comparison. McLeod paid off the cab driver, collected his holdall and walked up the tiled path.

He rang the door bell and waited. In the distance he could hear Rex, the family's wire hair fox terrier, barking and Mrs Stewart shouting at it to shut up. He could see through the large frosted glass in the front door; the inner door opened and he could see the silhouette of his tiny mother-in-law approaching it. The door opened and the dog leaped up on him excitedly, both front paws on his legs. He stroked the dog as he continued to try to lick his hand. He looked up; the face of Mrs Rosena Stewart was both sad and stern.

"Hello David. I am so sorry. I'm going to kill her when she arrives!" she said, offering her cheek for him to kiss.

"I had to come. I couldn't let ten years of marriage just dissolve." He patted the dog again and ventured inside, sitting himself down on the couch in the lounge. The dog jumped into his lap.

"I'm not surprised that you're here. I don't expect the removal van to arrive for another four or five hours yet. Margaret is following it in the car. I don't know what we can do for you David. This problem must be solved by yourselves without interference from Angus and myself. She wouldn't thank us for it. You know she has a mind of her own, she always has had. Spoilt I suppose, by her father mainly, the only child and a daughter and all that, but I must take some of the blame for not imposing greater restrictions and imparting some kind of balance." she said.

Dave McLeod looked hard at the little lady, focusing on her greying hair and arthritic fingers; people seem to age so much quicker when you don't see them on a regular basis. Mike tried to guess her age, he knew Angus and Rosena Stewart had become parents in their early forties and, with Margaret now at twenty eight both were now in their early seventies. He loved her dearly, she had always treated him as a son, especially after he lost both of his own parents.

"We shouldn't have moved down south. I was too stubborn. I didn't listen to her. I really thought that the move would be of great benefit, but unfortunately it doesn't seem to be working out. Along with our marriage." he added.

"I'm just going to ring Angus at the factory and tell him you're here."

McLeod sat looking around the room at the photographs. Pride of place over the large open fireplace was a large framed coloured picture of himself, dressed in a McLeod of Harris Tartan kilt, and Margaret looking stunning in her wedding dress. McLeod felt choked up looking at it. She returned minutes later.

"Angus would like to see you. You can borrow my car if you like. You know where the factory is don't you?" she asked.

He nodded. "What does he want?"

"Just to talk, before she arrives."

She left the lounge and came back with a set of car keys and a key for the garage. It was a struggle for a tall man to climb into the little yellow Fiat Tempra, he readjusted the seat and turned the ignition key. It fired second time. The factory was no more than ten minutes away, on the East side of Dunfermline next to a small trading estate. Stewart's Aerated Waters Co. Ltd sat on four-and-a-half acres of land with the buildings having 200,000 square feet of production facilities.

The factory manufactured every conceivable squash drink imaginable and a ginger ale of the highest quality, which had received several awards and whose ingredients were only known by Angus Stewart, his father before him and, prior to that, the founder of the company; his grandfather and his brother. After alighting from the car he could hear the chinking of bottles as they were loaded on and off the lorries and the constant humming of the bottling plant. Angus Stewart had seen him arrive and was waiting for him in the reception area. He was a serious, dour Scotsman with no sense of humour and his face showed his every mood. He wasn't happy. As McLeod walked through the door, Angus shook his hand warmly, but that was as much warmth as he was to receive from him.

"David."

"Mr Stewart." McLeod had never been able to call him Angus, and had never been invited to do so.

"Let's walk for a wee bit." he said in his broad Scottish accent.

"O.K."

They ventured into the bottling plant where the bottles were being washed, dried, filled with Stewartcola, capped, labelled and crated with incredible speed.

"David, I want you to turn around and go back home. Margaret has made her mind up and that is that. She's coming home after a bitterly unhappy period in her life, that she wants to forget. You being here will only cause trouble and bad feeling. And I don't want that. Please go before she gets here."

Dave McLeod couldn't believe his ears, Rosena didn't want to interfere but Angus had jumped in with both feet, cocooning Margaret in a protective cushion of so-called love.

"Sorry Mr Stewart, as much as I respect your intentions, I cannot let ten years of marriage just disappear down the drain."

Angus Stewart was not a man that one normally said no to. He looked extremely irritated.

"David. You are no longer welcome in my home and I do not expect to see you when I arrive there this evening." The words were said with considerable bitterness.

McLeod said nothing further but turned and walked in the direction of the car. The brief encounter was not what he had expected. He drove the Fiat back to Roland Street and, before bidding a farewell to Rosena, he told her what her husband had said. Mrs Stewart was sad at the outcome and took him into her arms, knowing that it was probably the last time she would ever see him. He patted Rex who was wagging his tail in delight. He left Rosena at the front door, sobbing uncontrollably. He walked to the local station and picked up a taxi to take him back to Turnhouse Airport.

The British Airways shuttle back to Heathrow was full and McLeod managed to get the last remaining seat as the last call was being made. He sat in the seat feeling feeble; he had allowed himself to be talked out of confronting Margaret; but he also realised that the marriage now was irretrievable. As he sat pondering what might have been, the man sitting next to him lent over.

"Excuse me but aren't you Dave McLeod?"

"Yes. I am." replied McLeod

"My name is Michael Ellison."

Dave turned and smiled. It was the first time he noticed the fair haired stranger and months later he would wish he hadn't.

An hour and a quarter later, a drunk Dave McLeod disembarked the aircraft; he had made full use of the free bar with his newly found friend and shared a taxi with him to Ealing. As he alighted, Ellison shook him firmly by the hand and gave him his business card. Dave slipped it into his pocket, bid him farewell and made his way to the local off-licence where he picked up a bottle of Famous Grouse whisky and a bag of ice. Michael Ellison continued his journey into London's West End.

The whisky bottle became his best friend in the ensuing months, along with a small casino in London's Soho district. The business card of Michael Ellison showed that he was General Manager at The Golden Wheel Casino. McLeod was already more than just speculating on the horses; it had now become a daily ritual; and, along with the free membership he obtained through Ellison, his gambling became progressively worse day by day. After training, Dave would spend the vast majority of the afternoon in the betting shops and the evenings in The Golden Wheel Casino in Greek Street. At the club his behaviour had changed, from a happy go-lucky character to a morose, unforgiving, argumentative recluse. The other players kept out of his way, avoiding him whenever possible.

The nightly sojourns to The Golden Wheel Casino had seen Dave run up a debt of £19,000. The fact that he was well-known to most of the general public guaranteed him credit and he was forever being recognised and constantly requested to sign his autograph, on one occasion signing a woman's bra strap. Dave, like most gamblers, always thought tonight was the night and that he would clear his ever mounting debts with one big flutter. But Las Vegas was not built with winners' money. The majority of times he lost; if he played red on the roulette wheel it would invariably come up white, and vice versa. The casino was not the only avenue for his speculations. On the eve of the robbery, which was later called *The Great Training Robbery*, McLeod had not taken long to place £250 of his newly gained windfall on Stable Lad in the 3.30 at Doncaster. He had sat staring at the various screens in the betting shop, watching the results and listening to the commentaries from the race courses around the country. The £250 was lost in less then three minutes when Stable Lad unseated his rider at the sixth fence, the betting slip found its way quickly into the wastepaper basket.

McLeod left the betting shop, leapt into his immaculate black 'E' Type Jaguar and headed to Greek Street. On entering the casino he emptied his wallet and exchanged the £400 for chips. He played black-jack all evening, at one stage being £1,265 to the good, but instead of quitting whilst ahead he tried to increase his winnings. He lost. Finally, worse for wear, he removed himself from the table after seeing the croupier scoop up his remaining chips.

As he left the casino he felt unsteady on his feet and only just managed to descend the concrete steps without falling over. At the bottom he observed, somewhat blearily, that Greek Street was soaking wet after a brief downpour. The reflections from the cars and street lights danced chaotically in front of his eyes, making him feel dizzy. He stumbled along the pavement, using the walls and lamp-posts for support. Each contact made his hands wet and his clothes damp. It didn't help matters that he continually wiped his hands down the front of his jacket. Greek Street was unusually quiet for a Thursday evening, except for the odd taxi. As he approached Soho Square, he reached into his trouser pocket and extracted a bunch of keys. He staggered a few more paces and felt relieved when he could make out his black 'E' Type, still parked at the meter he had left it six hours previously.

On reaching the car, he took hold of the door handle in one hand and steadied himself. He struggled to remove the keys from his pocket. He fumbled with them as he tried to manipulate the car fob correctly in his hand, but staggered and dropped the bunch. They fell to the ground with a metallic clunk. "Shit." he mumbled to himself wearily, as he crouched down to pick them up. At first he couldn't make out where they were. He began to search in the dark underneath the sill of the vehicle, on his hands and knees. He felt the rainwater gradually seeping through the knees of his suit trousers as he blindly ran his hand along the road surface, trying to locate them.

He was past caring, his senses now too dulled by the excessive alcohol in his bloodstream. As he crawled about he became suddenly aware of another's presence. His eyes blearily focused on two large black shoes. He looked up like a naughty schoolboy. The man stood calmly and spoke coldly.

"Mr McLeod we have been very patient. We would like a very substantial return of our investment. Repayment of 75% in the next seven days or your playing days will be a thing of the past."

Dave McLeod suddenly felt quite sober. Fear brought the rapid response of adrenaline, which pumped quickly through his body, as the realisation of what was about to happen dawned quickly on him. Self-preservation saw McLeod manipulate his body upwards with as much venom as he could muster. His teeth and fists clenched in the expectancy of imminent mortal combat. As McLeod's head reached the same height as the stranger's, the man crashed his head into his nose, cracking it open like a walnut. Blood spurted from the wound, covering his clothing. As McLeod started to reel backwards clutching his nose, he was caught with the toe end of a boot in the groin. He cried out in pain as his testicles took the full impact of the blow, falling backwards against the car at the same time as his body crouched, trying to relieve the agonising pain. His body hit the ground with considerable force. As he lay prostrate the man grabbed his hair, lifted his head up and whispered.

"Seven days my friend, or I'll break every finger on both hands."

The warning was followed up with a kick to the stomach and another to the head. McLeod lapsed into unconsciousness.

Ray Prince's telephone call, ten minutes after his 'business meeting' as he would have called it, was very short.

"I have dealt with our goal-keeping gambler friend and I'm sure he'll be of no hindrance."

The soft spoken voice on the other end replied;

"Good. Keep in touch."

Ray Prince was about to replace the receiver when he added hastily.

"The only problem is, somebody saw me do it, and ran off pretty smartish. If it hadn't been for some old cleaning biddy on a bike I would have had him."

There was a long thoughtful silence on the other end. Prince continued;

"Hello, are you still there?"

"Yes. Yes. I'm thinking. Have you any idea who he is?"

"Yes. I think I do." replied Prince thoughtfully. "He was in the club, so they must have his personal details, including his photograph."

Douglas Lowdnes coldly gave his most severe command so far.

"Find him and make sure that his mouth remains shut. Permanently. Bye."

Lowdnes poured himself a large gin and tonic, sat smugly back in his leather armchair and allowed himself a grimace of satisfaction.

Kirklees County vice Chairman, Douglas Lowdnes, along with elder brother Chairman James, had taken control of the club some ten years previously, after purchasing 65% of the share capital from the late club chairman's wife; a greedy woman who had no loyalties to the club whatsoever. The brothers had acquired their fortune by dubious means and despite the fact that fellow directors were suspicious of the legality of some of their business activities. The brothers had always managed to keep their dealings outside of the football club to appear legitimate. The huge interest-free loans made to the club; in excess of £6 million; had effectively stopped them from pursuing any form of witch hunt, believing that the financial rewards were of more benefit to the club. The Lowdnes brothers were disliked because of their directness and ruthlessness. Each director in turn had crossed their path, and each had fallen foul of their actions. They now remained tight-lipped and hoped that the club would never be involved in anything unseemly.

James and Douglas Lowdnes had successfully built up one of the largest franchise networks in the western world. Their chain 'Bigburgers' had been the first of its kind in Britain and had spread rapidly, now being found in every major town and city. The rapid expansion programme had seen new Bigburgers restaurants opening in Canada, Australia and the United States of America. The initial capital to finance the business was accumulated from protection racketeering in the North of England. Most shopkeepers paid, even major stores felt it more sensible to pay up rather than have their shop fronts decimated every few weeks. Non-payers would also suffer from physical attacks; the bravest of men soon succumbed to the continual harassment and coughed up.

The income from the protection racket was increased even further with the acquisition of a casino in Soho, The Golden Wheel, which led them into drugs, prostitution and, from these activities, easily into pornography. For several years, greed had seen them exploit lesser mortals than themselves and reach the position of minor celebrities and, more importantly to them, multi-millionaire status. A long way from barrow boys in the east-end. The gambling empire had grown to gargantuan proportions with the inclusion of 'Lowdnes' betting shops, hundreds now being franchised. The brothers realised early on that the pickings would be even greater if they could break the stranglehold of the mafia-type gangs in Las Vegas. The Lowdnes brothers and their highly paid assassins caused these gangs so much grief and loss of revenue that they allowed them a little latitude. It was a gesture they now regretted. Periodically, one or the other of the brothers had to jet off to the States to sort out a problem. Elder brother James was at present in Las Vegas doing just that.

Meanwhile, younger brother Douglas had taken it upon himself to utilise the syndicate to prevent Kirklees County from dropping out of the Premier Division. Instead of the investment of further capital to allow the manager to purchase additional players with the capability of preventing their relegation, Douglas had other ideas and had put into operation a series of events to neutralise the opposition. The club had been a leading contender for trophies since its formation in 1886. Relegation had never been experienced in its entire history. The gates, which exceeded

40,000 each home game, would fall drastically if the club fell from the top echelon of football and the spin-offs from the commercial activities would be affected too.

With two relegation spots still to be filled, it was a three horse race between themselves, West London Football Club and Sheffield Wednesday. Watford already looked destined to make the drop. Douglas had set himself a goal and was determined that it would not be Kirklees County joining them. He would ensure Premier Division football at Kirkless at all costs. The cost would fall to West London Football Club.

16

With son Bradley and daughter Michelle still living at home, and Sandra usually occupying the ensuite, mornings were sometimes fraught with the battle to occupy the remaining bathroom. John Crowther had won this morning and stood naked in front of the mirror, carefully shaving his upper lip and listening intently on the portable, along with three million others, to Capital Radio's 'Breakfast Show'. The effervescent Chris Tarrant, always playing many of the currrent pop records, threw in Chuck Berry's Maybellene and then another one of John's favourite artists José Feliciano singing Light My Fire. Immediately it began he started prancing around the bathroom singing along and playing a fictitious guitar.

You know that it would be untrue;
You know I would be a liar;
If I was to say to you;
Girl, we couldn't get much higher;
Come on baby light my fire;
Come on baby light my fire;
Try to set the night on fire;
The time for hesitation's through;
There's no need to wallow in the mire;
Darling we could only lose;
And our love become a funeral pyre
Come on baby light my fire;
Come on baby light my fire……..

As soon as it finished came the 7.30am news. The initial item concerned the A.A. with the suggestion that nearly 9.5 million members of the Automobile Association could well be in line for windfall payments of up to £200 after the demutualisation in 1999 and the eventual sell-off for £1.5 billion. A stuctural imperfection had been discovered in The Channel Tunnel, causing considerable concern and the likelihood of curtailment of services coming into effect immediately. A large fire had gutted an eight storey office complex in Clerkenwell which had caused the death of two people. It was thought to be arson. The next piece of news though caused him to stop shaving and stare at the radio in disbelief. The story echoed around the bathroom as the newsreader read it out:

"West London Football Club's Scottish International goalkeeper David McLeod was rushed to St.Thomas's Hospital in the early hours of this morning, after being found unconscious in London's Soho district by a passing taxi driver. It is thought that McLeod was yet another victim of a local gang of muggers, who have been terrorising the neighbourhood for some time. McLeod has sustained facial injuries and a fracture of the ribs, and is unlikely to leave hospital for several days. A spokesman for the club said that it was news to them and an official statement would no doubt be issued later in the day."

John Crowther rapidly wrapped his dressing gown around himself at the same time as the phone started to ring in the bedroom. As he approached the phone his wife Sandra had already snapped up the telephone and barked hello into it. She was not pleased at being woken up early on her day off. She held the phone up in the air with one hand, waiting for him to grab it, whilst still laying face down in the pillow.

"The Chairman." She said sleepily.

"Morning Chairman. Yes. I've just heard the news now. I'm about to contact the hospital to see how he is. No I don't know who they spoke to at the club. Yes of course I'll ring you when I have any news."

The phone call to St. Thomas's Hospital confirmed the news announced on the radio, but they refused to give any further details, only to the next of kin. It did not take long for Crowther to get dressed, jump into his Mercedes and travel to the hospital. He was greeted at the entrance by a barrage of newspaper reporters, cameras and the local regional television. As soon as they saw him the camera's started to click, the TV camera was hoisted on the shoulder of the operative, the boom mike and lighting all switched on. Various recording appliances were thrust underneath his nose as he attempted to fight his way through, whilst the waiting hoard fired question after question at him.

"Can you tell us what happened?"

"Is it drug related?"

"Is it true he was gambling?"

"How long will be in hospital?"

"What was he doing in Soho?"

"Is there a women involved?"

The questions came thick and fast, trying to get a response of some kind from him. John Crowther was experienced enough in dealing with the media, he knew not to stop and get involved, especially answering questions about something he did not yet know about himself. One wrong word could be totally taken out of context and then blown up out of all proportion.

"No comment."

"I have no comment." he repeated time and time again as he continued his plight to reach the large glass double doors entering into the hospital. At the reception desk the young nurse, dressed in a thin white overall, was busily fumbling through a large green metal filing cabinet, totally unaware of his presence.

"Excuse me." said Crowther.

"Oh. I'm sorry. Can I help you?"

"Can you tell me which ward David McLeod is in? He was brought in early this morning."

The girl sat down, gazed into the screen and commenced to tap into the computer keyboard.

"How do you spell his name?" she asked.

"M-C-L-E-O-D." Crowther replied slowly.

"Ward C8. Go through the swing doors, turn left into the next corridor and it's the fourth ward on your left-hand side."

"Thank you." said Crowther. He was through the swing doors and heading down the corridor before the girl had time to reply.

The staff nurse, a plump motherly fifty year old, was insistent that only family be admitted to see him, but after protracted explanations about the fact that McLeod's estranged wife was in Dunfermline and that he had no relations in or around London, she succumbed and allowed him a few moments to see the patient. Dave McLeod could not have looked any worse if he had been in a fifteen round contest with Frank Tyson. Both eyes were a deep mixture of red and black. His nose had been bandaged with a bridge support and the bed clothes were being held off of his body with a metal frame. He muttered a few almost incomprehensible words, hardly managing to form a sentence. But the little that John Crowther did make sense of concerned him greatly. After the words "When…..I…..left…..The….Golden…. Wheel… Casino………………." David McLeod lapsed into unconsciousness.

With the help of the staff nurse and a signed autograph, Crowther was directed to a side entrance, away from the parasites waiting for him. The car stood in the centre of the car park and appeared to have no-one in its vicinity. He made his way towards it, looking over his shoulder occasionally to see whether anyone had spotted his departure. The Mercedes had a small business card under the windscreen wiper. He took it out and glanced at it. 'Bruce Day, Evening Mail'. Written on it was 'We must talk, urgently' John thought if it is that urgent, why had he not waited?

Back at the Zion stadium, John Crowther sat in his office, contemplating the current situation; phone calls to the Chairman, the hospital and the police had not been encouraging. Chairman Alfred Wade was not pleased and accused Crowther of a lack of discipline, whilst the hospital confirmed McLeod had, in addition to the broken nose, three cracked ribs, badly bruised testicles and, more worryingly, severe concussion. The police confirmed the theory of mugging, although they admitted at this juncture that they were guessing, having still to obtain permission from the hospital to interview the victim. Crowther had passed on the short dialogue he had heard from Mcleod and the police were going to visit the club mentioned. They did confirm that he had no money whatsoever in his wallet. John sat and pondered the events of the day. Firstly the robbery. Then the episode with Mike Stephenson. And now the mugging of David McLeod. But, what was McLeod doing in Soho on an evening when he had been robbed? It didn't make sense. The lad's got a few things to explain thought Crowther.

John Crowther spent the remainder of the day on the telephone attempting to sign a replacement goalkeeper on loan, whilst coach Rob Dyson put the team through a gentle training session. It was imperative that he find a replacement quickly. Except for a brief break for a sandwich and coffee in the club's snack bar, John rang every Premier Division club but there was nothing forthcoming; no-one would make anyone available for a short loan without substantial payments, something West London Football Club were unable to afford. The non-availability of Dave McLeod had compounded an already weak area. Reserve keeper Alan Crooks was still nursing a badly bruised finger and junior keeper Paul Brown had never kept goal in anything higher than the one Premier Reserve League. Even in that game he had been found to be nervous and prone to making some quite eliminatory mistakes.

The day was continually interrupted by the switchboard.

"It's Bruce Day of the Evening Mail for you."

"Tell him I'm busy." replied Crowther.

The calls were made with monotonous regularity, with the same reply coming from Crowther on each occasion. He could do without Bruce Day sniffing around for a story for the local rag, nice guy as he was.

At the training ground Rob Dyson had heard the news and, knowing the position the club was now in, had taken young Paul Brown, along with Jim Fellows, Eddie Hirst and Barry Thomas, for shooting practice. Paul was having balls belted at him unmercifully from every conceivable angle. He was doing reasonably well, but the fair haired six-footer was still very inexperienced. Rob Dyson just hoped the boss would be in luck in getting a replacement. He anxiously watched the youngster picking the balls out of the back of the net and sighed in frustration. As the working day progressed towards its close, Crowther spoke to the Club physiotherapist, Tony Pullen, and

Alan Crooks himself. They both confirmed that any thoughts about his selection was a non-starter. John picked up the phone and dialled the internal line of Rob Dyson.

"Rob it's John. It looks as though we'll have to play Paul Brown at Spurs tomorrow."

"I was hoping you weren't going to say that."

"We've no choice have we. I can't get anyone on loan without breaking the bank and Alan Crooks is definitely out for several days. His recovery is really causing me concern. I know you are as concerned as me but can you have a word with Tony Pullen and find whether we can give him an injection or something."

"I've already pre-empted what you're asking. Tony doubted that he would be capable of handling the ball at all."

"I thought this would happen. I've put Paul through hell today in readiness."

"Is he ready?"

"Ready as he'll ever be. He's woefully lacking in experience."

"That, Rob, must be the understatement of the decade. Christ, this is every manager's worst scenario. A goalkeeper who's still wet behind the ears against one of the best attacks in the country. Will you ring him and give him the news?"

"Yes OK. One thing we haven't thought of though, what about the substitute keeper?"

"We'll just have to use John Summerfield from the youth team. He does quite well in the kick around."

"All right I'll give the two of them a ring and tell them to be here at 10.30a.m."

Crowther put his feet up on the desk and wished he still smoked. He imagined taking a cigarette from the packet, lighting it by drawing a deep breath, allowing the smoke to enter his lungs and feeling the soothing effect of the nicotine. He had packed it in some twenty years previously but he still longed for one in a crisis, and this was just that. He fought off the temptation, as he had done many times before, knowing that he couldn't just stop at having one. He flicked through the many papers on his desk, putting off the inevitable phone call to Alfred Wade. One bollocking in a day was enough, but without a goalkeeper he knew he was in for another.

He dialled the number and waited nervously for Wade's secretary to put him through. The gruff voice barked at the other end;

"Well, what have you got to tell me? I bloody hope it's good news."

"I'm afraid not Chairman. Dave McLeod will be out of action for the remainder of the season. Alan Crooks is injured and the only goalkeeper in the camp is young Paul Brown."

"Who the fuck is Paul Brown?" bellowed Wade.

There was a long silent pause from the other end. He knew this was going to be followed with some totally illogical outburst and sat and waited for it.

"So go out and sign one on loan!" Wade shouted down the phone.

"I've tried every Premier League club and they all but one said that they hadn't one available, the one that did actually wanted £30,000."

"I thought you had some influence in the football world. That's why we made you the manager. Now I'm beginning to wonder. It's just not good enough. Sort it out John or we'll be looking for someone replacement for you."

Before Crowther could reply the phone had been slammed down.

John knew the next day would be a nightmare. The old man would speak to everyone else but him. The old cold shoulder treatment.

17

Bruce Day cradled the telephone and carefully re-read his meticulously prepared report of the clandestine activities of Dave McLeod. The sports reporter from the local Evening Mail had, over the season, become very attached to West London Club. His work took him around the country, reporting on the club's fortunes. As a reporter though, he always felt that his first duty was to the public. Over the season his articles had caused a considerable amount of controversy. His remarks were often scathing; criticising tactics, club policy, the fans, and occasionally making personal attacks and comments about members of the club staff. His reporting was more in keeping with the larger national newspapers, the gutter press as they were often known. His lifetime ambition was to sit in a press office in Fleet Street, giving readers even tastier snippets of gossip and information than he was currently able to present.

The Evening Mail was located in a tiny back street in Hounslow; it was a long established local evening paper, which vied every evening for sales with the London Evening Standard. With a circulation of 31,000 it was hardly holding its own but struggling in the field of technology, some 20 years behind. The tiny cobbled street in which the Victorian building stood was far too small for the massive lorries that constantly delivered tons of reels of newsprint. It seemed almost a daily problem for one of them to be unable to either enter or exit, not helped by inconsiderately parked cars. There were continual problems throughout most days and, even on the easiest of days, one or another of the delivery vehicles required guidance back out of the street and into the High Street, where it would stop the main flow of traffic.

For several years, rumours had filtered through the various levels of staff regarding the company's likely move to more modern premises and the installation of new equipment. However, when approached by the trade unions, the proprietors always replied with a resounding denial, much to the frustration of the unions who knew only too well that, eventually, the old rotary letterpress machinery, the compositors, linotype and foundry would have to be replaced with cold web-offset lithographic presses, desk top publishing and automatic plate making facilities. Other regionals had already done so in the last fifteen to twenty years. Technology had seen the reduction of manning levels and the saving on overheads, many firms scrapping their production totally and keeping a minimal staff to report and generate copy direct to an external printing company specialising in the newspaper production industry. This had caused even further reductions in staffing levels.

For many years the unions had succeeded in thwarting the implementation of new technology. National newspapers were producing their daily papers at a far lower grade then most of the suburban papers. Those that had found the union insistent on maintaining old working practices, made any updated acquisitions financially impractical and impossible to work. Strikes had become prevalent and the late Robert Maxwell had often threatened complete closure of a number of new factories. It was inevitable that the unions would succumb before too long. Strangely enough it was Eddie Shah and Richard Murdoch who caused the biggest transition in the newspaper trade. Murdoch, an Australian, encountered the union in a headlong battle when he moved his entire operation to Wapping and utilised external contractors to transport the papers nationwide. For weeks on end the unions picketed the Wapping factory, the initial thousands dwindling down over a period of time to a militant few. The cost to the rate payer; due to the vast police presence; was enormous. Many of the police were drafted in from all over the country and the overtime paid for many a mortgage.

It was nearing three o'clock; the copy deadline set each day; and Bruce Day had already produced his copy for the evening's issue. He sat impatiently behind his desk, wondering whether to call John Crowther again. He had phoned on at least half a dozen occasions now and had still not had a reply. He pondered over David McLeod's predicament. He had followed McLeod on a number of evenings and had been surprised by his enormous consumption of alcohol and his compulsion for gambling. Discretely taken photographs of McLeod's acquaintances were given to a policewoman friend and the results of the 'enquiry' had astounded him. His associates were well-known criminals.

The situation both excited and terrified Day. On the afternoon of the robbery, Day had sat in his car in the car park of the training ground, carefully hidden from view by an enormous oak tree. His objective was to tail McLeod wherever he went, to monitor his movements and, if possible, to enlighten Crowther as to his findings. Whilst waiting he ate continuously. The car had become littered with empty chocolate bar wrappers and crisp packets. His enormous frame made the Ford Mondeo feel very small. His gargantuan eating habits had long been a concern for his general practitioner who had already prescribed tablets for hypertension and had warned him about the possibility of becoming diabetic if he didn't take up a strict diet.

He sat huddled, alert only for the departure of McLeod or the opportunity of speaking with the elusive Crowther. He didn't know that he had seen the arrival of the thief that robbed the players, nor did he realise that he had seen him leave either. He had sat impatiently in his car as the time ticked on; his enormous girth hanging heavily over his belt; watching various visitors arrive and depart, some in suits, others casually dressed and several track-suited.

Day saw the players finally curtail their training session and leave the field. He daydreamed as he awaited their departure, his mind conjuring up various episodes and endings, all with him finally achieving a major scoop. The arrival of the police car hurtling through the gates of the car park and shuddering to an abrupt halt on the ashfelt made him jump back into reality. He stared intently as the two police officers casually removed themselves from the white Vauxhall Vectra, placed their caps on their heads and meandered into the dressing rooms. Day was intrigued to know what had instigated the arrival of the police.

One of the last to leave was John Crowther and Day squeezed himself from the vehicle and waddled over in his direction.

"Mr Crowther, may I have a couple of minutes of your time?" he asked pleadingly.

Crowther stopped momentarily. He couldn't believe that the local press had heard of the robbery already and he was in no mood for conversation of any kind.

"No I'm sorry. No comment."

Crowther quickly departed in his Mercedes.

Day went back to his car, opened another bag of crisps and began stuffing his face. As McLeod left the dressing rooms, Day attempted to conceal himself from view, lowering himself as best he could. McLeod reversed quickly and the wheels span violently as the Jaguar accelerated through the gates and onto the main road. Day followed McLeod to a nearby betting shop where he spent the next few hours observing McLeod's behaviour. He watched in disbelief at the vast amount of notes he kept pulling from his pockets. He betted in extortionate proportions, with an almost total disregard for the value of money. Day kept having an occasional flutter himself, so as not to look out of place. In rough calculations, Day thought that McLeod had wagered near to £1,000.

On departing from the betting shop, McLeod was followed by Day somewhat hazardously in his clapped out Ford Mondeo. The tail led him to The Golden Wheel in Greek Street. Day managed to obtain a day membership and then settled himself by the bar, filled with intrigue as he watched Dave McLeod's stack of chips multiply and then gradually subside into oblivion as the black jack croupier continually retrieved chips from his winnings. When he had lost everything he tried in vain to carry on without any collateral, the croupier calling the management for assistance as he became more and more objectionable. He was finally asked to leave the club.

Bruce Day remained seated at the bar waiting for the right time to continue his pursuit when he noticed the manager of the club; dressed impeccably in a black evening suit, black bow-tie, black patent shoes, cummerbund and a frilly dress shirt; move swiftly from the end of the gaming table to the far end of the bar. He engaged himself in a quick conversation with a little man calmly sipping Perrier water and munching a packet of potato chips. The man listened intently, nodded, arose from his seat and made his way to the exit.

Day followed, keeping a reasonable distance away so as not to be observed. The little man seemed to be following McLeod. Day walked slowly, watching the staggering, stumbling progress of Dave McLeod and the graceful pursuit of his shadower. He watched helplessly as McLeod fumbled around on the floor for his keys and his shadower rapidly approached him. He wanted to scream out but fear stopped him; he was no hero and never had been. The realisation of what he was experiencing in front of his own eyes sickened him. He watched, feeling totally impotent as the little man tore into McLeod, leaving him a bloodied mess on the ground. It was over in seconds. Day stood, transfixed to the spot, wondering what to do. He didn't expect the little man to exit the scene so rapidly; suddenly he realised that the perpetrator of the attack was heading in his own direction. He turned quickly and at precisely that moment the little man spotted him. Day started running as fast as his body would allow. Panic raced through him as he tried in vain to propel his legs faster. His sudden departure made the little man question whether he had been seen and realise that maybe he had. He began to run in pursuit.

Day ran as he had never run in his life, his overweight body was not used to such exertion and sweat began to escape from every pore. His feet scuffed on the kerb as he slipped and stumbled through the puddles as though they didn't exist. As he reached Shaftesbury Avenue he crossed the road, leapt into an empty black taxi-cab which was just about to pull way from the traffic signal and exhaustively gasped.

"Waterloo Station,quick!"

The cab sped off towards Piccadilly Circus, with Day frantically staring out of the smoked-glass back window for his pursuer. He had been exceedingly fortunate not to have been caught. If it had not been for an unsuspecting charlady merrily weaving her way through the disarray of dustbins on her bike, he would now be more than just exhausted. But fate had, instead, led the little man into a collision with the bicycle, bringing the overweight char, the bicycle and himself crashing to the ground.

Day tried hard to regain his breath whilst the cab made its way around Piccadilly Circus, down Haymarket and past Trafalgar Square. As the cab entered the Strand, Day overcame his breathing difficulties and his thinking processes began to function rationally again. He realised he still had to retrieve his car from Frith Street, he lent forward and tapped on the screen which divides the passengers from the driver. The driver slid the window open.

"Yes. Guv?"

"Sorry. Could you take me to Frith Street?"

"Are you mad? We've just come from there!" replied the surprised cabbie.

"I'm sorry." Day said apologetically.

"Your money Guv."

The cab did a violent u-turn and headed in the direction it had just left. The road was clear. As he paid the fare, along with a huge tip, he looked around carefully to make sure that it was safe. He retrieved his Ford Mondeo and headed briskly for home.

18

The team coach departed from the ground at 11a.m, watched by a handful of supporters. On board, in addition to the players, were Manager John Crowther, Team Coach Rob Dyson, physiotherapist Tony Pullen, Chairman Alfred Wade (who, as expected, was not talking or even acknowledging Crowther), four other directors and Chief Executive Roy Peters. The party took their normal seats on the coach, with the exception of Paul Brown who didn't know where to sit until Jim Fellows said.

"Come and sit here lad, you look like a spare prick at a wedding."

The trip was too short for the four regular card players in the party to embark on their customary game of draw poker. They were scheduled for a light lunch at the Richmond Gate Hotel - on Richmond Hill in Surrey - prior to the game. The journey would take them forty minutes at the most. The hotel was a little out of the way but, with there not being a decent one en route and the Richmond Gate not being too far from the North Circular, it was thought to be the best one to utilise.

The pre-match lunch; a traditional occurrence for all away games; would not have satisfied the majority of food connoisseurs. Whilst the A La Carte menus were very often comprehensive, the food required by the players had to be light, easily digestible and full of vitamins. It was always pre-ordered by one of the office staff the day before, from a list compiled at the beginning of the season, and updated according to team selection. It also included the relevant details as to the hotel address, telephone number and contact details, as well as times and various pick up points, which also varied according to the venue of the game.

Jim Fellows always had lightly scrambled egg on toast washed down with a cup of tea, whilst Barry Thomas preferred rice crispies with milk, followed by coffee. Others had boiled chicken, pasta, omelettes or boiled fish. A very nervous Paul Brown plumped for boiled chicken. He ate it under sufferance; he was really too nervous to eat and normally didn't before games in the reserves. He felt sicker and sicker with each mouthful. He couldn't concentrate on the food or the endless banter coming from his teammates. Whilst they all vacated after the meal to the lounge area to watch Grandstand on the television, Paul Brown visited the toilet, where he was violently sick.

Grandstand's Football Focus's main feature was the game at White Hart Lane, including an interview with England goalkeeper Paul Robinson and clips of past matches. Included in the feature were action replays from the December meeting earlier in the season at Zion Stadium, which West London won 3-2. Football Focus's presenter Ray Stubbs was quick to point out it had been the last time that West London had won and laboured on that fact as the reason for the relegation battle they now found themselves in. Jim Fellows was shown towering above the Tottenham defence twice to head home, followed with a tap in from Billy Dowsett who had earlier in the season been transferred to Liverpool for £1.5 million. All the goals brought a roar of approval from the West London contingent who were now relaxed and feeling confident to take on their illustrious neighbours from North London.

Whilst the players were relaxing, John Crowther and Rob Dyson went for a short walk down to the River Thames to get some fresh air. As they walked slowly along the bank, the conversation centred around both Mike Stephenson and Dave McLeod. Neither man was able to comprehend what their problems were but they realised that, whatever they were, they had to be sorted out for the good of the club. On their return, the players were already boarding the coach to take the relatively short trip to White Hart Lane. The coach made its way out over Kew Bridge, up Gunnersbury Avenue and Hanger Lane, picking up the North Circular Road on the outskirts of Ealing at the infamous Gyratory System and continuing on it until they turned right at Edmonton, into Fore Street. The closer the approach to the ground, the more congested the streets became. Many cars were trying to secure parking spots as close as they could to the ground, with little success. The police had coned off many streets, including the High Road, to prevent them doing so. The programme sellers and many sellers of counterfeit scarves and other Tottenham memorabilia were out in force and hoards of Spurs supporters; already adorned in the club's famous navy blue and white; mingled with a few West London fans wearing the club's gold and blue, all making their way to the stadium.

As the coach slowed in the traffic, the home fans gestured mockingly at the players peering out through the windows, some crudely but most good-naturedly. The few West London fans that could be seen waved, clapped and cheered. The atmosphere was building up for an exciting local derby.

As the coach turned into the ground, two mounted policeman on huge Clydesale horses slowly patrolled the street, leaving behind them piles of hot steaming dung. The players began to admire the huge structure which dwarfed them. As the coach drew slowly into the quadrangle, three BBC TV vehicles with their cables and aerials stretching in all directions could be seen, making the occupants of the coach feel overawed and nervous for the first time that day. Paul Brown started to shake at the thought of making his debut in such intimidating surroundings.

The team disembarked from the coach and were ushered through the 'players and officials' entrance by a Tottenham official; smartly dressed in a navy blue blazer with the club emblem on the pocket, matching club tie, white shirt, grey trousers and highly polished black shoes. He directed them to the visitors dressing room. The room was large and square, a treatment table stood in the centre, surrounded by bench seating. Six toilets, a plunge bath and several showers were slightly off to the right. There was a huge coloured lamp mounted above the door and the white tiles would have looked clinical if they had not been offset with a series of navy blue tiles spelling out the words 'Tottenham Hotspur', plus a huge cockerel next to it. The team left their belongings and ventured on to the playing arena, examining the condition of the pitch and chatting together, with each deciding in their own minds the correct stud lengths or boots to wear. The pitch was soft and flat. Ideal for good footballing sides. The ground was virtually empty, the gates not being opened yet for the paying public. The stewards were in one corner being briefed, whilst the police contingent were at the other end of the ground having their own briefing.

A vast amount of people could be seen busily bustling around, organising the programme sellers, checking the safety requirements and organising the enormous amount of food and drink that is sold on a match day. The match officials passed the team as they made their way to the dressing rooms. They had already examined the pitch and the netting and would probably do so again prior to kick-off. On the return to the dressing room the shirts had been hung up on the hooks with the shorts and socks carefully folded up underneath them.

All players have their own way of preparing themselves for a match, whether it be a series of warm-up exercises, a perusal of the programme or a visit to the toilet. One by one the West London team changed and made their way onto the White Hart Lane pitch to warm up, getting themselves acustomed to the conditions and the environment. The crowd began to arrive and fill up the empty seats. The atmosphere began to buzz as the music bellowed from the loud speaker system, interrupted by an occasional announcement. The continual chatter of the spectators, along with their spasmodic chants, increased the tension in the players as the realisation of the enormity of their task, and the importance of it to the club, began to increase their awareness. Rob Dyson appeared at the end of the tunnel and beckoned them back into the dressing room. They filtered back, having a sneak look at the Spurs team going through their own warming up exercises on the way.

The team entered the dressing room and sat in their respective seats, listening intently as John Crowther and Rob Dyson reminded them of what was required. The talk was directed at building their confidence, with the odd tactical reminder thrown in. It wasn't heavy and, typically of both John Crowther and Rob Dyson, it contained a number of humorous anecdotes which had the lads grinning and laughing. It had the required relaxing effect. John knew that to bombard them with tactics would make them more anxious than they already were and, if they didn't know what was expected of them after a week's coaching and training, then it was far too late now.

The talk was abruptly interrupted by the sound of the buzzer and the coloured lamp on the wall flashing. The officials were ready to take the field. John Crowther stood at the dressing room door, giving each player a firm slap on the back and a word of encouragement as they lined themselves up to parade out onto the park. White, as captain, took the lead with the others (some superstitiously) taking up their positions in the line-up. Big Jim Fellows always went out last, whilst Barry Thomas always insisted on being fourth.

The referee confirmed that everyone was ready and, flanked by his two linesman, checked everyone's studs before leading both teams out of the tunnel, to be greeted with a crescendo of fans clapping and cheering enthusiastically. Paul Brown, cap and valuables bag in hand, ran to the goal behind which the West London fans sat. The fans all knew how nervous he must have been feeling on making his debut and stood and clapped him warmly, shouting words of encouragement. He waved back and managed a weak, nervous smile. He had butterflies in his stomach and a dry throat. He was excited, nervous, elated and terrified simultaneously. He hoped he would give a good account of himself and didn't make any stupid errors. He felt reasonably good in the kick-about, handling and catching the ball cleanly. He wished it to continue after the whistle was blown.

The game was not more than two minutes old before Brown was called into action. A high ball from the right by Darren Anderton was allowed to drift across the goalmouth with the defenders leaving him to collect it. He didn't! Fortunately, the ball evaded the Spurs attack and drifted behind for a goal kick. White and Brodie both remonstrated with him, telling him that this was his ball to come for. The pressure placed on the defence by the

Spurs front line, particularly Les Ferdinand, was continuous. The fact that neither Cameron Brodie nor Don White had any faith in their young goalkeeper made the situation even worse. With both the central defenders struggling with their form, the pressure was immense. Balls that would normally have been played to him were either being kicked into touch or the defenders were trying to get out of trouble themselves.

Corner after corner was conceded in the vain attempt to restrict the rampant Spurs team from scoring. After forty three minutes, from one of those many corners, Brown left his goal to punch clear the out swinging cross. He was caught in two minds; he ventured from his goal-line, paused and then decided to continue to attempt to fist the ball away. The uncertainty caused him to arrive too late; his right fist missed the centre of the ball, catching its underside, pushing it up in the air several feet directly above him. He watched, waiting for it to drop and hopefully catch it. Two Spurs players plus Don White were also waiting for it. White rose to head it at the same time as Brown jumped and stretched his arms out to catch it. The two collided into one another; Brown made only momentarily contact with ball, it falling from his grasp at the moment of impact.

As it dropped, White, along with both Ferdinand and Sherwood of Spurs, lunged despairingly at it. White's knee connected first, precisely the same time as the falling Brown knocked him off balance. The ball span awkwardly, rising towards the roof of the goal. Tim Wharton leapt in a brave attempt to head the ball over the crossbar, caught it squarely on the top of his head and watched it agonisingly continue its path, strike the underside of the bar and continue on its way into the unprotected goal. The ground erupted, as 40,000 fans went wild with delight.

Tottenham Hotspur....1 West London....0

Half time arrived with no further score. Although the West London defence was put under great pressure, they managed to repel the home side and prevented them from increasing their lead. The West London team looked physically and mentally exhausted when they returned to the visitors' dressing room. They had given their all in the first half but had still failed to take any advantage of their fortuitous luck. They should have been at least four or five goals in arrears instead of just the single goal they were trailing to. In the initial forty five minutes they had mounted only one threatening attack and looked inept up front.

John Crowther pointed to the various aspects of play they were failing in and where the danger was emanating from in the Spurs side. He instructed Eddie Hirst to drop deeper and the wing men; Dennis Harper and Barry Thomas; to venture out wider on the flanks and not to defend, leaving four men up front. The West London side, renowned for its football, was going to totally change its tactics in the second half and hit long balls from defence. It was a huge gamble and a method of play that neither John Crowther nor Rob Dyson believed in and had, in the past, criticised strongly in the media. But it was time for the introduction of a few desperate measures. The club needed to obtain at least a point to help with their Premiership survival.

The second half saw a continuation of the first half, with the West London defence under considerable pressure. Paul Brown caused a couple of scares when the ball was passed back to him, taking an inordinate amount of time to clear it on both occasions, once stupidly dribbling around Spurs forward Armstrong before despatching the ball up field. In the eighty second minute he received a number of slaps on the back, verbal praise from his teammates and applause from the crowd when he turned a point blank, goal-bound header from Ginola around the post.

With three and a half minutes to play the impossible happened; a long clearance from full-back Paul Sulley found the head of Jim Fellows, the ball was chest trapped and, before it dropped to the ground, deftly lifted over the Spurs defensive wall. Martin Gibbon sprinted in between two Spurs defenders who were struggling to turn, leaving them floundering at his heels. He ran forty yards towards the Spurs goal with the two defenders trying desperately to stop him. As he neared the goal Ian Walker, the Spurs 'keeper, ran out to close the angle. Gibbon dummied, the keeper went down at his feet and, as he did, Gibbon gently chipped the ball with the outside of his right foot over the diving body, sending it speedily into the awaiting goal.

To the West London fans it seemed to take an eternity reaching it, let alone crossing the line. This time it was the turn of the few thousand West London fans to celebrate and raise the roof. The Spurs contingent were silent and their players mortified. West London had equalised with their only worthwhile effort. The equalising goal knocked the complacent Spurs out of their stride and the long ball tactics adopted by West London suddenly saw the contest take a different shape. In the dying seconds another long ball, this time from Paul Sulley, found Jim Fellows in a similar position as before, but this time Martin Gibbon's strike rebounded from the foot of the post to safety. If he had scored, it would have meant two vital additional points, for the whistle blew directly afterwards to finish the game.

John Crowther stood and waited at the entrance to the dressing rooms, giving each player a slap on the back and a "Well done!" when they came in. He had never thought at half-time that they would salvage anything from the game. After a few moments, he left the elated team in the dressing room and raced up to the Dave Mackay Suite to watch the football results and, in particular, the fortunes of fellow strugglers Kirlees County and Sheffield Wednesday. He grabbed a cup of tea and ham sandwich and joined everyone watching the teleprinter on Final Score. It was already in full swing. John enquired of a stranger standing close by;

"Has the Kirkleses result come in yet?"

"No, not yet. But most of the others have." was the reply. Final scores continued as the teleprinter worked away, pausing only momentarily whilst waiting for the next one.

4.46
Div 3 Lincoln City 1 Scunthorpe United 2
Div 1 Stoke City 3 Norwich City 0
Div 2 Huddersfield Town 4 York City 3
Div 1 Birmingham City 0 Burnley 1
4.47 PREM DIV Chelsea 6 Sheffield Wednesday 1
Div 2 Rotherham United 2 Walsall 2

4.48
Div 1 Barnsley 2 Blackpool 0
Div 1 Bristol City 0 Swindon Town 0
Div 3 Carlisle United 3 Plymouth Argyle 1
PREM DIV Arsenal 2 Watford 0

There was a pause and Desmond Lynam broke in:

"A goal has been scored in the Kirklees County versus Liverpool game. We are unable to give any more details at this time as we have lost contact with our reporter at the ground. But Kirklees have taken the lead against Liverpool. The score is 3-2, but with two players from each side being sent off and an additional crowd problem, the final result won't be in for some time yet. We will let you know as soon as we can. Most of the results are now in and we'll go over to the Classified Football Results."

John Crowther sighed in disappointment, took a deep breath and waited for the inevitable.

He watched the Classified Football Results presented in its normal league fashion, commencing with the Premier League. The Kiklees v Liverpool game was still not in and was marked with an 'L' denoting a late result. This was followed by League Division One, Division Two, Division Three and then the Scottish League and Vauxhall Conference. The programme visited a variety of grounds, each commentator on the spot giving their opinions and reporting on the game in question. The league tables followed, displaying first the top half of the Premier Division then the bottom half of the table, still without the Kirklees v. Liverpool result.

The discerning guests in the Dave Mackay Suite seemed to be aware of the anxiety John Crowther was suffering, waiting for the one result that now mattered, and several wished him good luck. As the program credits and the familiar music began, John Crowther started to look around to see whether anyone had a radio. He was desperate to learn the score. The BBC left the popular sports programme for the day and commenced with their advertisements for the evening's viewing. Whilst most of the other guests had now drifted away, either reverting back to the bar or to one of the many tables, Crowther stood with his eyes transfixed to the set, waiting to be put out of his misery. After what seemed like an eternity, a newsflash appeared over the image of the new quiz game which had just started, Anyone Can Do It hosted by Noel Edmunds.

PREMIER DIVISION RESULT: Kirklees County 3 Liverpool 4.

John Crowther leapt up, one fist punching the air with relief and excitement. He left the room with a bigger grin on his face than he had had for sometime. There was still a slim chance of surviving, but it was going to be a nail biting finish. Crowther returned to the dressing room, where everyone was now dressed, and gave them the good news. It was a very happy journey back across the city.

When John Crowther arrived home that evening, his wife Sandra was busy in the kitchen, preparing the evening meal. As she fumbled to extract a casserole dish from the oven with an oversized pair of kitchen gloves, she looked up with a smile and said.

"Hello darling. A good result today."

As she gingerly placed the dish on the work surface, Crowther placed an arm around her waist and pecked the back of her neck.

"Yes. Let's hope we win the next two games. What's for dinner?" as he peered over her shoulder, taking in the aroma that was wafting from the contents of the casserole.

"One of your favourites. Stew and dumplings."

"Brilliant. Shall I open a bottle of wine? Where are the kids?" he replied.

"Yes please. There's one cooling in the fridge and glasses on the table. Michelle's gone to the cinema and Bradley's gone over to Jim's, helping to fix that old banger again."

He extracted a bottle of White Burgundy from the fridge and pulled the cork. He poured two glasses of wine, handed one to Sandra, took a large slurp of the other and continued towards the lounge. He switched on the teletext and began to study the league table positions at the end of the day:

	P	W	D	L	F	A	GD	PTS
WEST LONDON	36	8	9	19	37	66	-29	33
SHEFFIELD WED	36	8	7	21	34	64	-30	31
KIRKLEES CTY	36	6	12	17	43	69	-26	30
WATFORD	36	5	6	25	32	74	-42	23

As he did so, Sandra called from the kitchen.

"Oh, by the way, Bruce Day rang you. Would you please call him back. He said it was urgent. His phone number is on the pad by the telephone."

"What on earth does he want?" he said out loud.

The phone began to ring.

"Don't answer it." he shouted.

"Let the answer machine do its job."

19

On the Monday morning, Dave McLeod turned up optimistically at the club's training ground to resume training, his nose heavily protected with a bandage and plaster. If it had not been for the fact that no-one had expected to see him, he would have been fined for being late. Everyone, with the exception of physiotherapist Tony Pullen, was already training. When McLeod walked in through the dressing room door with his cosmetic bag dangling from one hand, Tony's first words were:

"Dave, you must be joking! You're in no condition to train."

"Oh come on Tony, be a pal. I can't just sit at home looking at the four walls. I need something to do to take my mind off everything."

"What happened?" asked Pullen as an after thought.

"I don't really know. I was getting into my car when some fucking animal just attacked me."

"Strip off and let's have a look at the areas I can't see. What I can seems pretty bloody horrendous."

Pullen winced as he looked at McLeod's body. He looked as though he had experienced fifteen rounds with Mike Tyson, and had certainly come off worst. His chest showed extensive bruising, just removing his shirt gave him considerable discomfort. His testicles were a bluish colour and extremely swollen and his stomach sore to the touch.

"It's ridiculous. There is no way I can allow you to train until the bruising and swelling have subsided. I reckon at least another week before you can even consider some form of light training."

McLeod looked totally deflated.

"I'm sorry Dave. No way. Go home, put your feet up for a week and relax. I know the boss would not like to hear me say that, but there is just nothing I or anyone else can do. The body needs time to recover. But one thing I do know is that he would like to see you. He's popped over to the ground to see Roy Peters, he said that he'd be gone for a couple of hours or so, so I suggest you go over there and see him."

McLeod slowly dressed himself, thanked Pullen for his time and left. As he approached his car, several of the players saw him and ran over, asking him how he was and enquiring what had happened. He virtually regurgitated the same information he had given to Tony Pullen minutes before.

Meanwhile Rob Dyson - in the middle of the park having split the players into four groups, all with different tasks to perform pushing them to limit of their endurance - blew his whistle hard and shouted to the absconders.

"You lot, get your arses back over here!!"

Virtually to a man they lifted their eyes to the heavens and responded immediately to the command. Dyson was not one to play around with. One of the tasks was a new free-kick which he and John Crowther had dreamed up the day before. The plan looked good on paper, but in practice it was awful. The approach work was good; the element of surprise would catch a number of sides out; but the finishing was woeful. The goal seemed to possess some magical power. In contrast to the Bermuda triangle where everything disappeared, the balls flew everywhere except in the back of the net. If their shooting was going to be as bad as this on match days, he didn't know whether he should have another dozen footballs or considerably more ball-boys to retrieve them. He amused himself firstly with the thought of sitting in the dug-out with masses of footballs around him, then with a hundred little track-suited infants forever despatching themselves to all four corners of the ground trying to retrieve them.

A quarter of an hour later, McLeod arrived at the ground, parked the E' Type in the spot reserved for Dyson and made his way to the reception. Again he was barraged with questions, firstly by Sheila the receptionist and then by every member of staff who passed through the reception area as they went about their daily business. He waited patiently whilst the receptionist repeatedly took the calls and transferred them in a professional manner.

"Good morning. West London Football Club. How can I help you? Just one moment, I'm just transferring you.", or "I'm afraid they're engaged, would you like to hold?"

'What a bloody boring job' he thought to himself as he hovered around, peering at some of the team photographs of the past years and the numerous action shots on the walls. Finally he was given the go-ahead to enter the inner sanctum. He pushed his way through the swing doors, made his way up the small flight of stairs and through another set of swing doors. John Crowther's office was situated on the left-hand side. On the door there was a brass metal plate with simply. 'Manager' on it. He knocked and the voice within said

"Come in Dave."

As he walked through the door, the phone rang and Crowther picked it up, gesticulating to McLeod to take the empty seat opposite him. It was unusual for Crowther to be in the office at this time as he was normally at the training ground with Dyson, Pullen and the players. The conversation went on for some time, McLeod began to feel tense and rather irritated at being kept waiting even longer. He liked John Crowther; it had only been his respect for the man that had enticed him to travel down to the South after playing most of his football in Scotland. But he now felt a certain amount of resentment towards him. He blamed Crowther, quite unrealistically, for the break-up of his marriage and the terrible position he was now in. He had to blame someone. He had never been able to accept responsibility for his own behaviour and that hadn't changed much since his childhood.

He sat impatiently tapping his fingers on the arm of the chair, looking around the office; it was small and basic. The directors certainly didn't believe in making it too comfortable. He listened as Crowther came to a close in the conversation, which he deduced was with a reporter.

"The rumour is certainly untrue."

"I cannot confirm or deny that particular observation."

"I'm sorry but you'll have to draw your own conclusion."

"Sorry. No comment."

"Again. I'm sorry, no comment."

John looked up and raised his eyebrows. McLeod could hear the incessant gabble of the reporter coming from the receiver. Occasionally, Crowther would remove the receiver from his ear and hold it as far away as possible, in an attempt to give his ear a rest. McLeod was becoming more and more anxious as the time slipped away. He began to feel like a patient who is due next in the dentist's chair. He gazed aimlessly around the walls. On one there was a large Sasco wall chart, meticulously covered with rectangular, square and star-shaped tokens, with each fixture attached to either a red or green rectangular sign, which was magically held on by magnetism. Green were home games and red away. All the reserve and Youth team games and meetings that he had to attend were marked. It was impressive. McLeod noticed that the arms on Crowther's leather chair were well worn and that there were heavy scratches on the top of the desk. He pondered as to what the desk was made of; teak, mahogany, oak, walnut? His patience was near to an end. 'It can be fucking balsa wood for all I care' he thought. 'Get off that bloody phone.'

Crowther finally said his goodbyes and replaced the receiver.

"Sorry about that. These blokes seem to think that you are at their beck and call all the time, once they've got through to you, they never stop."

There was a pause as Crowther studied the face of McLeod. Dave McLeod said nothing, waiting for him to continue as he knew he would.

"You don't look too well Dave. Are you sure you're alright?"

"Yeah, I suppose so. I'm a bit pissed off that I cannot train though."

"So tell me what happened?"

"I was just about to get into my car when this bloke jumped me. He knocked seven bells of shit out of me and nicked my wallet."

Whilst he spoke he shuffled nervously in his seat, his eyes wavered around the room, never once meeting Crowther's. His voice quivered.

"And that's it?" enquired Crowther somewhat suspiciously.

"Yes. I cannot remember very much else. I just blacked out."

"I've been wanting to have a chat with you for some time. I'm going to talk straight to you Dave and I want an honest answer. Rob Dyson tells me that your weight has been very difficult to maintain for a few weeks now. Have you hit the bottle or are you overeating, or what?"

For the first time, Dave McLeod's gaze caught Crowther's and he sat and stared defiantly at him, saying nothing.

"Well come on. What's going on? I know Margaret's gone home to her parents in Scotland and I'm really sorry to hear that, but I'm sure you will sort something out. Why did you not come and talk to me when it happened? We've been friends for a long time. I know you've been upset over it, and probably still are. But you are a professional footballer. Your livelihood depends on your fitness. Surely you can see that? If you're hitting the bottle it will increase your weight dramatically."

McLeod cut in abruptly. "You smug arse. Who the fuck do you think you are talking to me as though I'm a twelve year old. Just 'cos you've got a good marriage doesn't mean we all have. Yes, I was upset. Yes, I'm still upset. Yes, I've had a few drinks, as if you wouldn't if you were in the same situation."

"Firstly Dave, let's not start getting into a swearing contest. Don't swear at me and secondly, if you want to act like a twelve year old, I'll treat you like one! A twelve year old would probably react in a more responsible fashion than you have. What were you doing in Soho in the early hours of the morning anyway?"

McLeod stood up, and leaned over, placed both hands on the desk and glared at Crowther in an intimidatory manner.

"I've had enough of this fucking quiz game. I don't see what business this is of yours. You pay me to play football, I don't pay you to act as my nurse maid, so get out of my face."

"It's my business, because that is exactly what you are paid for. To play football. And that is exactly what you are failing to do. Because of your own stupidity, no-one else's."

McLeod turned away and made his way to the door, as he did so he uttered. "You'll have my written request for a transfer in the morning."

The door slammed behind him as he left and Crowther sat back dejectedly in his chair. He had handled the situation badly and had gained nothing from it.

True to his word, the following morning's mail brought the promised transfer request from Dave McLeod. Crowther read it carefully and put it to one side. The club stood very little chance of transferring McLeod until he was fit or until the season closed, the transfer deadline having all ready been and gone.

As he opened and read the many letters he recieved that morning, the phone rang. It was Sheila on the swichboard.

"Chairman for you John."

"Thanks. Morning Chairman."

"John I'm on my way in. I should be with you in about fifteen to twenty minutes, depending on the traffic. I want a meeting with yourself, Roy Peters and Paul McCormick as soon as I get to you."

Crowther rang down to Sheila.

"Get hold of Roy Peters and Paul McCormick. Tell them that the Chairman is on his way in and has called a meeting in the boadroom in fifteeen minutes. You'd better provide us with some coffee and biscuits."

"Alright." she said chirpily. She was in her early fifties with short grey hair and a dumpy little body. The lady loved her job and always had a smile and a laugh with everyone. Unlike others on the staff, she couldn't take the football too seriously and had only found out Saturday's result when the paper boy had left the normal cross section of nationals the club received on a daily basis.

"Great draw at Spurs Saturday."

Not to be embarrassed she had replied;

"Yes wasn't it." She had a quick look to see who had scored so that she was in the know.

When Crowther arrived at the boardroom, Chief Executive Roy Peters and Commercial Manager Paul McCormick were already there. They both sat without uttering a word, except to say good morning; both looked troubled. It was a strained atmosphere whilst they awaited the arrival of the Chairman. Sheila brought in the coffee and biscuits and John poured one for himself and grabbed a biscuit. Roy and Paul declined to have either.

The panoramic boardroom window overlooked the car park and John Crowther stood by it watching for the Chairman's arrival. John realised this was serious and, for the first time, wondered whether he was going to be sacked. There was no mistaking Alfred Wade's car; a silver Rolls Royce Corniche. It swept into the car park and parked in his own parking spot.

Five minutes later a bad tempered Chairman strode through the door. He removed his jacket and placed it on the hanger, talking rapidly at the same time.

"Morning, we have a major problem. Where's the letter Peters?"

Peters removed the open letter from a folder and gave it to Wade who read it.

"Arsehole!"

He threw the letter on the table and Crowther read it, McCormick didn't look at it so it was obvious that Peters had already shown it to him.

ZION ELECTRONICS PLC
Zion House, 155-160 Regent Street,
London W1T AL2 Tel: 020 7160 3775

West London Football Club Plc,
Zion Stadium,
Hounslow,
Middlesex
For the attention of Mr Roy Peters, Chief Executive

PRIVATE AND CONFIDENTIAL

Friday 21st April 2000

Dear Roy,

We have given careful consideration to the three-year sponsorship proposal formulated between ourselves over the past few months. Regretfully we feel the present financial climate prohibits the extension of the current agreement.

We have no alternative therefore but to advise you that this company will cease its sponsorship deal with West London Football Club on 1st September 2000, when the existing contract expires.

Thank you for your support in the past and we wish the club every success in the future.

Yours sincerely,
GM Shaw
Gregory Maurice Shaw
Managing Director

It was a bitter blow but, after the last meeting with Shaw after the Villa game, it did not come of too much of a shock to Crowther.

"A sponsorship deal to the value of £8.5 million is an awful lot of money to recover in a relatively short space of time. I was certain, like you were Mr Chairman, that we would pull it off. We've assumed that we would receive the money and have budgeted accordingly."

"I'm becoming more and more disillusioned with the competence of the people that work at this club. I pay you all fucking good money. To run, in comparison to my own multi-million pound organisation, a piddling little concern which brings me more than enough aggravation."

The three looked at him; he was beetroot red and he had not finished.

"My working life comprises fourteen hours a day, seven days a week; mainly it seems to keep this club afloat; and for what? If you three do not start functioning pretty soon you'll all be looking for another job."

Wade glared at the three of them, waiting for a response. None came.

"This friendly in Cyprus…. Cancel it immediately. Let's see if we can save some money somewhere."

Peters nearly had a heart attack there and then and was incensed; he had undertaken a lot of work to ensure the game would take place.

"But Chairman! We fly out tomorrow morning, it is totally impossible to cancel at this stage, it won't save us anything. We're totally committed."

Paul McCormick interrupted.

"Mr Chairman. Basically the money is spent. If you remember you signed the cheque some two weeks ago and it has already cleared through our bank."

"Well if we've spent it, we've spent it. I have to say gentleman that I'm seriously considering selling my shares and cutting my losses. If someone can take over my loan then that would be desirable."

Crowther had known that he wasn't as committed as he had been, Up until the Spurs match, Wade had not travelled away with the team for weeks. It had not gone unnoticed by the players.

Wade calmed down.

"What time does the coach leave tommorow?"

"4.30am Chairman." replied a relieved Peters.

"Bloody hell. The wife will have to get up and drop me. She'll be well pleased with that."

Wade retrieved his coat from the rack and left.

"See you at 4.30 tomorrow morning." he said as he disappeared out of the door.

The three sat round the table, horrified by the revelations. Crowther was the first to speak.

"Well I'm glad I never told him that Dave McLeod has asked for a transfer."

"He hasn't!?" said McCormick surprised.

"He has." Crowther replied, departing back to his office.

As he entered the room the phone rang and he picked it up.

"Hello."

"Bruce Day for you. Are you in?"

"Yes I'll take it."

The call was put through.

"Bruce, sorry I haven't got back to you, but I've been rather busy."

"Yes. I realise that. You're off to Cyprus of course tomorrow." said Day.

"Yes that's right."

"I'll be travelling out on Thursday morning to cover the game. John I must speak with you on a one to one basis, urgently."

"Don't be so dramatic Bruce. What's the problem."

"I can't talk over the phone."

"I can't spare any time for you today. Why don't we discuss whatever you want after the game. Are you in the same hotel as us?"

"No, I couldn't get in. You know how tight this lot here are. One minute they don't want you to go and the next minute they do. Well as normal they left everything too late. I'm staying in the Paphos Beach Hotel."

"OK, meet me after the game at the players entrance and we'll get the coach to drop us off at your hotel. I presume it's got a bar?"

"Yes of course."

"Ok then I'll see you Thursday night."

He cradled the receiver and wondered what on earth couldn't be said over the phone.

20

It was quarter-to-three on a damp and dismal Tuesday morning, a time that most of the players did not know even existed. The exception were the few that had newly born babies who, in addition to keeping them up at night, awoke them bright and early in the morning. The sun had not yet risen as the travelling party arrived one by one at the appointed meeting place. They awaited the arrival of the coach, sitting in their cars listening to the radio. It was even far too early for a glimpse of the morning newspapers. The Zion Park ground echoed eerily as each vehicle drove onto the concourse, casting ghostly shadows as their headlights penetrated through the gloom, lighting up different areas of stadium. With each arrival, the draught caused the surrounding litter to lift up from the ground and float gently in the air, before cascading back into an entirely different position on terra firma. The sky looked sinisterly black, with thick clouds blotting out most of the moon's reflected rays. The ground and offices were securely locked and in total darkness, The club's administrative staff still at home, tucked up in their cosy beds.

It was because of the economic plight the club now faced that they were up this early in the morning; to catch a 7am chartered flight from London Gatwick to Larnaca in Cyprus rather than a scheduled flight at a more reasonable hour (the fare for which was exorbitant). The players weren't happy about it. They knew that the supposed four day break in the sunshine meant a lot of hard work but the consolation to the younger players of the temptation of girls, booze and song had been sourly tempered by a stern lecture earlier in the week. They were told, in no uncertain terms, that no such behaviour would be tolerated by the management. It was pointed out that they were ambassadors, representing not only their club but also their country, and that they were responsible adults in a profession that many would love to have. They all felt that the lecture was over the top; making them feel like a bunch of schoolchildren; but whilst they all thought it and voiced their criticisms between themselves, no-one was man enough to stop John Crowther and Rob Dyson in their tracks by telling them so. A schedule had been set out for training every morning, with the rest of the day off. A strict 10pm curfew was set for each evening, with the friendly versus Anorthosis Famagusta in Larnaca due to be played on the Thursday evening. Some of the players with families were unhappy at leaving them, whilst some of the more flirtatious married men, and most of the bachelors, were quite keen. Well, prior to the lecture that was.

Coach Rob Dyson had been the first of the management to arrive. He alighted from his car, made his was to the laundry room, unlocked the door and turned off the alarm system. Once inside, he started to check the itinerary list against the contents of the four hampers containing the playing strip, training kit, cones, balls, medical equipment etcetera, which physiotherapist Tony Pullen had organised the previous evening. He was a bit annoyed that Tony hadn't yet arrived. He carefully examined the hampers, ensuring that all the travelling party's, boots and training equipment had been included. He remembered only too well once, when at Crystal Palace, leaving two pairs of boots behind on a trip to Italy and having to have them sent over by air with one of the office staff. It had caused him considerable embarrassment and leg-pulling from the players, and the club additional expense. He wasn't going to repeat the mistake. When Tony Pullen finally appeared, he looked tired and harassed.

"Sorry, I'm a bit late, the alarm didn't go off."

But when he observed what Dyson was doing, his apologies turned quickly to anger.

"What are you fucking up to? I spent nearly three hours last night sorting that out. Don't you think I'm capable or something?"

Rob Dyson physically winced at the onslaught and replied defensively.

"No, don't be stupid Tony, but I just want to be satisfied in my own my mind that everything is in order. I've been embarrassed before."

As he spoke the final few words he knew that they would be misconstrued, and he could have worded it better.

"Well, fuck you. You can sort it out yourself next time."

Tony virtually pushed him out of the way as he began re-strapping the hampers. Rob Dyson stood in silence watching his colleague fuss around like an old woman, trying to think of something to say to lighten the atmosphere. He was relieved when the silence was broken by John Crowther, who poked his head around the door.

"Morning fellas. The coach has arrived. Most of the boys are on board. There's still two to come, the Chairman and Don White."

"Morning. Don't worry about Don he's meeting us at Gatwick. It seemed a bit daft him travelling up here from Croydon, when he's virtually on the doorstep." Dyson replied.

Tony Pullen just said a curt "Morning." and pushed one of the hampers past them, through the door and out into the car park. Crowther looked quizzically at Pullen and then at Dyson with a questioning face and said;

"What's up with him?"

"Oh I opened my big mouth and upset him. Nothing to concern you."

"Well done, top marks for starting the trip off in great spirits." Crowther said sarcastically.

After loading their baggage (including several sets of golf clubs) onto the coach, the party sat patiently on board, waiting for the arrival of Chairman Alfred Wade. The coach driver left the engine running in an attempt to keep the vehicle and his passengers warm and to prevent the mass of condensation already formed on the windows from becoming any worse. Both Dave McLeod and Mike Stephenson were not travelling; McLeod due to his transfer request and hospital treatment and Stephenson because of domestic problems. All the other senior players were included and the party totalled eighteen. As time ticked on and there was no sign of the Chairman, Chief Executive Roy Peters used the phone in the coach to attempt to contact him on his car phone. The phone was switched off. He then tried the Chairman's home and his wife Audrey could be heard over the answer phone:

"Hello. This is the Wade household. We're sorry there is no-one in at the moment to take your call, but if you would like to leave a message after the tone, we will ring you on our return."

He waited for the tone and then said "Mr Chairman. It's Roy Peters at the Club. I've tried your car phone but there's no reply. It's now 3.45am and I'm afraid we cannot wait any longer. The flight is due to take off from Gatwick, bound for Larnaca, at 7am and the flight number…..... he paused as he fumbled through the travel documents ...... is BA0190 which leaves from the North terminal. Hopefully we will meet up with you there."

Confused and with a considerable amount of doubt, Peters instructed the coach driver to set off. The journey to Gatwick via the M4, M25 and M23 motorways was relatively quiet and the coach made good time, arriving at the North Terminal at 4.55am. The party collected their belongings, found themselves trolleys and proceeded to the check-in area. The queue for flight BA0190 had already formed with excited holidaymakers laden with suitcases all moving slowly towards the ever-smiling check-in girl, who was asking each one in turn whether they had packed their own suitcase, whether anyone had done it for them and whether they had left it at any time.

She monotonously tied the relevant baggage labels onto the luggage, issued the tickets and passed onto the next passenger. The West London party joined the back of the queue. Roy Peters had possession of all the passports, with the exception of the Chairman's. He waited impatiently for his impending arrival, wondering what mood he would be in after he had been left behind. He feared for his job; the months of continual criticism by the Chairman and the undermining of his decisions had given Peters an inferiority complex and an anxiousness when dealing with him. It was now 6.10am, still no sign.

Peters tried to ring Wade on his mobile but realised that he had failed to charge it the previous evening and it was dead. He broke from the party and made his way to a nearby public phone. He again rang both the numbers and received exactly the same response as before. He returned to the check-in to find that Don White had joined the queue, but there was still no sign of Alfred Wade. He waited to see his own luggage pass the check-in procedures. In his panic, he realised he'd left not only the mobile but some vital paper work in the phone kiosk.

Some of the players had now been recognised and were busily signing autographs as they pushed their baggage ever closer to the check-in desk. A couple of supporters were chatting to John Crowther; the two followed the club home and away, to all the league, cup and friendly games, and had booked the same trip as the club, staying at the same hotel. Not that the players knew where they were staying; everything was organised by the management and administrative side of the club.

By 6.20am the team party had checked in and ventured through customs into the departure lounge, making sure they bought their entitlement of duty free goods. Roy Peters and director Alan Proctor stayed landside, waiting at the check-in for the arrival of Alfred Wade. At 6.30am they heard the boarding announcement of flight BA0190 to Larnaca, but they both lingered in anticipation of his impending arrival. They stood listening intently to the continuing flight announcements, watching one of the many flight departure screens continuously updating flight numbers, expected departure times and gate boarding numbers. As one took off it would be deleted from the screen and all the flights jumped up a row. Their own flight kept flickering as well as the others. Flight BA0190 Larnaca Now boarding at Gate 36.

It was 6.45am. The public address system again interrupted their thoughts with the now familiar announcement: "Will passengers Proctor, Wade and Peters please make their way to Gate 36 for the immediate departure of flight number BA0190 to Larnaca. This is the last call for passengers Proctor, Wade and Peters, would you please make your way to Gate 36 for the immediate departure of flight BA0190 to Larnaca. This flight is now closing."

They could wait no longer and ran towards customs and the departure lounge, then down the travellators towards Gate 36. As they boarded the plane all the remaining passengers were already seated; strapped in waiting for take-off. There was a small round of applause from the West London contingent as the two frantically made their way to their allocated seats and struggled to find room in the overcrowded overhead baggage lockers. The Boeing 737 took to the air without the Chairman, much to the relief of everyone except Crowther, Peters and Proctor, who were concerned that he had not appeared nor made contact. It was an impoliteness that Alfred Wade did not possess himself and hated in others.

The flight was uneventful and landed on time. The short coach trip to the five star Coral Beach Hotel was far enough from the town of Paphos to discourage some from venturing from the resort and had sufficient facilities to cater for most tastes. It was also the cheapest five star hotel in Paphos. Because of the abundance of British squadies forever frequenting Ayia Napa in the evening, and the game being played in Lanarca which is in reasonable proximity, it was decided to stay in Paphos. Alfred Wade failed to appear at the hotel and, after a phone call to the club, it had transpired that they had not seen or heard from him.

The first of the daily two hour training sessions started at 3pm the same day and they were then due to continue at 10am each morning. It was hard. Some of the island's landscape is as rugged as can be found anywhere in the world and the players were introduced to it with a five mile run. This was followed by an energetic programme of physical exercises near the pool, which was watched with fascination by the hotel's holidaymakers who were predominately English and German. The end of the session saw the players take over the swimming pool as they continued their boisterous activity; continually jumping in and out, still in their training gear. This activity caused a few problems with the hotel management as they had strict rules regarding acceptable swimwear. The warnings had no affect on the players; they continued to abuse the hotel's hospitality.

The rooms, all equipped with satellite television, telephone, lounge areas and mini-bar, had twin beds. Unknown to everyone else this did not suit two of the players who always roomed together Paul Sulley and Eddie Hirst. Their good friendship had developed into something more, through their shared sexual experiences. It was one of the best kept secrets in the football world. The game had always been a man's game played by men, but the many years that had passed since the legalisation of homosexuality had seen an increase in the number of players who preferred their own gender.

Whilst the first few days saw the others pranking around, the two would escape to their room and make love. On the Thurday morning after training, instead of their lovemaking session, they decided to hire a moped and have a few hours sightseeing. Unusually, the hotel reception were most unhelpful in providing them with a suitable local hire company, due mainly to the inexperienced young lady not knowing where to find the relevant information. They managed to grab a cab outside of the hotel and the driver took them to a back street where one dealer had several mopeds for hire. He gave them an old Vespa on a cheap hire. Too cheap. No helmets were provided, as it wasn't a legal requirement. They mounted the bike and off they drove on their adventure.

Prince disembarked the flight from Heathrow on the Wednesday and picked up a white jeep at Lanarca airport. He had settled himself in the Coral Beach Hotel car park, watching intently the comings and goings. On Wednesday everyone stayed within the confines of the hotel, but on the Thursday he saw John Crowther, Rob Dyson, Don White and Jim Fellows pile into a mini-bus with a few bags of golf clubs. He spotted an opportunity when Paul Sulley and Eddie Hirst scrambled into the back of a cab some twenty minutes later. He followed the cab through the back streets and observed them hiring a moped from a pretty average hire company. He followed them at a safe distance. As time passed by Prince was becoming more and more impatient

They visited Paphos Harbour, Paphos Archaeological Park, the Tombs of the Kings and finally, after Aphrodite, they'd had enough of the masses of historical education and took the road through Paphos towards Limassol, turning off inland towards the Troodos Mountains. The two were too engrossed in the wonderful vista and each other to notice the white Jeep following their every turn. The climb up to the Troodos Mountains at first was gradual and the roads of reasonable width. Paul Sulley found the scooter easy to handle, but a little under-powered. Eddie Hirst just hung on tight, not being a great lover of bikes of any kind. The further inland they drove the steeper the gradients and the narrower the roads became, but it also became cooler, which was quite a relief.

The cliffs began to dwarf them on one side, whilst on the other it was a breathtaking view of the valleys below and in places a sheer drop. Whilst the sun was strong and bright, the higher they went the cooler it became. Paul was enjoying the drive, but Eddie was not. Not only did he dislike bikes, but he had a fear of heights.

Paul's occasional missing of a gear was not exactly reassuring; the scooter was past its best. Periodically, another car would appear around the corner in the opposite direction, causing his heart to miss a beat. He dare not look down his left-hand side as the drop was devastatingly worrisome. Paul would casually pull the bike further towards the unguarded drop and continue as if nothing had happened. The occasional coach caused Eddie even more apprehension; the vehicle taking up most of the road as it manoeuvred down the mountain; but Paul would change down a gear and guide the bike around it deftly, without concern.

As they approached a tight left-hand bend, Eddie looked at the drop in horror; the road was pot-holed badly and gravel was spitting up from the surface. He wished they had stayed at the hotel. The realisation that a vehicle was directly behind, negotiating an overtaking manoeuvre, made him stare in disbelief at the driver of the white Jeep as it accelerated past them. The driver seemed totally unconcerned at the danger he was putting them both in. Paul Sulley shouted an expletive.

"Bastard! What the fuck's this prat trying to do?"

"Get over you arsehole!" shouted Eddie.

As the Jeep drew alongside, it veered violently to its left and braked. The scooter was caught by its front wheel and, as it did so, the handlebar span from Paul's grasp. As his hands left the handlebars he lost all control. Eddie's head crashed into Paul's shoulder and, although totally off balance, he instinctively and unsuccessfully tried to grab his expensive Ray-Ban sunglasses as they departed from his head.

Eddie totally lost his hold on Paul; whatever stability he had felt previously had gone. Paul's body, along with his own, moved involuntarily as they started to part company with the machine. The riders, along with the bike, found themselves free-falling, floundering in mid-air, trying to catch hold of anything, but there was nothing. Nothing but air. They flayed their arms like drowning men as they dropped, screaming with fear. Shock, and the speed perpetuated by the drop, saw both pass out before they reached the bottom. Their bodies crashed into the earth at violent speed, breaking and shattering fragile bones. Their blood splattered the landscape as the rugged rock face inflicted enormous tears in the bodies. It took only seconds for the blackness of death to engulf them both.

Meanwhile, John Crowther, Rob Dyson, Don White and Jim Fellows' mini-bus had taken them to the 72 par championship golf course called Tsada Golf Club, in the Paphian Hills just outside of Paphos. Dyson, White and Fellows had brought their clubs with them, but Crowther had to hire a set from the club shop. All the sets were identical, surprisingly 'Ping', with the exception of the putter. He had searched each available set on hire for a decent putter, without luck. He then purchased a dozen golf balls and a glove and split the cost of the buggy with Rob Dyson. As he was about to leave, the golf pro noticed that he wasn't wearing golf shoes, so he shelled out again to buy the cheapest pair that he could.

"Bloody hell. This is costing me a fortune. I only want to play a round of golf, not to buy the place."

"Oh shut up moaning. You can afford it." said Dyson. They all laughed and waited while the buggys were made available.

Nearly four hours later, the fourball were on the 18th tee, waiting for the group ahead to get out of range. Don White was well out in front with a score of 74, playing off of a handicap of four. Having won the last hole he was fired up and first to play. He buried his tee into the ground and placed the ball carefully on top of it. He stepped backwards and made a couple of practice swings, talking all the time as he did so.

"I think Mike Stephenson's got a mistress." he said as he addressed the ball with his driver. He drew the club in a wide arch around his body and over his head, uncoiling his body and unleashing it downward and through the ball, with perfect balance and timing. The ball was fired through the air and disappeared into the distance, landing in the middle of the fairway, some two hundred and seventy yards away.

"Good shot." they all repeated begrudgingly, envying his talent that allowed him to repeat the same shot time after time. John Crowther approached the tee and, as he passed White, he looked at him disbelievingly. He bent down and placed his tee into ground saying "Why do you think that Don?"

"Well, after the robbery I'm certain I saw him pull a nude photograph from his wallet, and I think he saw me looking at him. He went white as a sheet with embarrassment. Excuse the pun."

The observance of Don White didn't help John Crowther's swing one little bit. As he pulled the club through to strike the ball, the right hand became more predominant than the left and the ball flew off down the middle, but the spin imparted on it saw it fade badly to the right. It ended up some one hundred yards away on the 18th fairway.

"Shit." he said, which was greeted with friendly agreement from the other three.

"Don you're a wind-up merchant." voiced Crowther as he retrieved his tee from the ground.

"I suppose you won't believe me when I tell you that Dave has got gambling problems then."

Rob Dyson place his tee in the ground and addressed the ball with a three iron saying "Now, that I am not surprised about."

"Why are you taking a three iron to this, isn't the fairway wide enough for you?" said Jim Fellows, standing with the biggest jumbo driver that could be bought.

"Bugger off Jim, I've just seen what John's done with his. I'm playing safe."

Dyson swung the club easily and the ball landed slightly to the right of the fairway, a distance of some one hundred and eighty yards from the tee. Jim Fellows marched up to the tee, placed his tee in the ground and, without any preamble, took an almighty swing and saw the ball glide off beyond Don White's. The ball took a bounce, bounced a second time and gently rolled into a bunker. Everyone wondered how Jim had become such a good golfer; his stance was wrong, his swing was wrong, everything seemed to be wrong, yet he still managed to bring the club head through at the correct angle and height to produce good golf shots.

"Hard luck Jim." They all said in unison.

"You don't mean that you bastards. All you want to do is take my money." he replied. "But going back to Mike and Dave. I think Don's got something you know."

Whilst John Crowther trudged off to the 18th fairway to play his second shot, his mind wandered from the golf match to the club's problems for the first time. The fact that both Mike and Dave had been left at home had, up to now, been of benefit to not only himself but to the rest of the squad. Both players had become a pain in the arse.

He waited for the players ahead on the 18th green to finish their game, hoping to land his ball where they were presently holing out. It was stupid to be thinking of anything else but the golf; it's a hard enough game to play when you're totally concentrating on it, but when you're not..... The ball squirted from the club head along the ground, colliding with several trees before finally coming to rest in a mixture of long course grass and sand; it took several minutes of searching before he finally found it. The shot was unplayable. His thoughts had ruined the end of an enjoyable afternoon. He picked the ball out of the grass, stuck it in his pocket and marched off to the green where the other three were waiting for him before putting out.

"What time are we leaving the hotel?" asked Jim Fellows as he lined up a three foot putt.

"5pm. But we've arranged a light meal at 4pm in the hotel before we go." said Crowther as he walked across the green towards them.

"Have you picked up then?" asked Rob Dyson.

"Afraid so." he replied.

"That's good, at least I'm not last then!"

The mini-bus back to the hotel was full of banter between the other three, talking about this shot and that shot, whilst Crowther sat thinking about what had been said.

On entering the hotel, Crowther was stopped several times and asked to sign autographs. It was a duty he always fulfilled; he had forever appreciated the fans that spent hard-earned money to support the team and had a lot of time for them. After a few words, he collected his key from reception and made his way to his room. His first call back was made to Roy Peters.

"Roy. Any news from the club about the Chairman?"

"I don't know how to tell you this, but he has been arrested for fraudulent activity. Seems the police arrived at 1 o'clock in the morning. Tuesday morning that is, and he's only just been released."

"You are joking?" "I wish I was."

"But surely it doesn't involve the club?"

"I'm not sure. Peter McCormick reckons that he has heard that he has used the company's pension scheme; some £45 million; to shore up shortfalls in some of his businesses. He's also been buying his own shares for Christ's sake."

"If he's done that he really is in the shit. No wonder he's been in some foul moods of late. As long as he hasn't used the pension money for the loans to the club."

"That is exactly what went through my mind."

"If he has, where does that leave us?"

"I don't know and I just can't bear to think about it. First we lose Zion and if we have a problem over the £10 million loan. ....Well we're finished."

"Oh well, it's just not worth worrying ourselves silly over it. We'll no doubt find out all about it when we get home. Did you manage to obtain the Watford result last night?"

"Yes they drew 0-0 with Man Utd."

"Bugger. I thought that Utd would win that. By the way, I don't think we should mention this to any of the players."

"No I agree."

"I'll see you in the restaurant at four."

They both hung up. Crowther stripped off and leapt into the shower.

As they sat for their meal, Dyson noticed that Paul Sulley and Eddie Hirst had not arrived.

"Anyone seen Paul and Eddie?"

There was so much banter going on between the players that no-one seemed to hear the question. Dyson turned to Crowther.

"Where the hell have they got to? I'll go and check with reception and see if their key's still there."

Dyson came back shortly shaking his head.

"The key to their room is still hanging up. The girl in reception says she hasn't seen them."

At 4.45pm the coach arrived, the kit was placed on it and the players started to gather in the foyer in ones and twos, ready for departure. Still there was no sign of Sulley or Hirst. They waited until 5.45pm but couldn't wait any longer. The journey to Lanarca was about 90 miles. Crowther left a detailed map of how to get the ground with the hotel reception and told them that the hotel should arrange a cab.

It was quite apparent, after half-an-hour of the journey, that the time allowed to make the coach ride to Lanarca had been drastically underestimated. The coach was nowhere near Limassol when it encountered its second delay due to extensive roadworks. Whilst the game was only a friendly, it was part of the transfer deal which had taken young Michael Charalambos to West London and Crowther didn't want to show any disrespect by kicking off late. He ordered the coach driver to stop and remove the playing kit from the luggage hold. The coach stopped on the side of the road. The hamper was far too big to squeeze into the seating area and Dyson, Crowther and Pullen removed the necessary playing gear and told the players to get changed whilst they travelled.

Typically, not one player had even thought of helping, they all sat in their seats mucking around like a bunch of overgrown schoolboys. With Sulley and Hirst missing, Crowther sat down to figure out what team to play. He had fined both lads for being late before, but usually it was just twenty minutes to half-an-hour. He couldn't imagine what had happened to them. As they approached the outskirts of Larnaca they could see the floodlights in the distance. The coach had difficulty in progressing quickly because of the immense volume of traffic, caused by the locals who had travelled from all over the island to see a class side play one of their own. On its arrival, the coach was surrounded by eager supporters trying to get a glimpse, touch, or autograph. But the club's security efficiently made sure that the players safely disembarked into the ground's miniscule entrance.

The ground resembled that of a semi-professional club, built mainly of breeze block. The terraces were made of compressed dirt with wood edging, which acted as supports, with a small stand which housed the dressing rooms, a small bar and offices. The stand had no more than four hundred tip-up slatted wooden seats and a corrugated iron roof. The pitch itself was in excellent condition; the grass was lush, a little longer than one might play on in the UK, and for a country with little rainfall it had been well tended and watered.

The game itself was witnessed by just over 4,000 fans who used every vantage point possible to watch the game. Prior to kick-off, the teams exchanged pennants and shook hands. The game, as expected, was a one-sided affair. If it had been a boxing match it would have been stopped after 15 minutes, when West

London led 3-0, but it got steadily worse for the Cypriot side as West London ran riot, winning by 8 goals to 1. Fellows scored a hat-trick, with Steggles (2), Harper (2) and Thomas also scoring. Don White sportingly handled the ball in the penalty box for the Anorthosis side to score their only goal from the spot. All the players got game time, including Michael Charalambos who had returned to Cyprus with homesickness. From the crowd's reaction to the goal, anyone who had just arrived would have thought it was the winner.

After the game, the Cypriots entertained the West London team and officials in their bar, organising an enormous spread of food and drink for their honoured guests. The players made themselves at home and got stuck into it. Sulley and Hirst had still not arrived and Crowther was now very concerned. He asked one of the Anorthosis officials if he could use the phone, explaining his predicament. The official obliged and rang the hotel for him, the conversation that followed in Greek was easily understood by the mannerisms adopted by the official. He cupped his hand around the mouthpiece of the phone.

"They have not returned to the hotel."

Crowther was so involved with finding out the whereabouts of the two boys that he totally forgot his meeting with newsman Bruce Day. He apologised to his guests and explained that, under the circumstances, they would have to cut short their stay and depart for Paphos. The Anorthosis contingent were very disappointed but understanding. When Crowther reached the coach, Bruce Day was there waiting for him. Crowther was polite but was still not prepared to discuss his problem with him.

The coach reached the Paphos Beach Hotel in sombre mood and Crowther again found Day waiting for him. Crowther told him that there was no way that he could think of anything but the two lads and that their meeting would have to wait until they arrived home. Day walked away from Crowther shaking his head in disbelief, still unable to share with Crowther the secret he held. The players filed off and re-assembled in the reception, eager for any news of their two teammates. There was none.

Crowther asked the receptionist to call the police. Within fifteen minutes they arrived and checked such information as was available. No-one could recall seeing either of the lads and, unfortunately, the one person who had seen them was a junior who had stepped in for just ten minutes when one of the reception staff had an emergency call involving the loo. With so much that normally happens in and around the reception area on a daily basis, the girl didn't even remember that this had occurred and the junior hadn't been questioned.

In broken English one of the policeman asked; "What about their passports. Where are they?"

"We have them. We always keep everyone's, so that we know nobody's left theirs at home or that they have expired. We travel as a party." Crowther answered.

The policeman gave him a quizzical look.

"Yes. Don't say it, we mollycoddle them."

The policeman looked at him again, even more confused. He didn't understand the expression.

"Sorry. We cater for their every need. They don't have to do anything for themselves."

The policeman nodded. He now understood. There had been a number of accidents that day and the police diligently examined each one in turn to establish whether any of them involved Sulley or Hirst, either together or on their own. None of the motor or scooter accidents involved two males and all those connected with accidents that night had been named. The police tried to find out whether anyone knew where the boys had been planning to go, but no-one could remember.

A few hours passed. The police were no further forward in establishing the whereabouts of either of them but, just when it looked as though all of their endeavours had been fruitless, one of the on-patrol policeman found a hire company who had leased a scooter to an Edward Hirst. He provided them with the the registration of the bike, emphasising that the bike should have been returned by 6pm.

Crowther, Dyson, Pullen, Proctor and Peters managed to get very little sleep that night. They hovered around the bar area and the reception as the police came and went. They asked more questions, but were devoid of any answers when asked for one themselves. A thorough search of the island would be made at daybreak, but it would be a thankless task with all the mountainous terrain that made up the island.

Daylight broke at 6am with the five sitting in the reception having yet another cup of coffee. The coach was due at 8am to take them back to the airport and the return flight to Gatwick. There was still no news from the police. They decided to return to their respective rooms and freshen up. Crowther dialled his home number to talk to his wife Sandra, but hung up before he had tapped in the final number, realising that they were two hours ahead and it was just gone 4am in England.

The two hours until the coach arrived had seen even more questions, this time from the players who couldn't come to terms with the loss of their teammates. Everyone was in a state of shock and confusion. The once happy group left from the Coral

Beach Hotel in total silence. The two players' belongings had been kept by the Police and Crowther had made sure that their passports were also left in their safe-keeping.

Flight BA0191 from Larnaca took off on time, at 10.04am, for the near five hour journey back to Gatwick. The party touched down just after mid-day, collected their baggage, made their way through the customs area and out into the main arrival concourse. Television cameras, photographers and reporters were in abundance, lights flashed and the camera lighting sparked into life as the West London group walked towards them, pushing their trolleys.

"Do you know what has happened to Eddie Hirst and Paul Sulley."

"No comment."

"Did you know Alfred Wade had been arrested for fraudulent activity?"

"No comment."

"Do you think that it could affect the club?"

"No comment."

The team had been told of the arrest of Alfred Wade prior to leaving the hotel and had been briefed not to respond to any questions asked about either the Chairman or Sulley and Hirst. Crowther said that there might be reporters at the airport but probably not. How he had miscalculated. The players though were responding exactly as he had told them to. As they made their way to the waiting coach, the media followed, questions still being thrown at them from every angle.

"Is it true that they hired a scooter?"

"No comment."

"How long have they been missing?"

"No comment."

"Rumour has it that the club could well fold. Is it true?"

"No comment."

The media were not getting what they hoped for and, as the players tried to get on the coach one by one, they had to fight their way past, until Jim Fellows finally broke.

"Why don't you fucking parasites leave us alone, can't you see we're all pretty choked up."

It was the little piece that would be continually shown on the news that night, with a bleep cutting out the 'f.....g'. It made good T.V.

Fellows sat in the coach realising his mistake and just said "Shit!"

When they reached the ground it was very much the same. The coach stopped and was surrounded by even more media, some had beaten the coach back and the others had already been there since early morning. Crowther stood at the door of the coach and told everyone to sit down and listen.

"We've all gone through a dreadful few hours worrying about Paul and Eddie and let's hope that they are found safe and well. They've probably pulled a couple of birds. I hope so. If they have they'll get the biggest bollocking they've ever had and some hefty fines to go with it, but I'll be relieved as you will. Let's hope that is the case and nothing serious has happened to them. As for the Chairman, we will know when we get off this coach what that is all about. I do not want anyone going into the club. Go straight home, get some rest. Do not respond to these arseholes out here. I want you at the training ground at 10am tomorrow, so that we can prepare for the Kirklees match on Sunday."

The players acted this time exactly as he instructed. Dyson and Pullen struggled with the kit hamper, whilst Crowther, Peters and Proctor fought their way through the media and headed for the reception door. It was locked. On seeing the three of them Sheila unlocked the door and let them in.

"Am I glad to see you. Have you heard the dreadful news about Mr. Wade? It can't be true can it?" she said, all in one breath.

"I don't know." replied Crowther.

"They've been camped out there all morning."

"Is Peter McCormick in?"

"Yes he's in his office."

The three of them went directly there. Peter McCormick looked relieved to see them all.

"This is a bloody nightmare. The Police arrived early this morning with a search warrant and they've taken with them a load of material. Phillipa is going ape shit."

With that Phillipa Scott, the club secretary, appeared at the door.

"The phones have not stopped ringing all morning. I just don't know what to say to anyone and you could have fucking told me that two of our players have gone missing."

It was unusual to hear her swear. She lit up a cigarette, usually most people would have reminded her that the office was a non-smoking area. But today nobody cared.

"Yes. I'm sorry. we've had so much on our plate we just didn't think."

"You could have rung me at home!" she continued.

"Yes. I'm sorry." McCormick interjected before Phillipa said too much.

"I've tried to contact the Chairman but his line is permanently engaged."

"Phillipa you'll have to contact the players' relations." said Proctor.

"Yes I'll have a look at their files and contact them."

"Have you seen the papers?" asked McCormick, handing them out. They looked at the various headlines; Crowther read to see if there was any reference to West London. There was very little, but tonight's Evening Standard, the T.V. and tomorrow morning's nationals would certainly have plenty. The phone rang and McCormick picked it up; it was Sheila.

"It's for you Roy."

Peters took the phone from McCormick as everyone listened to a one-way conversation. It was Barry J. Seymour

"Hello.You are joking. When?"

He looked up at the inquisitive faces.

"Alfred Wade's dead. It seems he committed suicide."

21

Jason Middleton was a tall, fair-haired giant of a man, standing six-feet-three. He was twenty eight and had bought Chalk Farm Leisure and Fitness Club seven years previously, working there as as a physical instructor since he took over. He was as much in love with Jenny Clarkson as Jenny was with him. They made a good couple. He first met her four years previously, when she joined the club's 'step-up' class. Like most fitness clubs, Chalk Farm always checked on each new member's fitness and enquired of them what they were actually trying to achieve. Stronger legs; flatter tummies; general fitness or whatever. Jenny was already in good shape and was interested only in remaining so. Jason recommended a variety of the club's equipment which would generate muscular competence and guided her around the machines, explaining what they did and how they worked.

"Swimming, of course, is another extremely good method of keeping fit."

"Anything but swimming." she had said.

"Why?"

"I'm just not very good at it. I came close to drowning in Spain several years ago, when I was on holiday, and since then I have lost all confidence in the water." She had smiled at him and he felt that he had fallen in love with her at that moment. But it took him another six months to date her.

Jason, a former Olympic four hundred metre breaststroke swimmer, suggested one of the intermediary swimming courses the club were offering, but she declined. He monitored her progress personally on each occasion she visited the club, which was normally twice a week, and sometimes she managed to get in a third visit. Jenny was a little suspicious as she thought that others had to pay for the sort of service that he was providing her, but the membership fee was all she had ever paid. In the shower, after one workout, she overheard a conversation between two other lady members which confirmed her suspicions.

"That Jason Middleton's a bit of a hunk."

"Don't, you're making me feel randy just thinking about him. He could put his shoes under my bed anytime."

"I thought he already had."

"Bitch. No he hasn't yet! But I'm working on it."

"Well you certainly get some individual attention."

"It's costing me £20 an hour, and still he hasn't made a pass!"

"You pay for his time?

"Yes. Of course I do."

"You must have it bad."

"No. I just fancy something a little more than sex with the old man. His idea of foreplay is to say "What about it?"

They laughed.

"Down girl, just remember that you're married."

"I know, but every other bugger seems to be doing it, except me."

"I'm not!"

"Pull the other leg. I bet you're having it off with the bloke next door."

"I'm not. But you can dream, can't you?"

As the hot water cleansed her body, Jenny was fascinated by the conversation and wanted to know why she didn't get charged. The weeks passed, no charges were ever mentioned, and Jason Middleton had remained totally professional. He had never made any indication that he wanted the relationship to be anything else. Maybe he never would have. Maybe he was too much of a professional to try to date someone whilst working. Like a doctor and patient relationship. But sometimes fate has to give relationships a helping hand.

Another session had come and gone and Jenny Clarkson sat in the Nissan Bluebird, as she had done many times before, and turned the key in the ignition. Every other time it had responded first time but on this occasion the battery was flat and there was very little response. The engine would not fire. She tried, many times, but the more she tried the weaker the battery became. She finally gave up and ventured back into the club's reception to seek assistance. She asked the receptionist whether any of the staff could give her a push. Jason Middleton and his partner John Sutton, another of the instructors, volunteered their services. But, when they approached the vehicle and opened the door, the two instructors just looked at each other, in a 'what a stupid woman' fashion.

"Jenny. The car is automatic." said Middleton.

"Yes. I know." she replied naively.

"You can't jump start an automatic."

"Can't you?"

"No. We need a set of jump leads."

With none being available, Jason offered her a lift home, with the promise that he would obtain a set from a friend and get her car back to her the next morning. Jason's car was a new black Mini Cooper S; soft top with a 2 litre engine. He always thought that a car of this nature should be driven hard. This particular night though he drove the car slowly, hardly reaching

30mph. The high performance engine was being well under-used and Jason was forever in a low gear. It didn't make sense to her, but it did to Jason; he wanted to prolong the journey for as long as possible. If the lights remotely looked as though they would turn from green to amber, he would slow down and stop. The red would then suspend any further mobility. When the signal turned from red, to red and amber, the majority of drivers would have been half way across the road, but not Jason; he waited until it was green.

The journey to her home in Primrose Hill took normally five or so minutes, but this one was nearing fifteen. Jason and Jenny never stopped chatting all the way back. The invitation to a coffee when he reached her house was a bonus he didn't expect. He asked her for a date that night and the relationship had grown since then. She had left RADA some three years before they met. He had followed her progress ever since. He loved watching her on the television, although he knew that she needed a little bit of luck to succeed. He had recorded the few times that she had appeared and continued to play them back. She was good, and looked good on the screen. There were too many actors trying to earn a living, some very good. Some would succeed, some would never be successful no matter how hard they tried.

Her parents had been generous with regard to finances and would never let her go short. But she was a proud young lady and had attended a Pitman training course for several years; she could touch type and was adept at shorthand. She worked as a temp as this gave her the opportunity to be flexible. She didn't share Jason's enthusiasm for watching herself. To her it was a job, admittedly one she enjoyed and would like to do on a much more regular basis. She had appeared on BBC's Casualty and Midsomer Murders, and had cameo appearances in Eastenders, Holby City and The Bill. She had been excited and privileged to work alongside both John Nettles and Judy Parfitt and felt that she had learnt so much from them in the two weeks they had been filming, as well as through the preceeding weeks at the rehearsal rooms.

She was one of the few actors that appreciated friends in other occupations and didn't mix socially with the acting fraternity. The couple were both excited at news that she had been asked to attend a casting interview for a new ITV series called Foyle's War, written by Anthony Horowitz. She had been provided with a script and a brief summary of the intended story line, and an address and time to attend.

Jenny was early and was shown to a waiting area where there were two other actresses. One of them she recognised; Honeysuckle Weeks. Neither spoke nor even acknowledged her. It was nearly an hour before the other two actresses had been seen and departed. No-one else turned up. She was ushered into a large square room, with a long table on the far wall sitting in front of an enormous picture window and two women and a man sat in front of it. It was explained that it was a detective television series for ITV about a Chief Superintendent carrying out normal duties in World War II and they were looking for young lady to play a prominent part alongside him; to play his chauffeur. She was asked to read several lines in a posh English accent and she thought she had performed well.

Their Saturday nights together had followed a regular pattern. A show or film in the city, followed by a meal somewhere in the West End and then on to dance the night away at one of the variety of discos in town, and finally back to his pad.

This particular Saturday night was going to be a little different to the rest; he had booked Quaglino's. He had decided to propose. The engagement ring, a diamond cluster, had set him back over £2,000 but she was worth every penny. Marriage had often been brought up in conversation between them but normally it was in relation to others. They spoke of friends whose marriages had problems; with either themselves or their children; and none of the relationships could be held up as the ideal. They had discussed their own fears of commitment and the bleak future without a stable partner. But never the two of them as a pair.

He had never given any indication to her that he wanted her, and she had never given him any reason to think that she wanted him, certainly not on a husband and wife basis. He had rung her several times on the Saturday afternoon but there had been no answer. He was beginning to doubt whether he was about to do the right thing. Would she accept? What if she didn't? Negative thoughts clouded his day as the time ticked by towards their 8pm date. When should I do it? After the meal? Before the meal? He was apprehensive as to her reply and, if it was to be a refusal, would the relationship continue? Eight o'clock could not arrive quickly enough.

Jason Middleton arrived at the door bang on time. He had left home early and had taken refuge in one of Jenny's locals. A whisky steadied his nerves; ready for what he hoped would be the most eventful evening of his life. He parked the car, walked up the path and knocked firmly on the door. As he waited on the doorstep he peered through the frosted glass, looking for her to appear. She came from upstairs, opened the door and flung her arms around him. She was never normally quite so passionate, certainly not at the beginning of the evening. As a rule, it required a couple of drinks. He kissed her gently on the lips before he stood back to admire her.

He placed his hand around her waist and they walked together into the lounge. They called a black cab and waited. Whilst he knew she was pleased to see him, the conversation from her frequently dried up, as her mind kept wandering off.

He wished he knew what she was thinking about. It worried him. They had never had 'pregnant' pauses in their conversation before. Maybe it was the wrong time to ask her.......

The cab arrived and whisked them to Leicester Square. They wandered around hand in hand looking for a suitable movie to see and found a romantic comedy at the Odeon called 'A Notation in the Night', with Julia Ormond and Tom Selleck.

"I've booked Quaglino's for 11.00pm." he said.

She looked at him strangely.

"Blimey, that's going overboard."

"Oh sorry, did you want to go somewhere else then?"

"No. No. Forget it." she said abruptly.

The film was amusing though neither of them enjoyed it, both for entirely different reasons.

They hailed a cab and this time it took them to Quaglino's, just off Piccadilly. Quaglino's is an ultra modern brasserie restaurant and bar in Bury Street, owned and created by Terence Conran. The entrepreneur ventured into the catering market after considerable success in his futuristic furnishing business.

They walked in, reconfirmed their reservation with the Maitre D' and told him where they would be in the bar when their table was ready. The bar and restaurant were already heaving and attempting to buy a couple of dry white wines was almost impossible. The bar was packed with those that had already managed to find a space by it and refused to move to allow anyone else near it. They also begrudged those who wished to do so. Considering the amount of people crammed into the eating house, there was insufficient room to cater for everybody in comfort. When Jason did finally manage to complete his drinks purchase, he and Jenny had to stand. They were jostled constantly, as the other occupants attempted to get by and obtain their own refreshment and then get out again to find a suitable space to stand or, if really lucky, sit. Whilst the restaurant's clientele were not the most affluent in the city, they would be classified as upper middle-class. The majority of the females wore short slinky dresses, some low cut, but a general description would be that they were people who wanted to be seen. The men had their peacock feathers on, and the women responded to them.

The white Sauvignon Blanc was cold and dry, with a subtle taste of the grape. They sipped their drinks and began to relax and enjoy the ambience for the first time that evening. She felt safe. Safe with him and safe in the surroundings. Occasionally they would spot someone they both knew and give a wave. Or try to have a long distance conversation, mouthing the words to each other and trying to understand what the others were saying, and probably getting it wrong. At long last they were called to their table. They were sat in the centre of some sixty tables. Jason picked up the menu and started to read it to her in a mimicking Italian accent.

"Tonight madam we have on our extensive menu Caviar; either Sevruga or Beluga. Oysters; Rock or Native. Or can I interest you in the Crustacea? We have Dressed Crabs with mirin and soy. But you can have them undressed if you so wish."

"Oh stop it" she said testily. "Stop mucking about and let me have a look at the menu."

He ignored her and carried on.

"Or we have Langoustines Mayonnaise or a half Lobster Mayonnaise."

The accent changed from Italian to French. She grabbed the menu from him and began to peruse it.

"I'll have some Beluga Caviar?" she said crossly.

"Alright."

"No don't be silly I was only joking."

"Thank God for that you sounded very serious." he said.

She gave a forced laugh.

"I'll have the Dressed Crab, followed by the chicken salad."

"I'll join you with the Dressed Crab and then the peppered beef salad. And we'll have a nice bottle of Sauvignon Blanc. Are you OK?"

"Yes of course!" she replied abruptly.

The waiter arrived and Jason gave him their order. He fidgeted around in his seat and periodically felt his jacket pocket to ensure the little box with the ring was still in it. It was. The conversation between them was beginning to flow as Jenny began to relax a little and then she suddenly became very serious.

"David you know people in the car business don't you."

"Yes. Why?"

"I want you to sell my car for me as quickly as possible."

"Why? You love that car."

"Just do it. Will you?" she used the same abrupt tone she had used in the cinema earlier in the evening.

"Yes. Of course." he said, quite startled. There was a silence that fell between them as her thoughts momentarily went back to the night before. She so wanted to tell him, but couldn't. She didn't know how he would react. Would he blame her? Would he feel betrayed? She felt defiled and momentarily depressed. She had to pull herself together.

The first course arrived to take her mind off of her dilemma, together with the bottle of Sauvignon Blanc. The waiter showed the bottle to Jason, turning it so he could read the label. After receiving a nod of approval, he carefully removed the cork and poured a mouthful into his glass; Jason took a sip.

"Very nice. Thank you."

The waiter acknowledged and filled Jenny's glass, prior to returning to top his up. He placed the wine in an ice bucket and wished them a good meal.

Jenny ate her crab slowly and delicately whilst Jason consumed his hastily, as though his life depended on it. Whilst she was finishing hers, he topped up both of their glasses. She was now suffering with violent mood swings. One moment she felt happy and contented and the next miserable and distressed. Her mind wandered and, with her thoughts sometimes elsewhere, Jason had to constantly repeat what he was saying. Jenny's behaviour was again giving him doubts about his proposal. At times he was going to abandon his plan, but he convinced himself that if she did say no, at least he would know her feelings and would be able to act accordingly. But would he? He knew he would be heartbroken if she turned him down.

The chicken and peppered beef salads arrived and the waiter poured the remaining wine into the two glasses.

"Why do you want to sell the car?" he asked.

"I just want a change."

"You've had it a long time."

"I know, but I want a change." she said irritably. "Can we change the subject?"

They finished their salads and Jason excused himself on the pretext of needing to go to the toilet. He searched for and located the wine waiter, but was finding it difficult to get his attention. He furtively hovered around whilst the waiter busied himself with the other diners, taking orders and disappearing into the kitchen area to provide them with their evening's tipple. At long last he gained his attention and requested a bottle of Moet Chandon champagne to be brought to his table, along with two glasses.

Meanwhile, Jenny sat people-watching. It was one of her hobbies. Listening intently to their conversations and placing the individuals into several categories. She watched the waiters busily fussing around the tables, either bringing in the food or taking away the empty plates. She mused at the cigarette girl who floated around with her tray. Her long nylon legs protruded from her micro skirt and her boobs were pressed up to show her cleavage in a low cut bodice. The men loved it. They often tipped far more than the cost of the items she was selling, just to have her near them and bending down so that they could get a better view. She was always polite and always volunteered a great big smile. Jenny watched her wander from table to table, as she was beckoned. She lost sight of her momentarily, as she made her way into the bar area. She changed her attention and began to watch the three couples on the table close to the main thoroughfare. Just beyond, the cigarette girl reappeared and she returned to watch her. As she did so she caught her eye. The girl smiled at her and held her gaze as she jauntily headed in her direction. The smile remained. She reached Jenny's table smiled and said.

"Jenny Clarkson?"

"Yes."

"I have a note for you from a gentleman in the bar." The girl smiled and gave her the note which she took.

"Thank you."

She opened the note, read it, and went cold.

'Hi Jenny, Nice boyfriend, Jason isn't it? Just a note to say that I'm always around. Have a good evening. I will be in touch. Your friend from last night.'

She looked in the direction of the bar but couldn't see him. She folded the note and placed it quickly in her handbag. She didn't want Jason to know about it. Her heart quickened in pace and her body temperature rose dramatically, as the fear from the previous evening returned. Her limbs felt heavy and she felt faint. She left the table and headed rapidly for the toilets. She found herself a cubicle, locked the door and sat down on the toilet seat with her head in her hands. She took ten minutes to recover her composure. She washed her face, refreshed herself with perfume and returned to the table.

Jason had already returned and was taken aback when he found Jenny not there. When she finally returned, he said:

"Where've you been? You've been ages."

"I needed to go to the loo."

"Are you alright? You look quite pale. You've been in an odd mood all evening."

The waiter arrived with the champagne.

"What's this?" she said rather bemused and not too impressed.

"Champagne."

"Yes I know that. But why?"

The waiter opened the bottle and the loud pop of the cork being released from the bottle made many look in their direction. The waiter poured the Moet Chandon into the two champagne flutes, placed the bottle in the ice bucket and retired. She placed the glass to her lips and took a sip. Jason held his briefly, took a sip and replaced the glass on the table. He reached inside his pocket retrieved the little box, flipped the top open and placed it in front of her. The ring glistened brightly.

"Jenny, will you marry me?"

Jenny was shaken. She had never for one moment even considered marriage to Jason; they were having too much fun, and she enjoyed a certain amount of independence. Probably, on any other evening, she might have said yes, but with the events that had occurred she couldn't even begin to contemplate it.

She looked at the ring and then up into his eyes. They were beginning to look sad. She didn't need to answer, her body language had said it all.

"I can't." her voice trembled as she spoke.

"I can't." she repeated herself, as though he hadn't heard the first time.

It had been a risk to ask, especially in the funny mood she was in. He retrieved the box with great embarrassment and placed it back in its box. He imagined everyone to be looking at him. Neither of them touched the champagne, as an embarrassed silence pervaded the scene. Jason acquired an enormous lump in his throat and had the sudden impulsion to leave.

"Come on let's go." he said dejectedly.

They stood up. He grabbed the ice bucket containing the champagne and placed it on the table of the three couples Jenny had been watching earlier.

"Enjoy." he said.

The whole table stopped talking and looked at him in stunned silence, and then back at the champagne, and then each other. In the foyer he paid the bill and exited down the stairs to the main street.

"I'll take you home."

He hailed a cab and the two climbed in.

"Primrose Hill Road please."

There was total silence all the way back to Jenny's house, both were struggling within themselves to think of something to say, but whatever it would be, it would not be sufficient to overcome the disappointment of the evening. He paid the cab driver and turned to say goodnight. After nearly four years it seemed that the relationship was now over. She placed her arms around him and held him close, whilst his were dropped by his side. He didn't now know how to react.

"Don't go, stay with me."

He was receiving mixed messages. Messages he could not fathom.

"No. I'm off."

"Please. Please stay. I don't want you to go. I'm scared to be on my own."

"Why?"

He brushed her arms away and tried to move away, he felt hurt and used. She clung back onto him with tears streaming from her face.

"Please Jason. Please stay with me." she was becoming hysterical.

"No, fuck you. I'm too upset. I'm going home."

"Jason please, I'm frightened. Don't go."

"Why are you fightened?" She didn't answer him and wouldn't let him go.

It took ten minutes before he finally succumbed, he wrapped his arms around her. She began to sob as he held her close to him. They went inside and he found the brandy bottle, he noticed that a considerable amount had been consumed since the last time they had imbibed. It was unusual for them to stay at Jenny's. The single bed, whilst nice to make love in, never allowed them the luxury of a good night's sleep. At the start of the relationship it was acceptable for the both of them, as they enjoyed the continual sex and didn't want to sleep. But the relationship had progressed well beyond seeing each other for their bodies. They climbed into the bed and Jason held her naked body close. He began to kiss her gently, waiting for her to respond and open her mouth. Her lips remained closed. His hands wandered over her body, wanting to coax her erogenous areas into a response. Her hand constantly removed his. He tried hard to arouse her, to no avail.

In the morning, Jason awoke to find that Jenny had already got up and he was alone in the bed. He put on his pants and went down the stairs to find her in the lounge, in her dressing gown, clutching a cup of coffee. Her eyes were red. She looked up.

"I've just percolated some fresh coffee if you want some."

He went to the kitchen, poured himself a mug full, returned to the lounge and sat opposite.

"Are we history Jenny?"

She looked up at him and slowly shook her head, a faint smile broke across her lips.

"No, of course not. Be patient with me. When I'm ready, I'll tell you things that I wish I could now. But I just can't. I love you very much."

He started to get up. She held her hand up in the 'stop' gesture.

"No, please don't. Stay there."

He sat down again.

"What is it that's bothering you? The commitment? What?"

"It's nothing to do with us. It's a small problem I have and until it's resolved I cannot make any long term commitment."

She looked at him in an eye to eye contact.

"I want you to go now and I don't want to see you for a while. Please don't ring me, visit me or try to get in contact, I need time and space."

She knew that if she told the truth he would commence an enquiry of his own and she didn't want to get him involved. She was frightened that his involvement might put both of them in more danger than they already were. Although he didn't know it.

She had been awake for the most of the night. She had considered all the options available to her and decided to take the £15,000 and do what was asked of her. Then she would return to a normal way of life, and possibly even marry Jason.

"I will ring you when I'm ready. If you haven't met someone else by then, propose to me, I might even say yes."

Part of him felt relief and happiness and another part felt frustration. He couldn't comprehend. He was trapped in a labyrinth of unanswered questions.

"How long will we be apart? And why?" "I don't know. Trust me. Please do what I ask."

"If I agree, then let's go upstairs and make love."

"No Jason. Don't put conditions on our sex life. Now, please get yourself dressed and go. Before I change my mind."

He again partly got up to go towards her.

"No, don't say anything, I'm not changing my mind. Please promise me that you will do what I ask."

"Yes. I promise." Jason said reluctantly.

He dressed and, as he put his jacket on, felt the bulge of the small box in his pocket. He removed it, opened the lid and carefully placed it under her pillow. He met her at the foot of the stairs, held her close, kissed her affectionately on the lips and left. Jenny found the ring not long after he had gone. She took it from the box and placed it on the third finger of her left hand.

She busied herself in the house for the next few days, waiting hopefully to hear whether she had been short-listed for Foyles War and also for the inevitable contact from Phil West. Ray Prince, alias Phil West, kept his promise. The contact was made as she manipulated her trolley around the local supermarket. Prince was a careful man and didn't trust her with any pre-planned meetings, preferring the art of surprise.

"Come with me now." he said as he approached her at the fresh meat counter.

"What about my shopping?"

"Leave it and walk out. You can do that at any time."

She did as he asked; she walked away from the near full trolley and followed him through the doors to the exit. A large chauffeur-driven Mercedes drew up at the kerb, Prince opened the door and Jenny clambered in the back. Prince joined her.

The car drove into central London, finally stopping at a block of apartments in Berkeley Square.

"Be back here in one hour." he said to the driver.

"This is where we get out."

"Where are we going?" she said.

"You'll find out soon enough."

They alighted from the car and headed towards an apartment block. Prince extracted a piece of paper from his pocket and tapped the number written on it into the keyboard at the entrance. The door unlocked, he pushed it open and they entered the foyer. They took the lift to the fourth floor and walked down the carpeted corridor to room 41. Prince unlocked the door, went into the kitchen and returned with two coffees. She was so nervous that she spilled most of it into her saucer.

"These are a set of keys to this apartment, on this piece of paper is the code for the front door. I want you to familiarise yourself with the flat. Live here for a week. Pick up as much clothing as you require from your home and only leave when instructed."

Jenny sat acknowledging his instructions as though she was being briefed at a rehearsal.

"Have you heard of Mike Stephenson?"

She wasn't into football, but knew who he was instantly.

"Yes, he's the England football team captain."

"Would you be able to recognise him?"

"Yes of course."

"Good. At least I haven't got to provide you with a photograph."

"Next Tuesday, Mike Stephenson will be opening a shop in Bruton Street. We will get you an official invitation to get in.

I want you to get Stephenson back to this apartment and, most importantly, get him in the bedroom. What you do in there is not in the script, but you will seduce him and act out everything on top of the bed. How long it lasts is up to you. But the longer you are in there, the more we can photograph."

"Christ. What makes you think that I can even pull him?"

"You underestimate your beauty Jenny, and the effect you have on men. Follow?"

He got up and went to the bedroom. One wall was totally mirrored.

"Behind this." (pointing to the mirror) "is a camera, so always act in front of it."

Prince took out and opened his wallet.

"There's £3,000 in cash, the other £12,000 will be yours once we have had a look at the video and we're satisfied that it's good."

"Who am I?" she asked.

"What do you mean?"

"What's my name?"

"That's up to you. But I wouldn't use your own name."

She thought hard for a name that she wouldn't forget, but could only think of her mother's maiden name Rastall.

Jenny did what was asked of her and situated herself in the apartment, after first collecting what she required from her home in Primrose Hill. She wrote three notes, placed each one into an envelope and wrote on the outside of each one. She found a fourth big enough to hold the £3,000; which was in £50 denominations; and a reinforced envelope big enough to hold everything. She sealed the envelope securely with sticky tape and, on the way back to Berkeley Square, popped into the local post office. She registered the envelope and handed it to the counter clerk with the required fee.

The invitation arrived as promised. On the day in question, she chose a small-print knee length skirt with a low necklined, pink, button-down blouse, pink high-heeled sling-back shoes, single pearl earrings and a small thin neckchain. She looked at herself, combed her hair in place and knew that she was ready.

She threw a black Burberry Mac around her shoulders and made her way to Redmand Art in Bruton Street. On arrival she presented her invitation at the door and was greeted with a glass of champagne. She looked around hard at the guests but couldn't see Stephenson. She had arrived in good time. She was concerned as to how she was going to get the opportunity of approaching and talking to him. She loitered, glancing at the paintings, but her mind was on the job in hand. She established who the owners were, as they constantly looked anxiously into the street and at their watches. She tried not get drawn too far away from them or into any deep conversation with anyone.

Mike Stephenson finally arrived and he was quickly whisked away into a corner. He was even better looking in real life. As more and more guests arrived, inquisitive pedestrians on the pavement outside began to stop and view the proceedings; staring in through the windows. When Stephenson appeared, the viewing public became animated and very excited. His opening speech was short and amusing. He cut out the formalities normally associated with such occasions, with the exception of cutting a huge ribbon with a large pair of gold engraved scissors. The champagne corks popped continuously as the celebrations got underway and the waiters toured the customers, refreshing their glasses. It seemed ages before Stephenson ventured from the main party and started to wander around by himself. The opportunity very quickly availed itself and she moved smartly in his direction and walked up to the side of him, pretending to view the picture he was looking at.

"That's awful isn't it?" she said.

"Yes it is." he replied.

She knew at that moment that Phil West was right. Stephenson could not stop looking at her. He was mesmerised and she thought 'Good looking too, maybe this won't be as bad as I first thought.'

He made the initial move, which Jenny was happy about.

"Look, I don't know about you, but I fancy a coffee. Would you care to join me?"

She accepted but was still concerned. At the risk of being too direct, how was she going to get him back to the apartment? They walked along laughing and joking, most of the cafes were full, those that weren't didn't appear too inviting. She knew that this was the time to be bold.

"None of these places appeal to me at all. My flat's just around the corner. You're more than welcome to join me for a coffee, or something stronger if you wish."

She led him away towards the apartment block, like a lamb to the slaughter. Jenny's only pang of guilt so far was that she was using her mum's maiden name; Rastall; as though she was contaminating it in some way.

When they arrived at the flat she started the coffee percolator, opened a bottle of Chablis in the kitchen and strode into the lounge with two glasses. She placed herself on the settee with her legs tucked up underneath her, knowing he would be watching every moment and that every movement was a turn-on. It was so calculated. A little more movement, a little more show of thigh. An exaggerated lean forward to pick up a glass provided him with a good view of her breasts. She had him. He was hers and she was actually enjoying the power. They emptied the first bottle and she went to the kitchen to open another. She returned to find him on his knees looking through the CD collection. She moved towards him, placed her hand on the nape of his neck and let her fingers fondle his scalp. His hands responded by clasping the back of her legs and, as she lowered herself, moving under her skirt and up her thighs.

The kisses and caressing inevitably ended up with their movement towards the bedroom and then onto the bed. She manoeuvred Stephenson in such a way that he was always in full view of the camera and set about making love to him. He was a nice, gentle guy and was actually better at lovemaking than Jason. The wine and satisfaction saw them both subside into sleep. She had enjoyed the sex with him and was now going to enjoy the money.

She was awoken by Mike hastily pulling his trousers on.

"Where's the fire?"

"It's half past eight. I've got to get home." he said.

She was feeling angry and couldn't understand why. Not for what she had just done, but at him.

'Fuck 'em and leave 'em.' flashed through her mind and she then illogically blurted out.

"Bloody married men. You're all the same. Have your fun and run." Jenny's reaction was more annoyance; annoyance that a happily married man, a nice man, could so easily be led astray. "You're a nice guy Mike and I'm really sorry."

"Oh come on Jenny. You knew I was a married man when you met me. You even knew who I was. Can I see you again?"

It was a request she didn't expect.

"What, do you want to bring your wife and kid? I think not Mike. Let's just say it was a nice interlude. Good-bye."

He left and Jenny dropped back into a deep sleep.

The camera operator handed Prince the DVD and the digital camera, which contained over eighty colour shots.

"What was it like?" he asked

"Fucking horny Ray. Fucking horny."

Prince looked through the two-way mirror into the bedroom, and could see Jenny was fast asleep in the dimly lit bedroom. The evening was closing in and the light fading rapidly.

" I'm off." said the cameraman.

"Thanks. See you." said Prince.

Prince switched on the television, placed the DVD into the machine, sat back in the armchair and began to watch the activities. It was a great performance with the opportunity of picking up some great shots. The more he watched the more he wanted her, but this time awake. He switched the DVD off and looked back through the two-way mirror. She was still asleep and the room had now lost most of its light. He pulled at the mirror and it slid open, allowing him access into the bedroom. He removed all of his clothes and slithered in between the sheets, manoeuvring his naked body next to hers. He put his crotch next to hers and pulled her on to him.

She was still in a semi-sleep and recovering from the vast amount of wine drunk earlier in the day. Her dreams were erotic and Jason Middleton was in the forefront of them. Prince could feel her becoming aroused. She responded to his every touch and it was not long before she rolled passively onto her back and her legs parted. He climbed between her legs and penetration was easy. It was the most gratifying sex he had experienced for a very long time. Her orgasm followed quickly. Her total loss of control also excited him so much that it brought him to a rapid and satisfying conclusion.

He hadn't for one moment ever considered that she had known it was him and was taken aback when she started purring in his ear.

"Jason, Jason, that was great."

Prince became angry. Jenny leant over to switch the side light on and seeing him, screamed in horror.

"No. No. Oh God no not you. You cretin."

Not only had she allowed this cretin to fuck her, she had actually encouraged it. Prince hit her hard with a punch to the mouth. The blow split her lip open and was so violent it loosened her two front teeth. The pain was severe and her head was spinning. She held her mouth as the blood seeped through her fingers. She was now close to unconsciousness. Prince was still extremely angry and gripped her neck. He squeezed it so hard Jenny was dead within a matter of seconds. He left her on the bed, stormed into the kitchen and washed his hands shouting out:

"You fucking idiot. You fucking idiot."

Prince made a quick call, prompting others to come over, to clean the mess up and bring him some fresh clothes. The body was removed from the room and, with the help of an electric saw, was cut into small fragments, placed in several black bin liners and taken to a nearby furnace to be disposed of. The premises were cleaned thoroughly and all the furniture, including the bed, was removed, along with all signs of Jenny Clarkson.

22

Audrey Wade had begrudgingly packed her husband's bags for the trip to Cyprus the previous evening. In all the years they had been married, it was still one of the few things that he was incapable of doing. She had retired to her bed at 10pm and Alfred had come up just before midnight. She set the alarm for 2.30am and had set the breakfast things out and made sure the car had a full tank of petrol.

They slept in single beds. It had been a long time since they had shown any physical love to one another, the marriage had diminished into a close friendship after her second miscarriage some thirty years ago. In that time, her sex drive disappeared totally, whilst his increased. Over the years there had been many mistresses, but none that he would have left home for. Home was an 18th century seven-bedroomed rectory which accommodated a games room with a full size snooker table, dartboard, card table, a bar, and an immense indoor swimming pool. It had a garage big enough to accommodate four cars, a tennis court and a helicopter landing pad and was set in twelve acres of prime pine forest in Wormley, Hertfordshire. It was guarded with eight foot stone walls and a remote controlled security gate.

Alfred Wade was one of those many people in life who lived to work. To make money. His success gave him celebrity status. He mixed with the famous; politicians, film stars and even some on the fringe of the royalty. His life was forever in the news, portrayed in the tabloids and on television. Unlike the majority of his contemporaries who would have stopped when they reached billionaire status, the accomplishment only fuelled his drive to increase his wealth even further. Wade continued to expand his business interests, ever more frequently buying companies with cash flow problems. With the majority of his wealth committed, he sought and gained enormous loans from major investment bankers in the City, without complication. His name alone was enough to guarantee immediate monetary assistance. His enormous ego, however, persuaded Wade to purchase 150,000 of the shares available to become the major shareholder of West London Football Club. Once established as Chairman, he offered them a £10 million interest free loan.

With diminishing profits, the share value of his major companies falling dramatically and interest rates rising to an all time high, Wade embarked on a strategy of complicatives to confuse the City. He began buying shares in his own company in an attempt to stabilise their share value. He placed on the market forty percent of his holding of Sacher Paper Plc and attempted to influence the market by purporting them to be valued at over £500 million. He raised far short of that when they were sold for £263 million. His vast capital was continually being eroded alarmingly quickly, as bank interest alone was accounting for £1 million per day. He raised further loans from a variety of financial establishments by offering shares as collateral. The same shares.

The lenders themselves were negligent in not seeking the proof of their existence. The loans were thereby unsecured. He continued to satisfy the ever growing interest repayments, but at considerable loss to his fortune He reached an all time low when, as a Trustee of the Sacher Paper Plc Pension Fund, he fraudulently misappropriated over £45 million of it, to help pay the interest and to support his companies ever falling shares. Wade had paid well for loyalty and silence. Salaries were enormous and backhanders were prevalent. He had already used the shares in West London as loan security and there was now very little left.

Wade had bullied his way through his life, and, whilst he had an enormous amount of people that looked up to him and admired him professionally, not many liked him personally. He had immense energy, a quick brain and a cruel tongue. He was an overpowering man. Those that worked for him were petrified of him and those that crossed his path in the business world always felt subservient to him. In this environment it was inevitable that he acquired many enemies. His major error was his continual chastisement of his assistant Martin Cummings. Martin had suffered his rebukes for too long, he knew the problems first hand and decided that enough was enough. He contacted the police and a thorough investigation had been set in motion, to verify the man's allegations. Once proved, the fraud squad were ready to pounce. Forty officers were deployed on the Tuesday morning in simultaneously arresting Alfred Wade and five of his employees, at various addresses in the home counties.

Alfred Wade was woken with a start by the hammering on his front door. It was 3 a.m. He could not imagine who it would be at that unearthly hour, or how whoever it was had managed to get through the security gate. He hurriedly donned his dressing gown.

"What is it?" asked Audrey.

"I don't know." he replied.

He opened the curtain and gazed across the drive area and was shocked to see the forecourt illuminated by three police cars' blue flashing lights, casting strange blue and white reflections over the darkened garden.

"It's the police." he mumbled.

Audrey immediately sat bolt upright.

"The police. What do they want?" she said alarmingly.

"How do I know."

To stop them from breaking the door down, Wade walked amenably down the staircase and opened it to the throng of police officers. The officer in charge produced a search warrant and read out the customary arresting caution.

"How did you get through the security gate?" he asked.

"We have ways." smiled the officer.

They allowed him time to get dressed whilst they searched the house and removed several files. Audrey asked if she could go with him, reluctantly the arresting officer agreed that she could.

Later that day the police visited every one of Wade's businesses, including his accountants, removing massive amounts of paper and folders.

Wade was held for forty-eight hours before being released on bail. The news of his arrest and release was slow in reaching the national newspapers; the London Evening Standard was the first to print what they knew on the Thursday evening. Most of it was speculative reporting and, whilst they had picked up some major elements of the fraud, they were way off the truth, or the depth of the deception. The seven major celestial television channels also missed out on their evening programmes and could only sit outside of Wade's house, waiting for him to appear and film anything that moved around the property, again only reporting on the events speculatively.

When Wade was released on bail he returned home to be greeted with a mass of the media in close proximity to the entrance and it took his good friend and solicitor Barry J. Seymour (who had picked him up from the police station) an age to get through. Seymour dropped Wade off, promising to return later in the day. His home from then on became a fortress and there were no visitors. On the Friday morning it was on every national paper's front page, with not much more information than had been gleaned the following day other than the addition of the others that had also been arrested and the volume of the raids that had taken place.

Wade had long since unplugged the telephones from the wall. Since arriving home the phone had rung continually and he felt that he had spoken to every reporter of every national and regional newspaper in the country. None of the reporters had gleaned any information from him and their frustration at failing do so had effectively increased the calls, which had now gone far beyond his endurance level.

The house was more than comfortable and the freezer was full. He estimated that they had sufficient supplies to last at least ten days if need be. He was in no frame of mind to face anyone, with the exception of his solicitor Barry J. Seymour.

Seymour returned early in the afternoon and was subjected to a barrage of questions from the media that still surrounded the exterior of the house. He had remained tight-lipped under the glare of the lights as the cameras rolled and the camera flashes from the still camera operators were incessant. He had enjoyed his moment of fame and wondered whether he might end up on the evening T.V. or in the papers. The discussions with Wade took over an hour and, when Seymour left, he was subjected again to the waiting media.

Wade was not left full of confidence by his solicitor friend; the information was full of ambiguity and lacking in truth. Seymour's response to the facts given to him was pessimism.

They had dealt with one another for the past forty years and it was due to Seymour that he had become a Freemason. He had studied hard, had attained the exulted position of Grand Master and didn't relish the thought of contact with any other of his brothers. The embarrassment and humiliation was too much for him to even confide totally with Seymour. If he couldn't tell his oldest friend then who could he face?

Audrey came down the stairs to find him deep in thought and clutching a brandy, she was in her swimsuit, had a towel over one arm and was carrying a bottle of water .

"I'm going for my daily dip Alf, are you going to join me?"

"No my love. You carry on."

For an hour every day, Audrey Wade swam in the indoor pool with the sound of the displaced water adding to the acoustics of Frank Sinatra repetitively serenading her. She religiously continued her exercise routines in her own little world. She always started with the crawl; head in the water, blowing out through her mouth and then sucking the air in as her she pulled her head to the side. It was a stroke that submerged the ears and muffled many of the exterior sounds.

He walked with her and saw her place her towel down on the bench, turn on the music and slide into the water. The echo of the water hitting the sides of the pool as it was displaced by the movement of her body gliding through it confirmed, along with the dulcet tones of Sinatra, that she wouldn't be able to hear anything.

He made his way to the master bedroom and unlocked the small bedside table. He felt to the back of the drawer and his hand found what he was looking for. He extracted the bundle containing the piece of equipment he had purchased illegally some months previously as a safeguard against uninvited guests. The pistol measured a little under five inches and weighed a mere ten ounces.

The .25 ACP Beretta 950 Jetfire felt comfortable as he held it in his hand. He searched around the drawer again for the ammunition. He found the small box of .25 ACP shells he had hidden away. He took them one by one from the box, carefully loaded eight into the magazine, clipped the magazine into the Beretta, flicked off the safety catch and sat on the bed. Even in death he never considered anyone but himself. There was no thought or compassion for the person who would find him, and who would then have to live with that memory for the rest of their lives. He sat on the bed for quite a time, contemplating his impending action.

He found that killing himself was not that easy. What else was there after life was extinguished? But to spend many years of his life in prison was an option he found to be unbearable to consider.

Finally, he placed the gun in his mouth, pointed it in an upward direction and slowly pulled the trigger. The gun made a tremendous explosion and recoiled dramatically as the hammer made connection with the bullet. The bullet ripped through his brains and skull and lodged in the ceiling. Masses of brain fragments and blood engulfed the bedding, ceiling and walls and his lifeless body fell to the floor.

Audrey found him an hour later.

23

Ray Prince hadn't bothered to go to the game, instead he had completed the task he considered was necessary to disrupt West London's team completely. It had been unfortunate for the two lads on the scooter. Unlike the others, they were the only ones to break ranks. The others always kept together wherever they went, so it had worked well for him. He wasn't worried whether they were alive or not, he knew they were out of action.

His plane left at the crack of dawn the next day and he was busily getting his hand luggage together. He hated rushing. He fancied a good meal and a nice bottle of wine, followed by a couple of stiff brandies in the bar. In the past, the hotel had probably been, if not the best, then certainly not far off the best in Paphos. The four star Paphos Beach Hotel. Its name certainly gave that impression, but it was tired and in need of refurbishment. He had purposely not stayed at the same hotel as the players. Always cautious, he had selected this location and hired a white Jeep, keeping them in range with a set of binoculars. The hotel was nicely situated in the main part of the town and just off the beach, it had its own swimming pool, bar-side pool and gymnasium and was set amidst eight acres of landscaped gardens.

Prince sat in the bar consuming large quantities of brandy and was absorbed by the little Cypriot barmaid. She had long dark hair, dark brown eyes, pleasantly rounded breasts of fair but not excessive proportions and a husky voice. He wouldn't let anyone else serve him. He continually tried to embark on a conversation with her but it was difficult; her English was poor and she could just about decipher what he or anyone else wanted to drink, let alone have a conversation of any kind. He was so entranced by her that he didn't pay any attention to one of the hotel guests who was at the counter, buying himself a drink from her male associate.

Bruce Day stood at the bar with a small beer, sipping it as he re-read his report of the game and the additional column or so about the disappearance of Sulley and Hirst. He had already rung the newspaper and read it over the phone to enable them to alter the headlines and meet the deadline for the following evening's edition. He looked at his watch; unlike the team he was on the first flight out of Paphos Airport in the morning and needed to get some sleep. He turned to leave and stopped suddenly in his tracks, a cold shiver exhumed his whole body.

Sitting in a comfortable armchair, staring straight in his direction, he recognised the face and physique of the man he saw physically assaulting Dave McLeod, and who had then chased him. The man put an arm in the air and was struggling to get up. Day retreated from the bar at its nearest exit. Fear and the warm evening air made his body temperature rise dramatically and sweat enveloped his every crevice. The exit had taken him onto the terrace and he began to run frantically. His brain was in panic, in self-preservation mode. He daren't look behind him. There was no logic in the direction he was running in, the area was dimly lit, tree-lined with masses of stacked, strategically positioned, sunbeds waiting for the following day's sun worshippers. It was deserted. He ran and then stopped, bravely looking tentatively back in the direction he had come. The door from the bar area opened and the silhouette of a man began to walk in his direction. He continued to flee and, as he did, his legs caught a sunbed which had been dragged into a secluded spot earlier by an amorous couple. He began to fall, helplessly out of control, unceremoniously into the swimming pool.

If Bruce Day had one nightmare it was this; he feared water as he couldn't swim at all. It would have been difficult enough for him in a pair of swimming trunks, the fact that he was fully clothed was a great hindrance to him. He flayed his arms and legs frantically in an attempt to get his head above the water and take a breath. The suddenness of entering the water had not prepared him and the water had already entered up his nostrils and down the back of his throat. He was struggling to breathe. Each time his head went under he experienced the gurgling sound of the water and every time he came to the surface he tried desperately to clear the congestion and take a breath, but the constant panic pulled him beneath the water again before he was able to do so. His lungs were bursting with the want of oxygen and his past began to flicker through his brain as he started to lose consciousness.

It had been one of the hotel staff who had come out of the bar and onto the terrace. His duty was to replenish the towels in a nearby hut, ready for the following morning's sunbathers and swimmers. He heard the frantic noise coming from the pool and, seeing the desperate body, jumped into the water. He swam to Bruce, quickly turned him on his back and pulled him into the shallower water.

He kept a hand underneath his limp body to support him, sealed his nose and administered mouth to mouth resuscitation. He pulled him from the water and placed him face down with his arms above his head, then administered pressure on his shoulder blades. He began to work from the elbows, pulling them upwards until they resisted going any further. He repeated the exercise time and time again in the forlorn hope that he could save him. He pressed again on his shoulders and, unexpectedly, Bruce Day choked loudly; his airways and lungs had freed themselves of the water and he began to breath without obstruction.

Ray Prince had not spotted him in the bar and happened to be trying to tell the Cypriot girl that he had left a big tip for her, and his room number. If he had, Bruce Day's last memory of life would have been his struggle in the water.

An ambulance was called and Bruce Day was taken to a hospital in Limmasol for an examination. He was kept in overnight and missed his early morning plane. He rang his editor from the hospital and told him of the previous night's incident and his current predicament, leaving out any mention of Prince or any other connection to him. He was then told of Alfred Wade's death. He was saddened to hear of it and the circumstances surrounding it and was even more determined than ever to speak with John Crowther. He attempted to ring the club on several occasions but the lines were continually engaged.

He caught his rearranged flight to Gatwick late on Saturday, retrieved his car from the long term car park and sped down the M23 towards the M25 and then to Hounslow and the Zion Park ground. Whether it was tiredness, stress, or he just was not capable of driving at excessive speeds will never be known. On the outskirts of Sunbury, as the M3 interchange approached, the car veered wildly and collided with the central reservation. The impact sent it somersaulting into the air, ripping the front end of the vehicle away like a chainsaw would rip through butter. The car twisted in mid air and finally finished up on its roof, a twisted disassembled mess of metal. It was hardly recognisable as a car, just as Bruce Day was unrecognisable as a human being. He was killed instantly and knew very little about it.

24

Jason Middleton's week without seeing Jenny Clarkson had made him miserable. He had rushed home from work every evening to wait for her to call. Every occasion the phone did ring, his heart took an almighty leap. He would answer it, only to be disappointed that it was not her. His conversations were always short and a little abrupt as he tried to end them quickly and replace the receiver. He always wanted the line free for her to get through.

He was living in a tip. He couldn't be bothered to wash up or tidy the house. The washing-up was piled high on the draining board in the kitchen. Milk had been left out so long that it had soured. His bed had not been made and his discarded clothes lay where they had been removed. He was having difficulty in finding any enthusiasm to go to work and his normal clean wet shave had been neglected for a quick shave whilst driving to work in the car. Invariably he was late and his work was beginning to suffer. He had never experienced anything like this before, it felt as though a huge part of himself had been cut off and without it he couldn't function. He drank endlessly; beer, whisky, brandy and wine. Whatever came to hand. His sorties to the local shops were infrequent and were only made to restock his ever decreasing supply of alcohol, or to purchase a microwaved meal.

On this particular evening he sat untidily on the sofa, with the T.V. remote control in one hand as he incessantly changed channels. His interest waivered dramatically. The phone rang, he lifted the receiver; it was from a source he least expected.

An elderly female with a brummie accent on the other end, she spoke slowly, with great distress in her voice.

"I would like to speak with Jason Middleton please."

"Speaking."

"This is Jenny Clarkson's mother."

"Oh hello. How are you?" he asked tentatively, fearing the worst.

"I have received a registered package from Jenny and it's just a....mystery. I can't explain it. I'm terribly worried about her." Her voice faltered as she tried to hold back the tears.

"In the package there are three envelopes. There is one addressed to my husband and myself, one to yourself and another to a WPC Fairbrother at Hammersmith Police Station!"

"She has explicitly requested that I contact you, if she hasn't contacted us by Thursday. Hence this telephone call. I'm terribly worried about her."

She began to cry. She had his undivided attention. She didn't give him an opportunity to reply and continued:

"Please come, both myself and her father are worried sick about her. We haven't heard from her for over a week. We normally speak everyday." She began to sob and a sharp pain shot in his ear as she dropped the phone. A male voice cut in.

"Hello Mr. Middleton this is Brian Clarkson, Jenny's father. I'm sorry but my wife is too upset to carry on talking to you. I think it would be best if you visited us and collected the envelope addressed to you, and maybe take the one addressed to this WPC Fairbrother as well."

"Yes, of course. Where do you live? Give me your address and I'll make my way over now."

"We live in the West Midlands, well Shropshire actually, a place called Bridgnorth. 22 Town Court Place. I'll give you our telephone number, just in case you get lost. It's 017467-622414." The phone number was followed by directions.

"It will probably take me about two hours, or maybe even three, depending on the traffic. The time is now 6.45pm so, with luck, I should be with you about 9ish."

He replaced the receiver, quickly grabbed his car keys and a coat and was on his way immediately. Kentish Town was still a little congested as the remnants of the evening's rush began to subside. He headed towards Hampstead, then Finchley and picked up the North Circular.

The M1 was flowing well and he quickly had the Mini Cooper S in the outside lane, moving swiftly. As he drove he worried and, with the speed he was travelling at, he needed to be fully alert. The speedo rose rapidly beyond 100mph as he pushed the accelerator towards the floor. He continually watched for the police, as he did so knowing that he was more likely to be overtaking them than the other way round. Within an hour and a quarter of leaving home he turned off onto the M6 heading towards Birmingham. The radio was at full blast as he approached and cursed at cars who were in the same lane and impeding his onward journey. He frequently braked as he approached the hindrance in front of him, flashing his lights angrily until they moved out of his way. His journey then took him down the M42 and off into the countryside of Shropshire. He crossed the Severn, rounded the sharp left-hand bend and drove up the hill into the old town.

The directions were good and it didn't take him long to find their road. It was on the outskirts of the town and was one of very few roads in the old town containing modern houses. He drove slowly until he found their home, it was a small cottage, surrounded by several three-storied town houses, in a small cul-de-sac.

He knocked on the door and waited for what seemed an eternity. Brian Clarkson finally answered. He was a great deal older than Middleton had imagined him to be. He was completely bald on the top of his head with grey hair at the temples. His face was hard and lined. His blue eyes were sunken, there were large bags beneath them and he looked tired. He stood no more than five and a half feet tall and was finding difficulty in walking. Jason guessed that he must be in his early seventies. They shook hands and Jason followed him slowly into the lounge. If Jenny's father had seemed old, then her mother could only be described as decrepit. Her hair was white and her body frail. She was riddled with arthritis, which restricted her movement, and could only walk with the aid of a stick. Her complexion was pale, she had wrinkled blue-eyes and a genuine warm persona. He could see a likeness of both of them in Jenny.

The lounge had an old grandfather clock in one corner and a three piece suite. The room was adorned with artefacts collected from all over the world and there were many photographs of Jenny through various stages of her life; from junior school to university and some a lot more recent, as she was today. It was a proud room. Jason could vaguely remember Jenny telling him that they had married late in life and she was an only child.

"Thank you for coming. I won't get up if you don't mind."

"Nice to meet you both."

"Brian, get the envelopes and show Jason. Would you like a cup of tea?"

"Yes please."

Brian Clarkson came in with the package and handed it to Jason.

"Brian will you make a pot of tea."

He disappeared obediently into the kitchen.

"Firstly, read the letter she sent to us."

Jason extracted the three envelopes from the opened package; they were all in her hand-writing. He looked at the registered package to see whether the postmark on the outside would give an indication of where it was posted. It read 'London NW3 - 5th April 2000'. He opened the letter marked 'Mum and Dad' and began to read.

Dear Mum and Dad,

In the envelope you will find £3,000, would you please be kind enough to place the money in my old Halifax Building Society account for me in Bridgnorth. The account book is still in my bedroom table drawer. You will probably think this is all pretty strange, but I've moved out of the house for a little while as I've gone on location with a film crew. I can't tell you where and I won't be able to ring you, as it's a secret documentary. There are two other envelopes; one's for Jason and the other's for a WPC Fairbrother at Hammersmith Police Station. If I don't manage to ring you by Thursday 13th, then please ring Jason and ask him to collect the envelope. Please do not send it! He can also take the other envelope off you and give it to the policewoman. Don't worry, it's

only my driving licence, which they require after a
little misdemeanour. Thanks.

    Always remember that I love you both very much.
            Jenny xxx.

Jason sat and began to read it again, whilst Evelyn Clarkson sat patiently waiting for a reaction from him. It was a strange and confusing letter. Why didn't she just bank the money locally and why all the secrecy? What was in the envelope for him, why hadn't she given it to him herself and why hadn't she just popped the licence into the police station? He couldn't recall her mentioning any traffic violation. The most important question was, where was she?

He put the letter down and looked up at Evelyn Clarkson as Brian came in with a pot of tea and a huge plate full of chocolate digestives.

"Milk and sugar?" Brian asked, as he began to pour the tea.

"Milk. No sugar, thank you."

"Biscuit?"

Jason helped himself to a couple and quickly devoured them as he began to slit open the envelope marked for his attention and take out the contents. As he did, something fell on the floor beneath his feet. He reached down to find out what it was. He ran his hand over the carpet pile until he found it. When he touched it he knew exactly what it was: the diamond clustered ring glittered even under the dim lighting in the room. This was not what he expected, though he wasn't sure what he had expected either. He opened the single sheet of paper and read it to himself. He could imagine every word being said as if she was there.

My darling Jason,

I have been so happy and I love you very much, although I have returned the ring and will never be able to wear it. I have worn it my darling and as far as I am concerned we were engaged to be married, and I wish I could fulfil that promise to you and bear you children. The fact that you're now reading this letter will mean that something really bad has happened to me and I most probably have lost my life. I can't even imagine the thought of death and it scares me. Please, please break this to my mum and dad gently. I love them very much and I so wanted you to meet them and if you hadn't done so now, you never would. Also, please deliver the letter to WPC Fairbrother at Hammersmith Police Station which explains everything. Please, please my darling don't get involved, leave it to the police. I couldn't bear it if I thought your life would be threatened in any way. I love you and will love you for ever. Your ever loving fiancee.

   Jenny xxx.

By the time he had finished the letter, tears were streaming down his face. He handed it to Brian Clarkson who read it in silence and then sat down in a state of shock.

"What is it? What does it say? It's bad news isn't it? Please tell me. What's happened to my daughter?"

Brian recovered his composure, got up and placed his arms around his wife. He spoke softly and slowly, showing an enormous amount of restraint and compassion as he did so.

"It very much looks as though Jenny has somehow lost her life."

"How? When? Let me read the letter."

He handed her the letter and, as she read through it, she repeated the same words as though they could change its content.

"No…. No….. Oh no." and continued to cry uncontrollably .

They stayed up for half the night, discussing the letter's content logically, and decided that, whilst they had received it, what she had envisaged might not have happened and there was still hope that this might be the case. Jason stayed over and left early next morning. The parting was traumatic but they were all optimistic. Until they found Jenny Clarkson's body she could still be alive, somewhere. He had collected all the letters and the package they had been sent in and was going to make Hammersmith Police Station his first call.

He had sat in a queue on the M1, stationary, for some thirty minutes after an accident had blocked all lanes just south of Northampton, with the package alongside him on the passenger seat. He had fought off the temptation to open the letter addressed to the police several times. He wanted to know the contents. He wanted to know what had caused her the problems. And he wanted to kill anyone that had harmed her. It was too much, he was unable to stop himself. He fumbled in the package and found the envelope. He ripped it open and found a similar piece of paper to the one that had been addressed to him.

Dear WPC Fairbrother,
I have requested that my fiancée Jason Middleton,
delivers this to you in the event of my disappearance.
He will have already seen my parents. I left a letter

with them with additional letters for Jason and this one for you, which hopefully will help you. I have no doubt lost my life. I am sorry that I didn't tell you everything from the beginning, but I was frightened and never thought it would come to this. The night I had attended the London Bravo rehearsal rooms in Acton. I was introduced to a man named Phil West - although I doubt whether that was his real name - by the owner Felix Simon. West offered me a sum of £15,000 cash to appear in a porno film. I refused. He left. When I went to my car later that evening he attacked me and knocked me out. He drove me to somewhere I didn't recognise. He threatened me with a knife, dumped me and told me he'd be in touch. I then aimlessly just walked until thankfully you found me. I discovered in the morning he was scaringly actually upstairs when I went up for a bath; when both yourself and your colleague were downstairs! He did later approach me when I was shopping in my local Tesco supermarket, he then explained what he wanted of me.

I was to approach the England football captain Mike Stephenson at Redmand Art in Bruton Street on 11th April. They provided an invitation for the opening of the gallery, plus accommodation at 41 Tennison House, Berkeley Square; I would be going to live there from 5th April and I was to entice him there and seduce him. I was given an initial £3,000 which I've sent to my parents to bank. The bedroom had the facing wall totally mirrored with cameras behind it. I know no more than that. I agreed to do it because they threatened not only me but mentioned Jason by name. On Saturday 31st March he followed us and sent me the enclosed note. We were eating in Quaglino's and the cigarette girl brought it to me. Jason never saw it and doesn't know anything about it. Please don't tell him anything. These people are dangerous, I might have lost my life, but I don't want him to lose his. I'm so sorry. In my defence, I had no option. He made it very obvious, with his various threats, that he would not be averse to killing me.

Jenny Clarkson

Jason Middleton sat trying to digest the contents of the letter and read the brief note left for her in Quaglino's. The letter had been written in great haste but explained so many things of that Saturday night in Quaglino's. Now he had murder on his mind.

It was an hour before the traffic began to move again and he made his way to Hammersmith. He noticed a Ryman's stationers on the corner so he pulled in, bought a box of Conqueror DL envelopes which were precisely the ones used by Jenny and paid for a photostat of the letter to WPC Fairbrother. On returning to the car, he carefully forged Jenny's handwriting on the outside of the envelope, placed the note and the original letter in it and sealed it, sticking the photostat in the glove compartment.

When he arrived at Hammersmith Police Station he asked for WPC Fairbrother, only to find she wasn't on duty until the following day.

25

Mike Stephenson had obtained permission from John Crowther to miss the friendly in Cyprus, his excuse; domestic problems. He hadn't wanted to discuss it at any great length and he hadn't been pushed into doing so. He hadn't discussed his predicament with anyone else either. The brown manilla envelopes containing photographs of himself and Jenny Rastall arrived with regular monotony. He had managed to be at the front door on each occasion one had arrived, purposely getting up earlier than normal to do so. He was living a nightmare. Knowing that Julia would not be able to accept his infidelity, to leave her to open the mail whilst he was away in Cyprus would lead down the road to separation and maybe, ultimately, divorce. Unknown to most, Julia had twice previously curtailed relationships with other women and had warned him that if there was ever another, she would leave him. A circumstance he could not now contemplate.

He had trained through the week with those players that had not been fortunate to have been selected, the reserves that had not even been considered for selection and the youth team. They were not a happy bunch, knowing whilst they were at home in the cold, their mates were in the sunshine having a good time. Tom Kettley, an ex-player and newly qualified as a physiotherapist, supervised the training and took care of the injured. Tom was always called upon when emergencies occurred, he worked on a part-time basis, doing the same for various clubs. In the afternoon, immediately after training, Mike Stephenson would travel to Berkeley Square and would sit and watch the entrance to Tennison House as well as the art shop in Bruton Street. Jenny Rastall had not appeared at either of them. In his time spent in surveillance he began to recognise regular key holders of Tennison House and customers of Redmand Art. He was beginning to think his efforts were a waste of time.

None of the faces that frequented the apartments were the same as those that frequented the shop, and vice-versa. There were no leads or connections, until the Friday. After spending a couple of hours there, Stephenson had driven from Redmand Art to Tennison House and begun another vigil. Within the first half-an-hour he had his first break. A tall, fair-haired male who had visited Redmand Art some forty minutes earlier, was attempting to gain entry to Tennison House, with considerable difficulty. Stephenson watched him closely, his pulse racing. The door opened and a resident exited, allowing the man to gain entry. Stephenson sat patiently watching the door.

He had thought about this moment many times before and was ready to react. Fifteen minutes later the stranger reappeared, looking around furtively before he began quickly walking back in the direction of Bruton Street. Stephenson followed slowly in the Alfa. As he did so, the volume of traffic increased and his speed dropped dramatically to less than a reasonable walking pace. He was rapidly losing ground. The traffic stopped and the gap between himself and the stranger he was pursuing increased, until he totally lost sight of him as he disappeared into an adjacent street. The traffic began to move again and Stephenson turned the car in the direction he had seen him go. He looked hard at all the pedestrians, in the hope that he might re-establish visual contact again. He had vanished.

He pulled the car into the kerb dejectedly, wondering what his next course of action should be. And then he spotted him. A Mini Cooper pulled away from a nearby parking meter, the tyres screeching from its violent acceleration and black smoke hitting the air from the friction caused by the burning of rubber. Stephenson quickly slammed the car into first gear and abruptly re-entered the traffic flow, making the queue of vehicles behind him stop violently.

He continued his pursuit, keeping as near as possible without appearing obvious, dropping back to a reasonable distance when he felt uncomfortably close. He followed the Mini as it left Central London. Every turn it made, Stephenson made. Night began to fall as the journey continued. The streetlights flickered into action and fine rain began to fall, casting reflections on the wet road surface. Stephenson switched on his wipers as he concentrated on the two red back lights of the Mini in front of him. The traffic in the suburbs became thinned and, as it did so, the speed of the Mini increased alarmingly. Stephenson found himself jumping traffic lights as they turned from amber to red as he struggled to keep pace with it. The Mini turned off the main road and continued travelling quickly through a series of minor roads. Neither car slowed for the sleeping policemen and the force of hitting them each time sent Stephenson in a violent upward motion, his head catching the roof. Suddenly the mini braked hard and stopped alongside a small house in the Primrose Hill area.

Stephenson stopped on the other side of the road. He watched as the glass on the front door was smashed and then the door forced opened. He remained in the safety of his car, looking on. The intruder explored the dark house by torchlight, the beam from it being caught in the windows as an occasional flash of light would strike one of them. Stephenson decided it was time for a confrontation.

He alighted from his car and reached the front door, ensuring nervously and frequently that he wasn't himself being followed or observed by anyone. The door was still open. He pushed it gently, it opened further and a hinge squeaked for the want of oil. Stephenson froze. He stood still, hardly moving a muscle, listening intently. All was quiet, except for the sound of his own heartbeat, which reverberated like a drum in the silence. He moved stealthily from the front door and into the lounge. He was finding it difficult to see in the darkness as he fumbled around in the room. It was cold and damp. He was unsure of what to expect and found himself wondering why he had been so brave. What was he going to achieve? He heard a sound from upstairs and began to make his way towards the bottom of the stairs. The vibration of feet running down the stairs made him move faster, only to be impeded by a sharp coffee table. The front door was opened and shut with the oil-less hinge screeching as it did so. By the time Stephenson reached the road the Mini was gone.

He returned to the house, jammed a chair against the front door, pulled the curtains and switched the lights on in the lounge. He started to search the house from top to bottom. He located many photographs, still in the same packages that they had been collected from the processors, as well as several albums. He sat and perused them all. The photographs in one album were taken over several years and included many generations. As he looked, he recalled his own photo collections, and these were not too dissimilar, just different people recorded in different parts of the world. Like his, they probably included grandparents, uncles, aunts, cousins, parents and friends. Some were sepia, some had deckled edges, some were black and white, but the majority were in colour as they became more recent. They were all in different condition: some edges missing or folded over, some creased and some cut and censored for some reason or another. As he turned the pages, he looked closely at the faces. Jenny Rastall's face became more prevalent as the photographs moved into colour and was the only one so far that he had recognised. He could see her pretty face and her body mature as time passed. She became a far better looking woman than she had been a girl.

As he reached the remaining pages, he looked hard in astonishment. The stranger he had followed was staring back at him. He turned another page and there he appeared, again and again. Sometimes he was on his own, in others with groups of people and sometimes just with her, Jenny Rastall. He removed one of the photographs and stuffed it in his wallet. He continued his search, finding a number of life assurance certificates and then a birth certificate. He unfolded it carefully. It was filled in ink. In the 'When and Where Born' it read 'Twenty Sixth September 1973'. 'Name if any' - 'Jennifer Anne'. 'Sex' - 'girl'. 'Name and Surname of Father' - 'Brian George Clarkson'. 'Name and Maiden name of Mother' - 'Evelyn Caroline Clarkson formerly Rastall'. He found a pen and a piece of paper and copied the information he required, noting that Jenny had used her mother's maiden name and her own Christian name.

He searched through a pile of letters and invoices, which did not help him any further. He found a small flip top index file containing telephone numbers. He decided to wait for her. He switched all the lights out and sat himself on the sofa. After an hour he became tired and fell asleep. He awoke hours later, uncomfortable and cold. He listened hard for any movement. The house was silent. The chair was still wedged against the front door, he had forgotten that he put it there and was curious to know whether anyone had tried to gain entry and failed. He removed the chair and left for home. It was well past ten when he arrived back in Sunbury. Julia was not in and a note was left on the table.

Mike,
I'm fed up with the your continual bad temper and selfishness. I've gone to Mum and Dad's with the Emma for a couple of nights.
   Julia.

The note hadn't surprised him and in some ways it came as a bit of a relief. At least she wouldn't be continually asking where he was going and he didn't have to keep lying.

Jason Middleton had made his way to Hammersmith Police Station and left the package addressed to WPC Fairbrother with the sergeant on the desk, deciding to do his own piece of detective work. Visits to Redmand Art Gallery and Tennison House had provided him with no information whatsoever. He had attempted to break into flat number 41 but the security was too good; he had made no impression on the door and gave up. He visited Jenny's house in Primrose Hill and found a slip of paper with Felix Simon's name and address on it in the bedroom. Whilst he wanted to carry on with his search, he heard the front door squeak. He panicked and realised he was not as heroic as he first thought. He got out quickly and set off to locate Mr Simon.

The luxury apartment on the Bayswater Road stood majestically overlooking Hyde Park. The white exterior magnified its historic importance. It reflected opulence to every onlooker. The foyer resembled a major hotel with its luxurious carpeting and furnishings. The commissionaire hovered in attendance, politely dealing with enquiries, opening doors and helping those that might require it. As Middleton entered he approached him.

"Can I help you Sir?

"Yes. I'm here to see Felix Simon."

"One moment and I'll ring up."

He walked back to his desk, picked up the phone and dialled. He placed his hand over the receiver.

"It's ringing, but there is no reply. I haven't seen him for a few days, he could well have gone away on location. He often does."

He continued trying to get through.

"No, sorry. There is no reply."

Middleton left; he knew he had to get into the flat somehow. Simon had introduced West to Jenny and he was the link. Somewhere in the apartment must be a clue to his whereabouts. He left the building, the rain had stopped and the pavement was wet. He meandered along the road, racking his brain for an idea. He crossed the Bayswater Road and ventured into the park, it was then that he saw his opportunity. Two winos were sat on the bench seat, slurping turps and having an animated conversation. They were unshaven with matted grey hair which looked as though it hadn't seen a comb in years, let alone a wash. Their clothes were covered in grime and he imagined they smelt to high heaven. He walked up to them. They looked at him through a drunken haze, one of them belched loudly.

"Would you like to earn a tenner each?"

"Yes, 'course we fucking would."

He explained what he wanted them to do. They agreed and he handed them each a crisp ten pound note. They got up and he followed them. They entered the building and, whilst one of them walked towards the commisionaire, the other walked to the side wall and proceeded to remove one of the paintings. The commisionaire flipped, he ran towards the paintings as the other tried to stop him. The planned distraction would give Middleton the opportunity to get to the lifts without being stopped. He entered the foyer. What had smelt so pleasant ten minutes earlier now smelt like a refuse tip of rotting food. He got to the lift without being spotted and the door opened immediately he pressed the button.. He selected the eighth floor and the lift responded, soaring upwards. It slowed, the door opened and he was facing the door to Felix Simon's penthouse suite.

He hit the door heavily with his foot several times and then with his shoulder. He looked around the corridor and noticed a heavy fire extinguisher, he lifted it from its holder and crashed it into the door just above the lock mechanism. The lock broke and the door gave way. He slowly made his way in, closing the door as best he could behind him. In front of him was a long corridor with three doors on each side and another one facing him at the very end. All the doors were open except for the one directly ahead. It was wall to wall carpeted and the walls were awash with photographs, memorabilia and awards. The furnishings were modern; all chrome and leather.

As he passed each open door he looked in. Three were bedrooms, two were en-suite bathrooms, one led into the kitchen. He opened the door at the end of the corridor and, as he did, his nostrils began to detect an offensive odour. As the door swung open, he was startled. There, in the dark, was a figure sitting by the window. Jason Middleton was transfixed.

The smell was very strong. The figure was motionless. He walked slowly towards it expecting the worst, but what he saw horrified him. The man was roped to a dining chair, a transparent plastic bag had been placed over his head and tied securely around his neck. He sat with his eyes open. The bag was full of condensation and, with his fight to inhale oxygen, he had sucked it into his mouth. The stench was now unbearable; Middleton began to heave. It was an uncontrollable reaction to a situation he had never experienced before. He vomited. The regurgitated food splashed his shoes and clothing as it settled on the carpet. He found the bathroom, washed his mouth and splashed cold water on his face. He took the stairs down to the ground floor, stopping spasmodically to regain his breath. The foyer was empty and he made a rapid exit.

26

The flight from Los Angeles was over two hours late arriving at London Heathrow, which had in turn meant that James Lowdnes missed the internal connecting flight to Birmingham Airport. Brother Douglas was prepared to wait for as long as it took. He needed to speak with his sibling as soon as he touched down. He knew he would be extremely annoyed that he had deployed Ray Prince to get involved in the problems of Kirklees County Football Club. Douglas himself had instructed Prince to hurt and blackmail, but Prince had well overstepped his brief.

He had done a good job on Dave McLeod, putting him out of action, and the blackmailing of Mike Stephenson had seen his form completely desert him. But Douglas had only discovered the killing of Jenny Clarkson because of the cleaning up operation some of his other staff had undertaken. Whilst other aspects of their various businesses required such undertakings, this one was far too close to James Lowdnes' lifelong love and he wouldn't want the club being involved in their underworld activities.

He sat in the arrivals waiting area of the airport, smoking endlessly and watching the airport come to life as the late shift departed and the early morning one took over. He had another hour to kill. He strolled towards the cafeteria to grab a coffee and a bit of breakfast. He stopped at the newspaper kiosk and bought himself The Daily Express, then picked up a plastic tray and helped himself to a ham and a cheese roll and a cup of coffee. He selected himself a seat and opened the newspaper, taking a mouthful of roll as he did so. What he saw made his throat dry up and the roll lodge itself firmly in his trachea. He grappled for a drink to wash it down as he stared in amazement at the headline:

WADE COMMITS SUICIDE.
TWO PLAYERS KILLED

He had paid for Prince to travel to Cyprus to cause a bit of mischief, but surely he hadn't killed again? He read the article carefully, the more he read, the more relieved he felt. The report indicated that it had been an accident. If Prince was involved, he had covered the deaths well, with no comeback on himself, his brother or Kirklees County. He was astounded at the death of Alfred Wade. He couldn't believe it, nor the alleged fraudulent activities he had become involved in. Both men had held a mutual dislike for one another and the dislike had grown into verbal hostility in the clubs' boardrooms when their respective teams had played each other. He was now confident that, through his efforts, Kirklees County would remain in the FA League Premier Division and that West London would be relegated. Kirklees County were three points clear of West London and, with an away game at Newcastle United followed by the final game at home to West London, the future was starting to look brighter. He couldn't see West London beating Coventry City the following Saturday. Their lack of class players and the problems they were now encountering would surely be their downfall.

The monitors showed that the flight James Lowdnes was on had finally touched down and Douglas waited until it showed that the passengers were in the baggage collection area before leaving the refreshment complex. He watched as the glass sliding doors continually opened and passengers emerged, pushing their trolleys, laden with luggage and gift bags. Each one looked around for their respective friends and relations, seeing them and waving or being met with big hugs and copious kisses. The wait seemed interminable until James finally came through; like all the others before him his trolley was full, brimming with gifts and duty free items. Douglas and he embraced affectionately.

"Good journey James???"

"No. It was bloody crap actually."

"I've done nothing but hang around at Heathrow and LAX. Where's the car?"

"In the short term parking area."

"Why isn't Philip here to pick me up?"

Douglas shrugged his shoulders. "I just decided I would come and get you."

"What do we employ a chauffeur for then? I'm not saying it's not nice to see you and all that, but that's what we pay him for. To just sit around for hours on end."

"I needed to speak with you."

"Couldn't it have waited 'til I was home?"

"No."

"Then what's the matter?"

"You won't like this very much, but you weren't around. So I made a decision which, well, hasn't exactly backfired, but I've become nervous about."

James Lowdnes stopped pushing the trolley and waited for the information to be divulged.

"I've done something that we have always said we would never do. But I did it because the situation was desperate."

"What? What have you done?"

"I cannot tell you here. It would be stupid. Let's wait until we get to the privacy of the car."

They walked on in silence, James knew whatever Douglas was going to tell him was serious.

The journey from the airport saw the brothers argue bitterly after Douglas had disclosed the various actions he had taken. James didn't believe that Prince was not involved in the deaths of the two players in Cyprus.

"You must be mad, Prince is a fucking psychopath! If you had to do something there are better equipped personnel on the payroll to employ than him. He hasn't got the fucking mentality to undertake something like this! Take care of him before we end up in the middle of this mess. He killed those two boys, it's too much of a coincidence. Sent to disrupt and this happens." James said tersely.

"Douglas, stop him from carrying out anything else. Enough is enough. I appreciate your reasons for doing what you did, but let's stop it now."

27

WPC Susan Fairbrother arrived at the station early. She changed into her uniform before entering the canteen for a coffee and light breakfast, comprising two pieces of toast and marmalade. She sat with two other male constables; Terry Spooner and Roger Smith; who were tucking into sausages, bacon, fried eggs, tomatoes, fried bread, an overloaded spoonful of baked beans, thick buttered white bread and a huge mug of sweet tea. To her it smelt and looked awful. They spasmodically dipped their bread into their eggs as they read their morning papers. She wondered which one of them would be the first to spill the egg on their tie; it inevitably happened when they gorged themselves in this way.

As she sipped her coffee and took delicate bites from the toast, she exchanged friendly banter with her two colleagues, while they turned the pages of their newspapers, scanning the news. The main stories were the suicide of Alfred Wade and the deaths of two West London Football Club players. She knew little about football but had always kept a keen eye on the financial markets and, like everyone else, she knew of Alfred Wade.

"This is a bit of a bummer for your lot Terry. Wade commits suicide and Hirst and Sulley are killed in Cyprus." said Smith.

"Do you support West London then Terry?" asked Fairbrother.

"Yep. If I'm not on duty down there, then I pay to go and watch them."

"What's the chances of them staying up now then?" Smith carried on; he was a keen Chelsea fan and disliked West London immensely.

"Not much. They've asked the F.A. to call off the game on Sunday, but they've refused because it's the televised game and the only one scheduled to be played. It's bloody ridiculous. It's not sport anymore, it's all about money, and we're going to suffer for it."

Fairbrother was bored with their conversation, it always either involved sport or sex. Thankfully, on this occasion, they were too preoccupied with the football to be pestering her about her sex life. She wondered why men always had a longing to know what colour pants women were wearing, she couldn't care less what colour 'y' fronts the men wore.

It was not until the early morning briefing that she was presented with the envelope from Jenny Clarkson which Jason had left. She had opened it immediately, along with the note left in Quaglino's. She had to read it several times before it had sunk in. She showed it to the sergeant who took it to the superintendent. In no more than fifteen minutes the police had despatched squad cars to each of the addresses detailed in the letter.

The Tennison House address was found to be empty, the occupant having moved out a couple of days previously. The apartment had been totally redecorated and recarpeted. The owner, a Mr. G. Kabranda, had leased the premises for a year to Mr. G. Townsend. No trace could be found; he had paid cash. The address he had given was ficticious. The place was fingerprinted but none of the prints matched anything on record. Jenny Clarkson's home was searched thoroughly and fingerprinted. However, besides a broken front door and a bodged repair to an upper floor window, nothing was found. The police took away a file of telephone numbers and a photograph album. At Redmand Art, the police interviewed both the owner Colin Redmand and the manager

Ron North and, not being satisfied with their stories, brought them both in for questioning.

Quaglino's was visited and the cigarette girl usually on duty on Saturdays; who Jenny Clarkson would have received the note from; could hardly remember anything, explaining that she had seen and spoken to so many people it was impossible to recall either the couple or the man who must have given her the note.

The London Bravo rehearsal rooms provided an interesting fact: Felix Simon had not appeared for work for several days, nor had anyone managed to contact him at his home.

Jason Middleton was found at his home in Kentish Town and brought to the station. They were finding it difficult to obtain the address of Mike Stephenson. There was no one available at West London Football Club in authority who were either willing to give his address, or knew it.

The interviews with Colin Redmand and Ron North proved nothing; they both kept to their story that it was their idea to contract Stephenson to open the shop. The pressure exerted from the police interrogators bore no fruit, but the explanations were not believed. The police released them both, knowing that they were not telling the truth and that there was a force that frightened them more than the law.

28

Jason Middleton finally turned up at Hammersmith Police Station. He told them very little. He provided them with the other two letters, which said nothing more than they already knew and admitted to breaking into Jenny's home earlier in the day and being disturbed by someone whilst there. Throughout the interview he looked nervous and jumped when he was asked whether he knew Felix Simon. He did not have a chance to answer. The door of the Interrogation Room opened and the two officers were beckoned to leave. The recording system was turned off and they left the room, leaving him with a uniformed officer.

Only one of the two officers returned, but this time he was joined with another.

"The time is now 6.37pm. I am Detective Sergeant French and I am accompanied by Detective Sergeant Musgrove, we are continuing with an interview with Jason Middleton regarding the disappearance of Jenny Clarkson."

"Jason, would you like legal representation."

"No."

"We would like to say for the record that earlier this morning Jason Middleton gave us a set of his finger prints of his own free will, so that we could eliminate his from others found in Jenny Clarkson's home. Is that correct?"

"Yes it is."

"You were asked just prior to the interview being curtailed, whether you knew Felix Simon. Did you know him?"

"No."

"Have you ever met him."

"No."

"Have you ever heard of him."

"Yes."

"Where have you heard of him?"

"He was a producer, Jenny was..."

"What do you mean was?"

"I mean he is."

"No Jason, you got it right the first time. You know, don't you. You know he's dead and that's why he became the past tense. Did you kill him?"

"No."

"But you have been in his flat."

"Yes."

"When?"

"Last night."

"Why."

"To see him."

"Why?"

"Because I knew he knew something about Jenny and this Phil West character."

"How did you know that?"

"I read.... I read the letter Jenny sent to WPC Fairbrother."

"And."

"With WPC Fairbrother not being on duty. I decided to make my own enquiries. I visited as I've said before Jenny's house, I also went to Redmand Art and Tennison House and then to his apartment in Bayswater Road. I broke in and found him. It scared me shitless."

"Why didn't you call us?"

"I was scared. I suddenly realised what I had walked into and remembered the warning left by Jenny."

"We wish you had come clean earlier. You've wasted a considerable amount of Police time. If we had had this information earlier we might be a lot closer to solving her disappearance. We will probably pick up your finger print match at Simon's flat, but we struck it lucky when the commissionaire recognised you from a photograph in Miss Clarkson's album."

When Paul McCormick drove into the West London car park to continue he was he surprise to see a Police car parked outside. In the reception two uniformed officers sat.

"What do they want?" asked Paul in a whisper. Sheila the receptionist replied.

"They want to interview Mike Stephenson."

"What for?"

"They wont say."

"They've asked me for his address, but I don't know it, and even if I did, I haven't the authority to give them it."

"Am I the first one in?"

"Yes, and Phillipa won't be in for sometime and it's Mary's day off."

Paul turned and headed towards them. They promptly stood up.

"Good morning, my name is Paul McCormick "Can I help you?"

"I am PC Spooner and this PC Smythe. We wish to locate Mike Stephenson. Is there anyone who can tell us his home address?"

"What do you want him for?"

"I'm sorry Sir but we can't disclose that information."

"If you would like to wait for a few moments, I'll try to get hold of someone and see if I can get his address for you."

He quickly rang John Crowther's number. Crowther answered.

"Hello."

"Hello, John it's Paul McCormick. I'm sorry to bother you, but there are two policeman in reception wanting Mike Stephenson's address."

"What for?"

"I don't know they won't say. There just asking for his address."

"I don't know it. Is Phillipa in yet?"

"No she will be late."

"What about Mary Davis in accounts?"

"No, it's her day off."

"Send them down to the Training Ground at 10 o'clock, I've got the first team squad training this morning, and with luck he should turn up."

"What do you mean with luck?"

"Sorry it's me being a bit facetious. I wonder what they want?"

"Goodness knows. Are you coming to the ground later?"

"Yes I'll be there about one-ish."

"See you later. Bye."

McCormick told the officers what Crowther had told him and the two proceeded to the Training Ground, PC Spooner didn't need any directions, he was one of the officers who had attended the robbery a few weeks earlier.

John Crowther and Rob Dyson were first to arrive at the Training Ground and managed to discuss the problems prior to them being confronted with the two police officers. If Crowther had been taken aback by recent events, Dyson was in perpetual astonishment. Within a month the club had been subjected to the most horrendous set of circumstances which only the Munich air disaster in February 1958, when the Manchester United team were decimated, could be considered worse. The death of two players and the Chairman, with the additional financial problems and relegation fears, had seen the club being catapulted from one crisis to another. Relegation was fast becoming a possibility, with extinction a probability.

The presence of the police when the players arrived brought more questions and concerns. Everyone showed up with the exception of Mike Stephenson. Crowther addressed the players and told them all the information that he knew and told them to forget, as best as they could, the problems and concentrate on the football. The police were made perfectly aware that the only person in the club who would be in a position to furnish them with Stephenson's home address would be Club Secretary Phillipa Scott. After radioing into base, they made their way back to the Zion Park ground.

Phillipa Scott was in her early twenties. An attractive dark-haired woman of slight build, she lived on her own in a small unassuming flat in Barnes, she was single with a small daughter. Even today she was still looking for Mr. Right, but had never found him and it would be unlikely that she ever would. She had not been without lovers and there had been plenty. But none of them attained the high standard for which she had set herself. If she didn't finish with them because of their imperfections, then they would finish with her because of her moodiness and selfishness. She had become sexist and difficult to approach.

254

She had arrived late and bad tempered, after a hectic morning sorting out a mischievous child and getting her to the nursery and then like everyone else before her, she had to run the gauntlet of the mass of media, which had again descended on the ground. Phillipa was subjected to a variety of questions before reaching the sanctity of the reception area, only to be faced with Spooner and Smythe and two police officers. She treated the two policeman with indifference and contempt, reluctantly providing them with Stephenson's home address. When the two officers arrived at the house in Sunbury, there was no reply.

Stephenson had meant to appear at training, but his sleepless night, had him continually worrying about the guy in the mini and his obvious connection with Jenny Clarkson. Unwashed and unshaven and dressed in a tracksuit, he found himself revisiting her home in Primrose Hill. He felt and looked a mess, but on arriving, it was the least of his worries. As he neared the house he noticed the activity surrounding the area. He stopped and watched at a suitable distance as the police carried out a thorough search of the front garden, digging up specified areas. Periodically officers would leave the house carrying plasic bags of varying sizes. Stephenson was confused. Why were the police involved?

Why had the guy in the mini undertaken the same search pattern as he had? Who was he and what did he want? Was he also looking for her? Was he in a similar mess as he was? Questions, questions and more questions, with so far, no answers. As he sat watching the police in their methodical search, the questions repetitively came to mind and he could find several solutions to each one, but which one, if any, was the correct one. Then suddenly the penny dropped. Jenny Clarkson was missing. Stephenson's stomach began to rumble as his body began to crave for the indulgence of food, he had missed dinner the previous evening and breakfast that morning and his system required nutritional input.

He drove slowly past the house and made his way to the centre in search of a cafe of some sort. He found a dingy road side cafe and ordered himself a large mug of tea, double sausage, bacon, fried egg and fried bread and sat himself in the corner. In any hotel reception in the country, normally dressed he would have been immediately recognised and surrounded by autograph hunters and admirers, but his attire and appearance, together with the surroundings he was in meant that no one gave him a second look.

As he ate he watched the cafe's clientele come and go. Some sat and consumed their purchases, whilst many utilised their take away service. He wished he had bought a paper to read to make himself even less conspicuous than he already was. He feared being recognised. He had set about the breakfast with some relish and as he fed another morsel of food in his mouth his eyes briefly caught the headline of the building labourer sitting opposite him on the next table as he folded the paper over. It was just a glimpse. Had his brain interpreted correctly what his eyes had just seen?

The labourer had involved himself with the fantasies of the unclad female on page three and continued to absorb himself in the articles surrounding her. Stephenson's initial visual impact impregnated his brain and he became desperate to view it again and hope that what he thought he had seen was in fact untrue. He sat patiently, as the labourer turned the pages. Typically of his kind the pages were turned and folded, the front page never coming back into view.

Stephenson's prime objective on leaving the cafe was to find a newspaper shop. On doing so, he bought one and stared unbelievably at the headlines. He was distressed as he read about the death's of Sulley and Hirst and the suicide of Alfred Wade. He decided there and then to visit the police. When Mike Stephenson presented himself at Hammersmith Police Station, the whole station seemed to stop. It was not often a well known celebrity entered through their doors, and every wanted to have a look. Not that he looked at his best, but to the women, he still was a pin-up. The interview took some three hours as the police interrogated him, but whilst a few more facts were compiled his testimony didn't possess very much more than they had gained from the Clarkson girls letters.

On leaving the enevitable happened Middleton and Stephenson came face to face. Stephenson never saw the punch and never had time to defend himself, the blow to the head sent him realing across the reception area of the station, colliding with a large glass partition. The second strike followed almost immediately and whilst the first connected with his chin the second caught him across the nose and the mouth, both areas spurted blood over his face immediately on impact. Stephenson dropped to the floor holding his face as Middleton kicked him hard between the legs. The pain generated by the first two blows were nothing to that of the third. The boot of Jason Middleton caught Stephenson in the testicles taking the wind out of him. He lay groaning on the ground as police officers managed to get from behind the partitions to stop the beating continuing any further. Middleton was taken to a cell in the basement and Stephenson to Ealing Hospital.

The police continued with there enquiries, but were eluded in every area. No fingerprints of any subsequence could be found, others than those of Felix Simon, Jason Middleton and Mike Stephenson. Every enquiry drew to a blank. Where was Jenny Clarkson? Was she still alive? or had she been killed as her letters suggested. Who was this Phil West? and where was he? and what was it all about?

Detective Inspector Ian Bevon sat contemplating all these questions, forever puruising the evidence. The more he thought about the case the worse his headache became and the more he smoked. He failed to see any connection. Why would you blackmail Mike Stephenson? and yet not to seek any money. And why would anyone go to such lengths £15,000 for a tart. As the ash tray filled he became more and more depressed. He had never been a liked copper and very rarely followed the book, but the only two people he could take issue with he felt were innocent victims. Middleton was just the girls lover, so was the, whatever it was, directed at Jenny Clarkson or Mike Stephenson? Or was it both? Another cigarette found its way into the already overburdened ash tray. He reopened the files and looked firstly at the facts surrounding Jenny Clarkson born 26th September 1973 Jennifer Ann Clarkson actress, acting name Jenny Rastall. She had used her mothers maiden name. Attended RADA, lived in Primrose Hill. He looked hard, but couldn't find anything that connected Stephenson to her. It all seemed totally meaningless. Devoid of any motives, yet this little scenario was not performed for nothing. But for what and why?

29

Ruth Corderoy was in her mid-thirties and was at the top of her profession. She had handled more than enough companies in administration and liquidations in her comparatively short time with Gillis, Freeman and Parker. She was a short attractive blonde, with large breasts and an equally inflated ego. She treated men as her equal, in fact no; she thought she was superior. She was unmarried and without a regular boyfriend, which was not surprising. Not that she hadn't had her fair share, but after a while most of them tired of her outlandish know-it-all attitude and curtailed their relationships.

She stood in the club's reception in a smart blue Dolce & Gabbana two-piece suit, a black Chanel handbag in one hand and a large leather briefcase in the other. Her two stooges, both men, were strategically placed one pace behind her. She proffered her business card and asked to to see Roy Peters. Susan, the new girl on reception who had only started that morning, rang his number and nervously fiddled with the card as she waited for a reply. Peters was involved in a conversation regarding the trip to Cyprus, with both director Dennis Proctor and Paul McCormick when his phone rang.

"Hello." Peters answered.

"Mr Peters, there is a Ruth Corderoy of Gillis, Freeman and Parker in reception asking to see you, along with two gentlemen." she said meekly.

Peters knew exactly who they were and had been expecting them. He had, along with Alfred Wade, agreed to place the club into administration a few days before.

"Do you know whether the boardroom is free?"

"Yes it is." she replied.

"Would you please show them up to the boardroom, and organise some coffee and biscuits. Oh and when John Crowther comes in, please tell him to pop in as well. Mr Proctor, Mr McCormick and myelf will make our way there now."

Both Proctor and McCormick were mystified.

Peters greeted her in the boardroom.

"Good morning. My name is Roy Peters, the Chief Executive. This is Dennis Proctor, one of the Directors and this is the Commercial Manager, Paul McCormick."

"Good morning my name is Ruth Corderoy of Gillis, Freeman and Parker and this is John Carr and Bob Ingham, two of my associates." They all shook hands.

"Please take a seat." said Peters.

At that moment a confused John Crowther, arrived and he was introduced to everyone.

Ruth Corderoy immediately began to explain the reason for their attendance.

"We are here as the administrators for Sacher Paper plc which, according to share certificates in our possession, owns seventy percent of this club. In addition, Mr Wade loaned West London Football Club a sum of £10 million, which is very likely not his own money. I cannot disclose any more information than to tell you that we are entrusted with the running of the club by Sacher Paper plc and various merchant banks in attempting to retrieve as much of the monies that have been misappropriated as possible. This letter of explanation informs you officially that I have the authorisation to carry out immediately the duties of the day to day running of this football club and I also have the jurisdiction of either making necessary financial adjustments to improve its viability, to hopefully generate a profit, or to improve its capability to be of interest to a prospective purchaser. Whether that be as a football club, a shopping mall, or for re-development. Firstly, would you provide me the personnel files of every employee and a set of management accounts within the next say two hours. We are already in possession of a vast amount of paperwork. We would also like a suitable office made available to us, one with at least four desks with sufficient telephone availability and power points."

Dennis Procter asked the question everyone was dreading. "How much is owed?"

"I don't know for certain yet, if I wanted to make a guess; not less than £50million."

There was a horrified realisation from all present that there was very little chance the club would survive for much longer.

Within no more than an hour, without any preamble or courtesies, she had taken the helm of West London Football Club. Dennis Proctor, Paul McCormick and John Crowther looked visibly shaken.

Peters lifted the phone and rang Phillipa Scott's number. There was a silent hush. The remaining attendees watched and listened intently.

"Phillipa. I think you had better come up to the boardroom." Corderoy quickly butted in.

"I didn't ask for a staff meeting. I will see the staff in my own good time, when I decide and not when you see fit." said Corderoy abrasively.

"But these people need to know. They are essential in the operation of this club." said Peters angrily, "and by the way,

Phillipa is the best person in this club to satisfy all your needs. She is the Club Secretary."

"Whether they are essential is for me to decide. They may have been in the past, but we have to look at this problem sensibly, explore every element of it, and then make necessary decisions to rectify and address those areas of concern as quickly as possible."

Roy Peters was visibly shaking with rage. His position of Chief Executive had given him total control of all the administrative aspects of the club and this upstart of a woman had usurped his exalted position with a few well chosen words. He knew that a look through his personnel file would show a salary of some £75,000 and, in comparison with Peter McCormick's £27,000, he could well find himself without a job, if she reacted as he thought she would. Dennis Proctor, a minor shareholder and board director, had no such worries. He had sat and digested the limited information that Ruth Corderoy had found it necessary to provide and chose his words carefully.

"Has Alfred Wade been found guilty without trial?"

"That is not of my concern. What is beyond any doubt is that the money West London Football Club have received in the form of an interest free loan was not his to utilise. It belonged to Sacher Paper plc and I have to ensure that money is, in one way or another, repaid in full, plus any additional losses which have occurred through non investment. The sale of the shares, I think, will be comparatively simple, but I must ensure that they don't drop in value too much. Inevitably they will drop, but with careful management we may be able to minimise that fall."

Proctor interrupted Corderoy again. "I must impress on you that the major assets of the club are the players and to decimate the team would, at this time, be detrimental to you and what you are attempting to achieve."

"Thank you, I do realise that. I know more about football than most women. I've followed it since I was a little girl."

For the first time since she arrived, she allowed a glimmer of vulnerability to creep through her guard.

"Actually, I've supported Arsenal from an early age and still do. I'm a season ticket holder."

The humour was wasted on Roy Peters, who mumbled under his breath;

"Bully for you."

"I beg your pardon?" she asked.

"Nothing."

John Crowther cringed at the thought.

The door opened and Phillipa Scott entered the boardroom.

"I'm sorry, I didn't call for you. My name is Ruth Corderoy, I am a senior partner with Gillis, Freeman and Parker, and these are my associates, John Carr and Bob Ingham. I have explained to all parties that I have taken control of West London Football Club as the official administrators on behalf of Sacher Paper Plc." Phillipa was so shocked, at first she couldn't speak.

"I have been instructed to ascertain the financial position as quickly as possible, which may well require some late nights working here at the ground. I therefore require the relevant keys to gain entry, the code number of the security system and someone to show me how it works and a set of current management accounts."

Phillipa Scott said that she could provide her with all the information she required and get her a set of keys. Within another two hours, Ruth Corderoy and her two associates were pouring over the files and examining the management accounts. Finally she knew what must be done first and she was aware the decision would not be accepted by John Crowther.

With folders underneath her arm she ventured along the corridor to his office. She knocked, entered, plumped herself down on the opposite chair and laid the files on his desk. She had each player's personnel file, on which she had written in pencil what she considered could be obtained for each one, in the current market. She sat, legs crossed, with a smug look on her face.

"I want to sell David McLeod and James Fellows, they are the only two players on the books that have any value. I reckon the total value of the whole squad would not exceed £11 million, which is somewhat disappointing. We should get £2 to £3 million for James Fellows and £1 to £1.5million for McLeod so, for a quick sale, £3million. It's a long way short of what is actually required, but it is a start, It's a shame Michael Stephenson's contract is so close to ending as he he would certainly be worth more than any of the others. I know that McLeod is currently injured, but I understand it's not serious and there's nothing stopping him from being fully fit for the forthcoming season."

"Probably not." agreed Crowther. Crow-ther had never made an approximation of the saleable value of the players and wasn't prepared to argue with her valuations, or to ascertain who had provided her with the figures.

Crowther continued. "They are not monkey's out there. One smell of the administrators and the valuation of every player drops like a stone."

"I agree." said Corderoy.

"I suppose the players are the only immediate assets, or are they? Is there not any other area where savings can be made?"

"I'm afraid not. The club has far less playing, coaching and physio staff than most of the others in the Premier League."

Crowther sat back and folded his arms, listening intently to what she had to say. He realised she had a difficult job to perform and was surprised at her quick grasp of the situation. He began to nod in agreement.

"McLeod has already requested a transfer, I haven't made that public yet. But Jim has never considered moving on, though we've had a few interested parties trying to buy him in the past."

Crowther thought for a moment.

"I'll speak with him on Monday. Let's get Sunday's game out of the way first."

"Ok. Let's see what we can get for him."

The phone rang and he answered it.

"Hello." He placed his hand over the speaker, it was Susan in reception. "Sorry for disturbing you Mr Crowther, but I have the Assistant Chief of Police in Cyprus, Steven Petrone, wishing to speak with you."

"Sorry about this." Crowther felt anxious as he waited for him to be put through. Corderoy smiled at him. She wished she hadn't mentioned to anyone that she had been a supporter of Arsenal since she was a little girl. It was unprofessional of her and something she had never divulged to anyone in a business situation before. She had to be in control at all times and show no weakness. She watched him closely, his eyes began to water and his face became ashen. He began to stutter.

"God…….almighty! Where….did….. they find them?"

He looked up at her, the tears starting to run down his face. He was finding it difficult to talk.

"Did they die... Did they die… immediately? Thanks. Thanks for all your help. I'll get our secretary to ring you, her name is Phillipa Scott. I have your phone number. She'll contact the police at this end and tie any loose ends up with you and their respective families."

He replaced the receiver, put his head in his hands and began to sob. Ruth Corderoy got up slowly, placed the files on the vacated seat and walked over to him. She placed a hand on his shoulder and gently squeezed it.

"Are you alright. Can I get you something?"

"What has happened?" she asked sympathetically.

"We came home fom Cyprus without two of our players; Eddie Hirst and Paul Sulley. That was the Cypriot Police to inform us that their bodies have been found at the bottom of a precipice."

"They're dead?"

"Yes, I'm afraid so."

"It seems that they hired a scooter and went up the Troodos Mountains and, well, went off the edge. If they hadn't have come across a pair of sunglasses on the side of the road, they may never have found them."

30

The news of the death of chairman Alfred Wade, along with the deaths of Hirst and Sulley, had shaken everyone at West London Football Club. With the additional problems of working within an environment of impending doom and the club being in the hands of the administrator, football now seemed to be an unnecessary intrusion. The club had tried in vain to have Saturday's fixture at home to Coventry City postponed, but the Football Association had flatly refused to comply with their wishes. Whilst they were sympathetic, monetary contractual agreements far outweighed compassion; they insisted that the game should go on.

The telephone calls between the two parties were endless, but fruitless. They had started off polite and logical and ended up strained and illogical; both parties in total disarray, shouting at one another. After the final call, West London considered calling the game off themselves and facing the consequences. But there was the veiled threat that points could well be deducted…. They remembered the plight of Middlesborough Football Club in 1997, when squad players had been decimated through a flu bug and an inordinate number of injuries. The management felt that they could not field a competitive side in the imminent away game with Blackburn Rovers and contacted the FA to request a postponement of the game, only to be denied. They decided reluctantly to postpone the game themselves, leaving the Ewood Park club high and dry when they did so just 24 hours prior to kick-off. They were fined £50,000 and had 3pts deducted. West

London Football Club were in too precarious a position to suffer such a punishment, the game would have to go on.

John Crowther sat at his desk scribbling names on a pad, thankful that the morning's training session had not added to his problems. All the players had come through without injury and only Mike Stephenson had not appeared, but he now knew why. Stephenson was hospitalised so already ruled out. Without McLeod, Stephenson, Sulley or Hirst, the choice was limited. His selection would also determine the tactics he would employ. With reserve keeper Alan Crooks still unavailable, Paul Brown would again have to play. Paul had perfomed well against Spurs but Crowther worried about him making his home debut. He knew of many occasions when young players had frozen in front of the home fans and never recovered. Indeed, very often the whole team preferred to play away; they expected to be criticised but at home too much was expected of them and they repeatedly failed to perform.

But his worries were really of no consequence, he had no choice in the matter. Paul was his only fit goalkeeper. He decided to play the Cypriot boy, Michael Charaiambos, in midfield. Michael had been homesick when he was first signed and had been sent home, but Crowther had to rapidly recall him. Eddie Dillon, who had not been selected in any capacity other than substitute for most of the season, and young Carl Solomons, a huge 6ft 5inch Nigerian centre back, would have to debut. Crowther stopped to reflect on his selection when there was a gentle knock on the door.

"Come in." he yelled.

Ruth Corderoy opened the door and stood motionless, she understood the problems John Crowther was experiencing and looking at him made her go weak at the knees. If there was one person in the world she could commit a discretion with, it was this man.

"Hello." She said sombrely.

"Hi." he replied.

He looked up at her, trying to understand why everyone considered this young women such an ogre when to him she was a kind, warm person.

"May I?"

She gestured to the empty chair facing Crowther. He nodded. She sat down, neatly crossing her legs, holding a file in both hands and resting it on her knee.

"How do you feel?" she asked.

"Devastated" he replied, shaking his head.

"I don't know whether the club can survive, even if we manage to avoid the dreaded drop!"

Corderoy, without any further preamble, went into business mode.

"I've been in contact with several clubs regarding Jim Fellows and Dave McLeod and, to be honest, I have had very little interest in either player. Only Birmingham City and Reading have shown any interest in Fellows and only Ipswich Town in McLeod. City offered £1.6 million, which is nowhere near our original valuation, but they do not have the funds to pay the whole sum up front. They are willing to pay 50%; £800,000; initially and the remaining 50% in six months, which is unacceptable. They are fully aware that if the club folds they might well get him on the cheap, or should I say, even cheaper. They're just trying it on. Reading are willing to pay £950,000 up front, which is to my mind the best offer. McLeod however is becoming a bit of a problem, the only offer has come from Ipswich, a meagre £140,000."

Before she could finish, Crowther leaped to his feet, sending his chair careering into the wall behind him and shouting. "Are you taking the piss? That's three million pounds less than our lowest estimate."

Ruth Corderoy was taken aback by his outburst and summoned her composure to make her retort.

"If you had let me finish…. If you remember the transfer deadline has been and gone, neither of these players are any use to clubs until next season. Hence the low offers, but they are firm and they have agreed to make payments into our account immediately after they pass their medical examinations. I honestly feel that this will be the best we'll get and it will show that we are serious about reducing the deficit, which will appease our creditors no end."

Crowther retrieved his seat from the wall and sat down.

"It's crap. Crap. Do you fucking understand the word? Crap."

He placed his head in his hands. "I'm sorry. I'm sorry. I'm losing it. I don't know whether I can take much more."

Crowther was finding it hard to look at Corderoy.

"Talk to them both and see how they feel." He said, reverting to the original conversation.

"OK." she replied and left hurriedly.

Crowther rang Dyson and asked him to come up to the office. The two examined the possible team selection, agreed it and decided what tactics to employ.

There was a knock on the door, it was Phillipa Scott again. She could not stop herself from shouting.

"The match has been postponed. There has been so much bad feeling and poor press that the FA have relented, we have been given a fourteen day reprieve."

John made a decision to call it a day. He was emotionally drained and badly needed the sanctuary of home. He rang and spoke with Sandra, briefly explaining what had occurred.

It took just under the hour to get home to Harpenden. It was a relief to be in the arms of someone he loved and who reciprocated that love.

Sandra poured him a large Johnny Walker black label with a mass of ice and sat and listened intently as John struggled to regurgitate everything that had occurred. Sandra was fully aware of the majority of the incidents, but John had intentionally left out some of the more criminal aspects. Both of the kids were out somewhere and wouldn't be back till late. Sandra took him by the hand and led him upstairs to the bedroom. In the loving interlude, John's blood pressure reduced dramatically and his mood improved significantly.

Afterwards, John busied himself in the kitchen preparing a chilli con carne, imbibing in red wine and having his tympanic membrane subjected to *Rod Stewart's Maggie May and You Wear It Well*, at high volume over and over again. Sandra entered the kitchen with the phone held high above her head shouting. "Turn it down John!" He did so.

"Who is it?"

"It's Phillipa."

"Hi John, I'm sorry to disturb you, but I thought I'd let you know before someone else does. Just to add to everything….. You won't believe it but Bruce Day has been killed in a car accident!"

It put a real dampener on his evening, but the alcohol intake lessened the shock. The food was good and they went to bed before the kids got home.

The bodies of Eddie Hirst and Paul Sulley were recovered from the Troodos Mountains and the British Consulate in Nicosia informed the next-of-kin of their deaths through the UK Police. The Consular staff in London had liaised with both sets of parents, organised air travel for them to fly out to Cyprus and identify the bodies and ensured their wishes were adhered to. Death certificates were provided by a Cypriot coroner and the bodies were embalmed and laid in zinc-lined coffins. It took several days but finally both bodies arrived back in the UK and were collected and taken to Fulham Public Mortuary for post mortem. However, the post mortems could not take place as the bodies had been embalmed. Because the deaths were not natural, an inquest was necessary. The inquests were held together and hastily arranged. It was short and, with very little evidence being provided, the coroner could only reach one verdict: Death by Misadventure.

The bodies of Eddie Hirst and Paul Sulley were transported to Brighton and Southampton respectively, the places of their birth and where their parents still lived. They were cremated, just two days apart. West London Football Club was closed on both days and a coach was provided for the staff and players who wished to attend. Many fans attended both ceremonies, some dressed in football kit representing a variety of clubs: Brighton, Southampton, Portsmouth, Arsenal, Tottenham Hotspur, Charlton, West London and West Ham United.

Alfred Wade was buried on the same day as Paul Sulley's cremation. The Club was represented by Roy Peters, along with a couple of staff members at his home town of Holmfirth in West Yorkshire, at St. John's Parish Church, Upper Thong. This was just yards away from the grave of Bill Owen, who played Compo in Last of the Summer Wine for 26 years, which was filmed in and around the area.

The church was full, with many not managing to get a seat. TV crews were in abundance but were respectful of the situation. A few of the celebrities who attended were spoken to and all spoke highly of him.

Bruce Day's burial was a little more convoluted, in Jewish tradition, burial should happen as soon as possible after death, and they usually take place in a matter of days, but Sports Reporter Bruce Day's was delayed due to him being killed in a car accident. A post-mortem and an inquest had to be conducted prior to doing so. Bruce was layed to rest at Willesden Jewish Cemetery attended by over a 100 people. No-one from the Club was invited.

31

The few days off in Cyprus, which started off as a relaxing break from the relegation worries, in hindsight now seemed inconsequential. The mood in the club had reached its lowest ebb, as everyone tried to overcome the major catastrophe which had almost immersed West London Football Club in the depths of despair.

Sandra Crowther was up early preparing a breakfast of sausages, bacon, fried eggs, hash browns, baked beans, tomatoes and toast, before she ventured into Oxford Street with Michelle for a little retail therapy. It was unusual as most Saturdays in the football season, John was either staying in one of the hotels somewhere in the country, after travelling up the day before with the team, or hurrying to get to the training ground in preparation for a forthcoming home game. Today would see the whole family have breakfast together. As they sat devouring the sumptuous treat, John was contemplating what to do. He could sit in the lounge in a state of nervous apprehension, watching the afternoon's goals being scored in real time and hoping Kirklees County and Sheffield Wednesday get beaten, or find a game to go to. Watford and Luton Town were the only decent clubs in the vicinity, but Luton were away and it was pointless going to Vicarage Road to watch Watford play West Ham, he might as well not bother. He made himself yet another cup of coffee and contemplated what he should do and then had a quick thought and searched the lounge fot the local paper. He had a quick search in the lounge, stuck his head back into the kitchen "Does anyone know where this weeks *Herts Advertiser* is?" he said impatiently. "Try the garage, I think I've thrown it out to take down the dump." Sandra replied. In the garage he searched the pile of old newspapers and magazines and finally located the copy he required. He looked in the sports section where there was a report of St Albans City's last match and established City had their final home game at Clarence Park, against Harrow Borough, in the Ryman Premier League that afternoon.

After the girls had departed for the station, Bradley despatched himself to one of the local hostelries for a few jars with a couple of his mates and John set off to Morrisons in St. Albans to pick up a few groceries Sandra had told him she needed. After grabbing a coffee he drove to the ground which was situated five or so minutes away. He was a little early so he managed to park without any problem. Quite a few fans had already arrived and were buying programmes from an overworked seller and purchasing hamburgers or hot-dogs from a stall set up in the front of garden of one the detached houses. John was tempted, but didn't succumb.

The Clarence Park ground had a capacity of 5,000 with 800 seats but normally achieved an attendance figure closer to the 1,000 mark. Whilst John could have phoned the management and they would have undoubtedly given him a complimentary ticket, he had decided not to and instead queued up at the turnstile to pay at the gate. He positioned himself on the half-way line and became absorbed in a really competitive match which both teams badly wanted to win. Aproaching half-time, St. Alban's centre-half Tony Moon leapt majestically to an in-swinging corner and his thumping header found the back of the net. 1-0 to The Saints. John had watched the young man closely in the first half and could see a lot of potential. In the half-time break, John lined up at a small stall and bought himself a hot Bovril and a steak and kidney pie. In doing so he was recognised by a number of the fans who nodded to him, and he nodded back. No one hassled him, knowing of the plight of West London. The speakers stopped playing the week's top pop songs and the announcer came on. He ran through the Ryman League scores and then announced that Manchester United, who had already won the Premier League, were winning 3-0 against second placed Arsenal at Old Trafford; third placed Leeds United were drawing 1-1 with leaders Sunderland at Elland Road; while at the bottom Kirklees County were 1-0 down to Newcastle United at St. James' Park and Sheffield Wednesday were losing 2-0 to Derby County at Hillsborough, which helped to calm his anxieties. John was beginning to suffer with indigestion, he was not sure whether it was his nerves or the pie he had eaten moments before. He had sporadically been experiencing bouts of dyspepsia over the past few months, so now always had a few *Rennies* tablets with him. He popped a couple in his mouth and, over the next ten minutes or so, the problem subsided.

The game was well into the second half when St. Albans scored another two goals to further increase their lead to 3-0. He was now really becoming interested in Tony Moon who was outstanding. The game and season finished on a high for the little club and John quickly made his way to the car to listen to the final results on Radio 5 Live.

He switched on the car's ignition just in time and caught *James Alexander Gordon's* familiar voice: "Here are today's football results."

"The Premier League:

Aston Villa 1 Leicester City 0

Chelsea 2 Liverpool 0

Everton 0 Southampton 0

Leeds Utd 2 Sunderland 1

Manchester United 3 Arsenal 2

Middlesbrough 0 Tottenham Hotspur 2

Newcastle United 1 Kirklees County 3"

John was astounded at the final result and shouted at the radio *"Oh No. No. No!"*

He only just managed to pick up the next result as he absorbed the second half comeback by Kirklees at Newcastle.

"Sheffield Wednesday 2 Derby County 3

Watford 1 West Ham United 2

West London v Coventry City match postponed."

"The Nationwide Football League Division One….."

The program continued with John only half listening, his mind very much on the league table; Kirklees County were now level on points.

	P	W	D	L	F	A	GD	PTS
KIRKLEES CTY	37	7	12	18	46	73	-27	33
WEST LONDON	36	8	9	19	37	66	-29	33
SHEFFIELD WED	37	8	7	22	37	67	-31	31
WATFORD	37	5	6	26	33	76	-43	21

He stopped at the local chippy on the way home. When he arrived home, Bradley was collapsed on the couch snoring and the girls were no doubt on their way home. He turned on the oven, unwrapped the fish and chips and left them to keep warm.

When the girls finally arrived home just after six o'clock, they had numerous plastic bags from several of the Oxford and Regent Street stores. Michelle was giggly, having had too much wine in a Tapas restaurant in Maddox Street, and for the next half-an-hour they paraded their new acquisitions in front of two largely disinterested males, before consuming a not very appetising fish and chips, which by this time had been in the oven for too long.

After watching the TV for a couple of hours John retired with Sandra to bed, leaving Bradley and Michelle watching a scary film; John had no interest in watching *Match of the Day*.

32

It was Sunday 7th May, which should have been the day of final games of the Premiership league programme. All the clubs were involved and every game had to begin at 12 noon precisely.

With the exception of two fixtures which had been postponed: West London v Coventry City, due to be played on Friday 26th May, and West London v Kirklees County, rescheduled for Sunday 4th June.

Sandra started preparing breakfast for everyone and John went upstairs to wake Bradley and Michelle. He came back.

"Don't bother about those two, they must have had a boozey night last night it smells like a brewery in both rooms and they are out for the count."

Sandra tried to talk John out of sitting around home all day engrossed in the football.

"Come on let's go to the pictures." she suggested appealingly.

"What's on?"

"Erin Brockovich with Julia Roberts and Albert Finney." she replied.

John turned his nose up. "Is there nothing else. What about Gladiator with Russell Crowe?" he asked.

"It isn't on general release until next week or the week after." Sandra replied, a little irritated.

"Oh come on, stop being a pain. It's on in Hemel Hempstead at 11.30 this morning. It's quite long, just over 2 hours. We could then go and have a long lunch in one of the restaurants. There's a hamburger joint, Italian, Mexican and a few others, even a Macdonald's."

She smiled, knowing exactly what he was going to say.

"Forget Macdonald's you'd have to drag me in there screaming."

"Come on, I'll drive and you can then have a drink."

He capitulated, she booked the tickets and they set off. They grabbed a couple of cokes and some chocolate and settled down in their seats in a near empty cinema.

The film was far better than he thought it would be and it took his mind off the football for three hours. By the time they had spent another two hours in the Mexican restaurant, the games were finished, and whatever will be, will be......

It wasn't until they arrived home that John found out the results that mattered:

Leicester City 1 Watford 2
Sheffield Wednesday 1 Middlesbrough 3

	P	W	D	L	F	A	GD	PTS
KIRKLEES CTY	37	7	12	18	46	73	-27	33
WEST LONDON	37	8	9	20	37	68	-31	33
SHEFFIELD WED	38	8	7	23	38	70	-32	31
WATFORD	38	6	6	26	35	77	-42	24

Both Sheffield Wednesday and Watford had been relegated. A win against Coventry City would mean Kirklees County would have to win on 4th June to stay up. A defeat would mean they would then have to beat Kirklees County. A draw would level the points, but West London's goal difference of -29 was worse than County's by two goals and so West London would be relegated

………… In short, West London would have to win. It was all in West London's hands.

He discussed with Sandra the merits of driving himself down to the funerals of Hurst and Sulley and maybe staying overnight in between. They had been arranged for Tuesday and Wednesday: Hurst's was in Brighton on Tuesday and Sulley's on the Wednesday in Southampton.

"Don't be daft. Go down on the staff coach, come back, and then take the coach down again on Wednesday. That way you'll come back home and sleep in your own bed. You can have a nap on the coach and not be stressed out."

What about Wade, his burial is on the same day as Sulley's?"

"Forget him. You can't make both, it's miles from the South coast to Yorkshire. Go by coach. Do you want me to accompany you? I will if you want me to."

"No, that's not necessary. You're right, as always, I'll go down on the coach."

33

The Coventry City game was rearranged for the evening of Friday 26th May with a 7.45pm kick-off, which meant the clash away against Kirklees was to be played on Sunday 4th June. Kirklees County FC were not impressed and insisted that the game should not be postponed, but played on the original date. But the FA held firm.

So, the final game of the season would be played on Sunday 4th June. On the morning of the Coventry game, John Crowther's journey to the ground was uneventful. The traffic was light and the weather mild. He stopped at the local newsagents and bought a Daily Mail. In close proximity of the ground the activity was immense; Sky TV had already set up their cameras for the evening's game, with additional cameras positioned on the exterior of the offices and main gate. The programmes were being off-loaded and many of the match day staff were busy performing their preparatory work in readiness for the expectant crowd.

Crowther's sleepless night was now followed with stomach convultions as nervous expectations began to envelop him. He wished he knew his fate now! It was better to to know you would hang tomorrow than not to know if, or when. He picked up a programme from reception and proceeded to his office. He started flicking through it and noticed that it had a four page loose insert in the centre, with the likely Coventry team and a blank where the West London team should have been, with a large black border surrounding it. Although now out of date, the content in many areas was far from digestible to those that were connected to the club. There were details regarding the deaths that had occurred and, as he continued flicking through the pages, of the postponed game. He realised he was looking at the original content. He understood, from way back in his printing days, how much work and paper was involved in producing a high class piece of literature, and reprinting it wouldn't be cheap. The Daily papers, however, were well up to date with all aspects of the club and most had pictures of Hirst, Sully and Wade.

He turned his chair to face the car park concourse and gazed out at the mass of turnstiles, which were virtually motionless, waiting for the mass influx of supporters. Some fans had arrived early and were busily adding their scarves and assorted apparel to an already colossal collection of tributes. The massive grey mainstand of the stadium was strangely quiet. The club flag, flying at half-mast in respect of those who had died, hardly fluttered. The football world was united in sympathy. The kick-off would be delayed by five minutes to allow for two minutes silence, but it looked as though many were already holding their own vigil. Crowther still couldn't comprehend the decision to allow the game to be played, with so much depending on its result. He wondered whether the team would be capable of concentrating on football, when he was finding it difficult himself. The three hours to the 8pm kick-off passed quickly, as he performed the many duties he was required need to undertake prior to kick-off. He finally left his office and took the back stairs down to the dressing rooms. Usually it was noisy with the players being boisterous. Not today. The quiet was overwhelming. The shirts hung neatly on their respective numbered pegs, along with their black arm bands, waiting to be donned and for the battle to commence.

John spoke to each player in turn and offered them as much encouragement as he could muster, then a team talk, before handing over to Rob Dyson. At 7.55pm the bell rang and the teams left the dressing room. The officials and both teams assembled around the centre circle. The referee blew his whistle, the players lowered their heads and the proceedings began.

The motionless crowed stood in an eerie silence; there were tears shed by some. As the seconds ticked by, even the birdlife seemed to have respected the dead, as none could be seen or heard. The wind was still. The two minutes silence seemed to last an eternity and, when the referee blew his whistle, the sharp shrill rebounded around the ground as though it was empty.

The game was never going to be an epic with so much at stake. The West London side kicked off and showed they were suffering from nerves by immediately giving the ball away to the opposition. The pattern continued with missed passes, putting them on the back foot. They were just not in the game. After only four minutes the ball was played back to Paul Brown, the pass was a little too strong and not as accurate as it should have been.

Paul raced from his goal with two City forwards also in hot pursuit. He connected with the ball firmly but the oncoming forward, Steve Frogatt, had limited his options considerably. It rebounded from him, agonisingly spinning over his left shoulder. Paul could only look despairingly as it climbed high in the air and curled towards the unguarded goal. It took a high bounce on the edge of the six yard box as it connected with the ground and looped back in the air, looking as though it would, at that moment, clear the crossbar. But it dropped and hit the underside of the bar; on its descent striking the goal line and sending up a puff of white dust, the spin on the ball taking it over the goal line; and came to a stop nestled in the back of the net. 0-1. It was the worst start they could have possibly made.

After the disappointment, the large crowd of 39,000 tried hard to lift their side, but worse was to follow after a further nine minutes, when City forced their first corner. The West London defence had failed to cover all the possibilities, a short corner ensued and the defence stood watching Steve Frogatt collect the ball and move swifly down the goal-line. Only then did Don White see the problem and try to intercept but he was too late; Frogatt had been afforded far too much room. His pass to Robbie Keane was deadly accurate and Robbie gleefully crashed the ball home. 0-2 and there was still a further seventy seven minutes to play. The stadium erupted into a crescendo of noise as the partisan crowd showed they were unwilling to give up; the team's spirits were lifted and they began to fight for their survival.

A hopeful punt by Jim Fellows just outside City's penalty box; he manouvered himself past two defenders and, with only Chris Kirkland to beat, he carefully side-footed the ball past him. The ball richocheted off the post and in his endeavours to reach the ball before Kirkland, Fellows's left foot accidently struck the keeper's head before he could reach the ball. The incident looked far worse than it actually was and the referee's whistle shreaked immediately, just as the animated City team subjected Fellows to intense verbal and physical abuse.

Three of the City players were booked and the West London team waited apprehensively as the referee called Fellows to him. He spoke at some length and booked him. It was a relief to all concerned that he hadn't been sent for an early bath. Maybe the referee thought West London Football Club deserved a little rub of the green - on most occasions he would not have remained on the pitch. It was suprising there were no more goals and the final whistle finished the evening for West London, leaving a final game away to Kirklees County.

West London 0 Coventry City 2

	P	W	D	L	F	A	GD	PTS
KIRKLEES CTY	37	7	12	18	46	73	-27	33
WEST LONDON	37	8	9	20	37	68	-31	33
SHEFFIELD WED	38	8	7	23	38	70	-32	31
WATFORD	38	6	6	26	35	77	-42	24

John Crowther spent very little time in the dressing rooms; there was nothing he could say or do that would change history and the players were inconsolable. He left them and made his way to his office. He sat quietly, peering from the window, watching the remainder of the unhappy spectators make their way home. There were no demonstrations, just sadness. He began writing his letter of resignation many times, each one finding its way into the waste bin.

34

Mike Stephenson left the patrol car which dropped him back at Hammersmith Police Station, where he had left his own car earlier. He hadn't been told anything more than Jenny Rastall was actually Jenny Clarkson and that he had been set up. He didn't know why. He recognised Jason (as the person in the Mini he had followed earlier) at the moment before he attacked him. He now knew that he was very probably her boyfriend. Mike was concerned Jenny was missing and felt responsible; if he had just gone home directly after the ceremony finished, he wouldn't be in the mess he was in now.

He arrived home and rang Julia's parents' number in Surbiton. He knew it would be her first port of call if anything serious happened in their marriage. She was there. They spoke for over an hour without agreeing any reconciliation. Julia wanted a lot more time, she admitted their daughter was missing him but never disclosed her own feelings. "I'll ring you Mike when I make a decision." she said.

"OK, my contract runs out at the end of the month. I've no agent, so I'm looking for a club in Yorkshire." There was a lot of bitterness in her voice just before she hung up.

"Please yourself, you selfish bastard."

Mike packed an overnight bag, made his way up to the outskirts of Sheffield and found himself a cut-price hotel. He had decided to have a good breakfast in the morning and then set off to Sheffield United, who he knew were interested in signing him. He sat on the bed watching TV and dropped off to sleep. He didn't sleep well, continually dreaming of being chased by someone. He finally gave up trying to sleep at 6am and pottered around before going down to an empty dining room.

His surprise appearance at Bramall Lane had everyone in a fluster; neither the manager nor his assistant were in and one of the staff told him how to get to the training ground. When he arrived, only some of the coaching staff were working, along with one of the medical team. They knew of the club's interest and the fact that his contract was expiring, but no-one had advised them that he was coming. When the medical was over he was informed that he had passed without any problems.

He was chuffed with the result and felt a lot more relaxed about the future. He spent the rest of the day in and out of estate agents in South Yorkshire, looking for a three or four bedroomed house. It had to be secluded and detached, preferably with its own driveway and a double garage, in a private road, or a cul-de-sac maybe. His vanity precluded him living in a road with ordinary people. The house also had to be within a reasonable distance from United's training ground and close to, or in, a hamlet. It was a tall order; most of the houses available were a lot further from the training ground than he would have liked; he wanted a journey of about half an hour but most were over an hour away.

Mike found two properties; the first, a Manor House in Ackworth near Pontefract, had 5 bedrooms and 4 acres of land and everything he required. Priced at £650,000, it was just within his means, but the property was enormous. He was not being realistic and Julia would have thought he was crackers, she always said that he had champagne taste and beer money. He used to take exception to her jibes, pointing out what he had provided her with since they had been married. He had no doubts that he would be back with her and their little daughter Emma soon.

Mike had always been inclined to think he was better off than he was; Julia controlled the purse strings. He finally settled on a modern 5 bedroomed property in Dronfield for £580,000 which had stables. He asked for a viewing, even though the price was still higher than his property in Sunbury-on-Thames. One of the agents there had suggested its value would probably be in the region of between £350,000 to £400,000, which was well below what Stephenson thought it would sell for as the market at present was good. Yorkshire was known to be one of the cheapest places in England to live, but it was not the case when buying homes at the top end of the market.

He drove back to his hotel despondent, now certain he would not be able to afford his dream house, but made an appointment anyway to view it the following day at 11am. On his way back he spotted another agent so he parked up 100 yards away and went in. He decided to come back down to earth and lowered his budget. He found a 4 bedroomed house with a reasonable sized garden valued at £395,000 in Whirlow, South Yorkshire. He arranged for a viewing at midday, after cancelling the one he had set up at 11am in Dronfield.

He awoke at 8am and opened the door to pick up the Daily Mail he had ordered. He threw the paper on the bed, grabbed a towel and climbed into the shower. He towelled himself down, placed his overnight bag on the bed and extracted a pair of pants. As he stepped into them he noticed the name 'Stephenson' in bold type on the back page. There were three pictures of himself and Jenny Clarkson; one when they were flirting with each other in Redmand Art and the other two showed them enjoying each other's company, laughing and joking as they strolled along, which must have been on Bruton Street.

STEPHENSON
AND MISSING ACTRESS

Mike Stephenson, the England skipper, is helping the police with their enquiries into the disappearance of a young actress, Jenny Clarkson, who he was recently seen walking around London with. It is rumoured Stephenson is involved in an extra marital affair with the 24 year old actress and his wife has moved out of their home in Sunbury, along with their daughter Emma. Stephenson was the last known person to see Miss Clarkson alive. In the past few days she has been declared a missing person by her boyfriend, Jason Middleton. Neighbours of Miss Clarkson in Primrose Hill said they hadn't seen her for over a week and stated that she was a nice neighbour, always willing to stop and chat and update them on what she was working on.

There was much more in the article, but most of it related to Mike's playing history and his achievements. Mike now was worried, not only for his future in the football world, but about what had actually happened to Jenny Clarkson, and about the people that were responsible for implementing the situation. He dressed and went down for an early breakfast; fortunately he was the first one down and so could avoid the other residents, who would have already read their newspapers, and save himself from having to go through the whispering and odd looks. Usually he would have stuck the TV on but this morning, after reading the article, he couldn't face it.

He was still going to view the house in Whirlow. The young man from the estate agents was due to pick him up at 11.30 am and fortunately he hadn't recognised him, or if he had, he hadn't let on. Mike went off for a stroll around to pass some time, mainly in the recreation grounds and park, away from the general public. His emotions were all over the place and his thoughts fluctuated repeatedly through Julia and Emma; Jenny Clarkson; the house in Sunbury; West London Football Club; Sheffield United; the house in Whirlow; the bastards that had set him up and why...... It went on and on. Three hours went by quickly and he made his way back to meet up with the estate agent, Bernard Aylott.

In half-an-hour they had arrived in the pretty village of Whirlow and parked in the driveway of the house he was viewing. He wandered around the property with the owners who were not friendly, in fact they were unpleasant. From the moment he had been introduced to them, he could feel that he wasn't welcome. Nearing the end of the inspection, when they showed him the downstairs loo, he knew why. On one wall was a large framed, fully autographed Sheffield United shirt and on another an England shirt with his own autograph on it. They said their goodbyes and got back in the car.

"What did you think? asked Bernard.

"I like it" replied Mike. "It's just what we're looking for."

"Good, they are looking to get the asking price. It only came on the market yesterday. I have one couple coming to view it tomorrow, so I haven't had any bids yet, but I'm certain that it will exceed the asking price. They were a strange couple; you would have thought that they were not interested in selling it."

Mike was so pleased that this kid had no idea what had just occurred, he now definitely knew that the shit had hit the fan. Typically Mike, without too much thought, offered a bid of £450,000.

"Are you sure?" asked an amazed Bernard.

"Yes I am." Mike replied.

"OK I will ring as soon as I get back to the office and let you know the outcome. You have all the details to show your partner…."

"My wife." Mike cut him off mid-sentence.

"Sorry, your wife."

"Yes thanks."

"OK I'll speak to you soon. What time will you get back home?"

"About sevenish."

He bade farewell at the hotel, picked up his car and started his 150 mile jaunt back down the M1 South. He purposely didn't listen to the car radio, playing many discs from his CD collection instead. The traffic was slow and he became desperate for a toilet. He was fast approaching Toddington so pulled into the inside lane and came off at the service station. He pulled in to a pump, filled the Alfa up with fuel and made his way to the tills. He glanced quickly at the newspaper stands and couldn't see anything on the front pages, which was a relief.

He paid, parked his car by the main building and and hurriedly made his way to the toilet. As he stood at the urinal, feeling great relief at getting there in time, he was pushed by someone passing by. He looked up and a tall, broad youth shouted out "You fucking wanker." He had to go into a cubicle to dry his jeans, the episode upset him; it was not that it hadn't been called for, it was the venom that had been used. When he came out he made his way to the M & S Food Store, picked up a Margherita pizza and a bottle of milk, ignored the paper rack and continued his journey back home.

He arrived home and picked up the mail from the doormat. There was nothing of any significance. He placed the pizza in the oven and grabbed a bottle of red wine. As he took his pizza out, the phone rang. It was Bernard Aylott.

"Good evening Mr Stephenson, I have spoken with Mr and Mrs Rodway and passed on your offer. Whilst they have not rejected it, they feel the house has only been on the market for a short time and wish to wait and see what other offers might materialise."

"OK, I really want this property Bernard, please keep me posted on a daily basis. Do you think they will get a better offer?"

"I'm not sure, sometimes you get surprised doing this job, you experience lots of clients getting gazumped late on and just do not want lose something they feel they would be happy living in for the rest of their lives. A chain of people all selling does sometimes put people off. No doubt your home will sell easily, I have made enquiries about it. If you have the finances to own both properties, you could get a bridging loan. Anyway we will see first of all what the couple who are viewing it tomorrow think of it. I will keep in touch."

"Thanks, we'll speak tomorrow then."

Mike put the phone down, and thought about his predicament. He worried whether the impending move to Sheffield United would be affected by the Jenny Clarkson situation. If it was and they pulled out, he would be incapable of contemplating very much; no job, no sponsorship, no income whatsoever. The mortgage on the house in Sunbury still had to be paid. He poured himself a large gin and tonic and turned the TV on, just to see what was being broadcast. The news, exactly as had he thought, was frightful; there was an underlying bias regarding her disappearance, the finger was pointing firmly in his direction.

At ten o'clock the next morning he was still in bed when his sleep was interrupted by the telephone, he felt weary, stretched over and picked it up. It was an annoyed Ralph Strivens the manager of Sheffield United. The conversation was very much one-sided, Mike listened intently, answered 'yes' and 'no' in various places and finally put the phone down devastated.

Sheffield United were no longer interested in signing him after the revelations now sweeping the world of football, meaning very soon he would be unemployed, and maybe unemployed.

35

At New Scotland Yard, DCI Derek Bingley and DI Andrew Wright were holding their first meeting in connection with the disappearance of Jenny Clarkson. Part of the team; DS's Doug Inman and Hilary Ford and DC's Peter Woods and Marcus Warren; listened intently and digested all the information divulged to them by Hammersmith CID. On the evidence board, a head shot of Jenny was the first to be pinned up, followed by those of Mike Stephenson and Jason Middleton. The letter from Jenny to her parents, the one passed onto Middleton and the remaining one to WPC Fairbrother were read and re-read, prior to being added to the board. With the evidence so far acquired, the possibility of Jenny still being alive was remote. Bingley suggested that they should strongly consider that Jenny had been murdered, but they should keep an open mind until her body was found.

Bingley; a blunt, no-nonsence Yorkshireman; bald, overweight and an impatient taskmaster; left after three hours and the more amenable DI Andrew Wright took control.

"Right, we need to act immediately, to find out what has actually happened to Jenny and find this bloke Phil West."

"We also need to know guv, why? Why was Mike Stephenson set-up?" DS Hilary Ford asked.

"A good point Hils. If we could establish that it would answer so much. Hils, you and Peter get down to Hammersmith and question WPC Fairbrother. Find out as much info as you can. Find out more about the apartment and the question of the filming of the event. It doesn't make any sense."

"Yeh… Stephenson. He must have known." said DC Woods suspiciously."He isn't that daft, surely." interjected DS Inman, annoyed with Woods' indifference.

"No exactly. I'm going to have a close look at the apartment. Doug, you come with me. Marcus, locate Stephenson and let's see what he can tell us." said DI Wright.

DS Hilary Ford contacted Hammersmith Police Station and arranged to meet WPC Fairbrother there with DC Peter Woods later in the morning. On arrival, they were shown into one of the interview rooms and offered tea and biscuits. It was very apparent that WPC Fairbrother was extremely uncomfortable. DS Ford was first to speak.

"You seem to be very nervous Susan. Do you mind if I call you Susan?"

"No, not at all. I would prefer it." she replied.

"Just relax." said Ford. "Sorry, I've never been involved with anything as serious as this before, I've only been working for the force for eleven months." said Fairbrother.

"We know that. Don't worry, just relax and answer the questions. I am DS Hilary Ford and this is my colleague DC Peter Woods. As you know, we've come down from The Yard this morning to learn as much as we can about Jenny Clarkson. I understand PC Merritt is not on duty today."

"Yes, I did try to contact him, but he wasn't in. But I did most of the interviewing and recorded everything."

"Ok, no problem. When did you first meet her?"

She opened her notepad. "We were out on patrol on the Chiswick High Road; that is PC Alex Merritt and myself; when we came across Clarkson wandering around in a daze. She looked as if she had been dragged through a hedge backwards;

she had dirt, grime all over her. When we asked her what had happened, her explaination did not add up. Everything she told us was, we felt, a load of lies. The only thing we felt was the truth was that a man was involved and he had sexually assaulted her quite badly. We were unsure whether she had been raped and she wasn't too sure herself, she stated he had driven off in her car and she was scared."

"You then took her to A & E and then questioned her at her home, and then again at the station the next day. Is that correct?"

"Yes. She stuck to her original story, she was still frightened and became very abrasive, wanting quickly to leave the station. We had found her car, a red Nissan Bluebird. She picked up the keys and drove off."

"What was she like?" Ford asked.

"What do you mean?" asked Fairbrother.

"Her personality. What was your impression of her?"

"Oh I see. She seemed to be a very nice, attractive lady."

Ford looked through some of the paperwork she had spread in front of her and asked "You were one of the four officers that were dispatched to Tennison House with a search warrant. Is that correct?"

"Yes. We found that the apartment had been vacated a couple of days before. The premises were finally opened after using an enforcer. The place had been repainted and recarpeted. There was nothing in there; not a pot or pan."

She flicked through her notebook. "Ah, here it is. She says she took him into the bedroom and had sex on the bed and all that, knowing that she was being filmed. It was a one bedroom apartment."

Where was the camera situated?" asked Ford.

There was a long pause as Fairbrother thought about the question before she answered.

"We were only interested in finding Clarkson. We examined the apartment thoroughly and then we left. Everything was then handed over to the CID, so that was my last involvement. It was then handed over to you guys. It's a good question though 'cos the place wasn't big enough to house a clandestine camera."

Ford looked at Woods. Fairbother looked at Ford. There was total silence as they all sat back momentarily in deep thought.

"Was there a large mirror or glass wall or something like that? Like we have in the interview rooms. You know, with the two-way mirror." said Wood.

"No it was just a wall." said Fairbrother.

"Then they must have somehow used the apartment next to it. Maybe the wall is a false one. It was replaced with a two-way mirror and then, afterwards, it was taken down and put back to how it was originally." suggested Woods.

"That's a thought. Thanks Susan, you've been a great help. Well done Peter. I'm going to give DI Wright a call and tell him what we think. Well done, that would explain a lot. I'll have a look, when someone lets me get in, and see whether what you have said is feasible. We'll talk later. Look, this is taking too much time. Take Woodsy and locate Stephenson, he's got a lot of questions to answer."

Wright and Inman finally obtained the keys to number 41. Wright went up in the lift to the 2nd floor and found himself in a long corridor with doors either side, very much like hotel rooms. He turned left and located 41 and 42 near the far end, but the distance between the two apartments was far greater than most of the others, with a fire door in between them. He knew that they were all one bedroom apartments and the specifications precisely the same, so the idea that the other apartment could have housed the film cameras looked suddenly quite remote.

Wright opened the door to 41 and walked through a small vestibule with facilities for hanging up coats on the right. The door directly in front of him led into what was the lounge; it was immense and it was empty. He could detect the smell of a newly laid carpet along with a distinct smell of fresh paint. Even though it was carpeted from wall to wall, every sound echoed. To the right was an enormous kitchen-diner. Except for the units and white goods, there was nothing in there. Nothing in any of the drawers, cupboards, freezer, fridge, washing machine or dryer. He turned and made his way to the far door where he found what must have been the bedroom. No bed, or anything else. It had been re-carpeted and re-painted replicating the lounge.

Behind another door he located an ensuite containing all the up to date appropriate facilities. It smelt new, clean and unused. It was obvious that it would not provide any forensic evidence. He left the ensuite and approached the wall that was thought to be false. He rapped on the wall with his knuckles and a hollow sound reverberated from it. The adrenaline in his system increased considerably. When Inman found him he had a huge grin on his face.

"I've got the keys to 42 Boss." said Inman.

"Firstly, don't call me Boss, and secondly this is a stud wall. Let's have a look at next door."

They walked along the corridor towards 42. "The apartment's occupants left at the same time as 41, but they are not connected." Wright stopped in his tracks. "Sorry what are you saying?"

"The people that rented 42 are not the same people that rented 41."

They continued walking, Inman fiddling with his keys in nervous anticipation, whilst Wright had the feeling of impending disappointment. Inman unlocked and opened the door and stood motionless for a few moments, viewing what he was seeing. The vestibule was positioned on the left and not the right, the lounge was exactly the same as 41, but the dining room was on the opposite side. The decoration was exactly the same as 41 and there was precisely the same smell. When they opened the door to find the bedroom on the right they knew that they had located where the camera had been.

Immediately, Wright contacted the forensic team and sealed the apartment until they arrived. The team spent several hours examining, in detail, every inch of the apartment, bagging a few things found.

Whilst the CID team waited impatiently for the forensic results, they again went over all the evidence they had so far accumulated and what possibles scenarios they could think might have happened. DI Wright commenced with his observations.

"We have to establish first whether Jenny Clarkson walked away from number 41. If not, we must assume that she was killed in one of the apartments. If that is the case, how was the body removed? The chance of removing her body without being observed would be too slim, so I don't think that would have been considered. These guys are obviously professionals and had, no doubt, carried out many similar operations. As bloody horrible as it is, she might well have been dissected into small parts and removed along with all the building waste. If that was the case, I think they would have used the ensuite to cut her up, and this would have been done in 42. The forensic team thoroughly examined number 41 looking predominantly for blood traces and there was nothing. It is more likely we will have more chance of finding the evidence we need in 42. We also need to ascertain the association between the occupants of both apartments: …..there must be one! Woodsy you've got that information. Who are they?"

DC Woods frantically attempted to find the information required and looked at Wright in total failure.

"Oh for fuck's sake. Go and find the names now." Wright was fuming. "This is serious. Get your arses into gear, we can't afford to let these bastards get way with this shit."

It was not long before the forensic team reported that they had found human traces of blood in the drainage system connected to the bath in 42. They knew no more, but they thought that CID knowing this would at least give an insight into what they were dealing with. It would take several hours to conclude all their investigations, including blood tests. The CID team again met to discuss the possibility that either Jenny Clarkson, someone else, both, or even several people had been murdered and their bodies disposed of.

DS Inman and DC Warren missed the meeting as they were in the process of trying to locate Mike Stephenson. They had visited the Zion Park Stadium, the training ground and his home, but to no avail. No-one had seen him in the last few days and their day seemed meaningless. They had heard the news that the forensic team had found human blood in the apartment next door to where Jenny Clarkson had visited but, although elated, were fed up of the tedious job of sitting outside Stephenson's home. They sat for four hours, the sun was going down and the light began to fade.

The Avenue in Sunbury-on-Thames is a long tree-lined road adorned with large detached 4 to 6 bedroomed houses worth £350,000 to £500,000. It sits in close proximity to Kempton Park Race Course. The road was not busy and every car that passed close by gave them a brief adrenaline rush, but when it didn't arrive at the anticipated destination, the boredom again set in. At one stage Inman nodded off, a slight snore emanating from the back of his throat and nostrils. Warren looked over at him and gave him an almighty dig with his elbow.

"Sorry about that....this is bloody boring. Nothing's happening, no-one's in. I'm going to report in and see how long he wants us to hang around.... my wife will kill me if I don't get home at a reasonable hour tonight."

Just as they thought they might get home at a reasonable time, DI Wright contacted them. Both Mike Stephenson and Jason Middleton had independently shown up at Hammersmith Police Station and inadvertently come face to face with each other. Middleton had immediately attacked and hospitalised Stephenson and was now being held in custody in one of the stations cells. Stephenson had been taken to Hammersmith Hospital, where they were instructed to go.

36

After nearly half an hour comatosed on top of the bed in his room, Ray Prince's hunger for sex had seen him return to the bar. His reappearance coincided with the departure of the ambulance carrying Bruce Day. The inhabitants of the bar were enthralled by the events of the previous hour, but no-one knew the name of the Englishman who had nearly drowned and who had kept himself very much to himself.

The pretty Cypriot barmaid was still on duty as Prince, dishevelled after his short sleep, approached the bar. He bought a beer and offered her a drink, which she politely declined with a practiced smile. He tipped her well and sat, again watching her every move, imagining what he would like to happen. At three in the morning the bar closed and emptied out. The staff tilled-up and began to leave to make their way to home.

Rulie Kyriakou was one of the few staff who had managed to secure a room at the hotel. The room was sparse, having just enough space for a bed and a dilapidated toilet facility which included a toilet, a cracked wash basin and a shower. The shower was spasmodic in its performance and the bed hard and uncomfortable. The air conditioning had failed some years earlier and did not function. Considering all this, it was a surprise that she could make herself look so presentable. She always dressed impeccably and always used just enough perfume to make her smell good. Her room, at the top of the building, was stuck next to the now deserted laundry room and access to it was obstructed by various trolleys full of unwashed towels and sheets, awaiting the early morning shift. The staff were always considerate about not disturbing her, knowing of her late nights and the occasional visit of her boyfriend from one of the neighbouring hotels.

As she placed the key in the door and turned the lock, she became aware of someone standing behind her. The door began to open and she felt herself projected forcibly through it. She stumbled and fell and, before she could recover, was pinned to the floor by the heavy weight of a man's body. She struggled as his hands tore at her clothes, ripping them from her body in several powerful movements and rendering her helpless. She attempted to scream, but his hand muffled her cries. He stuck the remains of her pants in her mouth, nearly choking her, then pushed her legs apart and forced himself into her.

The rape reoccurred time after time as the petrified girl endured the insatiable sexual appetite and fantasies of a madman. She knew that her life was in his hands, and life was more important to her than anything. Rulie was in a no-win situation. Prince liked women to struggle, he enjoyed taking them when it was obvious that they didn't want him, and the thing she didn't know was that he would take her life anyway.

With daylight breaking through the window, he knew it was time to go. The girl looked at him, her eyes pleading for mercy as he placed his hands around her throat. He squeezed hard and the life of another victim ceased. He arose from the bed and, as he dressed, he looked admiringly at the naked body laid before him. The pretty blue eyes stared at nothing as the body lay limp. Prince locked the door behind him and then carefully pushed the key back underneath it.

Back in his room, he disposed of the used condoms, packed his belongings, shower and put on some fresh clothes, he was concerned that he had lost one of his contact lenses. He found the nearest exit, jumped into his hired Jeep and commenced a convoluted journey back to London via Larnaca Airport; where he dumped the vehicle and boarded an Olympic Airways flight to Athens. On arrival, he took a further flight by Air France to Paris Charles de Gaulle and then quickly hailed a taxi to take him to Gare du Nord railway station, where he boarded the Eurostar to Waterloo International in London.

Back in London, Prince made several phone calls connected with the protection area of the business. The one made to Felix Simon at the London Bravo rehearsal rooms concerned him greatly. Not that Simon wasn't prepared to pay what was due, but his continual questions regarding the whereabouts of Jenny Clarkson, and the nervousness that accompanied them, was worrying. Would he crack under pressure? Prince decided to act. He arranged to meet Felix at his apartment overlooking Hyde Park.

It hadn't taken Prince long to overpower him; he hated faggots and anticipated the exhilaration of watching him die slowly. He produced several pieces of rope and a transparent plastic bag from his case. He tied Simon to a chair, placed the bag over his head, tied it around his neck and sat and watched the man suffocate to death. Attempting to inhale oxygen, Simon finally sucked the bag into his own mouth and, as he did so, lost consciousness and his life.

37

Frustrated and upset, John rang home and spoke with Sandra in some depth. She listened intently to his ramblings and waited patiently for him to pour out the ordeals of his day. Finally, when he had finished, she was quick to come to his defence.

She said softly "It is not your fault John! You have done your best for the club under extraordinary circumstances, no-one could have done more. Don't do anything rash, just come home and we can talk about it further. Would you like me to come and pick you up?"

"No, I will clear up quickly and be home in an hour or so."

By the time he reached his home in Harpenden, John felt a lot more relaxed. Over the course of the evening he repeated all of his frustrations and took to his bed inebriated, after drinking more than half a bottle of scotch.

The next morning he woke with a slight headache, rose early leaving Sandra in bed, and travelled to the training ground in Osterley. Those that had played the night before were not in; they were having their mandatory day off, which was always taken following any game. The only personnel around were physiotherapist Tony Pullen and his assistant Simon Grainger, the groundstaff and players Paul Brown and Tim Wharton, who were having treatment for a couple of niggles from the previous night's game. Suprisingly, everyone was in a reasonable mood, obviously realising that the past cannot be altered, and some of the black humour actually made him smile.

The training ground was pretty basic; an unused recreation ground with a set of goalposts and series of prefabricated huts, one of which housed a small office. It was poorly lit, freezing cold, damp in the winter and oppressively warm in the summer. It contained a desk, two chairs, a filing cabinet, a chalk board and a telephone that was hardly used; it seemed incongruous in the present set up. Suddenly it rang. It made John jump. He picked it up. "John Crowther."

"John, good morning it's Phillipa. I'm at the Club."

"Hi Phillipa, What on earth are you doing there today? You should be at home with your little girl."

Phillipa ignored the comment, she was worried; the mood of the staff back at the ground was poor, many of them thought they would soon be unemployed.

"I couldn't sleep. I've come in and opened up and I hadn't been in long when a man appeared in reception wanting to speak with you urgently." She went quiet for a moment as she had obviously placed her hand over the phone. He could just about hear her speak to someone.

"Sorry what did you say your name was?"

John heard a male voice reply.

"Terry Morris, tell him I'm the son of the late Len Morris."

Phillipa came back to the phone. "His name is Ter........'

"I heard, Terry Morris, the son of Len." Do you know what he wants?"

"No he only wants to speak with you, very urgently." she replied.

"OK, tell him to stay put and I'll be back shortly."

When he arrived back there were three people sitting in the reception area; an elderly couple sitting on a small couch and a handsome, tall, slender, short-haired blond man, probably in his early to late thirties.

He was wearing an expensive looking black suit with a waistcoat, a buttoned down white shirt and a plain black tie with a Windsor knot. He was must have provided him with. 'What a great secretary she is' he thought. The man was totally asorbed reading the morning papers – The Financial Times and the Daily Mail. John approached him quickly, with his hand out readily to shake his, saying;

"I can't believe it. I haven't seen you in years. How are you?" Terry smiled, nodded and stood up and they shook hands.

"What can I do for you?"

"Can we go somewhere with a bit more privacy?"

John was a little taken aback, as were the elderly couple who were overjoyed to see John. The woman was struggling to find a writing implement in her handbag and her autograph book, which she always carried with her. In unison, they approached John.

"Excuse me Mr Crowther, may I have your autograph please?" she said.

"Of course." John, as always, obliged. The grateful couple were overawed by having him in their presence, albeit for a short period; something they would be able to tell all of their friends. They were eager to start up a conversation with him, but could see that he was otherwise absorbed with the young man. They both shook his hand, wished him good luck for the future and returned to their seat.

He said his goodbyes and ushered Terry to follow him.

"Let's go up to my office."

When they settled down in the office, John asked Terry whether he wanted another coffee and he declined.

Terry immediately opened the conversation. "I would like to have a chat about the Club."

"OK, fire away, what do you want to know?"

"I haven't been home for thirteen years. I fell out with my Dad over something pretty trivial and totally insignificant. I've lived in Sydney, in Australia, ever since then. I married a lovely Australian lady, Ella, and have a 7 year old son who I named after my Dad. I missed my Dad's funeral and I have lived to regret it. At the time I was so concerned about the length of time I would spend away from the business that I decided not to return to England for it. Ella badgered me for days, telling me I should put all the old issues behind me and that the business wouldn't flounder. I relented, but I took so much time to do so that I was unable to get a flight in time so, as I said, I didn't attend. Ella was right; the business continued to flourish and has expanded far beyond comprehension. I have been extremely succesful. My stupidity caused a considerable rift in the family, and I became totally ostracised."

John remembered the day of the funeral well; the consternation of the family that Len's only child had failed to attend and his own sadness. He was an outsider and paid his respects but was not involved.

John fidgeted in his chair and began to wonder why he was being presented with all the personal history. Terry could tell that John was becoming a little impatient.

"Bear with me. I now own, and run, one of the most successful multinational technology companies in internet related service and products in the world, competing with the likes of Amazon and Apple. Our turnover was 30 billion US dollars last year, the name of the company is Wallaroo and it's been trading now since 1992. Our growth is considerable and is exceeding all the forecasts, suggestions are that it could actually reach a staggering 40 billion next year."

John's knowledge of the computer world was virtually non-existent, but he had actually heard of the company.

"I don't know whether you are aware that Mum died last week, after several years in a home."

"No, I'm sorry to hear that. I'm afraid I totally lost any contact after your Dad died."

"This is why I'm over here now. Yesterday she was cremated, bless her, and, at the wake, Graham my cousin, who is the only one still talking to me, (who, by the way was the person who actually contacted me originally to tell me she had died) said that West London Football Club were in financial difficulty and in the hands of the administrators. Is this true?"

"Yes, I'm afraid so. Personally I think the club will not survive. We owe a vast amount, the majority to Sacher Paper Plc, but the Inland Revenue are also owed a fortune and let's not forget the bank."

"How much does the club owe?"

"I really don't know, but rumours suggest from £50 to £58 million."

Terry winced. "Jesus Christ that is some debt!!!…….. Sorry I shouldn't be blaspheming. That's such a shock."

For a few fleeting moments, John had considered that there might be a slim chance of survival and that Terry would be what the club needed; someone with money. But Terry's reaction brought him quickly back to reality; the sum owed was enormous, who on earth would have the wealth to consider such a venture?

Terry recovered from the initial shock. "Can I speak with the administrators?"

This response surprised John and he began to wonder whether Terry's interest was purely financial or maybe he was interested in making a quick buck by buying the land the stadium sat on, which must be the club's largest asset and worth a fortune, or was he interested in the club itself?

"I don't know whether they will see you but if you ring the club switchboard and ask to speak with Ruth Corderoy of Gillis, Freeman and Parker on Monday, she has taken control of the administrators. No......, actually it would be easier to speak with Phillipa Scott, The Club Secretary, I will let her know you'll be calling."

"Is this 'Ruth' in? Terry asked, I really don't have a great deal of time. Is she in today?"

"I don't really know. They come and go, they spend as much time as they want here, gather information and then go back to their own offices in the City. Hang on, I'll find out." He picked up the phone and dialled, in a short time it was answered.

"Phillipa."

"Hi Phillipa, is Ruth in today?"

"Yes she is, she turned up a few moments ago. I don't know where she is now though."

"Can you please find her and get her to ring me, and tell her it's urgent."

"OK will do."

"Phillipa is going to track her down."

The phone rang ten minutes later and it was Ruth Corderoy.

"John it's Ruth. I'm a bit busy, what is so urgent?"

"I have a someone in my office who would like to discuss the club's financial situation and try to help in some way." John looked at Terry for some form of acknowledgment. Terry nodded.

"I'm only interested if he has sufficient capital to invest into the club, which will enable it to continue, I have certainly not come across anyone so far with the financial clout to take on this debt and I doubt that one exists."

"That is a pretty negative attitude to take." John said.

John was annoyed, "Hang on a moment and I'll put him on. His name is Terry Morris." Terry took the phone.

"Hello Ruth. May I call you Ruth?"

"Yes, Yes." she said impatiently.

"It's simple. I am interested in buying the club."

John was as stunned as Ruth was.

"It will take a considerable amount of capital to do so and any such investment would have negligible return, if any at all. But any investment must also include a heavy commitment for the future."

"I would still like to meet you, along with John, to discuss it. Today if at all possible."

"No chance, I am tied up until 2.30pm and then I'm off home. It will have to wait until Monday first thing. Say 9.30am." she replied.

John looked at Terry for confirmation. Terry nodded.

"OK 9.30 Monday it is."

Terry cradled the phone and looked over at the near speechless John. "Lunch?"

"You bet." said John chirply.

"Look, I need to have a shower and get out of this clobber into something a bit more casual. Meet you back at my hotel in say one hour, I'm staying at the Ariel on the Bath Road."

"OK, I have some gear here I can change into and a couple of things I can do." said John. As soon as Terry left, he rang Sandra and told her of the exciting news.

The lunch was a hamburger and chips with a beer. It was a light-hearted affair, with John answering many questions about the past, his own career and home life, whilst Terry did likewise, admitting that he could actually remember the evening that he came to John's house quite vividly, and recalling his mum lavishing him with lemonade. They laughed a lot and both had a similar sense of humour.

Terry became serious, "So what has happened?"

"You don't know, surely you have heard!"

"No I don't follow sport of any kind, strange really with my Dad earning his living from it all of his life. One of those odd things that happen in family life I suppose."

John sat back, took a deep breath and began to recount the events of the past month or so.

"It is probably the most depressing time of my whole career. Unbeknown to me, the bank refused to increase the overdraft facility and the Chairman was unable to provide any further funds. That was a couple of weeks back."

"We were committed to playing a friendly in Lanarca, Cyprus against Anorthoses Famagusta, as part of a transfer fee for a young Cypriot lad. Fortunately we had already paid the air fares and hotel some months before."

"The Chairman, Alfred Wade, was arrested one night and committed suicide some time during the day after. He should have been on the flight but obviously missed it and, to be honest, at the time no-one cared less; he was an arrogant, self-important bastard."

"Whilst in Cyprus, two players went missing and we had no option other than to leave without them. A few weeks later their bodies were found down the side of a cliff; they had hired a scooter. And, just to add to the misery, Ruth Corderoy's mob turned up. Rumour has it that our Chairman was using the pension fund at Sacher's to support himself and us."

Terry looked horrified and went quite pale. "I hadn't been told that. That's awful. It must have had a dreadful affect on everyone. How on Earth have you managed to carry on?"

"I really don't know, a very supportive wife I suppose. The game last night was horrible, no-one really wanted to play; their hearts were really not in it and it showed."

Terry spoke candidly about his interest in the club that his Dad had been so well-connected with. He admitted that the outlay of such large sums of money would certainly require considerable professional undertakings to be put in place, to ensure that his money was not wasted. John glanced at his watch. "Terry, I'd better get home. Why don't you come over to my place tomorrow for Sunday lunch and meet my family, say 2pm, and stay overnight?"

"I'd like that."

John left him with his address and Terry arrived in a taxi in Harpenden on the Sunday afternoon as arranged, with a huge bunch of flowers, chocolates and a bottle of Cotes-du-Rhone. It was a long enjoyable day; he told them all about little Lenny and Ella and told them she would be arriving on Wednesday to stay for a week or so. Many hours were spent perusing through a number of photo albums, one of which contained many of his father. Sandra, Bradley and Michelle retired to bed long before John and Terry.

38

The first thing Terry wanted to do was to speak with Ella, he had agreed to ring her in the morning but he couldn't wait that long. He threw himself onto the bed and grabbed the phone by the bedside. He rang home, knowing that in Sydney it was 2am, the phone rang and rang monotonously until finally it was answered.

"What time do you call this?" The voice was a little incoherent as Ella began to awake from her slumber. "….I thought you were going to ring me in the morning!"

"Good Morning Darling." Terry said.

"Oh it's you, I thought it was my lover." she teasingly replied.

She blurredly looked at the bedside clock. "It's two o'clock in the morning!"

"How would you like a week or so in England?"

"Yes, you know I would…… I've nearly booked it already, but why?" she asked excitedly.

"This would be a lot of work with a bit of fun." he replied.

He told Ella what had occurred and waited patiently for her response but, before she had the chance, he said. "Do you think that I'm doing this out of a guilty conscience. Am I being stupid? What would my Dad have said?"

"You probably are feeling a bit guilty, but I'm sure your Dad would be really proud of you."

"OK look sweetheart, I could possibly be with you in 48 hours, Lenny is with my Mum and Dad for a few days but they will love looking after him for a bit longer, you know how much they idolise him. Shall I ring British Airways or Quantas?"

"The one that gets you here quickest."

"OK, I'll let you know as soon as I get confirmation. Heathrow or Gatwick?"

"Heathrow; Gatwick is a about an hour or so away, but Heathrow is virtually next to the hotel."

By the way, the debt is £58 million. So it's a question of how we can finance it."

"That is big bucks Tel!"

"I know, and I know that when you arrive you'll tell me what you think we, or I, should do. I'll leave you with that thought. Speak soon, love you lots, send my love to Lenny and give him big hugs and love, and thanks to your Mum and Dad. Tell them not spoil him whilst we're away!"

"Ha ha, no chance of that." she giggled. "OK I'm going to ring the airlines right now, I'm sure that they're open 24 hours. I'll let you know as soon as I confirm bookings. Have you all the relevant phone numbers you need?"

"Yes I do. You'll need to bring with you, both our personal and business portfolios. See you soon. Have a safe journey. Love you."

They both hung up. Terry glanced at the room service menu and quickly perused it; the hamburger he had eaten earlier had been digested and he required a little bit of something or other to nibble. He phoned down to in-room services and ordered the steak and ale pie with a double portion of chips. He opened the fridge to retrieve a bottle of red wine but quickly changed his mind and instead extracted a bottle of water; he required a clear head to grasp the problems he would most probably have to overcome. He left most of the pie but devoured the chips

Ella rang within two hours; she had managed to book a first class flight out from Sydney at 10am - Oz time - on Tuesday; it was the earliest she could book. She would have a four hour stopover in Bangkok, which meant she would arrive at Heathrow at 1pm UK time on the Wednesday.

She rang her parents, and made arrangments with them to look after Lenny. She took him to the offices to clear up a few loose ends and contacted a couple the management team to inform them what was happening and packed a small brief case with all the financial details which would be required. Then she visited a couple of clothes and cosmetic stores, much to Lenny's dislike as he was more interested in the toy shops.

She then packed a bag for herself and a couple for Lenny, containing his favourite playthings. In the morning, she packed the car up and drove over to her Mum and Dad who lived locally. When she arrived at their home she quickly gave them an overview of what had occurred.

39

On the following morning, both John and Terry were up early and John drove them back to the ground. The car park was virtually empty; normally it held about 1,000 cars on match day but today, no more than twenty. On arrival, Sheila the receptionist told them that everyone was waiting for them in the boardroom. They looked at one another in bewilderment.

When they entered, they were introduced to the various people around the large table by Ruth Corderoy, starting with herself.

"My name is Ruth Corderoy, representing Sacher Paper Plc, and we are the administrators. This is Roy Peters, West London Football Club's Chief Executive, and this is Michael Book from Wilson and Wilson solicitors, representing the Club. This is Barry J. Seymour, solicitor representing the late Alfred Wade, and of course Phillipa Scott who I have cajoled to take the minutes. She looked at John with a smirk. Reluctantly I might add."

Terry quickly interjected "My name is Terry Morris, I made it quite clear that the meeting was to be with Ruth Corderoy and John Crowther, no-one else. I am not interested in speaking with anyone else at this juncture."

Tempers became frayed, with both sets of solicitors making their feelings known; they didn't appreciate being summoned to a worthless meeting. Terry got up, shaking his head, and walked out. John told them that they were stupid and also left.

John caught up with Terry in reception, in the process of attempting to get a taxi back to his hotel. "I am really sorry about that. Let me go back up there and see if I can extricate Ruth, and use my office for the meeting."

"John, I'm not prepared to be bamboozled by a group of overpaid lawyers trying to line their own pockets. I'm interested in getting down to the fundamentals without continued interruption and views I don't need. I've been involved in too many of these type of meetings and it invariably ends the same way."

"OK, just let me see if I can at least do something to retrieve the situation. Go up to my office and I'll meet you up there, hopefully with Ruth." John hurried back to the boardroom where the atmosphere was toxic. He cornered Ruth.

"Everything is not lost yet. I caught Terry in reception and he is going up to my office, if we go there now we might be able to have some meaningful dialogue with him. Tell me though, are you trying to sabotage these talks or what?"

She grunted "No of course I'm not."

"You could have fooled me."

Reluctantly she gathered all of her paperwork up and followed him down the corridor.

When they arrived, Terry had embedded himself on the couch. Ruth spread her paperwork out on the desk but there was no apology or any reference to the previous half an hour.

Terry asked the million dollar question. "How much is the club in debt?"

She located the sheet of paper required and read out. £57,283,564.43.

"So who is the major creditor?"

"Sacher Paper Plc."

"Of course it is. What figure is required to settle that debt?"

"£46,591,119.73, plus about £4 mill in fees, dependant on the length of time we would be acting on Sacher's behalf. The Inland revenue is owed £4,512,738. We have an overdraft with

Barclay's of £14,690.87 which we are unable at this point to increase, nor pay any bills from that account. In fact, we are not even in a position to pay any of the ever accruing interest, which is obviously increasing day by day. We also owe the rates, which amounts to £37,011."

Terry was scribbling the amounts down in a small book. He looked calm and showed very little reaction.

"Our catering company is owed £27,900.27. We have a problem with one of our own sponsors; NEM; and owe for electricity totalling £40,888.55 Also the coach company £18,940.88 and various other small debts which total £14,215. Not forgetting of course the repayments of two transfers, which is paid on a monthly basis and presently stands at £60,000. We also have to pay the wages which is £1,498,845 including bonuses etc. A grand total of £57,283,564.43 and growing, daily."

Terry studied the figures and looked up. "Have you thought about selling the ground?"

Ruth looked at him with contempt." Of course we have. We are professionals."

"So what's it worth?"

"£10 million."

"You must be joking, that won't even pay the overdraft at the bank."

"Look, no-one wants the stadium, it's highly improbable there is a club anywhere in the vicinity who would want to move into it. The closest club is Chelsea, or maybe Wimbledon but I understand they are already considering moving to Milton Keynes. No-one wants to build on it because it would cost a fortune to demolish, before they even do anything close to starting construction."

"So, if say I said I would buy it for £8 million, it would probably be accepted."

Ruth looked strangely at him. "Yes, we would snap your hand off."

John stared at him annoyingly. Terry winked at him.

"So, if I offered £21 mill, I'm not sure what you'd do!"

"Well you'd be a fool. What cowboy business do you run?"

Terry looked at her with disdain and replied confidently. "Not everything is about business, sometimes you do things in life because it makes you feel good."

"It seems that the Inland Revenue …..£4,512,738 plus the overdraft……….£14,690,87……." He added up the two figures. "Comes to £19,203.60. Not forgetting the staff of course. These must be paid as quickly as possible to allow us to continue."

"OK, now that I know what I'm looking at I will need to talk with a few people. Please let me have all written documentation within 24 hours; I'm staying at the Ariel Hotel and it has a fax machine. I will get back to you quickly. To proceed, it is necessary for me to become a director. When you speak with your directors, if they are interested in going forward, I would like you to call a directors' meeting. If they're not interested then no doubt you will let me know. Do you think it is possible to organise it for say 2pm on this coming Thursday? I have spoken to my wife and she is already flying over from Oz. She is very knowledgable in the financial aspects of the business world and is responsible for *Wallaroo's* success, she is due to arrive at Heathrow early Wednesday afternoon."

Ruth, momentarily, was deep in thought before she replied.

"OK forget the fax, I will have all of the relevant literature copied and sent over to you. I will contact all of the directors and relevant solicitors to tell them of the meeting."

After leaving all of his contact details with Ruth, Terry left in a cab to the Ariel, whilst John and Ruth briefly discussed over the meeting.

"It all could be hot air you know. His advisors might consider it a no-go. He could even change his mind. I mean, all this has happened in a matter of hours." she said

"I know. We can only hope that this is not a dream and I won't wake up in a minute."

They both laughed, it was the first time the two had ever been convivial towards one another. John finished the chat with "In the brief time he has been in my company, he has convinced me he is very serious."

When Terry arrived back at the hotel he picked up a message at reception from Ella; timed at 2pm; saying she was boarding the plane to Bangkok and that she would ring him when she arrived. He glanced at his watch and reckoned she would ring about seven o'clock, it was now just gone three.

He went up to his room, switched on the TV, found a *Mars Bar* and a bottle of beer in the fridge and laid on the bed. He fell into a deep sleep and was awakened by a loud knock. He leaped off the bed and hurried to the door. He looked through the spyhole, saw a man in a suit and opened it.

"Good Evening Mr Morris." The smartly dressed man, who was holding several envelopes, handed them to him and continued. "I am Graham Hollingworth, the assistant manager. These envelopes have been left at reception by Ruth Corderoy from Gillis, Freeman and Parker. I told her you were in and asked whether she would like to speak with you. She said she didn't, but it was important you recieved them immediately."

Terry took the envelopes and thanked him.

He carefully opened all of them, spread them out on the bed and spent the next few hours perusing them.

Ella rang at just before eight o'clock. After a quick catch up, she told him the take-off had been delayed for over an hour whilst they sat waiting clearance, but she had landed in Bangkok and was still in time to catch the flight to Heathrow.

40

Terry met Ella at the Arrivals gate at Terminal 4 and, after loving greetings, they made their way to the taxi rank and on to the Ariel Hotel. "How's Lenny and your Mum and Dad?"

"They're all fine and send their love. Lenny wanted to come with me!"

"I do miss him."

"Hey what about me?"

He just grinned.

"Do I really need to even endorse that? I have a meeting with the board of directors for tomorrow morning at 2pm. Well, what do you think?" he asked.

"I looked at all of our investments before I left home; a number of them don't include interest. I have recalculated them into UK pounds and at present we have £3.5 billion, the problem I see is getting hold of the money quickly. It's a shame that we invested only £13 million in the Barclay's Venture Business Wealth Account 'cos we could put our hands on that immediately. I say it's a shame because we could have invested up to £50 million and we can have the money in 3 days. One of our investments is with Credit Suisse; where we have 50,000 Swiss francs; which works out on today's exchange rate to £39,000 but, as you know, we can only invest or withdraw every 6 months, and we cannot do anything until June 1st. HSBC and UBS between them hold the remainder of our investments in bonds and shares; it will take some time to raise that capital; we'll have to find out. So, this may be a no-goer."

The taxi arrived at the hotel, Ella checked in and they went to their room, whereupon she fell on the bed and was asleep within minutes. She slept for just over three hours and, when she woke, was very apologetic. She showered and changed into some clean clothes and, feeling refreshed, joined Terry at the table where he was sitting with the paperwork spread out.

"Right. I can't see us completing this deal quickly; realistically we will have only £13 million to use from Barclays. We just can't get hold of the amount of capital required quickly enough. I'm starting to repeat myself now."

'We must be able to do something!' Terry muttered under his breath.

They spent a further hour contemplating various scenarios, until Ella came up with a solution. "Firstly, you need to become a director. Then arrange to visit the club's bank and agree to pay the interest at regular intervals. This figure is increasing by £1,000 per day I would think. If they agree then that will mean we do not have to pay the £14 million or so owing. This would give us the opportunity to pay the Inland Revenue the £4,500,000 that is owed them and the Council Tax £37,000. That would give us time to complete the purchase of the ground for £10 million and we would have sufficient capital to pay the staff and many of the other creditors."

'That all sounds good, providing the current board of directors elect me onto the board and that the bank see this as a way forward."

"Why not? Your net worth is 3.5 billion pounds and they will be getting the interest paid plus a guarantee that the whole overdraft will be cleared."

"OK let's leave it at that and find somewhere to grab some dinner; I don't fancy eating here again, maybe the concierge will know somewhere." He rang the concierge, who answered in a strong Italian accent.

"Good evening Mr Morris, how can I help you?"

"Good evening, do you know of a good restaurant close by?"

"Hang on a moment. I do not know locals that well."

"What about a pub? I've always wanted to go to an English pub." shouted Ella from across the room."

"Mr Morris, my name is Valerie Marshall I'm the Deputy Manager, can I help you?" It was a young girl's voice.

"Yes, myself and my wife would like to have dinner in a local restaurant or a pub. Can you recommend one?"

"There is a famous old pub called *The London Apprentice.* It's about half an hour in a taxi and it serves good food. It's on the River Thames, it is a Grade II listed building, built in the 17th century, and they say that *Henry VIII* used to frequent it. You'll love it. I used to work there a few years back."

"Ok can you please make a reservation for the two of us for an hour's time and a taxi immediately."

"Of course Sir."

41

At the 2pm Directors' meeting, Vice Chairman Ronald Sperry took the chair; his first ever opportunity to do so. In attendance were fellow directors Robert Miles, Dominic Welch, Sean Davenport, Alan Proctor and Andrew Border. Also in attendance were Terry and Ella Morris, Chief Executive Roy Peters, John Crowther and Ruth Corderoy as well as Phillipa Scott the Club Secretary, who was taking the minutes.

"As I understand it, we have been summoned here today because of a proposed offer to buy the club by Terry Morris, who is the son of Len Morris, who, as all will recall, was our first manager. Unfortunately, Graham Whitehouse and Tony Purvis send their apologies for not being able to attend due to other comittments which they couldn't get out of. They have, however, faxed me their voting rights, sort of proxy votes. I'm going to hand over to Terry and let him tell us what his plans are. Terry, over to you."

Terry didn't like the way this was going. "Thanks. I have sufficient capital to meet all of the creditors' debts in full, but unfortunately I am unable to raise the funds quickly enough. The club's existence is vulnerable to charges being set against our assets by Gillis, Freeman and Parker. The main asset, of course, is the ground itself which is valued at £10 million by them. Sorry Ruth, but I believe it is worth far more than that. The land is a major appreciable commodity and can be sat on for years. I will have £13 million available in two days, with which I wish to purchase the ground. I do have a strategy and, if it is acceptable to the bank, then I can achieve the objective we are all wishing for; the continuance of West London Football Club; and this will allow sufficient time for me to buy the stadium and be in a position to use funds as they become available. Firstly, I need to be made a director immediately."

Ronald Sperry butted in agitatedly. "I'm not happy with this arrangement at all. Do you realise, if you pay off the debt totally, you would own 2,430 ordinary shares out of 3,000? Would you be prepared to sell some of them back to the existing directors?"

"Yes of course I know that and the answer to your second question is 'don't be ridiculous'. You guys have not managed to come up with a single penny to help the current problem, so why should you benefit from failure? It seems to me that you have enjoyed the position of being directors with very litte input or due diligence. If you do not elect me here this morning, I will just walk out and leave you all to it."

Sperry looked totally perplexed "It might be a good idea Terry if you stepped outside for a few minutes or so, whilst we discuss the situation."

"Ella and I will go down to reception and grab a coffee."

Ella said "Blimey Tel, you really have put the cat amongst the pigeons. This could seriously backfire." Terry smiled. "I know, but they are such a load of pompous idiots, they needed a kick up the arse to make them realise the gravity of the problem."

It was over half-an-hour before Phillipa Scott came down the stairs to fetch them. She looked at them with her eyes raised to the ceiling. "Do you want to come up?"

When they reached the boardroom, Ronald Sperry was quick to announce that the Directors had voted and agreed to elect Terry onto the Board of Directors by 5 votes to 3 with immediate effect. They had spoken to the Club's bank and an appointment had been made for 4.30pm that afternoon. They had also ageed to sell him the ground for £13 million; Roy Peters and Phillipa Scott would immediately set the sale in motion, along with the Club's solicitors.

The meeting with the bank's top executives was a lengthy one; Terry went with Roy Peters and Ella. Terry outlined his plans in great detail, and proved to everyone that he could provide the funds necessary to placate all of the creditors, including the continual payment of all salaries. The bank were happy to continue the overdraft, on the proviso that a Credit Suisse Bank Guarantee would be available by the following morning and all further interest payments were made on a weekly basis. The remaining stipulation was the crunch one; the overdraft would have to be paid off in full by 1st August.

Roy rang Phillipa at the club and told her what had occurred; she was overjoyed. He then asked her whether she could come in early in the morning as Terry would need a lot of help. She agreed to be in by 7am. Terry, Ella and Roy made their way back to the ground and settled down in the boardroom to put together a plan of action.

Terry's first call was from the hotel early the following morning; he contacted Credit Suisse in Australia and instructed them to draw up a Bank Guarantee Form. They agreed to forward the paperwork to him via fax, for him to complete and return to them. As soon as he had done so, they would be sent immediately to the Club's bank; Barclays in Hayes, Middlesex; and a copy sent for himself to his hotel.

Terry had to wait several hours, consuming an inordinate amount of coffee, before the Barclays Bank branch in Chiswick

High Road opened for business so he could check his current account. It seemed to take ages while they went through various questions verifying his identity. Finally, they confirmed that his account had been credited with £13 million.

Meanwhile, Chief Executive Roy Peters and Phillipa Scott were in the latter stages of organising the sale of the ground to Terry Morris for £13 million. They were now awaiting the arrival of the Club's solicitor, Michael Book, from Wilson and Wilson. Phillipa began to prepare the invoice in readiness when she suddenly let out an expletive. "Oh shit!" Everyone stared at her. "What about VAT?" They all gathered around her desk. Phillipa was the first to answer her own question. "We need to make the invoice out for £13 million inclusive of VAT, but we can utilise the whole amount until we submit our tax return in June when we submit our next return. What's the calculation, anyone know?".

Ella was first to respond. "The VAT here is 17.5% so you divide the gross figure by 1.175. Phillipa quickly tapped in the figures into her calculator........ £13,000,000 divided by 1.175 = £11,893,617.71 so the VAT is £1,106,382.29 "How on Earth did we forget about VAT? I feel bloody stupid." said Roy Peters. "Thank God it doesn't matter."

When Michael Book arrived no-one mentioned the near calamity of earlier. All the relevant legal documents were completed and the transfer of funds made to West London Football Club.

42

Dave McLeod regretted his falling out with John Crowther; they had known each other a long time and had become good friends. They had first met at a Professional Football Association Union meeting in London, when Dave represented Newcastle United and John, Arsenal. John, at that time, was nearing the end of his illustrious career and McLeod just starting his.

When John arrived, he had searched for his name on the large school-type easel and looked at the u-shaped table plan. He made his way to his designated seat, saying 'hello' or nodding to those who were too far away and greeting others with handshakes. When he finally arrived at his seat, he found Dave McLeod sitting next to him; a young man with his future before him. They shook hands and Dave introduced himself, knowing full well who John was. He felt overwhelmed, nervous and excited.

He told John he was at the meeting reluctantly, because the normal Newcastle repre-sentative had been taken ill and, as no-one else was either available or interested in attending, he had volunteered. Although he had been thoroughly briefed, the anticipation of having to stand up, speak confidentally and show his disagreement on two particular subjects, in front of so many attendees, worried him and he wondered whether he was capable of doing so. In a brief conversation prior to the meeting opening, McLeod had told John his predicament and John had given him every encouragement to speak up, which, surprisingly to even himself, he did very confidently.

They retired to the bar and, although there was a great difference in their ages, the two enjoyed each other's company. Future meetings saw them always sitting together, as they soon realised the seating position on the tables were adhoc. Whoever arrived first would move their place card to where they wanted to sit so John and Dave quickly caught on and made sure they always sat together and lunched together.

The meetings finished when John's playing days finally ceased. They remained in contact, meeting up whenever they were in the same vicinity. Over the years, John continued to watch Dave's progress with a sense of pride and, when Mcleod was suddenly put on the transfer list at Rangers, he rang Crowther who was in need of a decent experienced goalkeeper. Crowther stepped in quickly to sign him; his transfer fee of £180,000 plus a £10,000 signing on fee was a bargain for someone with 36 Scottish caps and over 300 league games at the top level.

The one problem was his wife Margaret; she was determined to keep their house in Dunfermline and was worried that she wouldn't find a job in the south as a dental nurse. The club, however, had several luxury apartments available for immediate occupancy in nearby Ealing, which the two could utilise.

Not long after they moved into their two bedroomed apartment in Ealing, Margaret was offered a position at a dental surgery in Putney. It meant Dave could drop her off at Ealing Broadway to catch a train in each morning and and then make his way to the training ground in Osterley. In the evening, when she came home, it wasn't that easy. Dave experienced a hellish problem of parking or having to continually hover around the station, waiting for someone to vacate a parking spot. The traffic wardens were quick to wave people away that were parked illegally and, if you left the car, it was ticketed. After a frustrating three weeks, Dave told her that it would be easier if she walked home. It was the first crack in a relationship that most people considered perfect.

Dave himself was stuck sitting in the apartment for five or so hours a day, looking at the TV. His cooking skills improved; from egg and chips to Boeuf Bourguignon; but he was bored. Margaret was arriving home in bad moods, the petty arguments had begun and she wanted to pack up work and have a child. It was not long before Dave commenced something that many footballers have found to be their downfall; betting. The local bookmaker's became his port of call after every training session and, to make matters worse, the owner was an attractive forty-something mature woman, Jill.

It was not too long before Jill was leaving the staff to pop upstairs to her flat for half an hour for a quickie that wasn't determined by the date or the timing of her menstrual cycle. His life was a tangelled web of lies and deceit. The not-so-sudden departure of Margaret back to Scotland and the regrettable association with Mike Ellison, the General Manager at The Golden Wheel Casi-no, had seen his gambling increase dramatically and, whilst the afternoon in the betting shop used to leave him short of £500, the casino was seeing him lose over £4000-£6000 every time he went. It was surprising to him that they had allowed him credit, which they were now wanting to have repaid, and he was disturbed that he was being physically threatened.

Dave now regretted asking for a transfer; he wanted to stay and have his life back as he was becoming more depressed every day and had considered going to the doctor. West London Football Club had always treated him well, and especially John

Crowther. It was important to him that the club still be playing in the Premier League next season and, with the financial constraints now sorted, it seemed to be a sensible decision.

He decided to give John Crowther a ring, apologise and withdraw his transfer request. He also wanted to talk with Margaret on her own; her mum was lovely but her overprotective old man was a nightmare. He didn't like any kind of sport. He had never liked Dave, or people of his kind, who made vast amounts of money for just kicking a football around a park, whilst he grafted every hour, every day to run the family business, which had been started by his grandfather. It was hard; the staff were good but the larger the company had become the more he had to employ and then lately having to employ a personnel manager.

Dave McLeod was determined now to speak with John Crowther and try to sort everything out and also hoped Mike Ellison at the casino to see if he would be agreeable for part payment of the debt.

43

Mike Stephenson's life had seen a dramatic decline within the last couple of weeks, through the sacking of his agent, the meeting with Jenny Clarkson and the one-sided fight with her boyfriend Jason Middleton. He was sitting on his bed in Hammersmith Hospital; his injuries were nowhere near as bad as reported by the media and he was waiting for the relevant documents to discharge him from the hospital.

DS Inman and DC Warren from Scotland Yard had not yet been allowed to interview him and were waiting patiently to take him back to the Yard, as instructed by their superiors. They were both tired and and should have clocked off three hours ago. They had phoned their 'not happy' wives from the public call box in the main reception and returned like scolded children. They had consumed coffee continually and boredom had set in.

As soon as he was discharged the two officers had him in the back of their unmarked police car and were speeding towards the Yard with the wail of the sirens and flashing lights. When they arrived, they didn't take long in handing him over to the duty desk sergeant before hurrying home.

Mike was taken to an interview room, the recorder was switched on and Bingley commenced. "For the tape, the date is Friday 5th May 2000, and the time is 2100 hours. I am DCI Derek Bingley, alongside me is my colleague DI Andrew Wright ane we are interviewing Mike Stephenson concerning the whereabouts Jenny Clarkson. Mike, do you wish to have a solicitor present?" Mike was already confused.

"No."

"Do you know Jenny Clarkson?"

"No."

Bingley and Wright looked at each other with quizzical expressions. DCI Wright showed him a photograph.

"This is Jenny Rastall" Stephenson replied vehemently.

Bingley stared at him in disbelief. "No, this is Jennifer Anne Clarkson."

"Well that was not the name she gave me, she said her name was Jenny Rastall!"

"How did you meet her?"

"In a high-end picture gallery called Redmand Art in Bruton Street."

"Why were you there?"

"I was asked to open the store."

"You were the celebrity to cut the ribbon and intice likely customers."

"Yes."

"I presume you were paid a fee to perform this duty?"

"Yes"

"Can you give me a bit more information as to how this came about."

"Yes, I was approached by the owner, Mr Redmand, through my agent to open the shop, which is basically a high class shop selling original artworks, or limited prints by artists like Lowry. They offered me £20,000 for what was four hours of my time. It was a no brainer."

"Wow is that the sort of return that you guys get?"

"It could be anything really, but it was enough for me."

"How did you come to meet Jenny, Mike?"

"It was after the ceremony had finished. I was just aimlessly wandering around with a glass of champagne, looking at the paintings, and suddenly she was standing beside me. We chatted about various paintings for a while and I asked her if she fancied going somewhere for a coffee."

"So you instigated it!"

"Yes I did. She is a lovely looking lady, as you can see from the photograph, and I never had any inkling that she might be playing me. She agreed to join me. We then left and sauntered around, looking in at a few coffee bars, but they were either full or we didn't fancy them. I was about to just say goodbye when she invited me back to her apartment, which she said was just around the corner."

"Well she was an actress and, by all accounts, a pretty good one too. So what happened when you got back to her apartment? And what time was it, can you recall?"

"Oh it must have been about 5pm. We had drinks, far too many, and ended up having sex."

"Where?"

"She led me into the bedroom and we ended up on top of the bed."

"And then?"

"I went home."

"And what time was that?"

"About 6pm."

"And what time did you get home."

"7pm."

"Was your wife at home?"

"Yes."

"OK, we will check, on that in a moment. Will she be there now?"

"No she has left me."

"Oh I'm sorry about that."

"Did you hear from her again?"

"Who?"

"Jenny Clarkson."

"No."

"Going back to the bedroom. Was there a mirror overlooking the bed?"

"Are you getting some fucking thrill out of this?"

"No, but you certainly were." DI Wright said flippantly.

"Yes there was a large one covering the facing wall."

"Did you not have any suspicions at all when you saw it?"

"No, my mind was on other matters."

"You know Mike, I've been doing this for a long time and, even if I say so myself, I'm becoming pretty good at assessing people. You're not telling all of the truth. You are on edge, you're too nervous. What are you not telling us?"

There was a pregnant pause before Stephenson accepted he had to tell more and slowly continued.

"I don't know whether you're aware but there was a robbery at the training ground dressing rooms a few days ago!"

"No, I wasn't, but what has it to do with this?"

"Well, when we arrived back at the dressing room after we had finished training, it was in turmoil; clothes were strewn all over the place. Most of the players had had money stolen, including me. But stuffed in my wallet was a photograph of Jenny Rastall and me. On the back was a message: '*You Naughty Boy Mike*'

Bingley looked concerned. "How come, surely you have lockers?"

"We have a security guard who is supposed to keep guard but he was caught short, desperately needed to visit the loo and didn't even have time to summon a replacement. The players were outraged."

"Anything else?"

"No nothing."

"Do you still have the photograph?"

"No, I destroyed it, as I have all the others."

"And that is it?"

Mike sighed heavily. "I really did like her, my marriage has been a bit rocky for some time and I wanted, I don't know, maybe I was looking for something, distraction. You'll probably think that I'm a rubbish husband and an arsehole."

"I'm not here to judge you Sir. I'm only interested in finding Jenny."

"I tried to ring her on several occasions and the phone just continually rang out, the last time it was unobtainable. I even got through to the operator and she said that it was a discontinued line. I did travel up to the apartment, managed to get into the building and banged on the door, but there was no reply."

"So do you have the number you rang?"

"Yes I memorised it when I left the apartment."

"Can you still remember it now?"

"Yes it's 020 7340 4180."

Bingley smiled "Now we are getting somewhere."

"I really would like to speak with your wife to confirm when you got home. Where is she?"

Mike was quick to respond. "Actually it was closer to 8.30pm when I left London and I arrived home at around 9pm.

Jenny and I had a lot more sex and wine and both fell asleep, totally exhausted."

Bingley looked at the file in front of him and looked up at Stephenson. There was a knock on the door. "Come in." yelled Bingley. It was a uniformed PC holding an A4 sheet of paper, he walked over to Bingley, handed him the paper and whispered in his ear.

"Before we started this meeting you were asked to give us a specimen of your fingerprints, which you gave us voluntarily. There were no prints found in 41 Tennison House, the the apartment had been thoroughly cleaned, but what we would like to know is how your fingerprints were found in Jenny Clarkson's house in Primrose Hill." Mike didn't reply.

"Oh come on Mike. How did they end up in Primrose Hill, this really is a bit worrying for you."

Reluctantly, Mike started to tell the truth. "I decided to go back to Tennison House and stake out the place. I sat in my car and watched people going in and out for quite some time and then I saw some big blond guy looking suspicious, after he went in and out quickly. I followed him and he ended up in Primrose Hill. I watched him go into a house and decided to approach him. When I got to the front door it was open. I ventured in as quietly as I could. I had just started looking around in the lounge, when I heard him leave. I ran out after him but by the time I got out he had driven off. I went back to the lounge and had a good look around; there were many photos and there were a couple of the blond guy and her together, so I assumed he must be Jenny's boyfriend, which was confirmed after he put me in hospital. I must admit, I did know her name is Clarkson, but only after finding her birth certificate, where I also noticed her mother's maiden name is Rastall."

"So why all the lies, why did you not come clean from the outset? I understand that you went into Hammersmith Police Station of your own accord."

Bingley closed the file, thanked Stephenson for his time and told him if they required to talk with him again they would be in touch. After he had left he said to Wright. "Well we know he wasn't responsible, all that he's confirmed is what we already know from her letters. We are no further forward in this investigation."

44

Ray Prince had been very busy in the past few weeks. It had been more than a fortuitous coincidence that General Manager Michael Ellison of The Golden Wheel Casino in Greek Street had sat next Dave Mcleod on the plane from Turnhouse. Then there was the surveillance and exploitation of both Jenny Clarkson and Mike Stephenson.

Whilst he thought his venture to Cyprus was totally undetectable, and he felt very comfortable, he was maybe a little over confident. The murder of Rulie Kyriakou; the barmaid at The Paphos Beach Hotel; had been discovered very early in the morning. The Cypriot Police had moved swiftly and had unwittingly passed Prince on the town's perimeter. It wasn't long before they were provided with a copy of his UK passport from the hotel; under the name Robert Williams; along with his photograph. The authorities at both Larnaca and Paphos airports were immediately informed and they waited for his arrival at all of the UK boarding gates. Prince though had been quite canny - knowing that his visit would no doubt lead to someone's death, he had made a booking on a British Airways flight to Heathrow in the name of Robert Williams, and one as Philip Louest on an Olympic Airways flight to Athens. Both flights were leaving from Larnaca International Airport.

Prince opted for the Olympic Airways flight to Athens and then an Air France flight on to Paris Charles de Gaulle, where he picked up a taxi to Paris Gare du Nord and caught the Eurostar (under the name George Major) to Waterloo.

The room he had stayed in had been fingerprinted and, whilst Prince had been careful; somehow managing to put on a condom before he commenced his crazed assault on Rulie; he had dislodged one of his contact lenses when her hand had caught his eye. He had searched everywhere possible but had to give up as time was of the essence. The contact lens was found by the police on the floor at the emergency exit; Prince had missed it due to it being stuck underneath his shoe. The police were not convinced that the lens belonged to the assailant but, nevertheless, placed it in an evidence bag. The automated fingerprint identification systems (AFIS) made a positive identification from a partial print with a Raymond Spencer Prince, a UK, citizen born 13th June 1952 in Islington who had been sentenced for committing grievious bodily harm and robbery in 1971 and had spent 18 months in the HM Borstal in Feltham, Middlesex. He was now forty-eight.

The Greek authorities immediately contacted the respective authorities in the UK for their assistance in locating the suspect.

When the case file requesting assistance in locating Raymond Spencer Prince, and hopefully, when found, his extradition to Greece for murder. landed on the desk of DCI Derek Bingley of New Scotland Yard, it was received with derision. His workload was already immense and most of the overtime working had been curtailed dramatically. The contents of Prince's file had been compiled by one of the administrators and contained a photograph of him aged nineteen, when he commenced his sentence, It would be difficult to identify him now after such a time lapse. The report outlining his behaviour over the period in question authenticated his propensity for violence and, because of it, his original 12 month sentence had been extended on three occasions, until he was finally released in 1974. Between leaving

Feltham Borstal and his appearance in Pathos, there was very little information available.

Bingley closed the file and wandered off to the coffee machine where he stood with a few of his colleagues, chatting about football and particularly the missing West London players in Pathos. Abruptly and without a word, Bingley walked quickly away from his bemused audience.

Back in his office he opened the file. Was it just a coincidence; West London Football Club travel out to Paphos for a friendly match and Prince is also there? Why? Either he was there to watch the game, or he was on business, or to catch some sun. If he was going to catch some sun, would you go on your own? What business would warrant him to visit Pathos? The more he thought about it, the more he believed he was there for no good. What had happened to the two lads, could he maybe be involved? Could he be the Phil West who was involved with the Jenny Clarkson disappearance. He was interested to talk to the Cypriot police. He contacted the team that were working on the Clarkson case and called them in for a 12-noon meeting.

When everyone had settled down, Bingley began to tell them his thoughts. There were a lot of acknowledging nods as they thought that Prince could very well be the Phil West they had been searching for. They began to re-examine all the files regarding Phil West and started asking questions as to how he had managed to evade the Greek police. WPC Hilary Ford was the first to offer an opinion.

"So far, we know Prince has a forged passport under the name of Robert Williams. Maybe he has more."

Bingley leaned back in his seat, contemplating her suggestion. "I think you're right. What we need to know first is if any male passengers missed their flights, and which male passengers had booked one-way flights. I am speaking with the Cypriot Police in the next half an hour, and it will be good to obtain first-hand information from them. I want everyone to think along the lines that this man Phil West is actually Prince, and he has used another nom de plume.

The Assistant Chief of Police, Steven Petrone, rang and was astonished when Bingley suggested that Prince might well be involved with the disappearance of Paul Sulley and Eddie Hirst. There was no reason to associate the two incidents; two days had now elapsed and so far thinking was that the boys had most probably been involved in a road accident. They were presently undertaking a major search of the Troodos Mountains, which would be the most likely area where an accident might happen as, besides the passing traffic on the road itself, it was desolate and dangerous and if someone had lost control of a vehicle it could prove fatal. Bingley asked him whether he would contact the various airlines and ascertain all the male passengers who had travelled alone, as well as those who had not held return tickets.

Steven Petrone promised to get back to him as quickly as possible. Within a few hours, he rang back. "Hello again, I'm very sorry to inform you that the search of the Troodos Mountains for Mr Sulley and Mr Hurst have proved successful. Two male bodies have been found. I have just this minute informed John Crowther at West London Football Club. We have only two passengers who missed the British Airways flight to Heathrow; the first was Robert Williams and the other a George Major. No other no-shows on any of the flights to UK all day, but we did also, as you asked, scrutinise the passengers who had one-way tickets with all of the airlines. We found three, all on an Olympic Airlines flight to Athens; Two missed the flight - James Vickery and Christos Constantinides. We located them; they are an operatic singing duo who had been performing at The Rialto in Limassol and their contract was extended virtually overnight. The third, a man named Henry Louest, landed and caught a flight to Paris." Bingley threw his arms in the air in total ectasy. "Gotcha, this must be Prince!"

"Unfortunately not; he caught an Air France flight to Paris Charles De Gaulle, and he couldn't be traced after that. It is presumed that, if he were trying to get back to the UK, he would head for Paris Gare du Nord and pick up a Eurostar back to London Waterloo. I'm sure that you will be able to access any information directly at your end. We will get back to you when we have news. Bingley thanked him for all the information.

HM Passport Office in London were contacted regarding the identities Raymond Spencer Prince; Robert Williams; Henry Louest and George Major and a request made for all of the particulars relating to the passports. The results returned were disappointing: Raymond Prince was born on 13th June 1952 in Islington, the passport was issued in Peterborough on October 17th 1995 and was due to expire on October 17th 2005, which tallied with the information already provided in the records received from Feltham Borstal. The photograph, taken when he was 43, confirmed, without any doubt, his identity and in the four years since the passport had been issued his appearance couldn't have changed much.

The names of Robert Williams, Henry Louest and George Major provided nothing as each had had their passports stolen within the past few years and all were in their mid-twenties.

Their photographs in no way resembled Prince. One important piece of information that had materialised was the address Prince had entered on his application form, which was on the Uxbridge Road in Shepherds Bush. On further investigation it was found to be an apartment above a launderette. Three squad cars were immediately dispatched to the address.

A decision was made to surround the property as best they could and observe from a reasonable distance. After a few hours without any sign of life, the front door of the apartment immediately to the right of the launderette was approached by a woman who unlocked it and entered the property. DCI Bingley had remained in the office until he received this news and, along with DI Wright and WPC Hilary Ford, set off to Shepherds Bush.

On their arrival, each donned a bulletproof vest, stood a few yards from the door and waited patiently whilst one of the officers battered it with an enforcer. As soon as it gave way, armed officers ran up the flight of stairs shouting "Police... Police....Police..." When they reached the top, they could hear a women shrieking in fear. They located her quickly and searched the premises thoroughly but no-one else was found. The distraught woman began screaming at them "What do you want? What do you want?" DCI Bingley started questioning her. She was a slightly overweight, short blonde with a pretty face and a London accent.

"What is your name?"

"Sonia.... Sonia Madden."

"Is this your apartment?"

"Yes."

"Do you live here on your own?"

"Yes."

"We are looking for Ray Prince. Do you know him?"

"No, I've never heard of him."

"Who owned the apartment before you?"

"I don't own it, it is rented from Hart and Sons just down the road, but I did meet the previous tenant. He came back here looking for something. He scared the shit out of me. He was threatening; if I hadn't had a friend with me in the flat at the time, I can't imagine what might have happened. He was gross."

Bingley continued. "How long ago was this?"

"Oh, several weeks ago."

"Did you catch his name?"

"No, but it wasn't Prince."

"Williams?" She shook her head.

"Major? Louest? West?" She thought for a moment and her face lit up when she realised she recognised one of the names.

"West, that rings a bell."

"Was it Phil West?" Bingley asked.

"Yes, I think it might have been." she replied.

"Do you know where he lives now?" Bingley inquired; he could see the trail becoming cold again.

"No I don't, and I wouldn't want to."

In the meantime, officers had searched the property and had found nothing irregular. "Here's my card, if you think of anything please give me a ring." He wanted to tell her to be careful as Prince was a psychopath, but he thought better of it.

Not far away, on a back street in Acton, Ray Prince was watching the horse racing from Doncaster. He had moved into a furnished three bedroomed second floor apartment in a 17th century grandiose detached property. He was on the couch, watching his bets ebb away with each race. Prince was becoming bored; no work had materialised for a week and he was beginning to feel his sexual urges growing rapidly as he admired the little housekeeping girl who was presently polishing. She couldn't be more than sixteen and was well proportioned and, with her hair tied up in a bun, she could be even younger.

Before he could carry out any mischief, the phone rang. It was Michael (Micky) Pearse, one of his schoolboy chums, who, along with the Lowdnes brothers and Eddie Bezer, started the syndicate some ten years before. "Hi Ray, how you doing?" said Pearse.

"Hi Micky. OK, a bit bored." replied Prince.

"Look, we've got a problem in Shoreditch. There is a mob called the Endersly Gang and they are trying to muscle in on our drug business and they need to be stopped. We know where they meet up and we want to be there tonight. We need to be tooled up. Are you still OK in that area?"

"Hang on, I'll have to go into another room, I've got a cleaner in." He entered the main bedroom and shut the door. "Yes I've got a .22 Walther PPK with a silencer and loads of ammo."

"OK. Meet Eddie and me at The Water Poet in Folgate Street at 8pm, we'll have two other lads with us. You'll find us in the public bar, probably on the dartboard. There is a bit of wasteland ten minutes or so up on the left-hand side if you walk east towards Brick Lane."

"What's in it for me?" Prince asked.

"A Monkey." replied Micky.

"OK, see you there at eight o'clock."

Prince was excited, some more action at last. The young girl looked at him quizzically when he came back into the lounge. Prince wondered whether she had heard anything and pondered for an hour while she was finishing up. He gave her thirty pounds cash and thanked her, though even as she was just about to leave he was still contemplating having her, but then she was outside before he knew it.

He arrived in the vicinity of The Water Poet pub early, and parked up in the disused piece of land Micky had told him about. When he entered the pub, he bought himself a pint, positioned himself on a bench seat which allowed him a view of the entry points and began people watching. Finally, the four arrived; Micky and Eddie were first in, followed by two guys Prince had never seen before. Micky and Eddie shook his hand and introduced him to Bruce and Derek.

"Do you want another?"

"No thanks, I'll stick with this." Eddie bought drinks and Micky explained in detail what he was expecting to happen. Prince listened intently, he felt a bit guilty sitting with a pint whilst the others were drinking cordials. Everyone finally finished their drinks and meandered back to their cars. Next to Princes' car was an enormous 4-wheel drive black Dodge. Eddie was first to get back, opened its driver's door and started fiddling around in the footwell. He came out holding a pistol with a silencer. Prince had very seldom faced fear in his life but he did now; he froze and, as he did, Bruce and Derek had taken his arms.

Eddie pointed the pistol at Prince and said apologetically. "I'm sorry Ray, we've known each other for a long time, but you have become a problem Ray. We cannot afford to have you around, you've become a liability." Prince struggled to free himself, shouting "You double crossing cunts!" but soon found himself on the ground. Eddie fired, the first shot penetrated his left thigh leaving him floundering on the ground in agony, a massive outlet of blood spurting from the wound. The second went through his mouth; death was instantaneous.

They searched Prince's car for his artillery, found everything they needed, removed the car's number plates and anything that would not burn. They dragged Prince to the car, placed him in the driver's seat, saturated the interior with the petrol they had retrieved from the boot of the Dodge and ignited it. The car exploded into flames. The four left, having achieved their objective.

45

With the final game against Kirklees County in West Yorkshire on Sunday 4th June quickly approaching, the mood at West London FC had been lifted with the news of a rich benefactor appearing out of the blue to purchase the Club. The Club's existence was secured, providing nothing untoward occurred.

Terry and Ella Morris, with the help of the club's staff, worked intensively without a break for hours. They found themselves very often waiting for parties to return calls and then having to haggle before agreeing terms. Most of those they spoke to were pleased and amiable but others not so. It was tedious and at times frustrating, but finally the major issues were resolved to everyone's satisfaction and the takeover would be completed within the next few weeks, as well as sufficient money being made available to curtail the administrators' interest.

John Crowther made sure that the playing staff were well prepared for probably the biggest match in the club's history; the training had been extensive, with a thorough breakdown of the opposition's likely tactics and, just as importantly, a full explanation given of the takover situation. Everyone had clapped, cheered and embraced one another, sharing in the joy of the Club's future. Nevertheless, it was still essential that the team obtained all three points on Sunday and remained in the Premiership. A win by either side would see another season for them in the top flight, whilst a draw would condemn West London Football Club to relegation.

On the Saturday lunchtime, the team and its entourage met at the ground in buoyant mood and travelled up to the North to take on Kirklees County. They stopped on the M1 twice for toilet breaks and arrived at the Cedar Court Hotel, on the outskirts of Huddersfield, in the early evening.

Within an hour, everyone had assembled in the restaurant for a light meal. John had a quick word and then left the players to their own devices. A couple of pool tables, a dartboard and a table tennis table were available for their recreation and they made much use of the offer. John had reiterated that everyone must be in bed no later than 10.30pm and no booze should be consumed. Breakfast would be at 8am sharp and the coach would leave the hotel at 10am for the ground.

The following morning at 7am, the fans back home were gathering en masse in the forecourt of the staduim, scouring the forty-five coaches that the supporters club had organised, looking hopefully for the one that was allocated to them. It had been a logistical nightmare; not many coach companies had fleets large enough to accommodate their requirements, and the company that the club normally used was not able meet the demand due to other commitments, only providing eleven. A further five came from Uxbridge; fifteen coaches had driven all the way down from Blackpool; another eight from Birmingham and six more from Reading. The excitement was immense, but it was also mixed with a masked nervous anxiety. The coaches arrived within thirty minutes of each other and, although the concourse was large, it became difficult to manoeuvre so many of them at the same time into a desirable position. The supporters club officials worked tirelessly, directing the fans one way or the other, but it took longer than first envisaged and the entourage left half-an-hour later than originally planned. All of the coaches departed, adorned with huge flags and scarves on the back windows.

After a sober evening, the West London contingent met in the morning for a light breakfast and, when they had finished, John Crowther shared a few thoughts regarding the impending take-over and listened to, and answered, as many questions as he could. The coach left on time and arrived at Kirklees County ground within half-an-hour. The ground had a capacity of 45,000 and was only ten years old, it was one of the first grounds to have undersoil heating.

The match was a sell-out, with over 6,000 fans travelling up from West London, but when the players walked out onto the pitch prior to kick-off, there were very few spectators in the ground. A minimal number of West London fans had arrived and they were easily outnumbered by the home supporters who were extremely vociferous, shouting abuse and making objectional hand gestures towards them as they walked around, examining the pitch. They had experienced this behaviour many times before, but not prior to kick-off. It was scary and a number of the younger players were shocked and felt unprotected. They all left quickly for the shelter of the dressing room.

At kick-off, the away supporters' section was far from full as an accident on the M1 had delayed all those travelling by road, including all of the coaches that had left late. The game commenced with Kirklees kicking off; the atmosphere was electric. The limited away support could hardly be heard as the Kirklees fans roared their team with every move, they forced three corners in as many minutes and were unlucky not to have taken the lead.

After 15 minutes, the ball had hardly visited the opponents' half and only as a result of the defence hacking the ball out as far as it could go. The decibels increased even more as the away end started to fill up with West London fans beginning to arrive in numbers. Half-time came and the score, unbelievably, was still 0-0. When the team arrived back in the dressing room, John Crowther gave them as much encouragement as he could and made a few tactical changes.

In the second half, West London settled down and started to play a great deal better; they got forward with greater frequency, although chances were rare. As the minutes ticked by, Kirklees surprisingly became less positive, dropping deeper in defence and giving up much of the possession. However, they denied West London any space and frustration began to creep in with a series of fouls and yellow cards. The Kirklees fans began to believe they were staying up and started to goad the West London supporters, singing chants of "Who… the fuck are you?. Who… the fuck are you?"; "We're staying up and you're going down." and "You'll get the sack in the morning!"

Suddenly the noise level erupted; a long ball found Kirklees front man Darren Smythe, he outpaced West London's Don White and Eddie Dillon in defence and, as he ran into the penalty area with only Paul Brown to beat, was unceremoniously hacked down by the retreating Dillon. The referee immediately pointed to the spot and dispatched Dillon to the dressing room. It was all over, with only a minute to play. Smythe snatched the ball away from his captain Alex Cowling, whom he seemed to be having an altercation with. It took a while for the obvious disagreement to abate.

Smythe finally strode up cockily, placed the ball on the spot, stepped backwards and drove the ball goalwards. It beat Brown, crashed against the bar and came back out to the edge of the area where it was cleared upfield by Don White. With the Kirklees team statically frozen and watching on in disbelief (many had collapsed to the floor in shock) the ball landed close to Jim Fellows, who was standing on the halfway line with his hands on his hips, glumly chatting with John Crowther.

He suddenly saw his opportunity and took off like a greyhound. He retrieved the ball, ran over fifty yards, rounded the goalkeeper and calmy side-footed into the unguarded net. The clock ticked on with the players congratulating Fellows and, by the time everyone was back onside for the restart, the referee only allowed Kirklees to kick-off before immediately blowing his whistle. West London would be playing in the Premiership for another season and Kirklees County were relegated!

The 6,000 travelling fans went beserk, as did everyone connected with the club. The long journey home would be one no-one would ever forget. The car park was full of supporters embracing each other in unison. It took over an hour before everyone departed and the M1 going south was monopolised from the start to the finish with West London Football Club supporters, their cars festooned with club scarves draping from the side windows. Each coach that passed was greeted with a fanfare of car horns and flashing headlights. Considering that everyone had been up at the crack of dawn, the adrenaline was obviously keeping them all wide awake.

As the team coach reached home territory and pulled in to Zion Stadium, it became obvious; with the vast amount of excited celebrating supporters also heading in the same direction; that something special was about to happen. It was immediately surrounded by the happy, celebrating supporters as it crept slowly forwards, stopping and starting every few moments with the ever increasing mass surrounding the victorious team as it neared the reception.

Unknown to everyone on the coach, in the event of an unlikely win, the staff had organised the bars to be open. At 11pm, the staff were still trying to cajole the thirty odd stragglers to vacate the premises. A few of the players had remained to the end, fully aware that there would no training to worry about for another ten weeks or so, and were 'men behaving badly'; attempting to keep the bars open. It was all good fun. John Crowther, along with Terry and Ella Morris, left in a cab at 10pm; the three inebriated and very happy.

It was a good thing that the club closed the following day as John Crowther was suffering badly with a hangover. He had tried all the remedies but his headache just woudn't subside. Sandra told him to go for walk and buy a newspaper, a bottle of milk and some lemons. She really didn't want anything but she couldn't bear him moping around in his self-inflicted condition, moaning continually about his head.

The mile walk into Harpenden did him the world of good; the fresh air and the many congrats from members of the public out shopping perked him up considerably. He grabbed a basket in Marks and Spencer and wandered around the shop, picking up various items not on the list, including a bunch of flowers. Whilst waiting in the queue, he perused the back pages and was astonished to find four pages on yesterday's game which really cheered him up, with the exception of one single column article concerning the club's financial plight and the problems of any club going into any sort of insolvency restrictions.

It also mentioned the rumour that star player Mike Stephenson was in the process of finding a new club for himself after sacking his agent, and that he had already had a medical at Sheffield United. It explained it was his right to move, following the Bosman ruling, and that he would be able to sign for them without any fee changing hands after his contract lapsed at the end of July. It was annoying as protocol had not been observed, but Mike had never considered extending his stay at the club until the very last moment.

The next morning he made his way to the ground to tie up a few loose ends and, more importantly, to grab the holiday brochures he had been looking through as a surprise for Sandra. He also wanted to discuss both the Stephenson and McLeod problems. He opened the drawer and was thumbing his way through a Santorini brochure (he had not been in the office more than fifteen minutes) when the door crashed open. John was startled. It was Chief Executive Roy Peters.

"You will not believe it! The fucking league wants to dock us 9 points this season for going into administration." He showed John the letter. John slumped back in his chair in disbelief.

"The Premier League has never before deducted points for going into administration as far as I know, normally that has been reserved for major misconduct, like paying agents through a third party, or financial irregularities." Said John.

Peters carried on, "I know that I have made a few fuck-ups and should have been truthful about the administration situation. Months ago I was made aware of the likelihood that Alfred Wade had somehow embezzled a vast amount of his company's money and had secured his shares of the club with that money. That meant that the Sacher Paper company actually owned the major share holding of the club. The whole of the conversation was off the record. Sacher Paper wanted the money repaid and were considering applying to the court for liquidation of the club, but they did not want Alfred Wade to know this. He suggested that it would be better all round that we should apply to the court to go into administration, as that way they could possibly come to a reasonable settlement. However, if that was done, they would insist on having a company they used in the past to become the administrators. The company was Gillis, Freeman and Parker. I then contacted Vice Chairman Ronald Sperry and he told me not to tell anyone, but to place the company into administration. He swore me to secrecy, threatening me with the sack if I told anyone!"

John was deeply concerned at the deceit and presumed that all the directors had known about it, but why?

"Let me get this straight in my mind. You, on instructions from Perry, placed the Club into administration and presumably informed the Premier League. Surely you couldn't have managed to carry out all the paperwork that must be involved in doing this on your own!"

"No, Phillipa knew as well."

"You are fucking joking!" John was fuming.

"Yes she did and was reluctant to stand by me; I threatened her with immediate dismissal. I was desperate. I realised that she was struggling moneywise, she was paying out a hefty mortgage and of course was bringing up a little girl. I actually got her to sign a non-disclosure document as well."

"I can't say I'm not disappointed, 'cos believe me I am. Why are you telling me all this now? So all that 'some people have turned up in reception' surprise was a load of crap, you knew all along! I thought it was odd, but hey I'm no expert and believed it was maybe just the way things happen."

"I don't know why now. I've been living with a lie for too long and just want to get it off my chest."

"So the letter you've just shown me, that isn't a surprise either. They must have discussed the repercussions of administration with you and the possibility of points reduction?"

"Yes"

"So, Terry Morris has saved this club, without having all the relevant facts, and this one is huge. If he was aware of this, he might not have thought it worth it. Were you aware of how many points it would likely be?"

"No."

Roy Peters had never been one of John's favourite people in the world and the two had had many a row in the past. John looked at him with contempt and, very out of character, said;

"No, I know why you're telling me. You're looking for an ally. You're worried about your job. You're worried how our new owner is going to react. Terry is his own man You've no balls Roy, and never have had. Don't worry about me, I suggest you ring him now and tell him yourself. I won't get involved."

FA Carling Premiership League Table 1999-2000

	P	W	D	L	F	A	GD	PTS	
MANCHESTER U	38	28	7	3	97	45	52	91	
ARSENAL	38	22	7	9	73	43	39	73	
LEEDS UTD	38	21	6	11	58	43	15	69	
LIVERPOOL	38	19	10	9	51	30	21	67	
CHELSEA	38	18	11	9	53	34	19	65	
ASTON VILLA	38	15	13	10	46	35	11	58	
SUNDERLAND	38	16	10	12	57	56	1	58	
LEICESTER CITY	38	16	7	15	55	55	0	55	
WEST HAM UTD	38	15	10	13	52	53	-1	55	
TOTTENHAM	38	15	8	15	57	49	8	53	
NEWCASTLE UTD	38	14	10	14	63	54	9	52	
MIDDLESBROUGH	38	14	10	14	46	52	-6	52	
EVERTON	38	12	14	12	59	49	10	50	
COVENTRY CITY	38	12	8	18	47	47	-7	44	
SOUTHAMPTON	38	12	8	18	45	45	-17	44	
DERBY COUNTY	38	9	11	18	44	44	-13	38	
WEST LONDON	38	9	9	20	38	38	-30	36	
KIRKLEES CTY	38	7	12	19	46	46	-28	33	R
SHEFFIELD WED	38	8	7	23	38	38	-32	31	R
WATFORD	38	6	6	26	35	35	-42	24	R

46

A few days had elapsed and Mike Stephenson had spent much of his time ringing everyone he knew, in the hope that someone in the football world would give him a break but, whilst a few were sympathetic, no offers materialised and very little help was proffered. He had tried to speak to Julia on countless occasions and left many messages. He needed to know whether there was any future in their relationship. The remainder of his life was in limbo until some sort of agreement could be reached. It felt like he had been quarantined.

The possible move to Yorkshire had been curtailed after Bernard Aylott had rung to tell him that the house had been taken off the market, he had seemed quite embarrassed. Mike was sure that it hadn't and the owners were just not interested in selling it to him. His only asset was the house in Sunbury which would have to be sold or rented out, as if he did manage to get a club, it wouldn't be in London. If they divorced it would definitely be sold and the proceeds split between them, but even if they reunited it would still be the same outcome.

He had received a bank statement for the Lloyds accounts which both of them shared showing £2,553 in the current account and £12,862 in the savings account. Julia had removed very little. He reckoned the £4,000 per month to pay the mortgage could be continued for three months but the £2,000 rental for the two cars would eat into the funds within six weeks.

He had one old mate, Chris Maddox, out in Spain. He hadn't spoken to him or seen him for ten years and wondered whether he should contact him. He had to find the address book which

Julia used when sending out the Christmas cards each year. He couldn't even remember which club he was involved with, but he knew it was in Madrid. Madrid had two major clubs; Real and Athletico. It was a discussion he couldn't have with Julia. He was now thinking of number one and a life without her and little Emma; if it meant downsizing his life, he would.

He began methodically looking for the book and hoped, when and if he found it, that it would hold Chris's telephone number. He searched and found an old diary in a drawer which contained numerous bits and pieces that were mainly useless but he didn't want to discard. He flipped it open, thumbed his way to the M's and found Chris's address and telephone number quicker than he thought; he just hoped they were both still current. He rang the number, it rang for quite a while before finally an answerphone responded.

'Hola. No estamos en casa, por favor deje un mensaje y nos communicaremos con usted.'

Mike's understanding of Spanish was pretty limited, but the message was obvious. He didn't leave a message, he was just relieved the number was still in operation. He picked up his car keys and left the house to get some fish and chips. As he shut the front door behind him, he was confronted with cameras including the BBC, ITV, Zion and Sky. He quickly re-opened the door and disappeared back inside. He found a M&S chicken kiev in the freezer, defrosted it with some oven chips and waited until 7pm before he rang Chris's number in Spain again. This time the phone was quickly answered, it was a woman's voice.

"Hola."

"May I speak with Chris Maddox please?"

"Qué."

Mike spoke slowly. "May….I…. speak….. with….Chris….. Maddox….Por favor?"

"Lo siento. Solo hablo español. Voy buscar mi marido."

"Hola, ¿puedo ayudarte?"

"Hi Chris, is that you, it's Mike Stephenson."

"Bloody hell, how are you mate?"

"I'm fine, who's the lady?"

"It's my wife, María."

"You are a dark horse. Congratulations."

The conversation flowed as they remembered some of the antics they had got up to over the years when they knocked around together.

"Do you remember the night we got locked in the foyer and couldn't either get out or get back to the offices and farted around waiting for someone to let us out?"

"Yes the passersby wondered what on earth was going on."

"What about the time we all went to France and ended up in a club, I think it was something like The Bootles or something, not The Beatles, odd name, but a great club". Mike suddenly remembered what he was going to say.

"There we were, boys about town, standing with drinks in hand watching the French birds and as one them was just about to pass you, you said. 'Where have you been all my life?' and she said with a perfect English accent *'Avoiding you darling.'*

"Yes didn't I get some stick."

"Hey mate, María is beckoning me. Grub is on the table. It's been great to talk to you again, we must not leave it so long."

Just before he hung up Mike blurted out "Chris, I need your help."

Chris shouted out to María. "María, lo siento, cariño, ¿quieres poner la comida en él horno, Mike está en problemas y realmente necesito seguir hablando con él un momento." There was a loud scream from the kitchen, María was not happy.

"I've just asked María to put the grub in the oven. What's the problem mate?"

"I'm sorry to be a nuisance."

Mike poured out all of his problems and Chris listened to his every word.

"What a fuck up Mike. You could never keep your old man in your trousers."

"I retired from Rayo Vallecano some six months ago." said Chris.

Mike felt deflated.

"But I'm still in touch with them. I could have a word with Sergi Martinez, the manager, for you, I'm in no doubt he would be interested, but you won't get anywhere near the package that you are used to. It will be peanuts. The club is in the second division; La Liga 2; and it only gets gates of about 7,000. Nice little ground, holds 17,000. But on the upside, the cost of living is a lot cheaper out here. Let me talk with Sergi in the morning and I'll get back to you. Try not to worry…. Adiós, amigo."

Mike put the phone down feeling a lot more relaxed, went to the window and surreptitiously peeped out. The paparazzi were still occupying the pavement and road outside, but there were now only a few remaining. He was fully aware they would all be back again in the morning, possibly even more of them. It was a wonder no-one had so far been brave enough to knock on the door and try to interview him. No doubt someone would lose their patience and do so. It was a situation he was reluctant to face.

When he awoke the following morning his worst fear had been confirmed; the paparazzi was firmly entrenched outside, many with step ladders to gain better views. There were now so many of them the car was unapproachable and there was now somebody continually knocking on the door or pressing the door bell. He stupidly switched on the TV to see coverage showing his house and many press and TV companies sending reports back to their relevant networks or editors. He picked up the phone with the intention of calling the police, but couldn't. He replaced the receiver.

The phone rang immediately and he picked it up. "I'm Francis Bennington of the Daily Mail. Is it true……" Mike Stephenson slammed the phone down. It rang continuously for more than two hours and he decided to disconnect it. Mike was anxious to discover what the reaction was from Sergi Mertinez, but didn't want Chris to feel pressured. He hadn't given him his mobile number and now wished he had. The costs for foreign calls was exorbitant. He just hoped none of the media would find out what it was. He made himself a bacon sandwich and a coffee and deliberated over whether or not to ring him. He finally sucumbed and dialled the number. It rang for quite some time and then Chris's voice was heard; 'Hola. No estamos en casa, por favor deje un mensaje y nos communicaremos con usted.'

"Chris it's Mike, sorry to trouble you. I just wondered whether you had managed to speak with Sergi…………….……" there was a long pause…..sorry I can't remember his name. I hope to speak to you soon. Bye."

At the same time, Terry Morris had spoken with John Crowther. He told him of the conversation he had earlier with Roy Peters, regarding the withholding of information concerning the points deduction, and asked him to come over to discuss it.

Mike badly needed to get out of the house, away from the bedlam. He ruled out trying to use the car and thought of another way to escape. Beyond the bottom of the garden there was a small footpath which meandered through a small copse and then out to a small grassed area, then onto a back road and then onto a main road. One problem; he would have to scramble over the back fence, which was covered with various plants.

He redressed into a tracksuit and made sure he had his wallet, keys and mobile. He crept furtively down the garden, hugging closely to the 8ft wall, and watched intently for any sign of life. When he got to the bottom, he looked for a suitable place to climb up. He found the best one in the far left corner, where next door's fence connected with his own. It wasn't ideal and he would probably find it difficult, but at least there were no roses to worry about. He stepped backwards and then sprinted towards the fence, jumped and managed to secure the top edge. As he scrambled up he caught his tracksuit leg on a protruding nail, fortunately it didn't penetrate any further than the material, which had torn and so just missed his skin. He successfully dismounted, had a quick glance down at the damage and ran as quickly as he could. He started to jog as he reached the green and continued at that pace until he reached the main road. It had taken him no more than five minutes. He found the phone number of the local mini cab service, rang them giving a false name and arranged a pick up point. Within minutes, the cab arrived.

"West London Football Club please." The driver, wearing a turban and probably of Sikh origin, was not only lacking in conversational english but had limited knowledge of the locality. He had no idea who Mike was. There was no glimmer of any recognition. Mike was relieved.

"OK it's not too far from Heathrow, if you get me close to there, I'll guide you." As they made their way, Mike began to examine his hands, which were covered with small scratches, and one five inch cut to the inside of his right hand; not deep but it was bleeding and annoyingly positioned. The tear in his tracksuit bottoms was becoming worse and his knee and the top of his thigh were visible.

Half an hour later they were at the ground. Mike tipped him well and made his way to the club shop; it was empty with the exception of the manager who was in the process of placing 'reduced' signs on selected goods without even looking up. The tracksuits on show, whilst the same design, did not include an XL sized one. He picked up an 'L' and went to the till point. The manager only then realised who he was, but didn't let on.

"That'll be £130, less 25% off is £97.50. Mike paid in cash, walked out with it in a plastic club bag and started looking for a toilet. The first one he found was padlocked and the next one had a sign showing *Closed due to cleaning*. He entered, shouted out and listened; there was no response. He washed his hands and quickly pulled on the bottoms, they were a bit tight and short in the leg, but would have to do. He dumped the unwanted bag, the torn bottoms and the unused top and made his way to reception. Sheila greeted him like a long lost friend and asked him how he was. He made it obvious, politely, that he didn't want go any further with the conversation.

"May I see John Crowther please?"

"I'm sorry Mike he isn't here today, he is with our new Chairman at his hotel."

Then Mike turned on the charm. "Sheila you couldn't remind me how I get to the Skyline?"

Sheila, who had never spoken with Mike before, was absorbed and quite excited; she had never been the brightest of people and she blurted out. "Ariel!" She realised her faux pas immediately, her hand covering her mouth.

"Oh I shouldn't have said that."

"Don't worry, I won't say who told me, may I use the phone to ring for a cab?"

When he arrived at the hotel it didn't take long to locate John, Terry and Ella, deep in conversation in one of the hospitality lounges. It came as quite a shock to see Mike standing over them.

"I am really sorry to interrupt, but I am desperate to talk with you boss." John viewed him as he stood there in a tracksuit with the bottoms at half mast. He looked tired and out of place.

John was irritated as the discussion he had interrupted was vital for the future survival of the club; relegation would reduce the club's income drastically. Terry Morris had indicated that he expected the club to be self-sufficient in the future and, whilst the money he had already invested was a gift to the club, he would not be prepared to forever pour money down the drain.

John had a certain amount of sympathy for Mike; many big-named sportsman had committed an infidelity; and he knew only too well that fame brought a variety of problems. There were times you had so many friends of both sexes you did wonder, if you were a Mr Nobody, would they still be by your side?

"Mike, this is Terry Morris, who is now the owner of West London Football Club, and his wife Ella. This is Mike Stephenson who is the current England captain and whose contract with the club has just expired." Mike shook their hands and John offered him a seat. "If it's about anything to do with football, then you can speak freely."

"I know the last time we spoke our conversation was, to say the least, toxic and I apologise for that. But you no doubt know what I had stupidly walked in to. I would like, if possible, to sign another contract."

It was a situation that John had never ever contemplated before, most players whose contracts come to an end just say goodbye and move on. Attempts to re-negotiate his contract over the past six months had always been declined; he had not been prepared to discuss it. Terry Morris, Ella and John had been discussing Mike earlier, but it was about the media coverage of the missing girl. Terry admitted he knew very little about football. He looked at John, waiting for his response. "I presume that United pulled out."

"Yes. As soon as they found out." Mike said sheepishly.

Ella looked to be wanting to say something several times but held her tongue. Inside, she was seething. John was about to say something when a commotion broke out and raised voices could be heard. There was a cameraman, soundman and a reporter trying to enter the hospitality lounge, with three members of the hotel staff attempting to stop them. When two of the hotel management joined in the furore, the situation became even worse; a punch was thrown by the reporter as he was being manhandled and, before long, everyone was in one scuffle or another. The arrival of two police cars brought a modicum of order and the unwanted visitors were reluctantly escorted off of the premises.

John, Mike, Terry and Ella witnessed the whole incident in bewilderment, knowing the situation involved Mike.

"I need a drink after all that." said Ella.

Terry beckoned one of the waiters.

"What are we all having? White wine?" Four glasses and a bottle of Sauvignon Blanc soon arrived.

"Where were we?" asked John. "What you're asking me to do would involve the club and in some way endorse your behaviour. I think the only way you can possibly get out of this problem with any sort reputation intact is to come clean with the press; let them have what they want. That way, hopefully, you'll be able to tell them the truth and end most of the conjecture."

Mike was speechless. John continued.

"I'm not sure whether I could take the chance of re-signing you without a dramatic change in circumstances and would have to think very seriously whether I could trust you. If, however, I did, I would not be paying any signing-on fee or bonuses; the wages would be reduced drastically and I would only offer you a one year contract, with an option of a further year. One step out of line and I would have no hesitation in cancelling your contract. You're a great player Mike, who once had a tremendous reputation, now it's up to you to try and salvage something."

Mike was left in a quandry; on one hand John Crowther had left him a lifeline, and on the other an ultimatum. Mike stood up, shook hands with everyone and bade them farewell. Once he left, Ella was the first to speak, jokingly. "You are a hard man Mr John Crowther."

"He deserved it. If he could get his head out his......"

"I think the word you're looking for is arse."

"If he manages to reclaim his reputation, which I'm not sure he will, I would be interested in re-signing him, but on my terms; he cost us a fortune and still wanted more. Let him sweat. If he doesn't come good I'm not too concerned, I think I aready have a good centre-back near to signing, but Stephenson would save us quite a sum. Not sure about his marital situation. She has left him, but that is another matter."

Terry Morris resumed the conversation relating to the 9 point penalty that had been imposed on the club and the predicament it had placed him in.

"We will have to take the Football League to court regarding the point deduction, but I have a major concern as to who will run the club when I go back home. I'm not at all happy with Roy Peters or Phillipa Scott; the fact that even after Wade killed himself they still allowed me to carry on with the take-over, knowing the one thing we couldn't afford was relegation. What do you think?"

John didn't think it was his problem and was just about to say so when Ella chipped in; "Sack them both."

"OK then, who takes over as Chief Executive, advertise or promote someone from within?" asked Terry.

"Well I don't know." replied Ella. John kept tight-lipped.

"Come on John you must have an opinion on the matter."

"I do but it's above my pay grade."

"What on earth are you going on about, if it wasn't for you this club would be defunct now."

"It's you we have to thank." said John

"Will you two stop patting each other on the back and get on with it? I've given you my view." said Ella.

John pondered momentarily.

"OK, I think Roy Peters had a problem when Alfred Wade told him that he would sack him if he told anyone else and, likewise, Phillipa was placed in the same predicament by Roy Peters. I would get rid of Peters, in my opinion he has never had his heart in West London Football Club. He left Liverpool by mutual agreement, I always wondered why and what used to irritate me was to be faced with a bloody great mounted team picture of Liverpool staring at you when you went into his office!"

"You're joking."

"No I'm not."

"I would keep Phillipa though, she is a hard working Club Secretary, a professional and dedicated young lady with no other half, a mortgage on an apartment in Ealing, a small car and a little girl to care for. I should think we are probably paying her peanuts. I like her."

"Yes, me too. She was so helpful when the takeover was in progress." said Ella.

"I would promote Paul McCormick and advertise for a replacement, Phillipa will help you. Maybe have a chat with her and let her tell you about the problems she has been having to face. It will help her, she must feel emotionally drained, guilty and isolated."

"Right, if he is at the club now, I think I should make my way over to the ground and get it over with."

"Wouldn't you want the job?"

"No way, I'm a football man, Paul is the man for the job; he always works with a minimum amount of fuss and working with him would be a more pleasurable experience than Roy. I don't know anything about his contract so maybe you should speak to Mary Davies in the accounts office, she will have his contract ready before you arrive."

Mike had walked out cautiously; the police had made sure that none of the media were around; he picked up a black cab which new arrivals had just vacated and headed home. He thought seriously about John Crowther's advice and considered whether he was right. To face up to all the media would stop them continually badgering him. It would be embarrassing, but at least he could partly unburden himself of the guilt of his adultery and the responsibility of Jenny Rastall/Clarkson's disappearance. In no time he had arrived back and the cab was immediately surrounded by the paparazzi. He paid his fare and stepped out. Microphones appeared in abundance and questions came at him from all directions. He put his hands in the air.

"Please stop now." Immediately there was a quietness. "I'm willing to try to answer any questions which you ask, there will be exceptions of course. Why don't you elect one person to ask me the questions, that way everybody will get the opportunity; we will not be going over the same ground again and again."

Mike surprised himself at his own positivity. The sound of the continual camera clicks and the sudden collectiveness of the press discussing who should ask the questions came to a sudden hault when Frances Bennington of the Daily Mail, stepped forward.

"Thanks Mike, I'll kick off with questions I would like to be answered. How did you first get involved with Jenny Clarkson?"

"Firstly, she said her name was Jenny Rastall and I met her when I opened a shop in London which sold original paintings."

"Can you tell us the name of the shop?"

"No I'm sorry it is a part of the police investigation."

"How did you meet?"

"I was wandering around when we ended up looking at the same painting."

The questions seemed endless, but he answered them all honestly, up to the point of receiving photographs in the post. He did not answer any of the questions that the police had provided him the answers to, which were few but important in the police's inquiries,\ or those concerning his wife. He knew that Julia would find his behaviour unacceptable and his marriage would be over. The media slowly dispersed, leaving a few stalwarts behind. His interview went viral within half an hour.

Once he got through the front door he poured himself a large brandy, took the bottle with him and sat and watched himself on the news. He felt pleased with the outcome and hoped his revelations would have the desired affect. The mobile phone rang; it was Julia.

"Thanks for telling the fucking world that my husband is an adulterer. You have really made me look like an idiot. You know, I would have forgiven you for most things but this is outrageous. I'm filing for divorce, I suggest you get yourself a solicitor."

She rang off. He slumped on the couch in a morose state. He poured some more brandy into the empty glass, he rang Spain and, once again, he was greeted with the same recorded message. After a few more drinks, Stephenson fell into a deep sleep. He was woken with a start when the telephone rang. It was Chris Maddox.

"Hi Mike it's Chris. I am with Sergi Mertinez at the ground. You will be pleased to know, he is interested in signing you. He knows all about your problems and would like to meet you. What do you think?"

"That is good news, the best I've had today. Has he mentioned money?"

"No that's up to the two of you to sort out. Get yourself over as quickly as you can. Tomorrow if possible. You can stay with me and I will bring you back here."

Mike replied. "OK I'll see what flights are available and get back to you."

Within two hours, Stephenson had booked a British Airways flight from Heathrow to Madrid. As promised, Chris picked him at Madrid-Barajas Airport and drove him to Rayo Vallecano. The meeting went well although, as he had been forwarned, the offer made to him was less than he envisaged and the contract for one year was disappointing. Mertinez explained his club's financial situation and that Mike would need a visa. Chris was waiting for him in the car park. "Hi, how did it go?" he asked as he jumped in the car beside him.

"Well, I suppose it went well."

Chris interjected "But the remuneration was lower than you thought."

"Yes, much less."

"You've got to remember that the cost of living here is far less than in England, and very few people buy their homes, they rent and the weather is better, the women beautiful and …….."

"OK, OK you've sold Spain to me."

"Look, stay for as long as you like, I will show you some life; we'll eat well, drink well and I'll show you what properties you could buy. You'll love it. You'll have to learn Spanish. When do you have to give him your answer?"

Mike Stephenson signed for Rayo Vallecano, moved to Madrid and found himself a nice two bedroomed apartment in

Madrid. He received divorce papers from Julia, citing his sexual intercourse with Jenny Clarkson which he didn't contest, and was pleased when he was granted contact rights for Emma.

47

John Crowther left for home after a couple of hours leaving a dismayed Terry and Ella in his office at the ground. They were disappointed at the latest revelations, but were unwavered; promising their continued financial support in the future whatever transpired. They listened intensively to John's recommendations for the immediate future and without challenge agreed to initiate them immediately, John left them to it. He stopped off at M & S for a few groceries on his way home and not long after he had arrived, and shut the front door the phone rang; it was Terry Morris.

"Hi John, I've just had a rather turbulent meeting with Roy Peters. Mary Davis by the way was most helpul when I arrived, she provided me with his contract file along with those for Paul McCormick and Phillipa. Peters' had a three month notice written in, which I agreed to pay, and I told him at the end of the contract he would have to return the company car. We could have sacked him but it could have caused us legal problems. He is a nasty piece of work; he threw the car keys at me! I had to get Paul McCormick to help me get him evicted off of the premises; with his Liverpool picture stuck underneath his arm; I felt like hitting him with it! Anyway, the dirty deed is done and he won't be back. I then had a long conversation with Paul and he accepted the job without hesitation. We then called in Phillipa and told her what had happened. It's a long time since I've seen anyone so happy, she couldn't stop smiling. Do you know it brought a lump to my throat. John, we were paying her peanuts so I have promised her an additional £2,500 per year; she cried!"

"Good for you Terry."

"I'm now going to contact our solicitors and see what can be done about the 9 point penalty imposed by the FA. Do you want to come John? I'm going to take Paul with me."

"No, you don't want too many people, Paul's a good choice. Just let me know what the outcome is tonight."

"Ella and I are missing little Lenny, so I'm in a bit of a dilemma. I can't go home until this is sorted out one way or the other and I am being realistic thinking it could well mean that we, or I, might be here for another week or so."

John grinned and said, tongue in cheek, "I can only think of one answer. Why don't you get Ella's mum and dad to bring him over and you can all have a bit of a holiday!"

There was a long pause. "What a great idea. I'll see what Ella thinks. I'm not sure whether she will be able to endure the continual fuss they will make of Lenny. We'll see. Speak soon."

Terry made his way to meet up with the club's solicitors, Wilson and Wilson, and in particular Barry J Seymour. He took Paul McCormick with him, along with the letter they had received from FA.

When they had settled themselves in his office, Seymour started: "The first thing we need to discover is whether The FA have deducted points from member clubs previously. If they have then we need to establish what those circumstances were and, if they have not, then why have they made the decision to do so now? Being involved with the takeover, I know that all the creditors were paid up in full, including payments to two member clubs whose monthly payments for transfers were not settled prior to the takeover; both now have been and the settlements included interest. The club have proved that they are now financially secure. I will be writing to FA today, I'll send it by messenger to Lancaster Gate so they will get it by close of play. It will basically ask why they have decided to make this decision, especially in the knowledge that West London would be relegated regardless of the result of the final game. I will inform them that we will take them to court. I wonder whether they can afford to continue this discrimination; if their actions are not upheld it would be catastrophic. The case might not get to the court for some 6 to 8 months, halfway through next season. West London would be in the Football League Division One and then would have to be promoted back to FA Premiership. It would be totally incomprehensible. West London would be looking for hefty compensation, as would the the team that took their place, and many others. The Premiership would collapse like a pack of playing cards."

John was astonished to receive a call at his home early in the evening from Dave McLeod. Dave was apologetic about his behaviour when they last spoke and launched into an in-depth explanation of the predicament he had found himself in. The conversation continued for over an hour and, before he realised the time, Sandra arrived home. She gave him a peck on the cheek and whispered "Who's that?" John mouthed back "Dave McLeod." She grimaced and whispered "Cup of tea?" He nodded.

"How is Margaret?"

"Not happy the last time I spoke with her."

"How long is it since she went back to Scotland?"

"Five months. It is a pity she didn't settle in down here, she has never mixed well, or formed any sort of friendship. She just went into her shell."

"If you ask me, the only avenue you have is to go back to Scotland. You still have property up there don't you?"

"Yes, we thought it best to keep it."

"Have you rented it out"

"Yes"

"Get rid of the tenants as quick as you can and move back in and try to sort your marriage out. I obviously cannot give you a free transfer, but I will be happy to loan you out, until someone gives us a reasonable offer. Have a word with your agent and see what interest there is in Scotland, there are quite a few clubs in and around Edinburgh and Glasgow that would give their right arms for a class 'keeper like you."

"One other thing Dave, I'm troubled with the gambling problem that has materialised, you never gambled when we first met. I remember very clearly you saying to me it was a mug's game; it is! What started this off?"

"Boredom, but I do know I had a major addiction and I have recently commenced meetings with Gamblers Anonymous. It is helping me and I haven't had a bet for a while now, not saying it is hasn't been difficult."

"Good for you, keep it up."

"Thanks John, I do appreciate it."

John replaced the phone and strolled into the kitchen where Sandra was already sipping tea and perusing the newspaper. "How's your day been?" he asked.

"Same old, same old. And yours?"

"Problematical, I just hope that Terry has some good news from the solicitor regarding the points deduction. I think he might get Ella's mum and dad to come over with Lenny for week or so. Fancy a curry?" Her face lit up. "I'll ring Zaman and book a table for 8pm."

The phone rang and it was Terry. "Hi John. It was an interesting meeting with the solicitor, they have hand delivered a letter to The FA appealing against the 9 point penalty. They are also requesting a written copy of the protocol providing the Premiership with the relevant authority to take such action, when it hasn't been taken against a club going into administration before. It's unreasonable when no company or club, nor any of our own players, were owed anything and any late payments had been paid in full; many with interest. We will take legal action if they continue with their action. It will be interesting to see how quickly we receive a response."

"And what it is." remarked John.

"Exactly. By the way, Ella has bought your idea and is currently organising everything, her mum and dad were up for it. All three will be here in three days."

"Terry, I want to thank you and Ella, on behalf of everyone at West London Football Club, for everything you've done since you've taken control of the club, besides the obvious monentary input which has saved us. Your tenacity and enthusiasm have been endless and have rubbed off on the rest of the staff, who appreciate your continued support. A lot of people would have just walked away when The FA threatened to deduct the points, but you stayed with it. If we don't manage to win our appeal and are relegated, so be it. But the club will have survived to fight another day, thanks to you."

"Thanks, but I couldn't see a club that my dad cherished go under, and I hope he's looking down on us with a huge smile."

48

The FA acknowledged receipt of the letter from Wilson and Wilson; it took a further three days before a response was received. Their reply did not cover any of the salient points in question but continued to reiterate that the points deduction would be imposed and West London Football Club would be relegated to the Football League Division One for the 2000 – 2001 season. Barry J. Seymour covered every eventuality, as he had suggested earlier, and immediately filed papers with the court to appeal against the 9 point penalty. The document was five pages long.

Mike Stephenson settled himself into an apartment within close proximity of Madrid, after signing a two year contract with an option of a further year with Rayo Vallenco, and loved living in Spain. Divorce proceedings were initiated by his wife Julia.

Dave Mcleod was transferred on a year's loan to Raith Rovers. West London received 75% of his salary. He and Margaret reunited and moved back to their original home in Dunfermline which is also in Fifeshire, 25 miles from Rovers' home ground in Kirkaldy.

Jason Middleton became a depressive for many months after the loss of his beloved Jenny and finally sold his business, 'Chalk Farm Leisure and Fitness Centre', to his pal John Sutton. He emigrated to New Zealand, where two of his step-cousins lived, and set up a gymnasium. He began dating one of his clients, a Kiwi lady named Angela, not long after it opened and, within 6 months, they became engaged; he often thought about Jenny Clarkson and what might have been.

West London Football Club were deducted 9pts and relegated from the FA Premiership, but lived on thanks to the continual financial backing from Terry Morris. John Crowther and Sandra spent a fortnight at the Kastelli Beach Resort in Kamari, Santorini, to relax.

As soon as John arrived back from holiday, Terry invited the couple out for dinner and acknowledged he couldn't stay in England any longer; he was missing Ella and Lenny, who had already departed. He was concerned that he would not be comfortable in employing anyone other than John to be Chairman; he trusted him explicitly. They agreed a financial package which was well above John's present contract; he accepted the offer immediately and was left to organise his board accordingly.

The Scotland Yard search for Ray Prince was unproductive. Their efforts to discover his whereabouts were thwarted continually and, whilst the case remained open, with no further activity it began to become less and less important. There was some speculation, when they discovered a badly burnt body in a nearly unrecognisable 4-wheel drive vehicle located on a piece of wasteland in Folgate Street, Shoreditch, East London, that it could possibly be him, but no dental records were available to link a name to the unfortunate person.

Jenny Clarkson's DNA was found in 42 Tennison House and it was presumed her body had been dismembered, removed from the apartment and taken to a furnace somewhere.

Kirklees County were deducted 30 points after breaching Football Association agents' fees rules partway through the 2001 – 2002 season; they were unable to make up the deficit and were relegated to the Football League Division One at the end of the season.

Zion Communications' future originally looked bright as it continued its battle with Sky, but Sky eventually equalled and bettered Zion's financial aptitude and it could not compete with their continual competition, finally going out of business.

The court case against the FA Premiership League did not take place until early October and the judge, whilst sympathetic and feeling that the 9 point penalty was unjust due to the club meeting more than their financial obligations, was unable to find in West London's favour, stating his inability to overturn a decision by FA Premier League's rules and regulations which the club as a member and shareholder had committed themselves to at the outset of joining. Nor was he in a position to award any compensation for loss of income. He wished the club his best wishes for the future.

With a dedicated backroom team and a very determined playing staff, West London pushed on. The acquisition of the 22 year old, Tony Moon, from St. Albans City (who worked for Customs and Excise and played part-time) for £30,000 proved to be a great decision. He was chosen twice in the season for England's under 23 squad, playing against Denmark and Germany. Add to that the recovery of Adrien Belmonte from his serious injury and his link-up play with Jim Fellows leading to goals a-plenty, plus a couple of astute mid-field signings from Arsenal, and the team ran away with Football League Division One under John Crowther, being promoted back to the FA Premiership League after only one year's absence.

The promotion celebrations were held at The Hurlingham Club in Fulham and attended by the staff, players, supporters and many dignatories. After all the formalities, including a tribute to those that were 'no longer with us', the music began to play and, before long, the main table was empty apart from Sandra, John and their daughter Michelle. Sandra was itching to dance with her husband and, apologising to Michelle for leaving her on her own, took to the floor. As they shuffled around the dance floor, Sandra gave John a squeeze and said. "Hey, look over there." Michelle was dancing with Tony Moon. "They look good together."

"They certainly do." he replied, holding her tightly.

"What a couple of years."

ABOUT THE AUTHOR

Paul Lamond was born in Bristol in late December 1944 and brought up in Feltham, Middlesex. He lives in St. Albans with his wife Lynda, where they have lived for 30 years and are both in retirement. He became a Brentford supporter in 1955 when he was taken as a boy, and remains a season ticket holder to this day.

He left Longford Secondary Modern School in Bedfont, Middlesex to take up a position as an apprentice compositor at a legal printers in Fetter Lane in 1960, but ended up being given the opportunity to work in the office. He spent his working life in the printing industry, ending up in management.

Paul invented a board/computer game in the 80's called 'Superleague' which was sold in Harrods and promoted by Bryan Robson on TV. It was a bit before its time, and was unsuccessful as likely purchasers of home computers back then were limited - only Amstrad and Commodore existed. His name though has continued to be used and the company; *Paul Lamond Games Ltd* is very much in existence today. Paul no longer has any association with the company.

After giving up playing football in his early thirties, Paul spent five years as a Middlesex County referee mainly in the West Middlesex Sunday Football League, played cricket (mainly wicket-keeper), squash and golf (poorly).

He played a major role in the production of the book '100 Years of Brentford' - the first hard-backed book produced for the Club - along with the editor Eric White and acted as the publisher under Oldfield Press Ltd. Paul also had the privilege of acting as 'Mine Host' for the Bees, in the hospitality lounge at Griffin Park, for nine seasons in the late 80's and 90's.